TROUBLE IN HEAVEN

A Novel

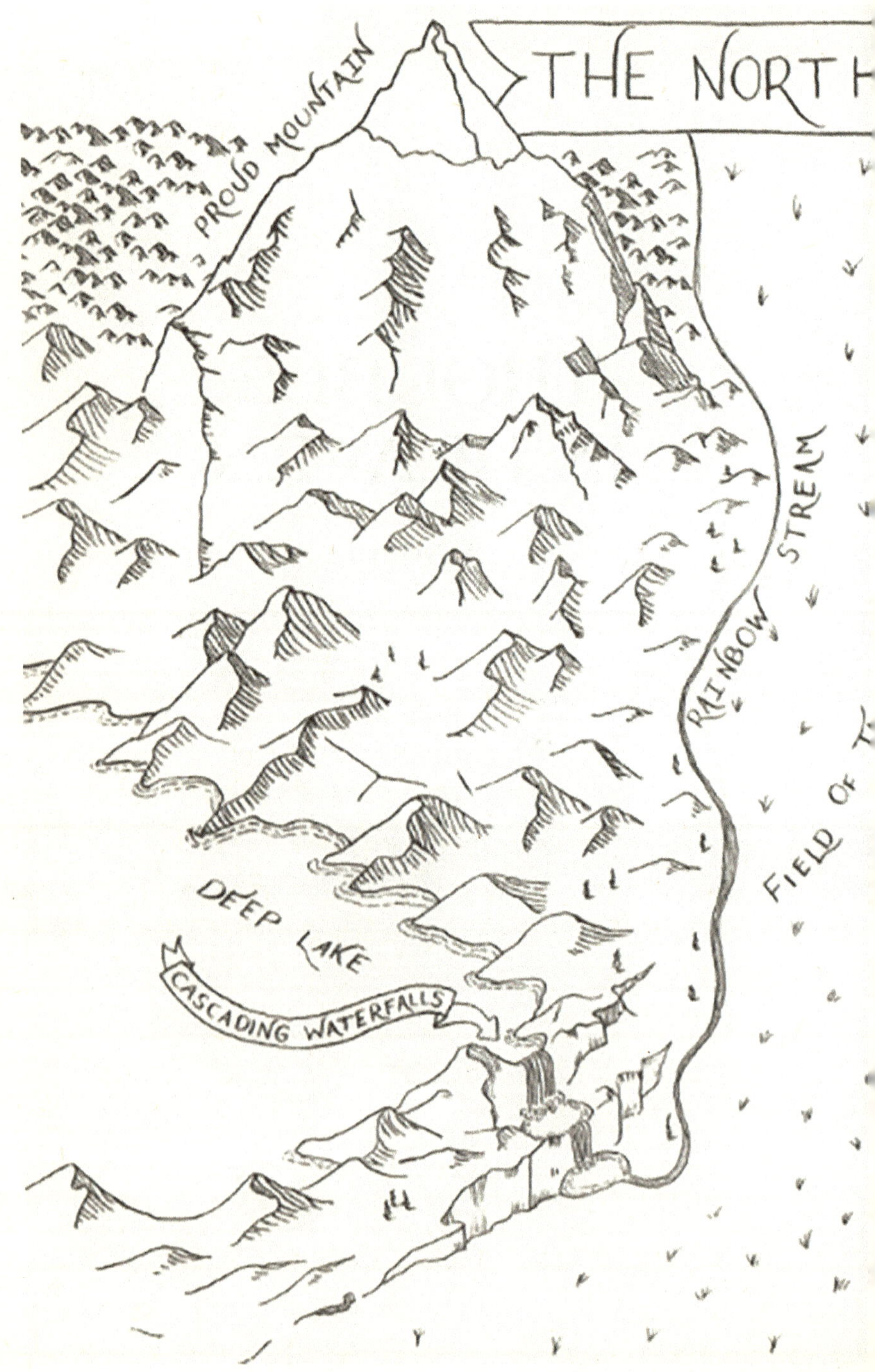
THE NORTH
PROUD MOUNTAIN
RAINBOW STREAM
FIELD OF
DEEP LAKE
CASCADING WATERFALLS

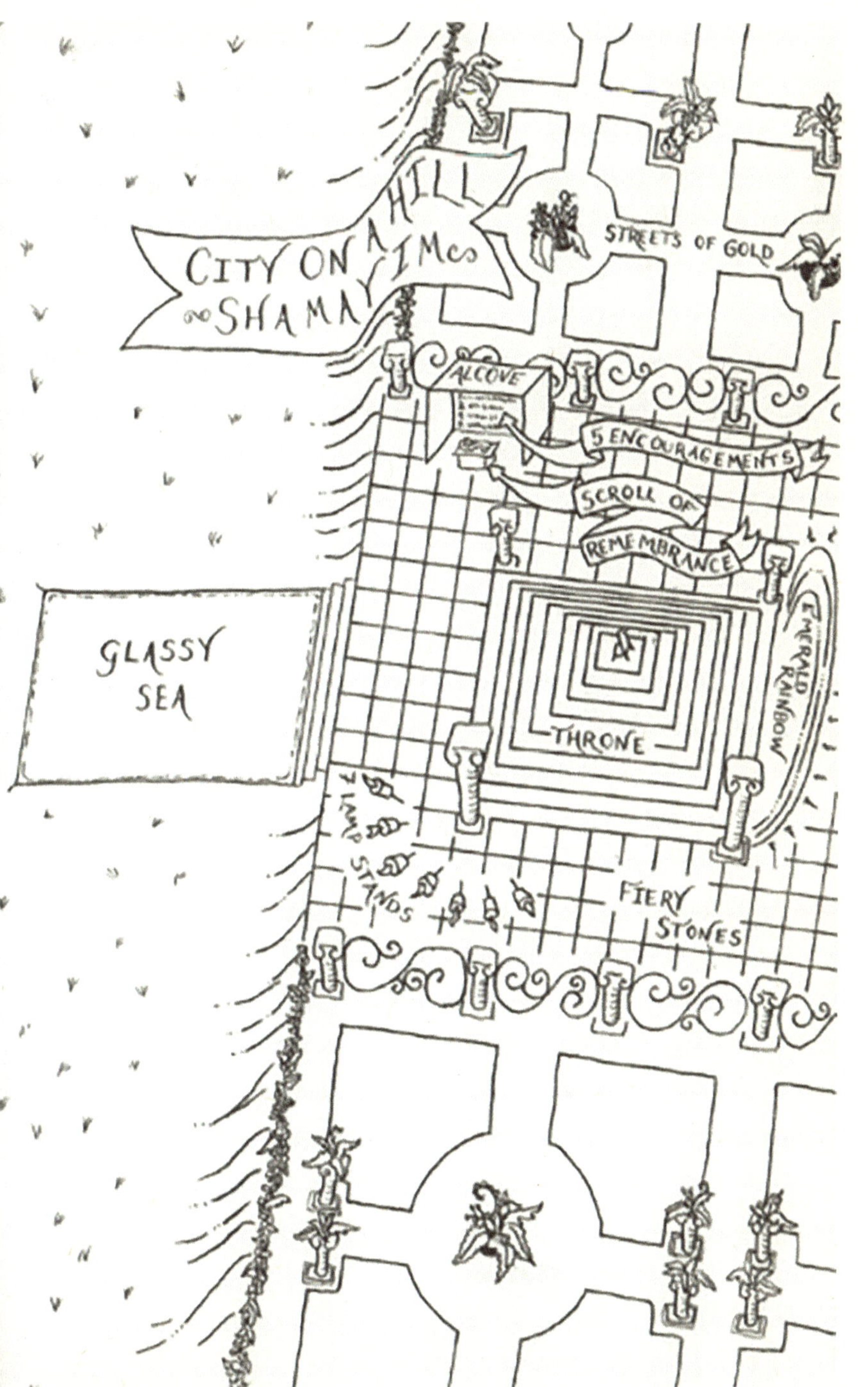
CITY ON A HILL
SHAMAYIM
STREETS OF GOLD
ALCOVE
5 ENCOURAGEMENTS
SCROLL OF
REMEMBRANCE
GLASSY
SEA
THRONE
EMERALD
RAINBOW
7 LAMP STANDS
FIERY
STONES

TROUBLE IN HEAVEN

J.C. Worthington
with
R.G. Ryan

Made for Success Publishing
P.O. Box 1775 Issaquah, WA 98027
www.MadeForSuccess.com

Distributed by Blackstone Publishing

First Printing

Library of Congress Cataloging-in-Publication data
Worthington, JC
Trouble in Heaven
p. cm.

LCCN: 2024946817
ISBN: 978-1-64146-888-6 *(PBK)*
ISBN: 978-1-64146-889-3 *(eBook)*
ISBN: 978-1-64146-890-9 *(AUDIO)*

Printed in the United States of America

For further information, contact Made for Success Publishing
+1425-526-6480 or email service@madeforsuccess.net

I sat me down to write a simple story
Which maybe in the end became a song
The words have all been writ by one before me
We're taking turns in trying to pass them on

Pilgrim's Progress
Keith Stuart Brian Reid

Dramatis Personae

The Alpha – He who has always been and forever shall be

Son of the Dawn – The Alpha's first and most beautiful creation

Michael – Warrior archangel, defender of the Realm, chief of the Archangels

Gabriel – Archangel. Leader of the messenger angels

Chamuel – Archangel gifted with strength and courage

Jophiel – Archangel designated "the Beauty of God"

Raphael – Archangel gifted with healing

Uriel – Warrior archangel in charge of the Scroll of Remembrance

Zadkiel – Archangel gifted with benevolence, mercy, and compassion

Kepteny – Warrior angel known for his riddles and light-hearted nature

Rok – Fierce warrior angel possessing exceptional athletic prowess

Taylor – Messenger angel

Schindaug – Messenger angel known for his visionary and sometimes clichéd yet God-honoring statements

Steele – Warrior angel gifted with the ability to gain the respect of others and original member of the Honor Guard

Wendly – Warrior angel and original member of the Honor Guard

Beleth – Angel assigned to Son of the Dawn, who becomes his "right-hand man" during and after The Defection

Dantanian – Angel loyal to Son of the Dawn during and after The Defection

Remashel – Angel who is part of Son of the Dawn's inner circle during and after The Defection

Semyaza – Angel assigned to Son of the Dawn, who is second in command to Beleth

Shamsiel – Fallen angel who once worked under the archangel Uriel, chosen to replace Semyaza

Apollyon – Name given to Son of the Dawn by The Alpha following The Defection

Adam – The first man formed by The Alpha from the dust of the Earth

Eve – The first woman fashioned by The Alpha from Adam's rib

Cain – Adam and Eve's firstborn son

Abel – Adam and Eve's second son

Awan and Azura – Twin girls born to Adam and Eve

The Serpent – A friendly beast befriended by Adam and Eve and eventually possessed by Apollyon.

In the beginning,
The Alpha created the heavens and the earth.
This story takes place before that.

Part One

The Birth of Everything

Chapter One

As it has at long last fallen to my lot to put pen to page and pass along words set down by a long line of those who have gone before me, I find I scarcely know where to begin. I first thought a simple retelling of that which had been given to me would suffice, but the more I toyed with that possibility, the more I found the notion left me unsettled.

You see, there is more to be told.

Much, much more.

And though some will think me foolish, I must recount not only what has been entrusted to me, but things that I've long suspicioned . . . things that have not been revealed.

Until now.

I know not why this knowledge has come to me, but it has, and I feel—oh, I don't know what to call it—mysteriously compelled to document the knowledge that has been given to me.

As with any tale worth telling, I suppose I should start at the beginning.

Somewhere in the long ago, and not yet in the eternal now, before time began, lived The Alpha. He who has always been and ever shall be and from whom everything else is derived. Beautiful in form, yet formless in His beauty, vast and yet contained, awesome in wonder and wonderfully complete. Singular, yet not alone. Spirit, pure and undefiled.

The Alpha stood in the vastness of His Spiritual Realm, in the center while at the same time, surrounding it. Then, He spoke. His voice resonated in the ether and emptiness. And that which was nothing became the something from which He would create *everything*.

He called this something *light*. Pure, unapproachable light.

Calling the light unto Himself, He watched as it began to shape and shift within His mighty grasp. Then, He hurled it, watching it circle the entire realm before snapping back to His hand almost as soon as it had been released. Laughing, He did it again and again—just like a lad with his baseball glove, tossing a rubber ball against a red brick wall of a house, feeling the same thrill, the same joy each time it returned to His hand. Finally, He tried to throw it so far that it couldn't return, but every time, it came back seemingly faster than before.

The way the light responded so completely to His will caused Him to declare, "Nothing I create will ever be faster than you, nor will there be anything more beautiful." Then, He paused, His eyes sparkling with joy, and added, "I will wrap Myself in you, and *you* shall become My glory as well as My dwelling place."

The light began splitting off into colors. Band after band, layer upon layer, shade within shade, exploding into an array impossible to fathom.

"This is wonderful—too wonderful to keep only for Myself." Pausing, He swept His gaze across the entire Spiritual Realm, saying, "Light, I need you to do something for Me." And the light stood still, awaiting His command. "I want you to fill this expanse—fill My Spiritual Realm. Let there be a feast of color for My eyes."

Before the light, there was only darkness. But where darkness once prevailed, the light moved in and was given authority to overtake it. Everywhere it went, a celebration broke out, the entire spectrum of light dancing before The Alpha accompanied by a sound impossible to describe. Melody, yes, but something more. It was light and sound together, showing off for their Creator, and their Creator was enraptured by it all.

He joined in the dance. Creator and creation in perfect union, twirling, spinning in wild abandon. Majestic melodies cascaded down like a mighty waterfall running throughout the whole of His creation. From this music, He knit together the fabric from which the entire universe was formed. Threads, strings holding everything in proper order, never to be corrupted or disrupted.

Stars began to separate out from the light, and as they separated, The Alpha called each one by name and then hung them in their own special place. As each one received its name, it began to vibrate, resonating in response to His glory.

Then, as He surveyed all He had done, He stretched His great arms wide and laughed.

He kept laughing, and then the heavens began to rejoice along with Him.

Colors danced.

A new song burst forth with melodies intertwining in and out and through the Spiritual Realm.

A song of joy. Creator and creation laughing and loving together.

As the heavens continued the celebration, The Alpha stepped aside to enjoy the spectacle, pleased that everything was in its place. But then He began to imagine a special place for Himself. A home. A resting place. His residence. A place He could fill with His Presence.

He smiled, "I know what I'm going to do."

The Alpha began to imagine a place within His Spiritual Realm—a place filled with trees and rolling hills and meadows covered with flowers and sweet grasses. He imagined a place with high mountains surrounded by lakes, rivers, waterfalls, forests, and all manner of metals and precious stones.

As soon as He imagined it, it came into being. There was nothing, and then there was something. As soon as it came into being, He began walking through this new country, loving the way the grasses caressed His feet in passing and how each and every blade seemed to sing for joy in His Presence, the trees bowing low at His approach.

"You are amazing," He said, and at His word, the trees stood taller and the grasses and flowers grew more brilliant in color.

Pausing in the midst of a vast and heavily-flowered meadow, He began to imagine a city set on a hill, with structures fashioned and formed from radiant light, its gates adorned by every precious stone, and the streets and avenues paved with purest gold, lined with trees both floral and verdant, swaying majestically in rhythm to a breeze set in motion by His very own breath.

It wasn't . . . and then it was.

"Oh, this is fantastic," The Alpha said as He approached the city, His smile causing everything around Him to brighten as He passed.

But He wasn't finished. As He entered the city, a reflecting pool appeared, stretching out before Him, the water so still, so peaceful, that it had the appearance of glass.

"I will call you the Glassy Sea," He said as He stepped onto the surface.

Everywhere He stepped, the surface solidified to accommodate His passage.

When He reached the end of the Glassy Sea, He stood still, imagining a palatial home within the city—a place for His Presence.

This time, He *spoke* it into existence, saying, "In appearance, let the palace be like jasper, as clear as crystal reflecting My light. And let there be a throne room and a throne where I can sit and enjoy My creation, where My creation can come and enjoy Me. To adore and be adored."

And there it was.

The palace was wide and as long as it was high, with an array of twenty-four stairs leading up to the entrance, each stair formed from the same gold covering the surface of the streets and avenues. The front of the palace facing the Glassy Sea was wide open, giving unfettered access to the throne room, while the side and rear walls were fashioned from material that, while opaque, became transparent as soon as you set your gaze upon it, providing an unhindered view of the entire Kingdom.

Outside the palace, hanging gardens of green, leafy plants formed a backdrop for all manner of magnificent flowers spilling over the edge, each with its own special color and scent. Water cascaded from somewhere high up on the walls, but as soon as it reached the bottom, it returned upward to its source, a cycle that made it appear as if the walls were in constant motion. If you got close, you could hear gentle melodies emanating from the falling water, melodies that were then echoed throughout the City on a Hill.

Inside, columns of white marble stood like sentinels lining each side of the throne room, rising seamlessly toward a ceiling of gold so pure, so brilliant, it almost hurt one's eyes to look at it.

Oh, the Fiery Stones. Sculpted like the smoothest river rock but perfectly symmetrical, and each one as alike as the one next to it. These Stones, a burnt amber in color, covered the flat floor of the throne room all around the throne. But when The Alpha approached, it was as if each one burned with an internal flame, turning them a blazing orange. Everywhere His foot trod, flames designed to respond to holiness and the pure in heart danced in His passing, rising high and then bowing low and yet giving off not the slightest bit of heat.

He stopped walking, turned, and swept His left hand in an arc. The Stones flamed high in response. He did the same thing with His right hand, and then both together as the Stones vibrated with a low and rumbling response.

"You are beautiful," He said, "and I love you. I love all of you."

When He spoke, the Stones put on a show. Fountains of liquid fire shot up, some as high as the ceiling, while others cavorted in an intricate dance, weaving in and out, turning the entire throne room into their own private dance floor.

The Alpha clapped His hands, shouting, "Bravo! Bravo, My Fiery Stones."

As He walked up the broad and shimmering stairs leading to His throne, light rushed to join Him from the furthest reaches of His Spiritual Realm in every color He had created, each desiring to be the one chosen to adorn the place of His Presence. Fantastic shapes, spinning, twirling, and filling the throne room.

As He sat on His throne, He pulled one color from among the others, saying, "Emerald." Vibrating excitedly, its radiance glistened throughout all His realm. "I want you to form an arch that will completely encircle My throne. Come on now, don't be shy. Show Me what you can do."

And it happened. A brilliant emerald arch formed around the throne. It rippled and moved as if in response to music only it could sense. The Alpha loved the color, and it loved Him back, expressing that love in the way it wrapped itself around His Presence.

Gazing out on all He created, The Alpha declared, "I shall call you Shamayim . . . the place of My Presence."

Seeing within and without, above and beneath, behind, beside, and beyond all at the same time, He sat perfectly still, surveying and delighting in the perfection of all He'd created. It was, indeed, a wonder to behold. Down the stairs of the dais and past the Fiery Stones, the Glassy Sea stretched to the furthest reaches of the City on a Hill, and everywhere The Alpha looked, there was beauty. All were made by Him, and without Him, nothing was made, and all that was made bore the marks of His essence, His own personal beauty and grace.

"This is good," He said, a smile of pure joy brightening His countenance. "In fact, this is brilliant, just brilliant. I love it."

Staring beyond the Glassy Sea and down the slopes from the City on a Hill, He imagined a vast field. And there it was. Covered in grass that was grayish green in color, it would be a boundary of sorts but also a training ground for that which was yet to come.

The Alpha declared, "You shall be the Field of the In-Between and beyond you the Rainbow Stream, which will encircle the base of Proud Mountain on the sides of The North, the Deep Lake, and the Valley Beyond. Let the Field stand between Shamayim and The North as a line of separation."

As He spoke, it all came into being. All of it. One by one, just as He said.

The Alpha became very still, projecting Himself outward and covering the entirety of creation with Himself, His essence, and His Presence.

"I am yours . . . and you are Mine for now and all eternity. Nothing shall ever separate us."

The heavens exploded with unconfined joy. The Alpha laughed. Then, He danced and laughed some more. And it was good.

But He wasn't finished.

Chapter Two

The Alpha walked across the perfectly level surface of the Field of the In-Between, the grass reaching the tops of His feet but going no further. Hands clasped behind His back and moving in a leisurely and unhurried manner, The Alpha crossed the Field in a northerly direction toward the Rainbow Stream.

It was called such by The Alpha because a rainbow of colors flowed bank-to-bank: deep blue transitioning to light blue and then peridot green, followed by yellow citrine, which flowed into orange garnet as it neared the north bank, and finally, ruby red. As the stream flowed, the colors never blended but remained separate and distinct. There were sections where it narrowed down to the point that, with a running start, one could've leaped to the other side, but those places were few and far between. Mostly, it was wide enough to serve as a middle ground between Shamayim and The North.

The Alpha reached the bank, sat down on the soft, grassy slope, closed His eyes, and listened to the music of the water as it flowed downstream. Tranquil. Restful. Meditative. It would become a place of peace for all who came after.

He opened His eyes and looked toward The North and saw Proud Mountain rising majestically from the landscape. Proud because its summit was the loftiest point in Shamayim.

With one thought, The Alpha was suddenly at the mountain's base, regarding the brilliantly colored waterfalls as they flowed into the Rainbow Stream—vivid hues and harmonious tones descending the slope from the white-capped peaks. The mountain trembled in His Presence, but whether from fear or awe, one could not say.

The Alpha then moved to the highest elevation of Proud Mountain, the summit from which He could see the Rainbow Stream, the Field of the In-Between, the full length of the Glassy Sea and its approach to the city, the palace, and the throne room, and finally, His glorious throne. Even at the farthest edge of Shamayim, the view was unobstructed.

The Alpha stood unmoving, simply staring lovingly over all He had made.

Finally, He said, "As much as I love My creation, I find Myself longing for something more. Longing for . . . some*one*. Like unto Myself, yet separate and distinct."

He was suddenly in the midst of the Fiery Stones, standing still as they rustled and flowed beneath His feet. His glorious face turned serious. Somber. Then, He moved up the stairs, turned, and sat, settling back against His throne in His new home. His brow furrowed as if in deep contemplation, consideration, and calculation. His eyes seemed to pierce to the farthest reaches of His Spiritual Realm and beyond.

It was hard to know how long He sat, but at some point, the atmosphere began to change, feeling like an open field before a mighty thunderstorm.

The Alpha leaned forward, His countenance shifting from deliberation to satisfaction as if having just solved a particularly challenging puzzle. Something was about to happen—something that had never been, nor would ever be exactly like this again. He weighed all the possibilities as far as they could go.

With joyful anticipation, He said, "I will . . . " and then paused, considering the importance of what He was about to declare.

He had created everything else without thought of consequence, for from His physical creation, He received complete and total cooperation. But this . . . this was pregnant with the possibility of consequence.

Rising to His feet, The Alpha descended from His throne, and as He moved, the throne room began to fill with a rushing, mighty wind. Unchecked, it would have been terrible in its force and substance. But, as with everything else in the Spiritual Realm, it had no will of its own. Only such as The Alpha commanded.

He stopped at the base of the stairs and stretched His hands outward, declaring, "I will now take of My essence and mix it with glorious light, creating a living being whose life force will be eternal. Like Me, but not in My likeness."

Many have had their own way of describing the being that suddenly appeared, but let's start by describing his appearance as, first and foremost, magnificent. Not in the way that The Alpha is magnificent, but magnificent nonetheless. His form was covered head to toe with all manner of precious stones—stones that hadn't previously existed but were imagined specifically for this new creation. Carnelian, chrysolite, topaz, onyx, lapis lazuli, turquoise, and beryl, all in a majestic array.

The Alpha stood back, marveling at what He had just brought into being.

"You are perfect in every way," The Alpha declared as Creator and creation regarded each other. "Just as I imagined you to be."

He knew joy, having experienced it at the creation of His Spiritual Realm. But this was different. Transcendent.

His new creation stood as if rooted in place, staring at The Alpha and then at the throne. He cast his gaze at the beauty of the surrounding throne room and then back to The Alpha again.

"Who are You?" he asked, his voice the pure personification of melody. "And who am I? And what is this place?"

Smiling at hearing His creation's voice for the first time, The Alpha said, "I am the first and the last, the beginning and the end . . . The Alpha. This is Shamayim, and you are . . . "

He stopped short of making the pronouncement, pondering what He was about to say.

Finally, He said, "You are Son of the Dawn, and I love you."

The Alpha was love, and love was The Alpha, and suddenly, that love had a new expression, reaching out and enveloping the new creation with all the passion and emotion He had to give.

Son of the Dawn understood what The Alpha had said, but more than that, he felt what He was feeling.

"You are The Alpha, and You are beautiful. Am I beautiful, too?"

"Oh my, yes," The Alpha said, stepping forward, throwing His arms around His new creation, and pulling him close. "Yes, you are. You are more than beautiful. You are the perfect embodiment of beauty."

Son of the Dawn was awash in his emotions for the first time. He also felt an intense sense of awe, respect, and admiration for The Alpha.

Returning the embrace, he said, "Even though I am unsure of what it means, I love You in return, Alpha."

Laughing, The Alpha replied, "And I accept that love."

"What am I supposed to do?"

"Come, learn of Me, and I will teach you My ways."

Son of the Dawn had a sudden and overwhelming urge to worship The Alpha.

"I don't know what this means, but . . . " he knelt on the Fiery Stones, bowing his head, and continued, " I worship You, Alpha. I offer all I am to You for Your glory."

The words he spoke and the emotions he felt were coming from a place deep within—a place completely unknown to him and yet very present in his mind.

Reaching down and pulling Son of the Dawn to his feet, The Alpha said, "And I accept your worship. Now, I'm sure you have many, many questions."

Son of the Dawn slowly turned in a full circle, taking in the majesty of the throne room.

"This place, it's . . . I don't even know how to describe it."

Smiling, The Alpha said, "Yes, it is rather amazing, isn't it?"

"In every way." Son of the Dawn allowed himself a small laugh. "I was about to say that I've never seen anything like it, but I've never seen anything like it or otherwise."

The Alpha laughed, saying, "That's true. And you will feel that frequently as you begin to experience My Kingdom."

Son of the Dawn grew thoughtful. "Are we the only two in Your Kingdom?"

"For now. But it won't always be like this."

"So, You will create others like me?"

"No," He answered quickly. "There will never be another like you. You are Son of the Dawn. The anointed cherub who walks amongst the Fiery Stones. Beautiful beyond description. Majestic beyond imagination."

Son of the Dawn opened his mouth to ask a question, hesitated, and then asked, "Is it possible for me to see myself? To know my appearance?"

"I can do better than that. I will reveal how you appear in My eyes."

Placing His hands on each side of Son of the Dawn's face, He stared deep into his eyes. As He did so, Son of the Dawn could see himself. Not a reflection, but a self that was pure and undefiled, untarnished as seen through The Alpha's eyes.

"Oh," he said, his entire body trembling under The Alpha's touch. "I really am beautiful."

"Yes, you are," The Alpha replied, stepping back and letting His hands drop to Son of the Dawn's shoulders. "But never forget that how you look is not who you are. Who you are comes from the thoughts and imaginations of your heart, for as you think in your heart, so you are."

"I understand, or at least, I believe I do." Son of the Dawn was silent for a moment and then asked, "Alpha, do I have anything to do, or am I just supposed to *be*?"

The Alpha started walking toward the open end of the throne room, beckoning for Son of the Dawn to follow Him.

He said, "Being is the most important thing there is. Doing will come, but for now, I want you to explore Shamayim."

"What is that?"

Sweeping His arms wide, The Alpha replied, "This. All of it."

Arriving at the broad and beautiful stairs, Son of the Dawn looked out on The Alpha's realm and asked, "Where can I go?"

"For now, walk the streets of the city. Get to know them by name. Then, I will help you move on from there until, little by little, you get to know this Kingdom, for it can be your abode . . . here with Me forever."

"I don't know *forever*."

"Yes, well, of all the things you will learn, that just may be the most difficult to comprehend. But you need not concern yourself with that at present. Just go. Have a look around, and when you return, we will begin your instruction."

With a nod of understanding, Son of the Dawn said, "Yes, Alpha." He walked slowly down the stairs, hesitated slightly before stepping out onto the broad avenue fronting the palace, and then walked forward boldly.

With a smile lighting his beautiful face, he said, "I'm going to love it here. I can feel it."

As The Alpha watched him go, He said quietly, "It is done. Set in motion. He knows so little. What will he do with what I give him, what I teach him, and the things I entrust to him?"

He returned to the throne, already imagining what came next.

Chapter Three

As Son of the Dawn slowly went down the avenue fronting the palace and wrapping all around it, he became aware of his movement. Although he had legs and instinctively knew what they were and what they were for, he realized he was moving without walking.

"What is this wonder?" he mused.

Training his gaze forward, he saw an interconnecting avenue ahead and thought that he desired to explore that avenue. Gliding smoothly over the surface of the golden pavement beneath his feet, he arrived at his destination almost as soon as the thought formed.

"Alpha?" he said, although no word was spoken aloud.

"Yes, what is it?" came the answer in his mind.

"I find that I can move without walking. Why is that?"

There was a soft chuckle. "Your mind is your method of movement, whether you choose to walk or simply transport to where you desire to be."

"Then, why do I have legs?"

"Because there are times when it is more appropriate to walk than to transport."

"Why is that?"

The Alpha replied, "Walking affords you the opportunity to slow down and observe everything around you more thoroughly and leisurely."

"How do You do it?"

It was a good question and one The Alpha hoped he would ask, for it demonstrated a desire from His creation to be like His Creator.

"Well, I do both, but actually, I prefer walking."

Son of the Dawn paused briefly and asked, "Would You come and walk with me?"

No sooner were the words spoken than The Alpha was standing beside him.

"Would you like Me to show you around My city?"

"Very much so."

"Come and see."

The Alpha began walking slowly down the avenue, hands clasped behind His back, gesturing occasionally at something of note and acknowledging the homage paid by various trees and plants as He passed.

Son of the Dawn remarked, "Those trees and plants seem to bow as You approach."

"Yes, they do. It's an expression of love and adoration."

"I see. And how do You return their love?"

The Alpha laughed, saying, "I breathe."

"I don't understand."

"My breath brings life to all, and without My breath, they could not live."

"Are they alive? Sentient?"

"In their own way, yes. A better way to say it is that they are aware of Me, and I am aware of them. It is a symbiotic, synchronous, and loving relationship. In Me, all things live and move and have their being."

"Am I that way?"

The Alpha stopped walking and turned to face His angelic creation. "You are much more. You are of Me, but I am not of you. You have My essence, but I do not have yours. We are alike and, yet, vastly different."

"That's very confusing to me."

"I'm sure it is. Perhaps, for now, all you need to focus on is the fact that I fashioned and formed you to love and be loved in return. To be with Me and like Me but fully yourself. To learn of Me while, at the same time, becoming who you were created to be."

"And what was I created to be?"

"Significant beyond measure. The first of many created beings to come. The pinnacle of My creation. Singular in honor and grandeur. Chief of all the angels."

"What is an angel?"

The Alpha laughed and commented, "So many questions."

"Well, I'm curious about many things."

"Indeed, you are," the Alpha said with a smile as He resumed strolling. "Think of it like this: angels are beings who will be like you but different, just as you and I are different."

"Okay. I think I understand. And when is this going to happen?"

"When I will it to be so."

Rounding a bend in the avenue, Son of the Dawn was captured by what he saw stretching out before him. The City on a Hill seemed to fill up the entirety of his vision. Majestic buildings rose in perfect symmetry as high as he could see, fashioned from gold and purest light. Gilded avenues, at once labyrinthine and ordered, wound in, among, and through it all. Flowering trees lined every avenue, every street, every boulevard, filling the air with a fragrance that was both enlivening and calming.

Finally finding his voice, Son of the Dawn said, "I feel compelled to say something but am unable to find appropriate words to describe what I am seeing."

The Alpha placed a mighty arm across his shoulders, saying, "That's the thing about wonder . . . if you could describe it, it would cease to be wonderful."

"Oh, yes. I understand. Not everything requires description. Some things are just too marvelous for words and should simply be observed and appreciated without comment."

"Very good. You catch on quickly."

Smiling slyly, Son of the Dawn replied, "Well, You did make me so . . . "

The Alpha laughed at his joke and said, "I want to show you something. Come and see."

Son of the Dawn suddenly found himself alongside The Alpha, standing before a thing of beauty.

"What is this?" he asked.

"This," replied The Alpha, gesturing with His hand, "is the Glassy Sea."

"It's incredible. What is it for?"

"You mean, what does it do?"

"Yes."

"Nothing."

Son of the Dawn said, "I don't understand. If it does nothing, then what purpose does it serve?"

"Its purpose is to make Me happy."

"And this is accomplished by just . . . being?"

"Exactly."

"I remember You saying something about that before—something about how being is the most important thing there is. Is that what You're talking about with the Glassy Sea?"

"In a manner of speaking." He paused and then explained, "I value two things above all else: relationship and truth. And the purest manifestation of truth is when you are true to yourself."

Son of the Dawn said, "So, You're saying that, for instance, for the Glassy Sea to be true to itself, it only has to *be*?"

"Correct. Further, for it to attempt to be anything other than that would mar the relationship we have."

Shaking his beautiful head, Son of the Dawn said, "I have so much to learn."

"You do, and you will. Come on."

The Alpha stepped onto the surface of the Glassy Sea and began walking its length.

"Am I supposed to follow You?" Son of the Dawn asked hesitantly.

"Yes."

"But isn't that liquid?"

"Only if you want it to be."

Son of the Dawn bent down and touched the water, watching his hand disappear below the surface.

"So, You're saying that if I want it to support my weight, it will?"

"Why don't you try it and find out?" Smiling, He added, "Walk by faith, not by sight."

"How deep is it?"

"What does it matter?" The Alpha replied with a laugh.

"Uhh, well, I'm not sure—"

"Come on. Just do it."

Son of the Dawn stepped tentatively onto the surface of the Glassy Sea and drew back as his foot slipped beneath the surface.

"Okay, did You see that? My foot went right in, and now it's soaking wet."

"That's because you have doubt. Get rid of the doubt, and you'll be fine."

As he stared at the surface, Son of the Dawn suddenly was able to see it for what it was and stepped forward boldly.

"Okay," he said, bouncing in place, "this is pretty amazing. It's almost as if it was longing for me to walk on it."

The Alpha smiled, pleased that Son of the Dawn had the courage to overcome his doubt.

He said, "You are going to encounter many things that will appear to be one thing, but for those with eyes to see and ears to hear, they are actually something else entirely."

Catching up to the Alpha, Son of the Dawn said, "I'm not certain I understand."

"What you *believe* is the most important thing about you. Because from that foundation, everything else is derived. You believe a certain thing, and that belief generates a whole way of thinking. And then, those thoughts produce feelings and emotions which, in turn, trigger actions."

Son of the Dawn shook his head. "I'm so young, and everything is so new. I am finding this to be quite overwhelming. But what You said makes sense . . . I think."

The Alpha laughed and threw His arm across Son of the Dawn's shoulders.

"You are young—there's no denying that—but I created you with a limitless capacity for knowledge and, beyond knowledge, wisdom."

"What's the difference?"

"I am so glad you asked. Knowledge, or knowing, is simply a collection of facts and information. Wisdom, however, is the ability to make sound judgments and decisions based on that knowledge."

"I see. And when You say limitless, You mean—"

"I mean that your mind is truly illimitable, inexhaustible, and infinite."

The two walked together in silence for a time—Creator and creation—comfortable in each other's presence as if it had always been so. Son of the Dawn was arrayed in all those precious stones, and the stones seemed alive in the light of The Alpha.

Gazing upon what appeared before him, Son of the Dawn asked, "What is this place?"

"It is the Field of the In-Between."

"In between what?"

“Here and there.”

“And what is there?”

The Alpha said, “The North.”

“Okay, and what is The North?”

“It’s over there. It is a different place than here.”

“What makes it different?”

The Alpha swept His hand toward The North, saying, “That incredibly tall peak you see in the distance is Proud Mountain.”

“I don’t know this term.”

“Proud?”

“Yes. It sounds bad.”

“Well, it definitely can be. But it can also be good. For instance, I created you. You are everything I hoped you’d be, and I am proud of you.”

Son of the Dawn said, “I see. So, being proud isn’t bad?”

“Not if it’s justified.”

“Help me understand the difference.”

The Alpha paused and then said, “Well, you can be proud to be My creation, proud of our relationship, proud of the way you love and honor Me—the way you reflect all of the beauty I instilled in you.”

“Okay, I understand that. When would pride not be justified?”

“If you were ever to develop a corrupted and self-idolizing love of your own beauty or an irrational sense of your own self-importance.”

"I'm not sure I fully understand what all that means, but it sounds like that would be very negative."

"Yes, it would."

"Well, I want to be just like You, Alpha. So, maybe, if I stay focused on that, I won't have to worry about anything else."

The Alpha stared at His creation before replying, "It is true. If you focus on being just like Me, you'll be fine."

Son of the Dawn stared toward Proud Mountain. "Could we go there? To Proud Mountain?"

"Of course. But we will walk because there are a few things I want you to see along the way."

"Great. I like the feeling walking gives me."

The Alpha motioned for Son of the Dawn to go ahead of Him, and as soon as he stepped out onto the Field of the In-Between, the dull gray-green grass under his feet turned to glowing chartreuse, causing him to halt abruptly.

"What just happened?"

The Alpha laughed. "Keep walking and find out."

The next step turned the grass turquoise and the next a brilliant citrine.

"I still don't understand what is happening."

"It's simple. The grass of the Field reflects a person's true emotions. You were at first hesitant, but as you continued walking, the hesitancy turned to excitement and then joy, which, in turn, made the grass glow brighter and with more intensity."

"Okay, I get it," Son of the Dawn said and began to move in a circle, causing different colors to appear, but none he liked so well as the citrine. He tried to make it reappear but couldn't do it. He became disappointed, which caused the grass under his feet to return to its former dull gray-green color.

"Did you see what just happened?" The Alpha asked.

"Is it because I was disappointed that I couldn't make citrine comeback?"

"Good observation. Now, watch what happens when you overcome the disappointment."

Clearing his mind, Son of the Dawn took off walking, moving faster and faster until he was running. Under his feet, a riot of brilliant colors rippled through the grass.

"This is amazing," he hollered from the middle of the Field and began laughing from the pure joy the phenomenon produced. As he laughed, the colors became more and more intense.

The Alpha approached the place where he was standing, and Son of the Dawn noticed the colors in the grass produced by His Presence glowed with a density of texture and intensity of color that overwhelmed his own, spreading out in concentric circles and covering the entire Field. Then, The Alpha raced ahead, beckoning him to follow.

When Son of the Dawn caught up, he asked, "How do You make the colors change so quickly? And why do You have so many more than me?"

"Well, I *am* The Alpha."

"Ah, of course. Maybe I should just concentrate on making my colors as bright as they can be instead of desiring Yours."

"Sounds like it'd be worth a try."

"But I still want all of Yours," he said with a playful grin.

Son of the Dawn felt happiness and joy beginning to rise within him, and immediately, his own colors returned, but not just his original three. An entire rainbow of color exploded around him.

"Okay," he said laughing, "this will work."

As he danced and spun his way around the area, The Alpha began moving toward the section of the Field that sloped downward toward the Rainbow Stream, pleased by how much Son of the Dawn was enjoying himself.

Arriving at the stream, He paused and waited for His young angel to catch up.

Son of the Dawn stopped by His side on the bank. "What is this?"

"This is the Rainbow Stream. It is the middle ground between Shamayim and The North."

"So, can I go across? What will happen to me if I do? Is it like the Glassy Sea, which will hold me up if I step on it?"

Laughing, The Alpha said, "Slow down. One thing at a time."

"Oh, sorry. I just have a lot of questions."

"First of all, yes, you can go across. As to what will happen to you, that's entirely up to you."

"What do You mean?"

The Alpha turned to face him, placing both hands on his shoulders as He explained. "The journey to Proud Mountain is not one to be taken lightly. There exists the potential for danger."

"Another word I do not know," said Son of the Dawn.

"Danger is when you are exposed to potentially harmful things or circumstances."

"Okay, but what can harm me?"

Leaning in until His face was only inches away, The Alpha said in a whisper, "Only yourself."

Turning suddenly somber, Son of the Dawn said, "Maybe I should wait until I know myself better before making the journey to Proud Mountain."

"That's definitely a choice you can make, but a better choice would be to *find* yourself on the journey."

Son of the Dawn hesitated only slightly before smiling and saying, "Okay, then. Where do we start?"

"Come, I want to show you the Deep Lake."

"But I thought we were going to Proud Mountain."

"We are."

"But—"

"We will get there. You just have to trust Me."

"I do trust You."

"But your focus is on seeing Proud Mountain."

"I can't deny that, but I don't see what—"

"When your desire conflicts with trust, it compromises relationship. You probably didn't notice, but when you questioned why we were visiting Deep Lake before Proud Mountain, the grass under your feet reverted to its original color. Take a look."

Son of the Dawn glanced down and saw it was true.

"My young angel, I created you to have marvelous vision, which means you can see everything. But you cannot allow everything you *see* to become the focus of your desire."

"Then, it's wrong to desire things?"

"Not if the focus of your desire is to do My will and be in relationship with Me. When you delight yourself in Me, I will give you the desires of your heart."

"Wait, so are You saying You will give me the desires of *my heart,* or that You will *give me,* meaning you will implant, desires in my heart?"

"Yes," The Alpha replied with a laugh.

Son of the Dawn shook his head and said, "Being alive is hard."

"You'll get used to it. Come and see."

Chapter Four

They followed the Rainbow Stream, sometimes splashing along in the center, sometimes walking along the banks, and sometimes, with Son of the Dawn racing ahead in anticipation and then racing back to share new things he'd discovered. Passing incredible rock formations, cascading waterfalls, and lush forests, they traveled, with Son of the Dawn's vision captured by each and everything they passed, his delight in every new discovery bringing a smile to The Alpha.

It is no small thing to leave Shamayim for The North, and as they journeyed, Son of the Dawn noticed an incremental, subtle change in the atmosphere. Where the air had previously been velvet-smooth, warm, and richly scented, here it felt colder, having a bit more of a bite. The ground was rockier. Harder. When you fell on the Field of the In-Between, your fall was cushioned. Here, if you stumbled and fell, it had a jarring impact. He thought it strange but was so filled with wonder that he immediately put it out of his mind.

Far upstream, they finally came to Deep Lake, the source of the Rainbow Stream. As Son of the Dawn stood on the shore staring into the deep, sapphire blue of its depths, he said, "Alpha, I have a question."

"Ask me anything."

"Back there on the field, why did You make the colors change when I became disappointed?"

"I didn't."

"But I thought You controlled everything."

"I do."

"Then, I don't understand. If You control everything, and the colors changed when I—"

"Think of it like this," The Alpha interrupted, sensing Son of the Dawn's confusion. "The grass, while completely passive and having no will of its own, still has the capacity to respond to changes in emotion."

"Is that what happened with the colors? It responded to changes in my emotions?"

"That is correct. And who is responsible for your emotions? You or Me?"

"Well, I suppose I am."

"Right again. Therefore, the grass responded in the manner you observed as a direct result of the choices you made. And, as you also observed, when you didn't like what happened, you made better choices that produced better results. That's called freedom of choice."

Son of the Dawn stopped walking, shaking his head. "That's almost too much for me to comprehend. So, You're saying I have the freedom to make choices, but I can't choose the consequences of those choices?"

"I'm not sure I would've said it like that, but that's pretty good. I might use that."

"So, that's a yes?"

The Alpha laughed and began walking along the shore. "That is a yes."

As Son of the Dawn rushed to catch up, he said, "I just want You to know that . . . well, I'm not sure how to say this." Son of the Dawn paused and then bravely said, "I'm so glad You created me."

The Alpha threw His arm around Son of the Dawn's shoulder, pulling him close as He said, "Well, that's great because *I'm* glad I created you as well."

"And . . . I love You, Alpha. I'm not even sure I really know what that means, but I do."

"And I love you back."

"What is beyond Deep Lake?"

"The Valley Beyond."

"And what is the Valley Beyond?"

The Alpha paused before answering, finally saying almost wistfully, "It's . . . for the *not yet*."

"So, You're saying that it's different?"

"I suppose you could say that," The Alpha replied with a secretive smile.

"You said the same thing about The North."

"It's because as I create, systems are put in place."

"Like what?"

"That's probably a conversation for another time."

With that, He turned and began walking toward the base of Proud Mountain with Son of the Dawn following closely on His heels.

As they began their ascent, Son of the Dawn asked, "What are these things You wish to teach me, Alpha?"

"I call them the Encouragements. It's a way of being—of living. Think of it as a pattern to follow."

"And will this pattern help me avoid making wrong choices?"

The Alpha stopped walking, turned, and said, "All I can do is provide you with the truth. What you do with it is entirely up to you."

Son of the Dawn shook his head, saying, "I have so much to learn."

"Yes, you do."

They were gradually ascending the slopes of Proud Mountain when Son of the Dawn suddenly found himself on a lofty, snow-covered peak from which he could see all the way to the City on a Hill.

"I thought we were walking, not transporting," he said.

"We were, but I really wanted you to see My Spiritual Realm from up here."

Gazing out on Shamayim from Proud Mountain's highest peak, Son of the Dawn said, "This is almost too wonderful for words."

"Indeed, it is. Tell Me, Son of the Dawn, what do you see?"

"Perfection. Down the slopes of Proud Mountain, I can see the Rainbow Stream and the Field of the In-Between. Beyond that, I see the Glassy Sea and the City on a Hill. And it's all perfect."

"What else?"

"The Palace, and within the palace, I see the throne room and Your throne."

"Anything else?"

Son of the Dawn extended his sight and saw something that hadn't been there before.

"I see seven lampstands in front of the throne and . . . is it an alcove set into one of the walls?"

"Very good. Yes, it is an alcove."

"Are You going to tell me why those things are there now when they didn't exist before?"

"Yes, but first, I am going to share the Encouragements with you."

"Okay, I'm ready."

"I am The Alpha and Omega—the beginning and the end. I do not change. You are My much-loved creation; I am with you; I am *for* you and am always working for your good. All that I am and all that I do is for your benefit. This is the First Encouragement."

"Can I ask questions as we go along?" Son of the Dawn interjected.

"Of course. It wouldn't be instruction otherwise."

"What is *my good*?"

"To give you every opportunity to be who you were created to be without constraint or compromise."

"Okay, I understand. What's next?"

"I am truth. I am always true to My words, for it is impossible for Me to be otherwise. This is the Second Encouragement."

"So, You're saying that there isn't the slightest possibility that You could ever be other than what You are? That what You say is always the truth?"

Draping His arm gently across Son of the Dawn's shoulders, The Alpha replied, "When I say that I *am* the truth, I am saying that what I speak cannot be other than what I am."

Son of the Dawn nodded in understanding, saying, "Who and what You are is manifested in what You say and do, right?"

"Correct."

"So, if You are love—"

"Then I can be nothing other than love in My thoughts, words, and actions."

Turning, Son of the Dawn embraced his Creator. "I want to be just like You, Alpha."

Returning the embrace, The Alpha said, "That is a wonderful choice, My young angel, and it actually leads right into the Third Encouragement."

Stepping back, he said eagerly, "I am ready to learn."

The Alpha continued, "Pursue Me. For when you seek Me with all your heart, you will experience unspeakable joy. This is the Third Encouragement."

"With *all* my heart?"

"Yes."

"Then, the possibility exists that my heart can be divided?"

"Your heart is yours to do with as you will. It's all part of having choice," The Alpha explained.

"And if I maintain my focus on loving You and remaining in close relationship . . ."

"Then there really isn't much room for wrong choices, is there?"

"Alpha, why would I ever choose not to love You? I cannot fathom it."

"Many things will seem unfathomable to you right now."

"They are. This is all so amazing. How do I learn to understand?"

The Alpha gazed lovingly at His creation. "Son of the Dawn, I have placed within you all the knowledge you will ever need in order to be who you were created to be. Your journey will be one of discovering and peeling back layer upon layer of that knowledge while at the same time acquiring the wisdom necessary to use it properly."

"It sounds like I am going to have a wonderful life."

"This is a good place to share the next Encouragement with you: I am always available. You may approach My throne with boldness and confidence, for I am never more pleased than when you are in My Presence. This is the Fourth Encouragement."

Son of the Dawn nodded slowly as if pondering what had just been spoken. Finally, he asked, "Alpha?"

"Yes, Son of the Dawn."

"I'm not sure how to ask this, but . . . "

He paused before asking, "Is there anything I could ever do that would make You not want to see me?"

Pulling him suddenly into a tight embrace, The Alpha replied, His voice thick with emotion, "I have made you; I have called you by your name, and you are Mine. I love you with everlasting love."

Son of the Dawn sobbed, saying, "You are my Father, and I am Your son. And I want only to serve You and to be with You for always."

Holding him at arm's length, The Alpha said, "I want you to remember this confession, Son of the Dawn. Remember it. Inscribe it on the walls of your heart."

"I will, Alpha. I promise You, I will."

"There is one more Encouragement, but I will save it for another time. I'm going to do something now that has never been seen before by anyone but Me."

"Okay, that sounds . . . intriguing. What is it?"

Smiling broadly, He said, "Come and see," and they went away to the throne room.

As they stood among the Fiery Stones, Son of the Dawn looked around the throne room. "Are You going to tell me about the new additions to the throne room now?"

"Yes. What would you like to know first?"

"Tell me about the alcove and the pedestal and the scroll on the pedestal, those words inscribed on the wall, and finally, those lampstands."

The Alpha said, "The Alcove holds the Scroll of Remembrance. Currently, the scroll is empty, but soon, it will be filled with worthy memories and significant deeds to remind others of what is important to Me. The words on the wall are the Encouragements I've just shared, written there so they may ever be before My throne and all those I create."

"And those seven lampstands in front of the throne?"

The Alpha paused slightly and then smiled. "That is where your seven archangel brothers will stand before My Presence."

"Wait, what? Archangel brothers? First of all, I thought it was just the two of us, and what is an archangel?"

"Son of the Dawn, you are now, and ever after shall be My highest creation. But you are the first among many yet to come. You will inhabit a place of preeminence among them and be their instructor—their example. As I have taught you, so you will teach them. As for what an archangel is . . . " He paused and ascended the steps to the dais before continuing, "Stand clear of the area around My throne."

Son of the Dawn moved well back, almost to the Alcove.

"And now, behold . . . "

The Alpha brought forth seven eternal pieces of Himself, directing each toward the lampstands. The throne room was suddenly filled with sound as the Presence of The Alpha came from behind the throne, circled the outer edge of the room, and then returned only to do it again and again, each rotation picking up speed and the pitch of the sound deepening. Ominous thunder clouds formed overhead. There were seven distinct patterns of wind swirling cyclonically throughout the throne room before forming around each lampstand where the flame from the lamps merged, turning into tornadoes of fire.

A tempest gathered over the throne of The Alpha as bolts of pure energy streaked across the ceiling, snaking up and down the tall parallel columns before escaping out the open end and upward into the sky, creating more tornados of fire and light. At the convergence of the two forces, lightning bolts formed, returning into the throne room and striking each lampstand's funnel of fire multiple times. And then, the Alpha breathed on each one, creating an instant calm.

When the smoke and clouds cleared and the tempest settled into a gentle breeze, there in front of each lampstand stood seven distinct and magnificent individuals, all of whom were staring back at The Alpha with expressions of pure love mingled with intense curiosity.

Chapter Five

The Alpha stood on the dais surrounding His throne, gazing down at the seven beings He had just created, each one in front of their own lampstand and each perfect in every way. Tall and athletically built with countenances that were fierce while at the same time filled with transcendent beauty, they stood in a semi-circle—the entirety of their vision filled with the form and Presence of The Alpha.

The Alpha spoke, His voice filling the throne room and resonating within every molecule of their beings, "Welcome to My Kingdom. I am The Alpha and Omega, the beginning and the end, and I love you."

The seven archangels gazed upon His face. They were beaming with pure pleasure and excitement as if enraptured. The largest one of them fell prostrate onto the Fiery Stones, followed in quick succession by the other six as they began shouting expressions of praise over and over. Standing to the left side of the throne, Son of the Dawn was immediately drawn into their worship, prostrating himself with the others and joining in the chorus of adulation.

It went on and on and seemed as if the created beings would never cease their praise. It would have been true had The Alpha not stopped them, saying, "Your worship is a pleasing act, offered in spirit and truth." He paused to absorb this new moment and appreciate the innocence of their hearts, then continued, "I accept it. Please, stand to your feet."

Son of the Dawn and the archangels stood, their attention captured by the Presence of The Alpha, but stealing quick glances at each other and seeing reflections of themselves, each one singularly unique and all clothed in swirling light.

Son of the Dawn said, "Alpha, I'm confused. As these archangels worshiped You, they used many names."

He replied kindly, "And I am all of those."

"But which one is Your true name?"

"My *true* name is one that no one can pronounce but Me."

"Then, how shall we address You?"

Smiling slightly, He said, "You may call Me Alpha, for I am the Alpha and Omega."

Descending the steps of the dais, The Alpha proceeded to a tall, burly archangel, and it was there that Son of the Dawn beheld a wonder. Thus far in his interactions with The Alpha, he'd been unaware of size differential, for he had simply been *there.*

Now, however, noting that the large angel was taller than him by a good margin, he marveled at how The Alpha's Presence dwarfed him. Not in an intimidating manner as if hovering over him, but rather, it enveloped and surrounded him, drawing him in close, ever closer, until they were almost as one.

The archangel said, "You are The Alpha, but what am I? What are these others? And . . . " he gestured toward Son of the Dawn, seemingly awestruck by his beauty, "Who is that?"

The Alpha smiled, saying, "You—all of you—are My archangels, and this is Son of the Dawn. He will be chief among you. Your teacher. Your guide. Listen well to his words, for he will provide a pathway to truth. And you," He continued, "I name you, Michael. You are the protector of My Spiritual Realm and the most powerful among your brothers."

Without being fully aware of it happening, Michael was suddenly clothed in brilliant, shining metal from head to toe, and on his side, a sword that flamed within its scabbard.

The Alpha continued, "This is your armor. None will ever be able to withstand or defeat you. Draw your sword."

Michael reached for the sword strapped to his left side, wrapping his right hand around the gleaming hilt. He withdrew it in one smooth motion, revealing a sword the likes of which existed nowhere else in The Alpha's Kingdom. Fashioned from pure energy, the blade flashed and sizzled, emitting a keening resonance as sharp as its edges.

"Behold," The Alpha said, gesturing toward Michael, "the Sword of Truth, within which I have placed My Word. And though some may contend against you—against My Kingdom—none shall prevail, for My word will pierce and divide asunder, discerning the thoughts and intents of the heart."

Giving a curt nod, Michael said, "I am honored."

Moving to the angel next to him, The Alpha stared long into his eyes and said, "And you. I call you Gabriel, My strength, My hero. You will be My messenger and My voice to all who are to come."

Gabriel was suddenly clothed in raiment nearly as bright as the light swirling around him. And when he spoke, his voice was so very like The Alpha's that all turned toward him, gazing in open wonder.

"I am humbled and honored, Alpha, to be entrusted as Your messenger."

Next, He came to one who was startlingly beautiful, only not nearly as radiant as Son of the Dawn.

"And you, My lovely one, I shall call you Jophiel, for you have the ability to make beautiful everything you see and everything you touch."

Jophiel was suddenly clothed in a high-collared garment that appeared to be made from strands of gold interwoven with particles of light. The beautiful angel, though nearly as large as the others, seemed to Son of the Dawn to be different. And when speaking, their voice resonated with a distinctly different timbre.

Jophiel said, "I worship and honor You and will carry the express image of Your beauty everywhere I go, both now and forevermore."

Unable to hold back his curiosity, Son of the Dawn asked, "Alpha, this angel seems different from the rest. How is that so?"

He smiled, saying, "I, your Alpha, am one, yet I have different expressions, while at the same time, I am not limited to one or the other. Jophiel represents a manifestation of My nature that is different from any of you. Gentler, weaker physically, and yet powerful beyond comprehension."

The Alpha then stood in front of the next angel and proclaimed, "You are Uriel, My fire. Bringer of wisdom and the angel of the Presence. You will shine the light of My truth upon all who need or desire it. To you is given care of the Scroll of Remembrance, to faithfully inscribe for all who come after the significant events and happenings of My Kingdom."

The light that already clothed him seemed to morph into raiment that was like liquid fire, with tongues dancing up and down his arms and legs and across his back and torso.

Uriel bowed slightly before saying, "I will burn brightly with Your truth and faithfully execute my calling."

Next, The Alpha stood in front of an angel whose very countenance seemed to cause Son of the Dawn to feel settled, peaceful.

He said, "To you, I give the name Chamuel, for you are one who already seeks Me. You will be a bringer of peace into troubled times and situations. Through you, My unconditional love will be made known."

Beginning with the hood that suddenly covered his head, his garment seemed to be formed from waters as still as the Glassy Sea. Deep blues and aquas intermingled, constantly shifting and rippling. All who gazed upon Chamuel experienced an immediate sense of peace and serenity.

Chamuel answered humbly, "I will be what You have named me, Alpha. Oh, how I bless Your holy name and offer my unconditional love."

As he finished speaking, it prompted another outpouring of worship, praise, and honor from all the angels.

Signaling for quiet, The Alpha moved on to the next archangel.

"And to you, I shall give the name Zadkiel, angel of mercy, guiding all who seek My throne of mercy."

His deep crimson garment hung from shoulder to floor with long, billowing sleeves that seemed to be woven without a seam.

Zadkiel bowed low. "This shall be my only purpose."

Stopping in front of the last of the seven archangels, The Alpha placed His hands on both of his shoulders and said, "Full of compassion, I name you Raphael. You will bring joy where there is sorrow, healing where there is hurt."

He was immediately clothed in a satin garment of deep emerald, undulating with the same textures and intensity as the arch surrounding the throne.

Trembling with overwhelming emotion, Raphael bowed his head. "I will honorably carry out that which You have created me to do."

Standing back, The Alpha said, "You seven are My archangels. Your allegiance shall ever be to Me, and Me alone. I will be your King, and you will be My servants in this glorious Kingdom. You will begin by serving each other." Turning to Son of the Dawn, He said, "As I have commissioned you, I now ask you to commission My archangels."

Son of the Dawn immediately stepped forward, joining The Alpha at the foot of the dais.

"I'm not sure I know what to say."

"Trust me," The Alpha said with a knowing smile. "It will come to you."

Then, Son of the Dawn stretched out his hands, gesturing toward each in turn. "Michael, you shall lead the archangels as the Great Prince and leader of the warrior angels. Gabriel, you are a Chief Prince of the archangels, and you shall faithfully lead The Alpha's messenger angels in service to your King, respecting the authority of Michael, your Great Prince. Together, in one accord, you will lead the other five archangels and oversee all their responsibilities. Do you both accept this commission?"

In unison, Michael and Gabriel responded, "With honor."

Continuing, Son of the Dawn said, "Uriel and Chamuel, in addition to everything your names entail, you are also warrior angels who will serve your King under Michael's command. Do you accept this commission?"

The two snapped to attention, saying, "With honor, Son of the Dawn."

Moving on, he said, "Jophiel and Zadkiel, you will be assigned to Gabriel and will serve your King nobly and notably as messenger angels. Do you accept this commission?"

Together, they replied, "We accept with honor."

"And lastly, Raphael, as The Alpha's healer, you will serve faithfully under the Great Prince, Michael. Do you accept this commission?"

Bowing low, Raphael replied, "I accept with great honor."

The Alpha thanked Son of the Dawn and then said, "From you I will build My Kingdom, and nothing shall ever prevail against it. It is everlasting, unshakable; nothing shall rival it. My throne is established in Heaven and will rule over all. It will be said of this Kingdom by all who come after, 'Come, let us go to The Alpha's realm, that He may teach us His ways and that we may walk in His paths.' From the North, South, East, and West, all will come and recline at My table."

Suddenly, the throne room was filled with shouts of praise. As Son of the Dawn and the seven archangels began dancing and leaping, the Fiery Stones joined in the celebration, with flames swirling between and among the celebrants.

The Alpha ascended the steps to His throne and sat down to enjoy the spectacle. So pleased was He with all He had created that His smile caused the emerald arch to ripple and undulate rhythmically in time with the angels' celebration.

They shouted, “Worthy, worthy is He to receive all glory, honor, power, dominion, and strength, both now and forevermore.”

Seeing the response of the emerald arch, the angels circled the throne as their praise increased in intensity and volume, linking arms and dancing with complete abandon.

Suddenly, The Alpha’s Presence began to glow with an intensity seen by none before, reaching out and engulfing, cradling, and caressing His creation, lifting each in arms of perfect love.

To them, He said, “I am yours, and You are Mine. So shall it ever be.”

Slowly, He began to draw back His Presence, returning the archangels to their original positions by the seven lampstands.

Turning His attention to Son of the Dawn, He said, “I have entrusted you to carry My light to all, and not only to carry it, but to soberly steward the light, ensuring that it remains available to all who seek both now and ever after.”

“I fully accept the responsibilities You have stated, but—”

“You are wondering about your position, are you not?”

Startled, Son of the Dawn replied, “Yes, I am. The archangels all have lampstands designating their positions, but I don’t seem to have one.”

“That’s because you are to be ever at My side. The only reason you would *not* be at My side is if you choose differently.”

“But why would I ever do such a thing?”

“Why indeed? Now . . . I’m going to take My archangels on a tour of My Kingdom. You may do as you wish.”

With a bow of his head, Son of the Dawn left the throne room, walked down the broad stairs surrounding the entrance to the palace, stepped onto the surface of the Glassy Sea, and then sprinted to the Field of the In-Between. He stopped suddenly, filled with deep contemplation.

Why would I ever leave The Alpha's side? It is a perfect existence. He thought, *I am His and He is mine. Who could ever wish for anything greater? The Alpha has entrusted me with so much responsibility. He values me. His trust in me feels wonderful, and I will not let Him down*.

"That is a noble thought," The Alpha said, suddenly appearing in front of him.

Son of the Dawn stepped back a pace. "I thought You were going to take the archangels on a tour."

"I was, and I am."

"What do You mean by that?"

"I mean, I am there and I am also here."

"I have no idea what that even means. How can You be both there *and* here?"

Laughing, The Alpha said, "I can be everywhere at once, or I can confine Myself to a specific place because I am omnipresent—everywhere at the same time. Since you left the throne room, I have shown them the Deep Lake, Proud Mountain, and everything I revealed to you. Now, I am back and enjoying being with them—and them enjoying being in My Presence and I am also here experiencing the same feelings with you."

Son of the Dawn expanded his sight and stared toward the towering spires of the City where he saw the seven archangels strolling down one of the grand avenues, and there, in front of them . . . The Alpha. He looked to where He stood in front of him and then back toward the City.

"Still there," The Alpha said playfully.

"This is too much for me to comprehend," Son of the Dawn said. "Here, there, and all around, all at the same time." His eyes suddenly filled with light and anticipation as he asked eagerly, "Can I do that?"

"No, for I have reserved it unto Myself."

Nodding in acceptance, Son of the Dawn turned and stared in the direction of the City and saw the archangels back in the throne room grouped around the wall containing the Encouragements.

Son of the Dawn said, "You appear to be instructing the archangels. Shouldn't I be there for that?"

"Yes, you should. In fact, how would you feel about teaching them the Encouragements?"

"It would be my honor."

And with that, Son of the Dawn found himself back in the throne room in front of the archangels, still standing at the wall where the Five Encouragements were inscribed into stone by a single finger of The Alpha.

Michael said, "What just happened? Son of the Dawn wasn't here, and suddenly, he was."

The Alpha said, "It's called transporting. It's how I took you to the various points around My Kingdom. You will all learn to do it on your own and have the opportunity to experience different forms of mobility that will allow you access to My Spiritual Realm. But first, Son of the Dawn is going to instruct you in the Encouragements."

Gabriel asked, "What are these Encouragements?"

"They are the truth," the Alpha replied.

"You mean they are true?"

"More than true . . . they are *the* truth."

"What's the difference?"

"Something can be circumstantially or factually correct and be true. But *truth* is transcendent of circumstances. Your perspective of something, as filtered through your experience, can be perceived as or feel true, but truth is immutable and unchangeable. It is objective, not subjective. Think of these Encouragements, these precepts, as the foundation for everything else you will learn, do, and be in My Kingdom."

As Son of the Dawn stepped forward and began to teach the archangels, The Alpha withdrew to His throne, where He sat marveling at the perfection of His creation, pleased with the interaction between them and planning for what came next.

As if combined into one image, He saw the past, present, and future all at the same time.

Overlayed.

Intermingling.

Interwoven.

Intertwining.

Combinations, permutations, possibilities of the future. All of it together in His mind.

He saw the legions of newly created beings yet to come. He saw the Physical Realm project laid out perfectly before Him and all that would entail.

The challenges and the triumphs.
The glory and the flame.
He saw it all and nodded His great head.
"As I have conceived it, so shall it be."

Chapter Six

Having completed their tour of the Kingdom and initial instruction in the Encouragements, Michael and the other six archangels walked down the center of the Glassy Sea toward the Field of the In-Between.

"So . . ." Chamuel said, "the Encouragements. They are a lot to take in."

"Yes, they are," Jophiel agreed, "but I thought the way Son of the Dawn presented everything was—"

"Amazing," Raphael said. "In fact, *he's* amazing."

"And beautiful," Uriel added.

"Well, he is the Chief of all the angels," Michael said.

"All the angels," Zadkiel mused. "Do you have any idea what that means?"

Gabriel said, "Well, we're archangels, and he's definitely Chief of us."

"Right. But The Alpha specifically said Chief of all the angels, not just us archangels."

"Perhaps The Alpha's not finished creating," Jophiel said.

"Well," Michael said, "He is the Creator, and wouldn't it follow that creators create*?*"

"Uriel," Raphael said, "what do you carry?"

Glancing down, Uriel replied, "It is the Scroll of Remembrance. The Alpha told me to carry it with me wherever I go and that I may add things of importance."

"Okay, but who gets to decide what's important?"

"Do you really need to ask that question? You know, we talk," he said playfully.

They strolled in silence for a bit before Zadkiel said, "Michael, The Alpha said that you are the protector of the Realm."

"What about it?"

"Well . . . protecting it from what? I mean, we're the only ones here, and I'm pretty sure none of us pose a threat."

Michael seemed to seriously consider his answer. "I'm not sure how I know this, but it occurs to me that The Alpha knows far more than any of us can ever know—even Son of the Dawn."

At the mention of his name, Son of the Dawn appeared alongside them, causing Jophiel to jump. "Okay, you have to tell us how you do that."

Son of the Dawn laughed. "I will, but first, as far as what Michael was saying, it's true. We only know what is knowable."

"I have absolutely no idea what that even means," Raphael said.

"Well, it's like this." He led them to the edge of the Field of the In-Between, pointing toward Proud Mountain in the distance. "What's on the other side of that mountain there in the distance?"

Gabriel said, "How are we supposed to know that? We can't see—"

"Exactly. You can't see because it's hidden behind the mountain. But The Alpha can see everywhere at the same time because He can be everywhere at the same time."

Uriel and Chamuel glanced at each other in confusion.

Chamuel said, "How can that be? I mean, we can't do that, can we?"

Son of the Dawn said, "No. I even asked. Only The Alpha can. Back to the point of what is knowable: we have limited capacity for knowing, but He is without limit. Therefore, Michael, if He has designated you as protector of the realm, then He obviously knows something we do not."

"Yes," Michael said, taking it all in. "I can see that. Thank you for the explanation."

"My pleasure. Now, I will leave you all to your exploration."

"By the way," Uriel said, "how did you know what we were talking about if you weren't here?"

"I heard you."

"You heard us? How is that possible?" Zadkiel said.

"Because nothing is hidden here in the Kingdom. The Alpha may know the thoughts and intent of your hearts—and before you ask, by the way—but you will find that your vision and hearing are exceptional. For instance, if you turn and look behind you, you'll note that not only can you see into the throne room, but you can see details."

"You're right," Chamuel said. "I can even read the Encouragements."

"Exactly. It just takes a little focus and concentration. All you need is to stay attentive and not let your mind become distracted by outside influences. Okay, enjoy your exploration."

And with that, he was gone.

Gabriel said, "He is extraordinarily beautiful."

"Yes," Jophiel agreed, "and those gemstones he wears. I could just stare at him . . ."

"All the time," Uriel said.

"I'll tell you something else," Michael added. "His voice. I don't know what it is about it, but I find it so alluring that I don't want to miss a word he says."

Raphael asked, "Are we, you know, *supposed* to love him? Or are we only supposed to love The Alpha?"

"Are you saying that you love Son of the Dawn?" Zadkiel said.

He hesitated, then answered, "Yes. That's exactly what I'm saying. Are you suggesting that you don't?"

"No, not at all. I do love him. I can't help myself. He's just so . . . so . . ."

"Fabulous," Gabriel said, "I admit it. I love him."

"Well, since this is a Kingdom of love, shouldn't we love everyone?"

Jophiel said, "Of course. How could we not since The Alpha made us all so lovely?"

Uriel said, "You're lovely for sure, and so are the rest of us. But Michael . . ."

"What about me?" Michael said.

"Well, you're kind of scary."

"Why, just because I'm a little bigger?"

"A *little* bigger?" Zadkiel said. "You are head and shoulders taller than the rest of us."

"So, you're saying that being the biggest and strongest immediately cancels out my chance of being beautiful?"

Gabriel said, "They're just messing with you. I think you're splendid."

Michael stared at everyone. "So that's how it's going to be, huh?"

"What, us messing with you?" Gabriel stared at the other archangels, who all began laughing. "I'm pretty sure you can count on it."

Without warning, Michael picked Gabriel up and playfully threw him toward the Field of the In-Between, causing him to cry out in alarm. But when he landed, the ground just absorbed his fall, allowing him to spring upright again.

"Wait a second," he hollered. "Do that again. That was amazing!"

"Gladly," Michael replied, racing toward him, grabbing him around the waist, and hoisting him high overhead before tossing him as if he weighed nothing.

This time, Gabriel flung his arms and legs wide, landing on his back and sinking into the surface.

Michael said excitedly, "Okay, now somebody, do it to me."

Uriel immediately grabbed him around the waist and lifted him with all his might, but Michael remained in place.

"What are you waiting for? Pick me up and throw me."

"I can't," Uriel replied. "You're too heavy."

Zadkiel said, "Let me try," and bent to the task with the same results.

Chamuel suggested that he join the two of them and that perhaps together, they could lift Michael. They tried. They failed.

Raphael said, "No wonder The Alpha made you the protector of the realm."

Michael shook his head, saying, "I guess I didn't realize there was that much of a difference between us. But now that I think about it, we are all unique in our commissions. I can't do what you do, Raphael, and you cannot do what Gabriel does."

Gabriel said, "And it's the same for each one of us."

"Well, Michael, you may be the strongest, but how fast are you?" Jophiel said and took off running with Michael close behind.

Then, when Michael attempted a tackle, Jophiel jumped—soaring high overhead and hanging suspended.

"Guys. Look at me! Look at what I can do!"

The other angels stared in wonder before attempting the same thing. They all jumped as high as they could, but Jophiel seemed to be the only one who could hang suspended while the others floated gently back to the field.

Uriel asked, "Can you move around up there, or just hang?"

"I don't know. Let's find out."

Leaning to the left, Jophiel's body began to move in that direction, then to the right, and then up and then down.

"This is amazing," Jophiel shouted, soaring high above.

Michael said, "Do you have to physically lean in the direction you want to go, or can you just think it?"

"Once again, let's find out."

Eyes closed and holding perfectly still, Jophiel began quickly moving backward, forward, up, and down, soaring high and then looping around and in and out.

While everyone's attention was on Jophiel, Gabriel stared toward the far end of the field and suddenly found himself there by simply taking thought.

"Hey," he shouted. "Look!"

They all turned to see what he had done. Chamuel said, "How'd you get all the way over there?"

"The same way Jophiel is flying around. I just thought about being here, and it happ—" As he spoke, he thought about being somewhere else on the field and found himself there. "That was amazing. You all should try it."

Focusing their attention on where he stood, all at once, the five archangels found themselves standing around him.

"This must be that transporting thing The Alpha was talking about," Michael said.

"Well, whatever it is," Gabriel replied, "I like it. Let's do it again."

With that, the seven archangels began zipping around the Field of the In-Between, first here, then there. Laughing, running, and jumping, brilliant colors followed them everywhere they went as the grass changed color to match their emotions.

Chamuel said, "Have you guys been paying attention to what's happening down around our feet?"

"You mean the color thing?" Zadkiel said.

"Yes. It's remarkable. I wonder what it means."

Son of the Dawn was suddenly there in their midst. "You're wondering about the grass?"

"Yes," Michael answered. "Why does it change color?"

"The way The Alpha explained it to me is that the grass perfectly reflects whatever emotion you are feeling in the moment. And, trust me, you cannot hide from it."

"What do you mean?"

Laughing, he replied, "Well, when The Alpha was first showing me around the Kingdom, we came out here, and He told me to walk on the field. I did and was amazed by the colors under my feet. All sorts of colors. My favorite was citrine, but it disappeared, and I wanted to make it come back. I couldn't do it and was disappointed that I couldn't, and the grass returned to its original dull, blue-gray color in response to my disappointment."

"What did you do?" Jophiel said.

"The Alpha explained what was happening, and as soon as I changed my focus to something else—something that got me very excited—the colors just sort of went wild and followed me all over the field." He paused briefly, smiling as he continued, "But you should've seen what happened when The Alpha stepped onto the field."

"Tell us," Uriel said.

"I don't know how to explain it. It was as if the colors exploded, dancing all around Him . . . as if they were worshiping His Presence."

"Well, I can understand that. I mean, who wouldn't worship The Alpha?"

"And it's more than that. You all haven't been around the City on a Hill that much, but everywhere you go, everything expresses worship in His Presence."

"Don't you mean everyone?" Gabriel said.

"No. Every*thing*. Trees, flowers, plants . . . the rocks and stones," he gestured toward the field, "Grass! Everything. All of creation worships The Alpha."

Jophiel had been standing still, listening and thinking. "Before you arrived, Son of the Dawn, we were all wondering what The Alpha meant when He said that Gabriel would lead the messenger angels and that Michael would lead over the warrior angels. Do you have any idea what that's about?"

"Not really, except I sense He will fill His creation with, well, more creation."

"That's exactly what I was saying," Michael replied. "Creators *create*. It's ridiculous to assume He's going to stop with us."

"You're right, Michael," Gabriel said excitedly. "And furthermore, we—all of us—were created by The Alpha, who took of Himself and formed us from Him. It would then follow that since He is creative, *we* can be creative as well."

Zadkiel said, "I'm not sure I understand how that would work."

Laughing, Son of the Dawn said, "Nor I, but, well, for instance. I was just thinking . . ."

As he paused to form his thoughts, the seven archangels pressed in closer, listening intently.

He continued, "I was just thinking, you know, how back in the throne room, there was a sound that spontaneously erupted when we all began to worship the Alpha?"

"Yes," Jophiel replied. "It was marvelous. What was it?"

"I believe it was music."

"What's music?" Uriel asked.

Son of the Dawn laughed, saying, "Before I answer, I need all of you to understand there are going to be many times when something will just appear in your mind that you have never even considered before, and then suddenly, it will be there, and you will have a complete understanding of what it is. That's because when The Alpha created you, He placed within you everything you will ever need to be who you were created to be. Layer upon layer, and as He explained to me, your lives will be one long journey of discovery. I know about music because of what I just shared. Now, as to your specific question, Uriel, music is what happens when you form sounds sequentially into something called melody, and then you add other sounds to it that are complimentary . . . harmonic . . . yes, that's it. Harmony. And then underneath all that, there is rhythm as the foundation."

"I have absolutely no idea what you're talking about," Michael said.

Raphael added, "Me either. What kind of sounds? Can you give us an example?"

"Maybe," Son of the Dawn replied, frowning in concentration.

Deep within his being, he began imagining what he had just described, and as if from far away, a sound was audible. Faint at first, simple, then growing in volume and complexity until it seemed to permeate the atmosphere around them as harmonic lines began weaving in and around the melody. It wasn't produced by any physical object but generated by Son of the Dawn's own spirit and perceived on that same level by the other archangels.

Suddenly, in addition to hearing, they began to see the sound as shapes and colors, with Jophiel leaping on top of a wave of sound, balancing on it, and riding it around the field.

"Look," Jophiel shouted joyfully, "look what is happening. I'm riding the sound!"

"It's a wave," Zadkiel said.

Gabriel asked, "How do you know that?"

"I don't know, I just do," he replied while leaping onto a wave of his own and riding right behind Jophiel.

Other waves appeared until all seven archangels were steering their individual waves all over the field, laughing joyfully.

Uriel hollered, "I love this, Son of the Dawn, and . . . I love you."

"I love you back, Uriel," he replied as a smile turned his already beautiful face even more beautiful.

"We all love you, Son of the Dawn," Chamuel cried out and was quickly joined by the others.

Gabriel said, "This makes me want to worship The Alpha. Son of the Dawn, can we take this back to the throne room?"

His smile broadened, and he replied, "Let's go." Without delay, they were all there before the throne, with the music eliciting melodies of praise born out of their own spirits.

On and on the celebration went, the music growing ever more elaborate and the rhythms more complex. Harmonies previously unknown were born as their voices layered one on top of the other; each archangel's voice perfectly matched in timbre and texture.

Finally, the melodies and harmonies merged into one as they sang in unison, "You are worthy to receive glory and honor and power; for You created all things, and by Your will they exist and were created."

The Alpha sat on His throne, reveling in the worship and adoration of His creatures and adoring them in return. When their song was over, He began to sing, rejoicing over them with joy. At the sound of His song, Son of the Dawn and the archangels fell onto their backs on top of the Fiery Stones as if slain, their faces alight in the glow of His Presence, bathing in the adoration of their Creator. Even when He ceased to sing, the song continued to resonate throughout their being, bringing peace, rest, and an unshakable sense of security.

From deep within Son of the Dawn's being, one word rose up. "Perfection." It captured his imagination to the extent that he could no longer lie there.

Not wishing to disturb the others, he stood quietly, bowed to The Alpha, and slowly exited the throne room without even knowing where he was going or why.

Once outside on the palace steps, he gazed toward Proud Mountain and felt something stirring within him.

He whispered to himself, "Everything I see is perfect. But what is it about that place that causes such disquiet in my spirit? I must find out."

Chapter Seven

Son of the Dawn walked around the City on a Hill as he had done before, only this time, he covered the entire length, breadth, and height. In the process, he discovered the city was built in a perfect square, its measurements equal on all sides. "Foursquare" is the way he'd heard The Alpha describe it.

During his wanderings, he had discovered many things. Luxuriant parks dotted with ponds and fountains, walking paths meandering throughout, overarched by trees both tall and verdant. Vast beds of flowers of all kinds, their scent carried to him on gentle breezes. Squares surrounded by towering buildings crafted from pure light and purest gold, and walkways soaring ribbon-like and connecting them all. As for what purpose the buildings served, he had the impression they were waiting for something.

Or someone.

Entering one great arena, he was impressed at the precision and order of construction, with everything existing in perfect symmetry and making perfect sense in relation to everything else. There were ranks and ranks of seats surrounding a central elevated platform—too many seats to be numbered.

Staring at the seating area, he mused, "I suppose this answers the question of whether The Alpha intends to do any further creating."

"Indeed, I do," The Alpha said from the platform, giving him a start.

"Alpha, I didn't see You there."

"That's because I was not, but then I was."

A bit embarrassed, Son of the Dawn said, "I suppose you heard what I said."

"Yes, I did, and I will address that. But first, I'd like to talk about what you were feeling when you left the throne room."

Son of the Dawn approached the platform, shaking his head and saying, "I don't know how to describe it."

"Try," The Alpha replied, smiling.

"Well, the only thing I can think of is that I found myself suddenly unable to reconcile what I can only describe as two simultaneous yet conflicting emotions."

"Go on."

"When we were all lying there on the Fiery Stones, and the worship toward You was so intense, the only thing I could think of was that we were experiencing perfection."

"And so, you were."

Son of the Dawn continued, "I found the thought so overwhelming that, as You know, I stood and walked outside. But when I walked out of the throne room and saw Proud Mountain in the distance, I was filled with a sudden uneasiness. And I don't understand why. Which is why I decided to go for a walk so I could just spend some time in contemplation."

The Alpha moved closer to the edge of the platform, saying, "And have you found any answers?"

Having arrived at an ornate bench situated under the verdant branches of a large tree, Creator and creation sat.

Son of the Dawn said carefully, "There is something about Proud Mountain—well, actually, The North in general—that troubles me, and I can't understand why."

"Can you describe the thoughts you have when you look toward The North?"

"I haven't tried putting them into words until now, so be patient and let me try to work it out."

"Of course."

Son of the Dawn gathered his thoughts and then said, "It's almost as if when I turn my gaze toward Proud Mountain, there is something pulling me toward it. And I can't understand it because," he paused to gesture grandly, "this is perfect and, as You said, The North is different."

"And you are wondering why that which is not ideal can represent even the slightest possibility of pulling you away from what is."

"Yes! Exactly."

The Alpha smiled. "As I mentioned previously, Son of the Dawn, I created you with limitless capacity and thirst for knowledge and understanding. The North is a mystery to you and is, therefore, tantalizing . . . arousing to your curiosity."

"Is that wrong?"

"Curiosity is necessary in order to acquire knowledge and understanding. But when curiosity turns to obsession—by which I mean that the object of your curiosity begins to dominate your thoughts—then you must evaluate your motives."

"Well, I can't really say I am obsessing over it. It's just so . . . *there*. So impossible to ignore. And I find there are times I cannot get it out of my mind."

"What specifically about it?"

"The fact that I don't understand it and want to go explore Proud Mountain and the Deep Lake and the Valley Beyond. To see for myself what it's all about and what makes it different."

The Alpha stood, gently pulling Son of the Dawn up beside Him. "You may go and explore any part of My Kingdom you desire."

"You would trust me to do that, even though I am so curious about The North?"

"Of course."

"Oh . . . then perhaps I will go."

"But not yet. I am about to do something, and you need to be there."

"What is it?"

The Alpha smiled, saying, "Come and see."

Son of the Dawn found himself transported to the Field of the In-Between, where he joined the seven archangels.

Moving over to stand beside him, Michael said, "Do you know what's going on?"

"No idea. The Alpha just said He was about to do something and I needed to be here."

"That's what He told us as well."

The Alpha said, "It's time for another level of My creation."

"Angels?" Jophiel asked excitedly.

"Yes, Jophiel, angels."

"We've heard You mention them, but what are they?" Zadkiel asked.

"Ministering spirits, sent out on missions to do My bidding."

Gabriel said, "Sent where?"

"Into that which is to come and also here in the Spiritual Realm."

"Will there be many?" Michael said.

Smiling and chuckling slightly, The Alpha replied, "Behold."

He waved His hand toward the Field of the In-Between, the breath of His mouth filling the length and breadth like a fresh and comforting breeze.

Son of the Dawn and the archangels stood in awe as beings began materializing before their eyes.

Myriads.

Thousands upon thousands, and ten thousand times ten thousand, emerging from the atmosphere and swirling above the Field of the In-Between, their faces alight with the glory of the One who had created them.

Son of the Dawn, seemingly caught up in the moment, began a song of worship the newly created beings immediately picked up and began to sing.

With high, soaring melodies and intricately interwoven harmonies, they sang, "Worthy are You to receive glory and honor and power, for You created all things; by Your will they exist and came to be."

Over and over and over came the refrain as The Alpha, standing with arms outstretched and His countenance radiating pure pleasure, welcomed His new creatures to Shamayim.

"I love you, My angels. I love you all," He proclaimed over and over.

So great was the spectacle, Son of the Dawn and the archangels stood in a group around The Alpha, too awestruck to speak or even move, marveling at the scene playing out in front of them.

Finally, Gabriel said quietly, "This is . . ."

"Indescribable," Jophiel added.

The Alpha gestured with both hands, and the angelic host began to settle onto the Field of the In-Between, rank upon rank, until it seemed that the field wasn't large enough to hold them all. But then, wonder of wonders, as more angels spilled from the atmosphere, it seemed as if the field grew to accommodate their numbers.

With Son of the Dawn beside and a little behind The Alpha and the archangels arrayed in a line behind him, they stared out at the field now filled with the luminous, angelic host. Similar in size but with individual characteristics, their raiment was The Alpha's glory, swirling around them from head to toe. Perfectly symmetrical faces were turned toward The Alpha in awe and reverence, eyes burning with the fire of unbridled, passionate love. Throughout the ranks ran a constant undercurrent of murmured praise and worship as various individuals bowed low or prostrated themselves on the surface of the field as the grass beneath their feet blazed with colors too brilliant to imagine.

The Alpha proclaimed in a loud voice, "I have awaited this moment when I would finally look upon My entire angelic host.

You have been in My heart, and now you are here before My realm. You will be My watchers, My builders, My messengers, warriors, helpers, and champions—ministering spirits sent to do My bidding amongst those who are to come. But first, there is much you must learn.

He paused and turned to indicate those who stood behind Him.

"This is Son of the Dawn, Chief of all the angels. His job is to teach you of My ways and lead you into all truth. No one is higher than he."

Moving on, He said, "And this is Michael, the Great Prince, leader of the archangels and warrior angels, the protector of My Realm, and the most powerful of all. Some of you will train in the ways of battle with him. Beside him is Gabriel, Chief Prince of the archangels and leader of the messenger angels. Some of you will train with him."

Turning toward the others, he continued, "Then, there is Uriel, the bringer of wisdom and angel of the Presence, and Chamuel, the bringer of peace into troubled times and situations. They are also warrior angels serving under Michael."

Gesturing toward Jophiel, He said, "There are those among you who will learn many things from Jophiel. And this is Zadkiel, My angel of mercy and compassion, guiding all who seek to My throne of mercy. They also serve under Gabriel as messenger angels. And finally, there is Raphael, who will bring joy where there is sorrow and healing where there is hurt. He also serves under the Great Prince, Michael." Turning His attention back to the adoring throng, He continued, "They are here to teach, guide, correct, and direct you. Learn well from them that your paths may be straight."

The archangels stared out at the vast throng of angels, feeling overwhelmed at the sight before them.

The Alpha continued, "I am dividing you into thirds: one-third will be under Michael's direct instruction, one-third under Gabriel, and one-third under Son of the Dawn. Michael will instruct in the ways of the warrior, Gabriel will instruct in the art of communication, and Son of the Dawn will instruct in the ways of creativity and beauty." He paused before continuing, "Never forget that, in this Kingdom, we are a family ruled by love. You will work together, you will learn together, and you will play together. You have a responsibility to watch out for each other, care for each other, and love each other as I love you. Respect and follow your leaders as those in authority, for I have bestowed it upon them. When you honor them, you honor Me."

One of the newly created angels, who was tall with short, spikey blonde hair, stood in the front ranks. He seemed unable to contain himself and blurted out, "Alpha, I love being in Your Presence, and I-I just want to stay here with You."

The Alpha smiled, saying, "Steele, I love you in return. I have loved you since I first thought of you. Long before anything you see existed, I formed you in My heart and in My mind, carefully imagining what you would be and what you would become after you were created. And now, having you here with Me brings such joy that I cannot contain it."

Steele quickly glanced to his right and then to his left, concerned with what those standing around him would think of this exchange with The Alpha, but no one seemed to have heard, for none were taking even the slightest notice of what was transpiring.

The Alpha said, "If you are wondering whether anyone else can hear us, the answer is no. I speak to you within the most private place in your being . . . the place no one knows but the two of us. It will be a place of meeting, a place of communion, and a place we will converse as if face-to-face."

Steele began to tremble all over as he felt the weight of The Alpha's Presence.

"I am yours, Alpha," he said, his voice quivering with emotion.

The exceptionally large angel to his right said suddenly, "I'm Rok," and then looked as if he immediately regretted it.

The Alpha laughed and replied, "Yes, yes you are, son. And you, though being of few words, will be rich in thoughts and feelings. Long ago, when you were still just a stirring in My mind, I saw you as you are here before Me, and I loved you so much."

Rok's jaw trembled as he tried to form words, but he only succeeded in falling to his knees in worship.

To Steele's left was an angel named Wendly, who stared at The Alpha in open awe and devotion.

Suddenly, deep within, Wendly felt rather than heard, "Hello, Wendly, My precious one. I'm so glad you are finally here, for I have been waiting for you. You are taking the first steps on an amazing adventure. Look to your right. These two—Rok and Steele—will become your best friends. Look after them, for they are going to need you."

"It will be with me as You have said, Alpha, and . . . and . . ."

Wendly couldn't complete the sentence, falling to the ground with Rok. Steele followed quickly after, prompting the entire assemblage to do the same. It was an awesome sight, all those legions of angels bowing before their Creator in silence, broken only by the sounds of many angels weeping in response to the extreme emotions they were feeling at the moment.

Son of the Dawn stepped forward and began to sing, his voice stirring the angels as deep cried out to deep.

"Glory in the highest," he sang, "to the One who was, and is, and is to come. All creation is filled with Your glory, from everlasting to everlasting."

As he repeated it, he was joined by an innumerable company of angels. Then, resonating throughout the Spiritual Realm, trees bowed, light danced, flowers released their fragrance, and plants trembled in awe. The water in the Rainbow Stream shot up in multicolored geysers, and the stars sang for joy. Those standing on the Field of the In-Between noticed their feet beginning to move as if of their own free will as they began dancing. They moved in pairs, in groups, and in long lines, weaving in, out, and through the assembly.

Some were lifted off the ground as if by an ocean swell and began to ride the music around the field, joyfully beckoning others to join them. Some stayed aloft on the waves of sound quite nimbly, while others rolled or slid off, hitting the ground and immediately catching the next swell that rolled past them. So infectious was the overall sense of joy that the archangels joined in the reverie, challenging their subordinates to friendly swell-riding competitions—competitions that Jophiel, by the way, had no trouble dominating.

As The Alpha raised His hands, the music quieted, merging into one final, glorious chord reverberating throughout the realm, then settling over everything like a cool, calming mist.

"Your praise is a sweet-smelling aroma to Me—pleasing, honoring," The Alpha said. "Uriel, record this moment so that it may be remembered."

As Uriel unrolled the scroll and began writing, The Alpha continued, gesturing grandly, "And now, I want you to explore the whole Realm, for I made it for your pleasure. But before you go, never forget that I have called each of you by your name, and you are Mine. You may come boldly before My throne, for I am your Alpha, and you are My angels."

The Alpha's Presence faded away, and the archangels were left facing the throng.

Raphael said, "What now?"

"Now," Son of the Dawn replied, "we do what The Alpha instructed us to do. I take my third, Michael and Gabriel each take their third, and we show them around the Kingdom."

"No, I meant, what do *we* do? You know, the rest of us who haven't been assigned to any specific task."

"But you have. Don't you remember when I commissioned you? Uriel and Chamuel are to serve under Michael; Jophiel and Zadkiel are to serve under Gabriel; and you are also to serve under Michael. But, for this tour of the Kingdom, why don't you come with me as I would welcome your company."

"I'd like that," Raphael said.

Gabriel said, "We should decide where we're going to start so we don't all end up in the same place." He glanced at the milling multitude before them.

He added, "It could get a bit crowded."

"Good point," Son of the Dawn agreed. "Where would you like to start?"

"I'll take my angels to the City on a Hill and work outward from there."

"Michael?"

"I think we'll stay here on the field, maybe work in a little training as well. Where are you going, Son of the Dawn?"

"The North," he said, surprising himself.

"Why there?"

"Why not there?"

Jophiel said, "I can think of quite a few reasons, not the least of which is that it isn't as pleasant as here."

"Perhaps, but it's still part of the Kingdom, and they need to experience it. Besides, I haven't heard The Alpha say anything that would stop us from changing it to our liking."

Michael nodded. "He's right. In fact, when The Alpha took us there, it was strictly to give us an overview of everything, and we really didn't have a chance to do any exploring. I'd like to go back and do that at my own pace."

"I know exactly what you mean," Zadkiel said. "I'd like that opportunity myself."

"Besides," Uriel added, "it makes all kinds of sense to start at the extreme end and work back this way."

"Which was exactly my thought," Son of the Dawn said, and then stopped speaking, staring around at the multitude as if unsure of what came next.

"What are you thinking?" Raphael said.

He laughed, saying, "I'm not sure how we do this."

Stepping forward, Michael said, "Leave it to me." He addressed the host in a loud voice. "Angels, give me your attention, please." He waited for the commotion to die down. "You have been divided into three distinct and separate groups. As The Alpha said, one-third with me, one-third with Son of the Dawn, and one-third with Gabriel. These will be your permanent assignments."

Jophiel stood beside him, saying quietly, "How do you know what you're doing?"

He shrugged. "I just started talking, and things came to me, almost like I've always known what to do." He started to say something to the angels but then turned aside to Son of the Dawn. "Do you want to do the actual divisions?"

"You're doing fine. Keep going."

"Right, but how do we physically divide this many angels?"

Uriel said, "Why don't you just ask them to do it?"

"Do what?"

"Separate out into thirds."

"I don't see how that's possible."

"You never know until you try."

Michael seemed to assess the vast assembly, his attention finally resting on the three angels in front of him, "You three—Rok, Steele, and Wendly, was it?" All three nodded. "You will be with me along with a third of the host. So . . . go ahead . . . divide."

No sooner had the words been spoken than a group of angels separated out and formed behind the three.

Uriel whooped, "I knew they could do it. Now, what's left on either side should be equally divided into thirds."

"Looks like it to me," Raphael said.

Michael allowed a small smile as he gazed at the divisions. "That was pretty great. Thank you for thinking of it, Uriel."

"Hey, it's what I do. I'm a thinker."

"But you're also a warrior."

"Who thinks," he added with a smile.

"Fair enough." Turning back to the angels, Michael said, "All right, I'm not sure how this is going to work, but Gabriel and Son of the Dawn's third, gather around them and their assistants. The rest of you, stay here. We've got some things to sort out."

A loud rustling sound arose from the field as the legions of angels moved to follow Michael's instructions.

Since Wendly, Steele, and Rok were right in front, they stayed put, with Wendly asking, "What do we call you?"

"Call me Michael."

"But you are the Great Prince and leader of the archangels and warrior angels. Shouldn't we call you Prince or something?"

"Michael. Call me Michael."

"Okay," Wendly said, with a smile, "Michael, it is."

The archangels and Son of the Dawn watched in wonder as the vast host of angelic beings seemed to merge into three single, incredibly bright, and glowing lights.

"What is happening?" Chamuel said.

"I'm not sure," Zadkiel said, "but it's amazing."

Son of the Dawn said, "It's like many becoming one."

"How is that possible?"

"With The Alpha, everything and *anything* is possible."

Gabriel said loudly, "My group, with me. We're going to the City on a Hill." Then, he and his group, along with Jophiel and Zadkiel, suddenly vanished.

Michael said, "I don't know if I will ever get used to that."

"What?" Chamuel asked.

"The fact that you can be somewhere, and then just like that," he snapped his fingers, "you're somewhere else."

"And my group," Son of the Dawn announced, "is going to The North."

"You going to do the vanishing thing?" Raphael said, "Or are we going to walk?"

Son of the Dawn said with a smile, "Why walk when we can transport?"

And then, they were gone.

"How'd they do that?" Steele said.

"You will learn," Michael said, suddenly realizing that even though the angels had formed into one source of energy, he could still see individual faces and forms.

"Michael, you said that we would stay here on the Field of the In-Between and do some training," Wendly said. "Training for what?"

"No, I said we *might* do some training, but now I'm thinking that was a bit overeager on my part."

"So, we get to look around?"

Michael asked his archangel assistants, "Uriel, Chamuel, what do you two think?"

“Since thinking is what I do,” Uriel replied, “I *think* we should give them the tour. It’s called context.”

“How do you know that?” Chamuel said.

“What, context? It just came to me. It’s like putting a frame around something so you can see it better.”

Michael said, “Sounds good to me. What do you think, Rok?”

Rok stared at him for a moment, his mouth working to form words, and then he simply nodded energetically, his face enlivened by an excited smile.

“Okay, then. Tour it is. Follow me.”

Michael led his class of angels toward the center of the Field of the In-Between, the grass beneath their feet evolving into as many different colors as there were angels.

From His throne, The Alpha smiled. He smiled at the delight and wonder being expressed by all the angelic host throughout His Kingdom as they saw Shamayim for the first time, loving the joy apparent on their faces—*all* their faces. For even though there were myriads upon myriads of angels, He knew them each by name and loved them passionately as individuals. He loved the way they thought, the way they smiled and laughed, and how they responded to Michael, Gabriel, and Son of the Dawn’s authority.

Most of all, He loved that what He had conceived in Himself in long ages past—that for which He had so meticulously planned and longed—was now a reality. And when He thought of what came next, His smile caused rays of glory to radiate throughout all of the City on a Hill.

And then, The Alpha laughed.

Chapter Eight

Son of the Dawn gathered with his third of the angels at the back side of Proud Mountain on the shore of Deep Lake, staring toward the Valley Beyond. He permitted the angels to explore Proud Mountain and Deep Lake at their leisure. As he stood, contemplating while the others explored, he felt those same inexplicable longings to go further . . . to see the Valley Beyond, if for no other reason than to discover why it was thusly named. It had to mean something, for everything in The Alpha's Kingdom had meaning, often layers upon layers of meaning.

"Son of the Dawn," a deep, gruff voice behind him said.

He turned to see one of the angels standing patiently and awaiting his acknowledgment. Son of the Dawn paused to assess him before replying. He was slender and dark-haired, and his eyes burned with an unusual intensity—an intensity that immediately drew him in.

"Why do you interrupt my repose?" Son of the Dawn asked. "And what is your name?"

The angel answered hesitantly, "I'm Beleth, and . . . well . . . I interrupted your tranquility because I . . ." His nervousness seemed to get the better of him, and he laughed before continuing, "I suppose I just wanted to tell you how happy I am to have been given the honor of serving under you.

I hope it doesn't bother you that we all stare at you. You are just so beautiful, and I, well, we all love you."

Son of the Dawn couldn't explain why, but Beleth's pronouncement brought him an immense amount of pleasure.

"Well then . . . you can interrupt me anytime you want," he said with a chuckle. "I must admit I *do* love hearing things of this sort. Tell me, Beleth, what do you think of The North so far?"

Beleth started to answer when he was joined by a larger angel who was built more sturdily, with flaming red hair that fell in tight curls to his shoulders.

"Son of the Dawn," he said, interrupting his fellow. "I'm Semyaza. Beleth here has probably already told you, but we're—well the two of us anyway—are very happy to have been assigned to you."

"Yes, but I enjoy hearing it again. So, I put the question to both of you. What is your impression of The North?"

Beleth said, "I don't really have anything to compare it with, but I really like it here. It just feels like . . . I don't know, like—"

"We belong," Semyaza said.

"Yes. That's it exactly. It's like we belong here."

"I agree," another angel said, stepping forward. "I'm Remashel." He pulled another angel forward. "And this is Dantanian. And being here is the best thing we've experienced since The Alpha created us."

Staring at the two dark-haired, solidly built angels, Son of the Dawn was taken aback by their response, for it exactly mirrored his own feelings.

"It's interesting you say that because I really like it here as well. However, I feel it is only fair to inform you that it's not The Alpha's favorite."

"Why not?" Remashel asked.

"I asked Him that, and His only response was that it's *different* here."

Beleth stared around him, taking in the landscape. "I agree. It is different, but it's the differences that I find so compelling. For instance," he gestured at the Deep Lake, "there's nothing even close to this back at the City on a Hill. And this is amazing."

"Yes, it is," Son of the Dawn agreed.

"What is on the other side of Deep Lake?" Semyaza inquired.

"It's simply called the Valley Beyond."

"Beyond what?" Dantanian pressed.

Son of the Dawn laughed. "That's a question I had just decided to ask The Alpha before you four interrupted my repose."

"And we're so sorry to have done that, Son of the Dawn," Beleth said hurriedly.

"No, no, think nothing of it. In fact," he glanced toward where Raphael stood talking to a group of angels. "I'm going to need a few assistants to help Raphael out. Are you four interested in that?"

The angels looked at each other, their eyes wide with surprise.

"Oh yes," Beleth replied. "We would be honored. What do you want us to do?"

"To start, stay close to me. Watch what I do. Listen to what I say. Learn. In short, imitate me."

Semyaza said, "That sounds wonderful. Are you going to tell Raphael, or—"

"I will tell him. Just as The Alpha has me and the seven archangels surrounding Him, there may be others I find amongst the company who show special aptitude or initiative and will be joining you and surrounding me. Kind of an inner circle, I suppose you'd say."

The four chosen angels bowed low before Son of the Dawn, with Beleth speaking for the group, "We are honored to serve you, for we love you."

"Oh, don't make a fuss. Stand up. Thank you, though. That is very meaningful to me. Now, off you go. Enjoy yourselves."

As Son of the Dawn stood watching them merge back in with the hordes of angels, Raphael approached and said, "What was that all about?"

"That? Oh, just some angels eager to please."

"I see. It looked like you told them something that made them very happy."

Son of the Dawn smiled. "I did. I told them I wanted them to become your assistants under me. To help with whatever you find that needs doing."

"Interesting. I never thought of that, but that's a really good idea. It will allow us to delegate responsibilities."

"My thought exactly." Son of the Dawn looked toward Deep Lake and then asked, "Raphael, do you ever wonder what is out there?"

"Where, the Deep Lake?"

"No. The Valley Beyond."

Raphael chuckled. "Not really. I've been a little busy. Why do you ask?"

"I'm not sure. It's just, for some reason, I find myself fascinated with going there and exploring."

"Have you discussed this with The Alpha?"

"Yes, I have," Son of the Dawn added quickly, "And to be clear, I would never even think of doing it unless He granted permission."

"And do you think He would? You know, grant permission?"

"He already has."

"Then what are you waiting for?"

"Well," he gestured around at the angels, "I, too, am a little busy at present. Besides, it just hasn't felt like the right time." Moving to the front of the assemblage, he said loudly, "Now, we will ascend Proud Mountain. You are not going to believe the view from up there."

Taking thought, the entire company was suddenly on its peak, staring out over the wonders of Shamayim.

"Is that the City on a Hill in the distance?" Semyaza asked.

"Yes. And if you expand your sight, you can see clearly into the throne room, which is where we will be going next," Son of the Dawn replied.

Beleth said, "It's beautiful." He frowned and added, "Is there another word for beautiful because I feel it doesn't quite describe what I'm seeing . . . kind of like the way we feel when looking at you."

While Beleth's pronouncement gave Son of the Dawn immense pleasure, he played it off, saying, "Raphael, how would you describe the City on a Hill?"

Raphael said, "Gorgeous. Stunning."

Son of the Dawn picked it up, "Spectacular. Remarkable—"

"Extraordinary. Astonishing. Shall we go on?"

"No, I think I've got it," Beleth said with a smile. "Like I said, all terms that would apply to you as well, only . . ."

"Yes, Beleth?"

"Only none of those words do you justice."

"Listen," he said, commanding the attention of all assembled. "I believe there is a teachable moment here. I have nothing to do with the way I appear. The Alpha created me, and I am merely a reflection of His purpose. It is what I do with what I've been given that determines my true beauty—my true value to the Kingdom. You would all do well to remember that."

As the angelic host murmured their approval, Semyaza stood a little apart from the others, staring out over the wonders of the realm. "I'm overwhelmed. Absolutely awestruck."

"I know what you mean," Beleth said. "It's almost as if, I don't quite know how to describe it . . . but from up here, it feels as if I am more than I am."

"Yes," Semyaza replied quickly, excitedly, "that's it exactly. Being up here does give you that sense. Is that good, Son of the Dawn?"

"As I mentioned, The Alpha created you to be amazing, so I'm not sure what the next level up from amazing is."

"We get that," Beleth said, "but this is something else. From up here, it's as if . . . as if we can see everything, and in seeing everything, we can know everything, and by knowing everything—"

"You can be more like The Alpha?" Son of the Dawn asked.

"I mean, that isn't what I was going to say, but isn't that something to be desired? You know, being like The Alpha?"

Son of the Dawn gazed at the legions of angelic beings swirling around the mountaintop. "The Alpha created you, so since you came from Him, you're already like Him. I'm not sure you can be closer or more like Him than you already are."

Semyaza said quickly, "It's just that we love The Alpha with our entire being and just want more of Him."

"As do we all, and I promise you, that will come. For now, there is more to see, starting with the Rainbow Stream."

Back in the City on a Hill, Gabriel guided his group of angels toward the twenty-four stairs leading to the palace and the throne room beyond.

He paused and said, "You now stand on the Glassy Sea, and in front of you is the royal palace, which houses The Alpha's throne room. After we ascend the stairs and move into the palace, you will find yourself standing on the Fiery Stones, which cover the entire surface of the throne room floor. These Stones are sentient, having a special delight in and sensitivity to holiness. In other words, they are aware of the thoughts and intents of the heart and will react accordingly to whoever is standing on them. As such, when you step foot upon them, you will see a reaction—somewhat like we saw back at the Field of the In-Between. Don't be concerned, though; they are just overjoyed to finally feel your presence."

Gabriel turned and started up the stairs with Jophiel, Zadkiel, and the throngs of angels following close behind. The angels had their first glimpse of The Alpha's throne and the Fiery Stones. It was as if their arrival had not only been expected but anticipated, for the Stones began to react to their presence by shooting out tendrils of fire, which danced with a choreography known only to them.

Instinctively, the angels found themselves drawing back, unwilling to move forward.

Smiling, Gabriel said, "You feel it, don't you? The Alpha's Presence."

Almost as one, the gathered light representing his group of angels responded with a murmuring of affirmation.

"It is natural, for this is a high and holy place, the place where we stand in the Presence of The Alpha. He is everywhere, and we are ever in His view, but this is where we come to see Him . . . the place of His manifest glory. What you are feeling is a sense that even though He made us and called us each by name and knows us better than we know ourselves, He is still completely other. Set apart. For there are none like Him. Holy is His name."

The angelic throng began repeating, "Holy is His name."

Gabriel allowed the praise to swell and then signaled for quiet.

"Before the throne are the seven lampstands of the archangels, whose flames shall never flicker, nor shall they ever grow dim. These lampstands," he paused to include Jophiel and Zadkiel, "signal our place in the Kingdom."

One of the angels said in a barely audible voice, "Is . . . is He here right now?"

"He is everywhere. As to whether He will choose to manifest His Presence, that is entirely up to Him."

The angels gazed in awe at the raised dais at the far end of the throne room, and the emerald arch swirling in the atmosphere completely obscured the throne.

Gabriel said, "It is good to feel a sense of holy awe in the Presence of The Alpha, but He also wants you to be comfortable—at ease—when you're with Him. Believe it or not, as you will quickly learn, He actually loves to laugh and enjoy Himself *and* His creation. He can be rather playful. Now, come gather 'round, and I will teach you the Encouragements."

The same angel who had spoken before asked, "What are the Encouragements?"

"That's what I'm going to teach you . . . what is your name?"

"Oh. Schindaug."

"You're serious?"

"About my name?"

"Yes."

"I guess. I mean, that's the name The Alpha gave me, and, you know, you do the best you can with what you've got."

"Ooookay. Schindaug it is."

Schindaug stood a little shorter than the other angels and had long, blonde, wavy hair and dancing eyes, and his mouth looked as if it were very used to smiling.

"So," Gabriel said, "the Encouragements."

Before he could continue, another angel stepped forward.

"Hi, I'm Taylor."

"Okay, Taylor. What is it?"

"Oh, nothing. I just wanted to introduce myself."

Grinning, Gabriel glanced at Jophiel and Zadkiel. "I'm so glad we got that out of the way because we've all been wondering who you were."

Taylor's countenance brightened. "Really? You were?"

Jophiel said, "He's just joking with you, Taylor. You'll get used to that. Seriously, though, it's nice to meet you. I'm Jophiel, and this is Zadkiel. Welcome to the group."

"Thank you. It's nice to meet you all as well. But shouldn't Gabriel be teaching us something right now?"

Gabriel replied patiently, "Good point. Alright, here we go . . ."

As Gabriel led his group through the instruction, he kept sensing that something was off. Not necessarily wrong, just off, as if everything around him was waiting in anticipation.

He had just finished speaking when he noticed Michael and Son of the Dawn had come into the throne room with their groups of angels.

"What's going on?" he asked Michael.

"I don't know. I was summoned."

"As was I," Son of the Dawn said.

The Presence of the angelic host, though clustered together into spheres of light and energy, seemed too much for the throne room to contain. Then, just as at the Field of the

In-Between, the volume of the room began to expand, growing ever larger to accommodate the throng.

"I keep wondering whether there's going to come a point where I will cease being amazed," Chamuel said as he observed what was happening.

Uriel replied, "I'm thinking, no."

They heard a low and undulating rumble as smoke suddenly began spewing from behind the throne. The emerald arch elongated, encircling the throne while rotating cyclonically, slowly at first and then picking up speed. Flashes of lightning snaked across the ceiling, winding down the pillars and connecting with the Fiery Stones, who responded in kind, adding their own inner fire to the spectacle.

Raphael said, "As incredible as this is, I'm not afraid."

"Nor am I," Jophiel added.

From the midst of the smoke, The Alpha appeared on the throne and, with a voice like thunder, said, "Behold . . ."

There, in front of the throne, weaving in and out, among and through the lampstands, were four pillars of fire, the center of each glowing as if composed of molten gold. Intermingling with the fire, the gold began to slowly take shape, but what emerged was so dissimilar and distinctive that the angels and archangels had no capacity to describe what they were seeing.

Son of the Dawn moved to his position beside the throne and said through the din, "Alpha, what is happening?"

Smiling broadly, He replied, "Come and see."

Son of the Dawn turned his attention back to the area around the lampstands. Each pillar of fire began forming circular patterns toward the bottom, patterns that swirled rapidly, throwing off flashes like lightning, which were absorbed and returned by the other pillars. And then, they were moving, almost faster than the eyes of those assembled could follow—here and there, up, down, and all around the throne of The Alpha. And in the midst of the fire were living creatures, each having six wings. With two, they flew; with two, they covered their faces; and with two, they covered their feet.

"Who are they?" Gabriel muttered in awe.

"Seraphim," The Alpha said. "My burning ones. The keepers of the flame on My altar."

As they flew around the throne, they cried out with loud voices, "Holy, holy, holy," as the beating of their wings created whirling patterns in the smoke.

Through the smoke and the fire, Michael could barely make out the faces of each one of the creatures, but only one was recognizable. The other visages were of a form and fashion he did not understand, nor did he understand the eyes, which seemed to cover them from head to toe.

Then, from behind the throne, an even greater wonder.

Four more creatures began to emerge. Impossibly large creatures, each having four wings and four faces: one toward the front, one on each side, and one toward the rear. But, as was true with the Seraphim, only the face in front was recognizable, eyes flaming with fire, fierce of countenance. Fire moved back and forth between the creatures, with flashes of lightning arcing over the angelic assembly. Beneath each creature was a spinning circle filled with eyes, deep topaz in color, and above them an expanse, the surface gleaming as brightly as crystal.

They took flight as one, the sound of their wings like the waterfalls spilling from Proud Mountain. In intricate patterns, they flew, the many-eyed circles beneath them spinning faster and faster until the lower halves of their forms seemed to be made of pure light and energy.

The Alpha cried out in a loud voice, "Behold, My Cherubim. My mighty ones riding upon the Ophanim, the guardians of paradise."

Suddenly, they stopped and let down their wings, hovering over the majestic throne of The Alpha, and from their midst came the voice of many waters singing, "Holy, holy, holy are You." The phrase immediately echoed throughout the vast throne room by the innumerable company of angels.

Then, Gabriel, Michael, and the other archangels felt a weight, but not the weight of something to be borne or even carried. It was wrapped around them. Comforting, warming, settling, like a thickly woven blanket on a cold winter's night—something you never wanted to be without ever again.

Michael said, "Alpha, what is this we're feeling?"

"The weight?"

"Yes."

"That's My glory."

"I never want it to leave."

"Good, because it won't. And now, arise and regard the Merkabah, My throne angels. They ever live to worship Me before My throne and to provide an atmosphere of worship, rest, and security for all who enter here."

The entire assembly fell on their faces before the throne as the song of the Merkabah washed over them, too awestruck to even join in, just basking in the Presence of The Alpha.

Son of the Dawn stood to the side as the Merkabah flew wildly above him, grabbing handfuls of the emerald arch and pulling it after them, intertwining, encircling, and intermingling until an elaborate pattern emerged, and then they began to play with the lightning emanating from the core of their beings until fantastic shapes rose and fell all around with more rising up to take their places.

As a holy fear settled over the archangels and the angelic host, The Alpha said, "The creation of My Spiritual Realm is now complete. Go now and continue with your training. You will need it for that which is to come."

Chapter Nine

Michael gathered his group of angels on the Field of the In-Between for basic training in swordcraft, dividing them between Uriel and Chamuel, whom he had personally taught prior to the official start of group instruction, and lastly, assigning part of the group to himself.

"No, not like that, Steele," Michael chided gently as he watched Steele and Rok walk slowly through a bit of elementary swordplay. Grabbing Steele's sword, he assumed a stance and continued, "The way you were standing," he said, demonstrating Steele's stance, "left you wide open to attack and lessened the power in your strokes. Remember, left foot ahead of your right. Why is this important? Wendly?"

"Umm, because unless you position your body properly, you can't execute the different angles of attack."

"Very good," Michael said. "And since you brought it up, what *are* the different angles of attack?"

Wendly thought and then said, "Straight down from the top, straight up from the bottom, diagonally down to the left, diagonally down to the right, diagonally up from the left, diagonally up from the right, and left and right strikes horizontally."

Smiling broadly, Michael said, "I hope you were all listening because Wendly was spot on. And you cannot execute any of those maneuvers by squaring off with your opponent. Okay, what else?"

Steele said, "Something . . . something about a melee."

"Environment," Rok blurted out.

Michael slapped him on the back. "That's right, Rok. You must assess your melee environment. And what does that mean exactly? Anybody?"

An angel with shoulder-length, light brown hair raised his hand.

"Yes, you. What is your name?"

"Kepteny."

"Okay, Kepteny. You have the answer?"

"You need to always be aware of where you are in the confrontation."

Pleased with the new angel's answer, Michael pressed him further, "Why is that important?"

"So, your environment can be used to your advantage."

"That's right. Because if you give your opponent a foothold, it can quickly become a stronghold."

"I remembered something else," Wendly cut in.

"Go ahead."

"You said that we should never stand still—to keep moving."

"What direction?"

Rok answered by pointing his finger to the right.

Michael said, "Very good, Rok. You move constantly away from your opponent's dominant side, which will almost always be toward his left and your right. Okay, now, let's talk about defense." Handing Steele's sword back to him, Michael drew his own fiery blade from its scabbard. "Wendly, face off with me and thrust your blade straight at my chest."

"But what if I stick you?"

"First, you won't, and second . . ." he smiled and pointed at himself, "immortal."

"Oh, right. Okay."

Wendly faced him and drove the sword point straight toward his chest, a thrust Michael easily deflected.

"Avoid thrusting your sword straight at an opponent," he said to the angels watching.

"Why? Because once you commit yourself to the thrust, it leaves you wide open for a counterattack. Do it again, Wendly."

This time, after deflecting the thrust, Michael quickly executed a back cut designed to take out an opponent's legs.

"See what I mean?" As the angels murmured their understanding, he continued, "But the most important lesson is this: hold your sword high overhead. This will allow you to parry any and all attacks. Rok, on me."

Rok came at him with a series of vicious sword strikes, which Michael easily countered.

"See what I mean? An overhead defense will defeat any attack. Now, pair up and try it. Take turns. Do it over and over until it becomes instinctual."

While the angels began carrying out their assignment, Michael moved over to observe Uriel and Chamuel's classes.

"How's it going?" he inquired of Uriel.

"Pretty well, although there are a lot of questions as to why this makes any difference. You know, like why we need to train for battle when there's no one to fight."

"I figured there would be."

"So," Uriel said, gesturing toward the field, "what do I tell them?"

It was a good question and one he had asked of The Alpha before instituting the training regimen.

Overhearing their conversation, Chamuel walked over to join them.

"Yeah," he said, "what do we tell them?"

Michael replied, "I can only tell you what The Alpha told me: we live in the *now* and the *not yet*. It is the *not yet* for which we train."

Uriel shook his head rapidly. "That makes absolutely no sense to me."

Michael laughed, saying, "You're not alone. But the more I thought about it, the more I began to understand something I feel is elemental to our existence. You know how The Alpha is everywhere at once?" The two archangels nodded. He continued, "Well, what if His knowledge is the same way?"

Chamuel said, "I'm not sure I follow."

"If He can be everywhere at once, why can't His knowledge be just as all-encompassing? What if He knows things that are so far above and beyond our comprehension that even if He were to share it with us, we'd have no context and, thus, no understanding?"

Uriel turned and shouted toward his trainees, "Hey! What did I tell you? Angles, angels, angels!"

"Seriously? Angles, angels?" Michael said.

Uriel shrugged. "It's what came to mind."

"Back to the knowing thing . . ." Chamuel prodded.

Michael said, "I mean, I'm not sure how else to explain it further."

"Well, we're archangels, so we know a lot—more than the angels in our charge."

"Right."

"Can they know what we know?"

Michael hesitated, then replied, "That's a good question, and I think the answer is no, they can't."

"Then I get it," Chamuel said. "It's a matter of degrees—of different levels of understanding."

Uriel said, "So, you're saying that no matter how hard the angels in our charge try, there's no way they could ever know what we know, and that's the way it is with us and The Alpha?"

"That's exactly what I'm saying," Michael said. "This whole thing about the *now* and the *not yet* is really confusing, and I wish The Alpha would explain it to me. But I'm beginning to see that no matter how badly I want to understand it, to fully comprehend all the ins and outs, I can't. It's just . . . beyond me. And I trust the Alpha, so I'm okay with that."

"Back to the original question of why we do this when there are no foes to fight against," Uriel said. "I think it's all about being in a state of preparedness."

Chamuel replied, "That's really good, Uriel. We prepare for what may come, with preparedness being the goal, *not* the anticipation of battle."

"Exactly."

Michael asked, "With that being settled, how are your classes performing?"

"Overall, very good, with a few exceptions," Uriel said.

"Define few."

"Oh, you know. There are certain individuals whose comprehension and execution levels aren't quite up to what you expect."

"Tell me about it," Chamuel said. "There is a whole group in my class who would fit that description. And frankly, I'm not sure what to do about it."

"I understand. I've got a few myself," Michael added.

"So, how do you handle it?"

"Peer instruction. I put them with angels who are excelling, in hopes that seeing excellence in their peers will encourage them toward greater effort."

"And?" Chamuel said.

"So far, it's working. And if someone is really struggling, I put them with Rok."

"Is he the one who doesn't say much?"

"He doesn't have to. He talks with his sword," Michael said.

"That good, huh?"

"Better than good. He's exceptional."

Uriel asked, "Why didn't The Alpha create everyone with the same abilities?"

"I actually asked Him that question," Michael said.

"And what did He say?"

"That He made us all as individuals reflecting different elements of His character and nature. If we were all the same, where would the individuality be? Together, we are unbeatable. Besides, part of His design is that the strong help those who are weaker."

"And what about the . . . the less perceptive?"

Michael laughed, saying, "Nicely put. It's the same. Those who have greater understanding should help those who struggle."

"Well, I think half my class would fall into that category." Glancing at the field, Uriel added, "I've got to go. I mean, look at that mess. Hey! What are you guys doing? That's completely wrong."

As Uriel hurried onto the field, Chamuel said, "I think The Alpha also did it to teach us patience."

"That's a fact. He told me that we are to help carry each other's load and that the Kingdom only works when we think of others more than we think of ourselves."

Chamuel repeated, " 'Think of others more than we think of ourselves.' I like that. Excuse me, I have to go pass that along to my class."

He walked past Kepteny, who was observing Steele and Wendly as they worked through a series of defensive maneuvers.

Out of nowhere, Kepteny suddenly said, "So, I have a riddle for you."

"Now?" Steele replied, backpedaling to avoid a thrust.

"Sure. Why not?"

"Well, we're a little busy, Kep," Wendly said.

"This won't slow you down. So, remember when we were touring Proud Mountain?"

"Yes," Steele said, ducking under a counterstrike. "What about it?"

"Do you remember how high Michael said it was?"

Wendly disarmed Steele, saying triumphantly, "That's three," then to Kepteny, "I don't know, something like eighty-thousand spans."

"A span being the distance between your elbow and the tips of your finger," Steele said.

"Correct. So, here's the riddle. Let's say that Steele started up the mountainside but knew he could only make it five-thousand spans before tiring."

"Okay. Go on."

"But every time he stopped to rest, he slid back four thousand. How many tries would it take Steele to get to the top of Proud Mountain?"

The two looked at each other in confusion.

Steele said, "And remind me why I'm trying to get to the top."

"It doesn't matter, Steele. You just are. Now, what's the answer?"

"How am I supposed to know?"

"But that's the fun of it," Kepteny said. "You have to figure it out."

"Kepteny," Wendly said wearily, "we're right in the middle of training—and so are you, by the way—and Michael wouldn't be pleased if he saw us doing anything other than that."

"Fine. Let's train. But do try to figure it out."

Steele said, "Why?"

"I don't know. Because it's fun."

"Said the angel who already knows the answer." Steele paused. "You *do* know the answer, right?"

Kepteny grinned. "Of course I do. I made it up. So, any guesses?"

"No idea."

Wendly said, "Okay, hang on. This is simple. If the mountain is eighty-thousand spans, and he makes it a thousand spans with every try, then . . . eighty."

"Wrong."

"Wrong? How can it be wrong? It's logical."

Kepteny laughed. "Logical or not, it's wrong. Work on it, and get back to me."

Steele and Wendly glanced at each other, realizing Kepteny had bested them both without even drawing his sword. Then, with a shout, they attacked him playfully, sending all of them to the ground. They rolled around laughing, drawing a sharp rebuke from Michael.

Back on the slopes of Proud Mountain, Son of the Dawn was standing on an outcropping of rock, speaking to the host of angels below him and explaining the formation of the waterfalls that fed into the Rainbow Stream.

One of the angels interrupted him.

"Son of the Dawn, why couldn't we stay in the throne room? I loved being there in the Presence of The Alpha."

"Me too," said another. "In fact, I never wanted to leave."

The sentiment was echoed by all.

He replied, "Since I have had the unique privilege of being with The Alpha more than anyone else, I know what you mean. But there are things to learn. Things to experience and explore. And you all have jobs to do and responsibilities to perform. While it would be wonderful to just be in The Alpha's Presence all the time—worshiping Him—if that were to happen, well, nothing would ever get done, and there is so much to do."

They seemed to hang on his every word, something he found fascinating. Exciting.

He thought to himself, *I'm sure I could persuade them to do almost anything.* A thought followed quickly by, *But why would I want to?*

Enraptured by his beauty, the angels under his authority were quickly falling in love with Son of the Dawn, adoring him, each unknowingly and on a subconscious level feeling that if he said it, they would do it without questioning. Even Raphael found himself more and more susceptible to Son of the Dawn's magnetism.

The Alpha, of course, knew all of this and pondered it in His great heart.

"Son of the Dawn," He said, "come here."

Having heard the summons in his spirit, Son of the Dawn called Raphael over.

"Raphael, The Alpha has bidden me come." He allowed himself a private moment of exhilaration before adding, "He needs me. And I need you to take over. Oh, I don't know how long I'll be, so carry on."

"It would be my pleasure. Anything you want me to focus on?"

"Yes. Take them down to the Rainbow Stream. I want them to see the colors. Oh, and give Beleth, Semyaza, and the other two something to do—some responsibility. It will help establish their place with the angels."

"It will be done."

Suddenly, Son of the Dawn was in The Alpha's Presence.

Standing at the foot of the dais, he stared upward toward the manifest Presence of The Alpha, feeling a slight tremor of trepidation.

"Yes, Alpha. What do You wish of me?"

"The thoughts you were having. The ones about persuasion?"

"Yes," Son of the Dawn replied. "Were those thoughts wrong?"

"Remember our discussion about thoughts?"

"Yes. But I wasn't thinking about it in such a way that I was planning to—"

"I know," The Alpha interrupted. "It was the second question I found intriguing."

"The one about why I would want to persuade them to do what I wanted?"

"That's the one. Here's what I want you to remember: I created you with tremendous, nearly incomprehensible powers of persuasion. It is necessary for you to have that in order to fulfill your role in My Kingdom. Without persuasion, how can you lead?"

"I'm certain that I could not."

"This is true. You would have no way of knowing this, but because of who you are, the angels under your care adore you and have already decided in their own hearts that they will follow you anywhere, do anything you *say* without questioning."

"They have?" he said in alarm. "But—"

"I know that wasn't your intent. My point in this discussion is to further teach you about the intricacies of cause and effect. In this instance, just you being you is the powerful cause, and the *effect* is devotion, loyalty, and adoration."

"But I didn't ask them for that."

"Once again, I know that. And, once again, that is not My point. I want you to understand your identity and the power it brings."

"To just be me, or are You talking about identity in general?"

"A little of both. I made you to be a certain way because, well, it's what I conceived in My heart and mind, and what I conceive, I bring forth. It's the same with each and every one of My creations. Call it purpose. By being who you were created to be—that is, by walking in your identity—you fulfill My purpose for you."

Son of the Dawn touched his temples. "I feel like there is so much I still don't understand."

"And the more you learn, the more there will still be to learn."

"So, my ability to persuade the angels You assigned to me is not a bad thing? Rather, it is simply me being true to my identity?"

"That is correct."

"Cause and effect," Son of the Dawn repeated. "Is it automatic?"

"If you are asking if every cause has a corresponding effect, then yes."

"And everyone is subject to this?"

"Everyone."

Son of the Dawn paused, considering whether he wanted to ask the question that had formed in his mind.

Before he could articulate it, The Alpha said, "Even Me."

"I don't understand how that is possible. You created everything. Why would You choose to subject Yourself to the governing principles?"

"In order for Me to be true to who I am, I have to abide by the same principles I have set in order for My creation. Otherwise, nothing would make any sense. I want to live with you—with *all* My creation—and experience everything you experience because only by so doing will I feel close to you." The Alpha then said tenderly, "Never forget, My beautiful angel, My greatest desire is to be *with* you.

Son of the Dawn replied soberly, "You subjected Yourself to Your own principles—gave up the freedom and ability to do whatever You wanted—just to be with me, to be with everyone, and to show us Your love? That's almost too wonderful to comprehend."

Having always known what His decision could potentially cost Him, The Alpha had done it anyway. If His creation made poor choices, it was because He had given them the option of doing so, and—with foreknowledge of all possible choices and resulting consequences—He had already made provision to deal with them appropriately. For defined and delineated deep within the Archives, and yet remaining in plain sight to any who cared to investigate, were provisions for things such as cause and effect, decision and consequence, rules and rescue, redemption, and life forces. All were encoded into the very foundations of His Spiritual Realm long before the creation of beings with free will.

"Now," The Alpha said, "get back to your group. They need you."

"Yes, Alpha," Son of the Dawn replied as he transported back to Proud Mountain, his entire outlook having changed.

"What was that all about?" Raphael asked when Son of the Dawn reappeared.

"That, my friend, was about the most important conversation I have ever had."

"Really? That sounds serious."

"It was."

"Anything you can share with me?"

Son of the Dawn turned his head to regard the archangel. "What if I told you that . . ." thinking better of it, he said, "Oh, never mind. It's too deep to get into right now. We've got things to do. How are my two assistants doing?"

"Semyaza and Beleth? They're great. Real naturals. You tell them once, and they've got it."

Son of the Dawn heard what Raphael said, but his mind was so filled with what he had just learned that he didn't respond. He couldn't stop thinking about the fact that The Alpha had subjected Himself to the same restrictions of cause and effect as the rest of His creation just so He could be with them.

Then, there was the matter of the Alpha's revelation about the power of his own influence over the angels in his care.

Drawing in a deep breath of sweetly scented air, Son of the Dawn said, "Let's go back to the far side of Proud Mountain. I wasn't quite done showing you around, and it's time for your first lessons in the creation of music."

Chapter Ten

As Taylor took the stage in the great arena in front of the assembled messenger angels, Gabriel stood backstage with Jophiel and Zadkiel, observing his young charge. He felt all along that Taylor was a quick study, and he was about to learn whether his instincts had been correct.

The purpose of the exercise was to address the assembled host of angels and make your voice audible and understandable and yourself likable. All the previous angels had struggled with at least one of the three, the latter being the most common downfall.

Taylor stepped forward nervously to a spot downstage center and surveyed the vast host of angel spirits filling the arena.

He began, "Hello, my name is Taylor, and along with you, I have the great honor of being a messenger angel. We have the unparalleled honor of being The Alpha's voice to all in this City on a Hill and throughout His Spiritual Realm, as well as to those who are still to come. We are the watchers, ever living to do The Alpha's bidding. We make known His plans and precepts and His principles and passions while being mindful that nothing of ourselves is passed along, for we serve only as a conduit for His voice."

Having finished speaking, Taylor turned and walked toward the wings where Gabriel, Jophiel, and Zadkiel stood. "How'd I do?"

"In my opinion, the best so far," Jophiel said with a smile.

"I agree," Gabriel said. "You were immediately engaging, and your voice was clear and articulate. I give you high marks, Taylor."

Zadkiel said, "Jophiel is right. You *were* the best so far. Good job."

Taylor thanked them and walked to the steps leading to the arena floor.

He met Schindaug on his way up to the stage.

Taylor said quietly, "You've got this."

"Thanks, but I'm not going to count my chickens before they hatch."

"Schindaug, what's a chicken?"

"What? Oh, umm, I don't know. It just popped into my mind."

He made his way to the designated spot downstage. Following a couple of calming breaths, he said, "I'm Schindaug, and like you, I am a messenger. While thinking about what I wanted to say, many things came to mind. But let me simply say this, for it is the core message we are tasked with carrying to our fellow angels and all who come after. The Alpha alone is worthy of our praise." His voice began to rise in volume as he continued. "He is good, and He does good. He who has ever been and ever shall be is *our* King, and we are His creatures. His Kingdom is from everlasting to everlasting. Holy is His Name. Holy is His Name. Holy . . . is . . . His . . . name!"

His words suddenly ignited a glorious expression of praise and worship among the assembled host of created beings who spontaneously added their voices with shouts of, "Holy is His

Name," resonating throughout the great arena as angels fell on their faces in worship to The Alpha.

Overcome by what was happening, Schindaug bowed his face to the floor with Gabriel, Jophiel, and Zadkiel quickly following, and little by little, a sweet fragrance filled the room. It was as if every flower in the Kingdom had simultaneously released its scent as an act of worship.

Suddenly, smoke began to billow from every corner of the great arena.

"It's The Alpha," Taylor cried out. "He's coming."

The face of every angel turned toward the rafters as the cloud gathered, filling the space until it hovered just over their heads.

Flashes of lightning and rolls of thunder filled the arena, and out of the midst of it all, The Alpha spoke, "I am yours, and you are Mine, both now and forevermore. Your worship is pleasing to Me, and I bless you."

Then, the cloud descended, engulfing the entire company of angels and archangels in manifest glory.

When, at last, it finally lifted and they were able to move again, Zadkiel shakily stood, saying, "Well, that was pretty good."

Gabriel stared toward center stage where Schindaug still lay on his face, unmoving.

He went to him, bent down, and helped him to his feet. Gabriel said to the assemblage, "Now *that* was a message. You are to be complimented, Schindaug."

He was a bit unsteady and struggled at first to find his voice, but he eventually said, "I appreciate it, but it wasn't what

I intended to say at all. I took a breath, opened my mouth to speak, and that's just what came out."

"You simply gave voice to the passions of your heart," Gabriel said. Turning to the auditorium of angels, he continued, "While there will be specific messages for us to deliver on various occasions, as Schindaug so perceptively stated, our core message is always to extol the attributes of The Alpha, and you cannot speak from your heart unless you feel it in the center of your being."

As murmurs of assent rippled throughout the great arena, like the sound of wind rippling through a field of tall grasses, Gabriel dismissed his charges to do as they liked until the next session.

Leaving the great arena, Taylor walked beside Schindaug, who was still not fully recovered from the experience.

"What are you feeling?" Taylor asked.

"I don't know how to describe it. It was as if The Alpha placed His hand on me in the most comforting way you can imagine. Both a covering and a caress, if that makes any sense."

"Yes, Schindaug, it does. I didn't feel His Presence in exactly that way, but I definitely felt it."

When they reached the broad avenue running in front of the great arena, Shindaug asked, "Can you describe it?"

Taylor laughed lightly. "I doubt it, but I'll try. It was like being in a warm, velvety liquid—not floating, but total immersion. And I was absorbing it through my skin and into the very core of my being."

"You know, I'm pretty sure if you asked all of our classmates what The Alpha's Presence felt like, they'd all have a different answer."

"Yes, just as He's called each of us by name, we each have our own unique and individual relationship with Him."

Schindaug shook his head. "I'm not sure I will ever be able to comprehend how that can be. I mean, you saw how many of us there were. How can He be one-on-one with all of us?"

"We were just talking about that," said a voice off to their left.

Taylor and Schindaug turned to see four warrior angels strolling along the avenue.

"Oh, hey, are you guys finished with your session, as well?" Taylor asked.

"Thankfully. I'm Wendly, by the way."

"Taylor. Nice to meet you. And who are these three?"

"Steele, Rok, and Kepteny."

"And this is Schindaug."

As greetings were exchanged, Steele said, "So, you messengers had a pretty amazing experience from what I hear."

"It was beyond amazing," Taylor replied. "It was . . . I don't even know how to describe it."

"What happened?" Kepteny said as they resumed walking.

"Well, we were all in the great arena, practicing being messengers by speaking in front of everyone."

"Everyone?"

Taylor laughed. "Yes. It was intimidating. Anyway, I did my bit, and Gabriel seemed impressed."

"That's because it *was* impressive," Schindaug said.

"I don't know about that, but after I finished, Schindaug came up next, and, well, when he started to speak, smoke started pouring from the corners of the arena, up in the rafters, and continued until everything above our heads was filled. And then, The Alpha spoke."

"What did He say?" Wendly asked.

"It was something like, 'I am yours, and you are Mine, both now and forevermore. Your worship is pleasing to Me, and I bless you.' "

"No, that wasn't it at all," Taylor said.

"Yeah, it was. I was there, and I heard it," Schindaug said. "Why, what do you think He said?"

"I know exactly what He said. It was, 'You are more precious to Me than silver or gold.' "

Wendly said, "Could it be that what He said was personal to each one of you? The reason I ask is because that's what we were talking about before we ran into you two."

"That has to be it," Kepteny replied.

Taylor said, "If The Alpha can be everywhere at once, then why not also be personal to each one of His creations?"

Steele turned to Rok and asked teasingly, "Hey! What do you think, Rok?"

Rok stared past him without speaking and then shrugged.

"He doesn't say much, does he?" Taylor asked.

"He speaks with his sword," Kepteny said.

"So, he's good?"

Gesturing toward Wendly and Steele, he said, "He could easily take all three of us at once."

Rok turned to Kepteny and said, "Seventy-seven."

"Nope," Kepteny replied.

"What's that about?" Taylor questioned.

Laughing, Wendly said, "Kepteny posed a riddle, and none of us have been able to answer."

"Really?" Schindaug said. "I love riddles. What is it?"

Kepteny stared at his fellow warriors. "Shall I let them in on it?"

"I don't see why not," Steele said.

"Okay. Here it is: Proud Mountain is eighty-thousand spans in height, and Steele wants to climb it. If he can only climb five-thousand spans before tiring, and every time he stops to rest, he slides back four-thousand spans, how many tries would it take Steele to get to the top of Proud Mountain?"

"You're kidding, right?" Taylor said.

"Totally serious."

"It would take him eighty."

"Wrong."

"Hmm, then I have no idea, but I'll definitely think about it because I really like rid—"

Rok suddenly placed himself in front of the other angels, facing toward a group of four walking toward them.

Wendly asked, "What's wrong, Rok?"

He just stood, staring as the group approached.

The short, dark, slender one in front stopped walking and said, "Looks like we're all on break at the same time. I'm Beleth."

Steele stepped forward. "Well met, Beleth. I'm Steele. Who are you assigned to?"

"Son of the Dawn. These are my associates, Semyaza, Remashel, and Dantanian."

Before Steele could introduce the others, Rok leaned in toward Beleth, saying curtly, "Go!"

Beleth stood staring at him. "What's your problem? We're just—"

"Go," Rok repeated strongly, pointing down the avenue in the opposite direction.

Wendly said, "Rok, what's gotten into you? They're just—"

He silenced Wendly with a fierce look and then repeated, "Go."

Semyaza stepped forward and confronted Rok. "Hang on. Why should we do what you tell us to do? We're all free here. We'll go when we're ready."

Kepteny said, "I'd maybe consider doing what he says."

"Why is that?"

"Because of all of us warrior angels, he's the toughest."

"Is that a fact?"

Wendly said nervously, "I'm not sure what's going on here, but I'd listen to Kepteny if I were you. You guys are all about beauty and creativity. We're warriors. You're no match for any of us, let alone Rok."

"Whoa, whoa, whoa," Schindaug said quickly, hoping to mitigate the escalating tensions. "Let's not make a mountain out of a molehill here."

"Tell that to your friend. He started it."

Dantanian said, "Maybe we should just move along, Beleth. Son of the Dawn wouldn't be pleased with any of this."

Beleth stared hard at Rok. "Okay, we'll go, but this isn't over."

And with that, he turned and walked away, with the other three following close on his heels.

When they were out of earshot, Wendly said, "Rok! What is wrong with you? Why did you try to provoke a fight? You need to apologize to our friends here and to those other angels."

Rok stood rigidly in place, staring after Beleth and his friends.

Finally, he turned and said, "No."

"No? What do you mean, no? You were completely out of line."

"What's going on?" Michael asked as he approached the group from behind.

They all turned. Steele said, "Some of Son of the Dawn's guys came up and started talking to us, and for some reason, Rok got really defensive."

"How so?"

Taylor said, "Hello, sir. I'm Taylor, and we—Schindaug and me—are with Gabriel. I wouldn't call what Rok did defensive. More like protective."

"That's right," Schindaug added. "As soon as they came up, he put himself between them and us like he was going to stand his ground and protect us."

Michael said, "Why did you feel the need to do that, Rok?"

Rok shrugged in reply, staring at the departing angels.

Michael followed Rok's stare. "You should all take advantage of your break because training will only get more demanding from this point forward. Now, move along . . . except you, Rok. Stay behind."

As the others moved on down the avenue, Michael said, "I know you don't have much to say, Rok, so I'll make this easy. Did you sense something about those other angels that caused a disturbance in your spirit?"

Rok nodded slowly.

"And it was strong enough that you felt it necessary to protect the others?"

Rok nodded again.

"Then, that's good enough for me. I'll look into it. Now, go join the others."

As Rok walked away, Michael said, "Alpha, can we talk?"

"Of course," came the immediate reply as he was carried away to stand before The Alpha's throne.

He continued, "I'm sure You saw what just happened."

"Indeed, I did."

"Then, I need some insight. Why did Rok do that?"

The Alpha moved down the steps and stood with Michael, inviting him to walk with Him across the Fiery Stones.

"First of all, you have to know that when I created Rok, it was with an enhanced level of discernment."

"Discernment of what?"

"Of thoughts and intents."

"Are You saying that Rok knows what people are thinking?"

"He cannot read their minds, but he can definitely sense their intent."

"So, if he suddenly felt protective, it was because of something he was sensing in one or all of those angels?"

"Yes."

"The implications are difficult to accept, especially since they are Son of the Dawn's angels."

The Alpha placed His arm across Michael's broad shoulders. "Remember when you were telling your fellow archangels about your confusion over the concept of the now and the not yet?"

"Yes."

"Perhaps this circumstance can be illustrative. You all live in the now, but Rok can sense some of the not yet. As a result, his actions were not necessarily related to the now."

Michael shook his head. "Okay, I'm getting closer to understanding that. What confuses me, though, is trying to imagine what Rok could've possibly seen or sensed that would make him feel so protective of the others."

The Alpha walked a bit without speaking. Finally, He said, "There are many things that can be known to you, Michael, but there are far more which will continue to be a mystery. It is far better to rest in what you do know and embrace the ever-present mystery of what you don't know than to allow it to distress you any further."

"Are You saying I should suppress my curiosity?"

"Not at all. Be curious, for that is how I have created you. But temper your curiosity with acceptance when you encounter that which apparently has no answer."

Michael stopped walking and gazed at The Alpha. "Then tell me this: The thing Rok was seeing or sensing, is that why we train?"

The Alpha placed both hands on Michael's shoulders, staring directly into his eyes. "You train, My mighty warrior, because that is what you were created to do—you and all the angelic host under your supervision. You see, in giving My creation free will, I introduced the concept of choice. And with the introduction of choice came the potential for wrong."

Michael pondered The Alpha's statement. "But You did it anyway."

"Yes."

"But why? Why not just set up Your Kingdom where everyone obeys all Your precepts and the capacity for wrong doesn't exist?"

"Because that would violate free will."

"Then take away free will."

"Love gives freedom. I will not take away free will, and love cannot take away free will."

Michael said, "But why? Is it really worth all the potential for wrong that comes with it?"

"Without question. Because in the end, those who follow Me—those who love Me and are devoted to Me—will do so because it is what they have chosen, not because I have commanded it."

"Alpha, this is a hard teaching, and I won't pretend to understand all of it."

"Nor do I expect you to. Just consider this: where would the value be if everyone loved Me because it was what was required of them, and they had no opportunity to choose to do otherwise?"

“I think I’m beginning to understand.” He paused, then said, “Alpha, there’s something else. Within the context of this conversation, is our preparation in vain, or is something coming that will require our preparedness?

The Alpha stared long and hard at His mighty warrior and smiled.

“The Angel Games, Michael. The competition will be more intense than you can imagine.”

With a bow of his head, Michael replied, “Ah, yes. I think I understand. It will be as You wish, Alpha.”

He suddenly found himself back on the avenue in the midst of hordes of angels, who were walking, laughing, and sitting in groups on the lush green grass. He tried and failed to imagine what could possibly disrupt such serenity, such beauty, such perfection, concluding finally that The Alpha was right: it was better to rest in what was knowable and embrace the fact that there would be some things simply too steeped in mystery to comprehend.

“Michael,” someone called from behind him.

He turned to see Uriel and Chamuel walking toward him.

“Hey, there. I was just going to come and look for you.”

Chamuel said, “We were looking for you as well. We ran into Son of the Dawn.”

“Did you now? And did he mention anything about what happened between his crew and ours?”

Uriel replied, “Yes, and he was just as confused about it as we were.”

“I’m sure. But I talked to The Alpha about what happened, and there’s a reason Rok did what he did.”

“What did He say?” Chamuel said.

"It's too complicated to get into. For now, just know that The Alpha is aware of what happened and seems fine with it."

"Perhaps there's an opportunity here," said a voice off to their right.

They all turned, watching as Son of the Dawn approached them with Beleth and Semyaza in tow.

Chapter Eleven

"Son of the Dawn," Michael said in greeting. "So, you obviously heard about what happened?"

"Yes, I did. And while I don't understand what Rok did—nor do I think it appropriate—like I said, perhaps there's an opportunity here."

"Okay, I'm listening."

Son of the Dawn took his time to continue, "Think about all the training and instruction we've been putting our angels through."

"Yes," Michael replied, "it has been very intense."

Gabriel approached. "Is something happening I need to be aware of?"

Son of the Dawn put his arms around their shoulders and walked away from the other angels, with Beleth trailing a short distance behind. Son of the Dawn asked, "You heard about the encounter between Rok, Beleth, and Semyaza?"

"Yes," Gabriel said, "which is why I came to find you both and see if you had any insight into what happened."

"I was just about to share a few thoughts with Michael about all that. We have been keeping a very rigorous, demanding schedule, and from what I've observed, all of our angels are responding beautifully."

"I have no complaints with my group. Michael?"

"Well, mostly no. But go on."

Son of the Dawn continued, "Before any of you were created, The Alpha and I would do things together that served no other purpose than to bring joy and a sense of . . . I don't know, call it . . . fun."

"Okay," Michael said, "I'm with you so far. What do you have in mind?"

"What if we instituted a series of friendly competitions between our groups and maybe even created some champions?"

"The Alpha calls them Angel Games," Gabriel said, "which is exactly what we will have."

"Exactly," Son of the Dawn replied. "It would go a long way toward alleviating any tensions that have arisen due to the intensity of training."

Michael added, "It would also provide an opportunity for our groups to get to know each other. I mean, with the way things have been, there is virtually no interaction."

"When do you want to start?" Gabriel asked.

"Why not now?" Michael asked.

"Why not, indeed. I assume we will conduct this exercise on the Field of the In-Between?" Son of the Dawn added.

"Seems the most logical."

Michael nodded his agreement. "This is good. I will summon my group and meet you there."

As Gabriel and Michael moved off to gather their groups, Beleth stepped forward and said, "I thought we were going to settle the conflict between Semyaza and Rok."

"We are."

"But—"

"Patience, my dear angel. Patience."

When they were all assembled, Son of the Dawn strode to the middle of the Field, which expanded in size to accommodate the myriads of angels as it had on other occasions.

All eyes were upon him. Attention fixed.

An atmosphere of expectation was pervasive throughout those gathered on the Field of the In-Between.

In his mind, Son of the Dawn thought, *They're all looking at me. Waiting for what I have to say. This is something I could get used to.*

Finally, he said, "I'm sure you are wondering why your leaders have summoned you here, so allow me to explain. Since tensions seem to be running a bit high among some of you." He paused to pierce Semyaza and Rok with hard stares. "We thought it wise to provide an opportunity for those tensions to be worked out in a positive manner. Michael?"

Michael walked to the center and stood by Son of the Dawn. "We are going to engage in what The Alpha has so astutely dubbed The Angel Games—a series of competitions designed to not only test your individual skills but also the extent to which you are able to work together as a team."

In the midst of a loud murmur arising from the angelic host, Gabriel joined the other two at the center of the Field and motioned for quiet. "I know you all have questions, but please be patient and everything will be explained. Now, we have designed the competitions so that no one will have an advantage based on their areas of expertise. Being an intensely creative member of Son of the Dawn's group will not give you an advantage over Michael's warriors, nor will a warrior have an advantage over one of my messengers."

Michael said, "To get things going, you will notice there are a few obstacles laid out at the far end of the Field. There will be other challenges proceeding simultaneously, but this is where we will begin. This first competition involves one angel being blindfolded while his partner talks him through the obstacle course. To make things even more interesting, your partner won't be chosen from among your group. The team pairs will then proceed two-by-two through the challenge until all have competed."

As another hum of conversation arose, Son of the Dawn said, "However," he waited for the tumult to die down and said, "Whatever score you achieve together will be added to your group total. So, it is to your advantage to do everything in your power to succeed."

Semyaza asked, "Who decides who our partner will be?"

"Me," Son of the Dawn replied with a smile. "In fact, I'm glad you asked that question because, as it turns out, you are first up in the competition."

"Me? But—"

"And your partner will be Rok."

Steele whispered to Wendly, "This should be good."

Semyaza said, "I don't suppose it would do me any good to protest the pairing."

"None whatsoever," Son of the Dawn said as he began walking toward the far end of the Field, beckoning all to follow him.

When they all arrived at the area where the obstacles had been set up, Michael pulled Rok out of the crowd and blindfolded him, saying quietly, "I'm not saying any of this was your fault because I know why you did what you did, but there are a significant number of angels who believe it was."

"Understood."

"And it is far better to work toward unity than to perpetuate conflict."

Rok hesitated. "Agreed."

As Michael positioned him at the beginning of the course, Son of the Dawn said, "Those of you who have been given other assignments are to wait for this one to start before beginning your own. Now, Semyaza, it is your responsibility to guide Rok through this course using only verbal commands. You can describe the obstacle in front of him, the approximate number of steps between obstacles, how high or how low the obstacle is, but you cannot provide physical assistance, even if he veers off course."

Gabriel added, "And remember, the score you achieve in this competition will be added to your individual team scores. So, I suggest you take this seriously."

"Oh, and one more thing," Son of the Dawn said, "if your partner falls at any time on the course, your team is disqualified."

Semyaza shook his head and walked up to stand beside Rok's hulking figure. He said quietly, "Look, I don't like this any more than you do, but we need to set our differences aside for the sake of the team. You good with that?"

Rok nodded his head once.

Son of the Dawn said, "All right, only the angels assigned to this competition are to remain in this area. All of the rest of you, go to your starting points."

There were six other competitions lined out at various points around the Field for a total of seven, and every team of angels had to complete all seven in order to have their scores recorded.

Michael shouted, "Those of you not involved in this competition, once you are all assembled in your assigned area, one of the other archangels will provide you with instructions." He waited for the other angels to gather around their assigned starting points and then for the instructions to be given. Then, he said in a loud voice, "All right . . . begin!"

The Field of the In-Between exploded into activity as pairs of angels, one after the other, entered into the competitions.

As the spectators around Rok and Semyaza's competition began yelling encouragement, Semyaza said, "Okay, here we go. Six steps in front of you is a pile of tree limbs stacked up about to your knees. You'll have to step over them and then be careful because there's a pool of water on the other side."

Rok moved forward quickly for six steps, hit the barricade, and almost fell, but managed to grab onto a log and get his legs over, plunging up to his knees in the pool on the other side.

"All right, the pool is about four steps across, and when you climb out, you've got about ten steps before you come to another section of logs that are laid out in a crisscross pattern with random spaces you have to step through."

Rok moved across the pool, pulled himself out, and walked quickly forward, with Semyaza warning him when he got close to the next section. Arms held wide for balance, he began stepping carefully through the logs.

"Great. You're doing great, big guy. Just about four more steps."

Rok made it the rest of the way without falling and emerged on the other side.

"Okay," Semyaza said, "now you've got a labyrinth in front of you made up of slabs of gold that are about as wide as your feet are long and about a half-step end-to-end. There is grass about the length of your foot between each. It winds around quite a bit, so you're going to have to listen carefully to my instructions."

As Rok began laboriously making his way across the labyrinth, Michael said to Son of the Dawn, "I have to say, I didn't know if this would work or not."

"Yes, well, whether it will have a lasting impact on their relationship is anyone's guess. But for now, anyway, the former confrontation seems to be forgotten."

Gabriel said, "Even if it's not forgotten, it is set aside, which is no small thing."

Rok finished the labyrinth and was working his way through the final obstacle: an irregular ladder that led to nowhere. Upon reaching the top, the contestant had to leap blindly, trusting his partner to guide him to solid ground. Otherwise, he would land in another deep pool of water, at which point he would be disqualified.

As Rok neared the top, Semyaza shouted, "Okay, you will have to clear a distance equal to your height in order to avoid the water."

"Can't," Rok replied loudly.

"Why not?"

"Heights."

"Wait a second," Semyaza said. "Are you telling me you're afraid of heights? You?"

Rok clung to the top of the ladder as if his life depended on it.

"Look, it's no big deal. The worst that can happen is you miss the ground and land in the water."

"Disqualification."

"Well, there is that. Okay, listen. You can do this! Big strong angel like yourself? This is nothing compared to the opponents you've already faced and conquered, right? So just step onto the top rung and then jump as far as you can. Even if you fall, the ground will cushion you."

Rok stood frozen in place and then slowly stepped one foot and then the other onto the top rung.

As the assembled angels cheered him on, Semyaza hollered, "Now, jump!"

Rok took a few quick, deep breaths and then launched himself outward, landing in an ungainly heap on the other side of the pool. He immediately ripped the blindfold from his eyes.

Semyaza came running toward him, arms outstretched as if planning to give him a hug, but was stopped by a stern look.

"Right. No hugging. No problem. Good job, Rok."

Son of the Dawn said, "Well done, both of you. Well done indeed." Then, to the spectators, "Now *that* is a perfect example of teamwork, and I expect all of you to follow their example. Rok and Semyaza, you may now move on to the next phase. Okay, who's next here?"

In response to directions from the three group leaders, teams ran the obstacle course and completed the other competitions. Some pairs did better than others, and scores were kept and points awarded accordingly. But who won or lost wasn't really the point. It was all about camaraderie and providing an opportunity for individuals to interact on a level that was ordinarily unavailable.

As the competition was winding down, Beleth approached Rok, who was standing with the three archangels.

"Something on your mind, Beleth?" Son of the Dawn said.

Staring up at Rok, he replied, "I would like to test Rok in a battle of wits."

Gabriel said, "I'm not sure this qualifies under the terms of The Angel Games."

"Why not?"

"He barely speaks," Michael said. "How would that be fair?"

"I agree," Son of the Dawn said. "Besides, this feels to me like an unnecessary attempt on your part to satisfy your damaged ego, and I—"

"Willing," Rok said.

Son of the Dawn said, "You don't have to do this."

"Do."

Appealing to Gabriel and Michael, Son of the Dawn asked, "What do you think?"

"If Rok is willing to do it," Michael said, "then I have no problem."

"Nor do I," Gabriel said.

"Okay," Son of the Dawn said. "Did you have something in mind, Beleth?"

"It'll be quite simple: Questions of logic are posed, and we are each provided with an opportunity to answer. The one providing the best answer will be declared the victor."

"And who gets to decide the correct answer?"

"It will be self-evident," Michael said. "Rok, are you sure about this?"

Wendly, Taylor, Steele, Kepteny, and Schindaug all gathered around Rok in a tight huddle.

"You don't have to do this," Kepteny said. "You have nothing to prove."

"Kepteny's right," Taylor said. "Just walk away."

Rok stared intently toward Beleth.

"No."

"But how can you debate someone when you barely speak?"

Rok glanced at Wendly. Something seemed to pass between them, and Wendly said, "I will serve as Rok's, uh, second."

"But," Beleth said, "you cannot speak for him."

"I won't have to, will I, Rok?"

"No."

Schindaug asked, "Who will be the moderator?"

"I will," Gabriel said, striding onto the Field.

Curious about what was happening in the center of the Field, angels gathered around as the rules of the challenge continued to be refined.

"Oh, that's hardly fair," Beleth said. "You will be unbelievably biased."

Kepteny said, "Then let me do it. I'm pretty good with riddles. In fact, let me pose the riddles to both of them; that way, there will be no chance of bias. I haven't told anyone these riddles."

"Gabriel?" Son of the Dawn said.

"I am agreeable to that."

"Then it is settled. Kepteny will pose three questions to each contestant."

Gabriel added, "How about this: if one contestant cannot answer within a reasonable amount of time or simply gives up, the other contestant will be given an opportunity to answer."

"Okay," Son of the Dawn said, "let the contest begin."

Kepteny closed his eyes in concentration for a moment and then said, "Rok, imagine that you are at the top of Proud Mountain, climbing toward the loftiest peak, and your foot slips on the frosty surface and you begin to fall. How would you survive?"

"Stop," Rok said immediately.

"Stop what?"

"Imagining."

"Very good."

Rok's friends applauded his answer. Kepteny turned to Beleth.

"Beleth, what ends everything?"

He thought briefly, and said confidently, "G. *G* is at the end of everything."

"Nicely done. The score is one correct answer each. Okay, Rok, what is so fragile that saying its name breaks it?"

Rok hesitated only slightly. "Silence."

"Correct. Two to one. Here we go, Beleth: the more you take, the more you leave behind."

Beleth repeated the question to himself several times. "Oh . . . footsteps. The more steps you take, the more you leave behind."

"Correct," Kepteny said. "The score is now tied at two apiece. Rok, your next question is this: what word is always spelled incorrectly?"

Rok paused, then answered slowly, "Incorrectly."

"Very perceptive. The score is now three to two. If Beleth answers this next question correctly, we will have a tiebreaker." Kepteny thought for a bit before saying, "Beleth, how long is the answer to this question?"

Beleth wrinkled his brow in concentration. "But you haven't posed a question."

"Oh, but I have. How long is the answer to this question?"

"But that's not a question."

"What is your answer?"

Clearly frustrated, Beleth replied hotly, "I have no answer because you have posed no question."

Turning to Rok, Kepteny said, "Rok, can you answer?"

"How long."

"Correct."

Beleth fumed, "What? That's not an answer."

"Yes, it is. *How long* is the answer."

"Son of the Dawn," Beleth said, "this is not fair!"

"Hey," Son of the Dawn replied, "this wasn't my idea."

Gabriel said, "Rok wins."

As the angelic host erupted in applause, Beleth bellowed in frustration, stalking off in the direction of Rainbow Stream.

Son of the Dawn said, "I apologize for my student's attitude. Rok, you are to be congratulated on your victory."

Having returned to the back slopes of Proud Mountain following The Angel Games, Son of the Dawn stood off by himself in quiet contemplation.

"Son of the Dawn?" said a tentative voice from behind.

Turning, he saw Semyaza approaching nervously.

"This is getting too predictable, Semyaza. Do you not realize that I value my private contemplation above all else?"

"I do, and I apologize for interrupting you."

"Again."

"Yes . . . I apologize for interrupting you *again*, but there is something I have to say."

"Then you'd better get to it."

Glancing around the area to make sure they were alone, he continued, "It's this thing with Rok and Beleth."

"What about it?"

"Beleth isn't letting it go. He keeps talking about getting him back for publicly humiliating him."

"Rok had nothing to do with Beleth's humiliation. He did that all on his own."

Semyaza said, "Agreed. But he doesn't see it like that, and I think he's planning something."

"Okay, you finally have my complete attention. You'd better tell me everything."

"I'm not sure I know everything, but I'll tell you what I know and also why I think you need to let it happen."

"Fine. Let's hear it."

Semyaza took a breath to compose himself and then said, "Remember when we were here before on Proud Mountain?"

"Of course."

"And we were talking about how we all felt like this is where we belonged even more than the City on a Hill?"

"Do get on with it, Semyaza. Just tell me what you have to say."

"I think Beleth—okay, not just Beleth, there are a number of us who think we should just do it."

"Do what?"

"Leave the City on a Hill and come here."

"Permanently?" Son of the Dawn asked, surprise coloring his voice.

"Permanently."

"Because?"

"Partially because Beleth doesn't want to have to face any of the other angels—too embarrassed and all that."

"I don't blame him."

Semyaza continued, "But more than that . . . and this is very hard for me to say."

"Just get it over with."

"Okay . . . well, a number of us have been talking, and—"

"How many?"

"Many. And, well, we'd rather be here with you than back in the City with everyone else."

Son of the Dawn came to the sudden and stark realization that there was something about what Semyaza was saying that he found intensely pleasing, and he wanted to hear more.

"But . . . why?"

"May I speak freely?"

"Certainly."

"It's you."

"Okay, but what about me?" Son of the Dawn knew he was fishing for compliments, anticipating the response, but he couldn't help himself.

Semyaza answered evenly, "Everything. Your voice, your beauty, your persuasion. There's just something about who you are that we all find irresistibly compelling."

When Son of the Dawn didn't respond immediately, Semyaza added, "We could create our own training camp here . . . our own place to be."

"You know, that's not the worst idea I've ever heard. It does get crowded back in the City on a Hill, and we all do feel more comfortable here. Besides, there is much more room to be alone, and creativity requires solitude. Knowing what I now know regarding your gratitude and appreciation of my leadership, I will bring it up with The Alpha."

Chapter Twelve

Following his victory over Beleth in the battle of wits, Rok's reputation among the other angels grew rapidly to the extent that there was virtually nowhere he could go in the City on a Hill where he wasn't stopped and congratulated. Being the reluctant conversationalist that he was, such encounters typically ended quickly and awkwardly. No matter. He knew who he was, and, more importantly, he knew his purpose.

Purpose.

It was a topic he frequently visited on his many long walks around the City. He felt more and more that his purpose was to assist Michael in protecting the Realm. Protect against what, he couldn't say. Actually, he couldn't say much of anything, but that was okay with him. He had already decided it was far better to listen than to speak. Besides, there were plenty of other angels who were only too eager to tell what was on their minds.

Like Schindaug.

And Kepteny.

Even though, most of the time, he had absolutely no idea what they were talking about.

The thought of his friends made him smile.

Walking on top of the Glassy Sea toward the Field, he spotted Uriel on the side of the Glassy Sea with his ever-present

Scroll of Remembrance. Since he was often placed under Uriel's instruction during training exercises, Rok walked up behind him and peered over his shoulder to see what he was writing.

Uriel glanced up, anticipating his question. "What am I writing? Well, my mighty warrior angel, I am chronicling the occasion of the battle of wits between you and that Beleth fellow. Wonderfully amusing, by the way. As for why I am doing it, it is because The Alpha desires it." Pausing to stare into Rok's eyes, Uriel continued, "He has me write down nearly everything in the Scrolls, which are then placed on the pedestal in the Alcove where they become part of the archives."

"Archives?"

"Yes. Archives are typically a room, or in our case an Alcove, where the records of significant happenings and events are kept along with The Alpha's teachings—foundational truths, precepts, and newly discovered principles—from which are drawn the very threads that knit the Realm together."

"Knit?"

"Uh, yes. Knitting is . . . never mind. Everyone has a scroll, you see, and no, I don't write everything down myself. The Alpha began our personal scrolls when we were created, scrolls upon which everything we do is recorded. My role is to keep track of Kingdom-wide happenings."

There were many questions in Rok's mind. Questions he couldn't quite put into words.

After trying and failing to utter a sentence, he finally managed, "Who?"

"Who what?"

Frustrated, he pointed to his eyes and then at the scroll in Uriel's hands.

"Are you asking who can read the scrolls?"

Rok nodded once.

Uriel continued, "Well, the things I write are open to anyone who cares to read. But the scrolls kept by The Alpha are open only to Him and Son of the Dawn."

"Why?"

"I don't know." He then added whimsically, "And I wish I did. But that's just the way it is, so I'm not going to trouble my spirit over it." He added quietly, "I will tell you, however, that I've been seeing Son of the Dawn in the Alcove quite a lot. It's almost as if he is researching—you know, gathering information."

"Why?"

"You know, that's a good question, and I don't know the answer."

Kepteny walked past, offering a casual, "Hey Rok, Uriel."

Rok said, "Fifty-three."

"Nope," Kepteny said and kept walking.

"What was that all about?" Uriel asked.

"Riddle."

Uriel shook his head. "You angels can be very strange at times. Now, I need to know whether it bothers you—you know, the fact that Son of the Dawn has been in the archives?"

"Yes."

"Can you tell me why?"

Rok stared at the palace. "Trouble."

Then, he resumed his walk toward the Field.

Uriel called after him, "Trouble? What does that mean? Rok!" Watching Rok's retreat, he said to himself. "That was very odd."

On the far side of the City, Son of the Dawn sat in the sweet grass under the giant canopy of a tree whose branches spread as far out as the tree was high. Beleth and Semyaza lounged with him.

He said, "I spoke with The Alpha about our desire to move the training camp to the other side of Proud Mountain."

"And?" Beleth said.

"He said He would consider the request."

Semyaza asked, "Did you get any feeling one way or the other?"

"He didn't say no, so that means He is at least open to it."

"I can't really think of a reason He'd be opposed," Semyaza commented.

Son of the Dawn said, "On another topic, Beleth, have you come to terms with your defeat?"

"If you are asking if I am okay with it, then the answer is no. If you are asking whether I am willing to let it go and move on, then . . . yes."

"Good, because attempting to perpetuate a feud with Rok would not be beneficial to us getting what we want from The Alpha."

After hearing his own answer, Beleth seemed to question himself and his true motives, which seemed to surprise even himself.

Beleth began processing out loud, "I understand. But what if I wasn't willing to let it go? What if, for instance, I wanted to provoke another encounter with Rok?"

"First of all, that would be disastrously foolhardy."

Hoping there might be an alternative reason to the obvious, Beleth asked, "Because he's supposed to be so tough?"

"Beleth, my young charge," Son of the Dawn sighed. "*Supposed to be* indicates there is a possibility that he isn't what he is purported to be. And I assure you, Rok is the mightiest angel in the Kingdom next to Michael."

"Okay, granted."

"Additionally, were you harboring such ridiculous notions, The Alpha would already know about it."

"Because He knows about everything?"

"Precisely."

"Then, if that's what Beleth was thinking," Semyaza said, "The Alpha would try to stop him?"

Smiling, Son of the Dawn shook his head. "No, He wouldn't."

"Why not?"

"Because He will not violate the natural order of His Kingdom."

"Meaning?"

"Meaning that He has given everyone free will. So even if He knows someone is contemplating a choice that is not in line with His principles and precepts, He may provide a warning, but He won't intervene and try to stop them."

"Even if it produces an outcome that does not align with His plans and precepts?" Beleth asked.

"Even then. The Alpha's belief in the principle of free will is so strong that even if someone makes a wrong choice, He believes He can somehow redeem it back into a positive outcome."

"That makes no sense whatsoever."

"It's not about making sense, Beleth. It's about The Alpha and the things He has set in place that are foundational to His Kingdom."

Semyaza asked, "Are you going somewhere with this, Son of the Dawn, or are we just engaging in philosophical discussion?"

It was a good question. One for which Son of the Dawn had no ready answer.

"There's nothing wrong with philosophical discussion. It frees the mind. Opens insight into possibilities. Takes you from being content with what *is* to considering what *could* be. Allows you to pull the *not yet* into the *now.*"

"And . . . is that what we're doing by pressing The Alpha to allow us to move our training camp?"

Son of the Dawn was silent for so long that Beleth started to repeat the question when he finally replied, "It's a fair question, my friend. The only answer I can provide is this: I'm not entirely sure what we're doing, but what *I'm* doing is attempting to get us into a position where we—all of us—can be who we feel we ought to be."

Semyaza said, "This has been a very confusing conversation, Son of the Dawn."

"I know, and I apologize for that. But take heart, the confusion will all vanish when it is appropriate for it to do so."

The Alpha stood on the Fiery Stones with Gabriel and Michael. Behind them, the Merkabah flowed in and out from the emerald arch.

Ever since The Alpha had divided the angelic host into thirds, the friendship and affection Michael and Gabriel felt toward Son of the Dawn had strengthened. They were completely enamored with their leader, and he with them. When not directly instructing their charges, one would often find the three of them together walking, talking, inventing their own "angel games" for themselves, and discussing challenges they were having with various students. It would not have been even slightly out of order to say their friendship was unbreakable.

"Son of the Dawn has petitioned Me to allow him to move his training camp to the far side of Proud Mountain," The Alpha said. "What do you think? Would it be beneficial?"

Michael said, "I'm glad he finally said something to You because I know it's been on his mind."

"Not in a negative way," Gabriel added quickly. "It's just that . . . well, the way he explained it to us was that creativity requires a certain level of serenity in order to be maximized, and he felt it was way too crowded here in the City on a Hill with far too many distractions."

Michael added, "You know this already because, well, You know everything, but Gabriel and I encouraged him to approach You."

"I see. I love Son of the Dawn and want only what is best for him and those under his care. And I agree that what he does requires a vastly different environment than what either one of you does."

"So," Michael said, "are You going to let him do it?"

"Why wouldn't I?" Then, The Alpha added with a smile, "Especially when the two of you are campaigning so vigorously on his behalf."

Son of the Dawn was suddenly there in their midst. He laughed and said, "You know, I don't know if I will ever get used to this."

"What, being transported suddenly into The Alpha's Presence?" Gabriel said.

"Exactly. Why am I here, Alpha?"

"I was sharing your petition with your friends."

"About moving the training behind Proud Mountain?"

"Yes. I wanted to solicit their thoughts before rendering My decision."

"Perfectly understandable. And have You come to a decision?"

"I have. You may do as you desire."

As Son of the Dawn danced a happy jig on the Fiery Stones, Michael and Gabriel joined in the celebration, causing the Stones to respond in kind.

The Alpha watched the three, pleased their relationship was so close, so strong.

"Thank You, Alpha," Son of the Dawn said, a brilliant smile lighting his perfect countenance. "Thank You. You will not regret this."

Leaning toward him, The Alpha said, "See that I don't." He turned and ascended the stairs to His throne. "Now, gather 'round. There's something else I wish to discuss."

The three approached the stairs, where they stood in an uneasy silence.

"Tell me," The Alpha said, "do you find there are angels under your care who aren't particularly well-suited for the training you offer?"

Michael said quickly, "I can answer that. Yes, and it has been a point of frustration. It seems that no matter what Uriel or Chamuel or I do, they just don't seem to learn past the basics."

"I have the same issues," Son of the Dawn said. "I have angels who would be far better off under Gabriel or Michael's tutelage."

"Same with you, Gabriel?"

"Without question."

"What if I gave you the option of circulating among each other's groups, identifying those who demonstrate an aptitude for your areas, and recruiting them?"

Michael said, "That would be very helpful, Alpha."

Son of the Dawn and Gabriel added their agreement.

"Then, so be it," The Alpha said, "Beginning now."

After the three took their leave, they stood on the outer steps of the palace, discussing what had just happened.

"This will change everything," Gabriel said excitedly.

Michael said, "In my mind, I have already identified many in my group whose minds are as sharp as the swords they wield who will make amazing, gifted messengers and quick-witted creatives."

"Likewise," Son of the Dawn said. "How should we approach this, though? I mean, it seems odd to just show up and start pulling angels out of each other's groups."

Gabriel nodded. "I agree. Perhaps a general assembly would be in order. You know, gather everyone at the Field and explain what The Alpha has given us permission to do."

"I like it," Michael said. "Why wait?"

Gabriel, Michael, and Son of the Dawn stood at the center of the Field of the In-Between, myriads of angels all around, their energies combined yet individually distinct.

Son of the Dawn began. "I know you all must be wondering why we have ordered this assembly, so I will get right to it. Michael, Gabriel, and I met with The Alpha. During the meeting, He inquired as to whether there were those under our care who didn't seem to be particularly well-suited for what we were teaching. Gabriel?"

Gabriel stepped forward.

"As a result of the meeting, The Alpha gave us permission to circulate among each other's groups, identify those we feel would be better suited to our areas of expertise, and recruit them for our instruction."

As murmurs of approval rumbled through the assemblage, Michael said, "I know just from my classes that there are significant numbers who will welcome this change. So, we aren't waiting. This happens now."

Son of the Dawn said, "In discussing how best to approach this, we've decided that those of you who are certain you are where you belong may leave and go back to whatever it was you were doing. Those of you who feel you belong with me, meet me at the Rainbow Stream. Those of you who wish to be with Michael, meet him here in the center. And those who wish to be with Gabriel, meet him at the Great Hall. For those who are unsure, we would be happy to set individual appointments to discuss options."

Gabriel said, "The Alpha's heart is always for you. We are for you. And whatever it takes to provide the best opportunity for you to be who you were created to be, we will do that."

The angelic assemblage erupted in sustained applause and shouts of praise for The Alpha.

"That worked well," Michael said.

"Indeed," Son of the Dawn said. "It will be interesting to see the results."

Chapter Thirteen

Immediately following the reassignments, Son of the Dawn moved the training camp for all creatives to the back side of Proud Mountain, where the first order of business was to construct a suitable facility to house and instruct myriads of angels. Having been given free rein by The Alpha to do whatever he felt suited his needs, he unleashed the full force of his creative powers, designing an elaborate complex of halls and meeting rooms devised to facilitate instruction in various disciplines of music, art, writing, and sculpture, all of which resulted in a much more contented group of students.

Beleth and Semyaza stood with Son of the Dawn in the Central Plaza, admiring the finishing touches as they were being applied to the last building in the complex.

Semyaza said, "It is truly magnificent."

"It is, isn't it?" Son of the Dawn replied immediately. "I really stretched when conceiving the design, and I must say, I really outdid myself."

"Breathtaking," Beleth said.

Dantanian and Remashel joined the group.

"So, what do you think?" Son of the Dawn asked.

Remashel said, "Absolutely and stunningly beautiful while at the same time not sacrificing functionality. I am impressed."

"Impressed because you didn't think I could succeed at something of this magnitude or impressed by the outcome?"

"Oh, no, I didn't—"

"Relax, Remashel. I was just giving you a hard time. And thank you. I accept your praise."

Dantanian said, "I think it's brilliant the way you've created a place that is . . . well, kind of the way Rainbow Stream has banks and yet remains free flowing."

"Excellent observation, Dantanian."

Beleth said, "It is a perfect reflection of your own beauty. I'm not sure The Alpha could have done any better."

"Careful, Beleth," Son of the Dawn said.

"Why? I'm just expressing an opinion. Besides, tell me you haven't thought the same thing."

The statement caught Son of the Dawn so off-guard he was rendered momentarily speechless—not an easy thing to accomplish.

"Well," he finally said, "I'm not sure how to answer that, and I am equally unsure as to whether I even wish to do so. But I will tell you this: The Alpha made me the highest expression of His creative abilities, so everything you see here is merely a manifestation of His imagination through me. Therefore, anything I do is what *He* would do. There's no competition here, Beleth."

"Then why has your countenance been so troubled?"

Semyaza said, "No one is closer to you than the two of us, and we see things that no one else can see. We have been noticing subtle changes and wondering what's going on."

Son of the Dawn thought about rejecting the notion entirely, but then that wouldn't have been truthful. And he wanted to be truthful with his closest associates.

"Dantanian, Remashel . . . can you give us some privacy, please?"

Watching the two angels depart, Beleth said, "We're not trying to pry. We honestly just want to know if there is anything we can do to help."

Son of the Dawn trained his beautiful eyes on each of his associates, smiled, and then answered, "I know that, Beleth, and I appreciate the concern. But I'm not sure there's anything either of you can do."

"Well, you'll never know unless you try."

He thought it over and said, "Okay. The Alpha made me the most beautiful, the most creative, and the most powerful of all His creation."

"More powerful than Michael?" Semyaza said.

"Ah, yes . . . straight to the point." Son of the Dawn paused, considering the question. "I am loathe to admit this, but the simple truth is I do not know. And, quite frankly, I'm not interested in finding out. Besides, Michael and I are quite close, and I am sure nothing could ever happen to change that. Apart from that, I find myself being more and more, well . . . I'm not going to get into it."

"Hey, you've come this far, might as well tell us everything."

"He's right," Beleth added. "What's the point of having someone to trust if you never put it to the test?"

"That is a very eloquent point, Beleth. And you are right. Okay, if you really want to know . . . have you noticed the way the angels and archangels respond to me?"

"I'm not sure what you mean."

His frustration obvious, Son of the Dawn repeated, "The way they respond—the way they look at me, tell me how beautiful I am, how powerful . . . you know."

"Well, of course," Semyaza replied. "There is no one more beautiful than you. No one's voice is more compelling. No one is more persuasive. Everyone in the Kingdom readily acknowledges that."

"Not all the time."

"What are you talking about? There is never a time when they—"

"In the Presence of The Alpha."

"Excuse me?"

"Whenever we are gathered in His Presence, it's like I'm invisible."

"And that bothers you?" Beleth said.

"I am ashamed to admit that it does." Shaking his head in frustration, he added, "I haven't said anything about it because, well, I'm struggling to understand why it should matter to me."

"But," Beleth said, "didn't The Alpha make you beautiful? Make you powerful? Make you the Chief of all the angels?"

"Yes. What is your point?"

Semyaza said, "I think Beleth is trying to say that if The Alpha made you all of that, then wouldn't it follow that He expects His other creations to love and adore you on a level above everyone else?"

"Quite obvious," Son of the Dawn replied with a weary smile, "is the fact that I have not made myself clear. They do."

His two associates appeared confused.

Beleth said, "Then, I'm not sure I—"

"Weren't you listening?" Son of the Dawn exploded. "Do you know what it's like to have unbounded love and adoration and then be completely invisible? Of course, you don't. Why would you?"

"Son of the Dawn," Semyaza said carefully, "it was not our intent to—"

"Well, let me tell you . . . it would be far better to have never been adored than to have been and then not be."

"I'm not sure I know what—"

"And I'll tell you something else," he said, "if I am being truthful—and I strive to be truthful—it has always bothered me. I've just ignored it and tried to shove it down and not deal with it."

The sudden and drastic change in their leader's demeanor was confusing and worrisome to the two angels.

Beleth said, "This seems to be upsetting you. Maybe we should—"

"And here's another thing: who do you think spends the most time in The Alpha's Presence?"

"You?"

"No! Not me." He was suddenly shouting and found he had no capacity to dial his emotions back. "I am Son of the Dawn. The first creation. Chief of all the angels, including archangels. I should be the one who has nearly exclusive access to The Alpha's Presence. But I don't. And it's frustrating, and I want to know why."

"Why it's frustrating, or . . . "

"I already know why it's frustrating. I want to know why the situation exists."

Semyaza said, "Why don't you ask The Alpha?"

"Why don't I ask The Alpha?"

"It's a fair question."

"Fair or not, it's not something I'm prepared to discuss at present." He asked dismissively, "Don't the two of you have somewhere to be?"

The two angels shared a worried glance before departing, feeling very troubled by what they had just seen and heard and yet not knowing what any of it meant.

As Son of the Dawn watched his associates depart, he heard a voice from behind. "There you are. We were hoping to find you."

Turning, he saw Michael and Gabriel walking toward him.

"Michael, Gabriel," he said in a pleasant greeting. "Have you come to admire my new training facility?"

"We have," Michael replied. "And I must say, it is quite impressive."

"I agree," said Gabriel. "It is absolutely magnificent."

Suppressing his sudden and troubling outburst, Son of the Dawn gestured grandly, saying, "It is everything I had hoped for and more. I wanted to create something representative of who The Alpha created me to be."

"Well, you have succeeded."

Michael said, "Listen, that's not all we came to talk to you about."

Waving them toward a set of ornate benches, Son of the Dawn said, "Then perhaps we should sit. Now, what's on your mind?"

Gabriel said, "You are on our mind."

"Really? In what way?"

"Well, I don't know how to say this without sounding insulting, but—"

"Insulting? Oh dear, now I am concerned. What's going on?"

Michael said, "That's what we want to know. What's going on with you?"

"I'm not sure I know what—"

"Come on. It's us. Do you really think you can hide anything?"

"Hide? What could I possibly have to hide? This is beginning to upset me."

Gabriel said, "While that wasn't our intent, whether you find what we have to say upsetting or not is the least of our concerns."

Before Son of the Dawn could reply, Michael said, "We have seen changes in you—changes that are quite troubling."

"Such as?" he said, already knowing where the conversation was headed.

"Such as growing subtly yet incrementally more and more taken with yourself and your own importance and beauty."

Son of the Dawn stood abruptly. "My own importance? Do not forget who I am. I am the anointed Cherub who walks among the Fiery Stones, the highest of The Alpha's created beings, the Chief of all the angels. Importance? Of course, I'm important. I am the first, and there will never be another like me. I am—"

"There is only one *I Am,*" Michael said forcefully, "and you would do well to remember that fact."

Son of the Dawn stood perfectly still except for a slow blink.

"Yes," he said, "of course. You are right. And I freely acknowledge that. As far as my other statements go, please forgive me as I am facing deeply troubling challenges of late . . . challenges with which I seem ill-prepared to deal."

"Is there anything we can do to provide assistance?" Gabriel said.

"I appreciate the sentiment, Gabriel, but no. This is something I am just going to have to puzzle through on my own."

"Son of the Dawn, with everything The Alpha has provided, there is always a solution. And we're here for you. You know that, right?"

Pulling them both to their feet and hugging each in turn, he said, "Yes, I do. And you have no idea what level of comfort I derive from that knowledge. Now, I must be off. There are a few final items to which I must attend."

With that, he walked off toward a structure in the final stages of construction.

As Michael watched him go, he said, "What did you make of that?"

"It is as we suspected. He grows ever more self-obsessed."

"Should we speak to The Alpha?"

“We may have no choice. But before we do that, I’d like to send a couple of our angels to check things out and report back. You know, just to gather more information and—”

“Help us know whether we are just being overly sensitive?”

Gabriel smiled. “Exactly.”

“Anyone in mind?”

“Taylor and Schindaug.”

“Why them?”

“Well, of all my charges, they are the most perceptive, especially Schindaug. Don’t let his jocular nature fool you. He’s very deep,” Gabriel said.

“Are you sure you can spare them?” Michael asked.

“No, but I will make arrangements to cover their assignments. This is important.”

Son of the Dawn stood alone, trembling under the onslaught of strong emotions generated by the encounter he’d just had with his two closest associates. While everything he confessed was true, he was troubled by how quickly and easily the confessions had come. Having harbored them deep within his being—trying and failing to completely eliminate them, and ultimately, coming to accept them as legitimate—now that they had been spoken aloud, he found they had taken on a life of their own.

A life and a power. A power that manifested at odd moments in very inexplicable ways. Like the throbbing he had just experienced in his abdominal region. Probing gently with his fingers, he was horrified to feel a bulge forcing his garment outward.

"What is happening?" he mumbled to himself.

Taking several deep and calming breaths, he noticed the bulge receding.

"This is very odd."

As he considered what could be causing the strange manifestation, it occurred to him that perhaps his bulging abdomen had been the result of the powerful emotions running unchecked through his being. But why? Why would his body respond in such a bizarre manner? Then, a thought presented itself, leaving him staggered by the implications.

"What if this is something I can control?"

Summoning the emotions to the surface, he focused his attention on the same spot and was shocked to find his abdomen began to swell outward almost at his command.

"But what if I do not desire this?"

Consciously willing the swelling to subside, he turned his gaze downward, focusing on his legs.

"Okay," he said shakily, "let's see if I can grow as large as Michael."

Suddenly, he found his legs growing not only in length but in girth.

As he returned to his normal size, he whispered, "What if I can be whatever I want to be and look however I wish to look?"

The implications were nearly overwhelming. But what to do with this newly discovered power? No one could know. At least, not yet.

The inescapable challenge, as he currently saw it, was that if he were to continue down this pathway, his two most cherished relationships would be lost. Was he willing for that to happen?

And then there was The Alpha.

Just after leaving Michael and Gabriel's presence, a pronouncement from The Alpha pierced like a white-hot dart, burying itself deep within his consciousness. The sensation had been so intense that his footsteps faltered, causing Beleth to reach out to steady him. Shaking off his help, he stumbled away to find his present place of solitude.

"I know your plans," echoed through his mind, which initially prompted a response of, "Well, that's good. Perhaps you could share them with me because I don't. In fact, I don't know much of anything anymore."

But it was disingenuous to the core as he knew full well what The Alpha was referring to.

Then came, *"Better to have me as a partner than an adversary."*

Was that where this was all headed? Was this the path he had set his feet upon? A direct conflict with The Alpha? Why would he do something so foolhardy?

Second only to The Alpha.

Every other created being under his authority.

Beautiful beyond compare.

Powerful beyond measure.

He already had more than everyone else by far. But at some point, he realized that more was not enough. He wanted it all, a reality he had only recently allowed himself to embrace. And why not? Isn't this how the Alpha made him?

Why deny the deepest longings of his heart just to maintain appearances?

Michael and Gabriel.

That was why.

As irritating as the emotion was, he found he loved them both intensely—loved them so much he had purposely repressed his true feelings, his true longings, for the sake of their friendship. But he couldn't have it both ways. Something had to go. He could either maintain his friendships or pursue the calling of his heart. He knew which one it would be. He had, in fact, known all along.

He felt as if he were standing at the peak of Proud Mountain. While he loved the view, he knew he couldn't remain. He had to leap. But once he launched himself outward, there was no going back. He turned to face the finely chiseled pillar he had been leaning against, running his fingers over its smooth surface and reveling in the tactile sensations.

"Sensation," he muttered. "That's it. I want—I deserve—the opportunity to experience the sensation of true power."

But to get where he wanted to go, he would have to risk everything. And if that were the case, he determined he wasn't about to do it by himself. Others would come along, and they would come willingly, for he would persuade them to do so.

Persuasion.

The Alpha Himself had affirmed that it was one of his surpassing abilities. He had even tested it out on several occasions, choosing an angel or group of angels at random and filling their heads with nonsense just to see if he could influence their thoughts and actions.

It worked every time.

They did exactly what he said without questioning why. Brimming with confidence, he even tried it out on Raphael. Gentle, kind, loving, peaceful Raphael. Though he had proven to be more of a challenge than others, in the end, he had come around as well. Of course, every persuasive thing he said—every single thing—was all a complete fabrication, much of it made up on the spot, almost like it was a game. And who was to say that it wasn't? If he were, in fact, the highest created being, and he most definitely was, then did it not follow that every other being under him was there for his amusement?

Transporting himself into the great hall he had constructed for large assemblies, he stood in the shadows at the side of the stage, watching the angels under his care clustered in pockets of energy, sparkling like the starry host, each prepared to literally hang spellbound on his every word.

Look how they adored him.

How they loved being around him.

Hearing his voice.

Basking in his musical creations.

Often simply sitting and staring at his beauty, unable to turn away.

They were his to do with as he pleased, just as The Alpha told him they would be.

"Son of the Dawn," Beleth said. "Why exactly have we all been summoned?"

Chapter Fourteen

The question snapped Son of the Dawn out of his reverie.

"Ah, yes, why indeed." Calling the four angels comprising his inner circle, he continued, "I have brought you together to bear witness to a revelation—a revelation that will change the course of our lives forever."

Beleth, Semyaza, and the other two shared nervous glances. Something was different about their leader. They had been noticing it for a long while but had been unable to identify exactly what had changed.

"Is that what has been on your mind all this time?" Semyaza said.

"Yes, Semyaza. Something known only to me that is now about to be revealed."

Son of the Dawn moved past the four and out to the center of a vast cavern hewn from the inside of Proud Mountain by the labors of his following, staring out over all his host before him and noting familiar faces. He could feel their adoration, which gave him a tremendous sense of power. He was especially pleased to see two of Gabriel's most ardent followers, Taylor and Schindaug, in the crowd.

Motioning for quiet, he began.

"I have called you all here today because I have something to share with you. But first, I want to make sure you understand and appreciate all that has already happened. I am, of course, referring to our beautiful new training center, which is uniquely ours, separate and distinct from everything else in The Alpha's Kingdom."

A mighty wave of applause erupted, rolling across the hall. Rather than signal for quiet, he let it go on, basking in the adulation. He suddenly felt his body rippling from head to toe. Similar to what he'd experienced earlier but much more intense.

As the applause finally died down, he continued, "Now, in case some of you are wondering whether The Alpha is all right with us being here, put your minds at ease. The Alpha doesn't care for The North and has told me so Himself on a number of occasions. So, if He doesn't want it, would it not follow that it is ours for the taking, ours to develop into something we can all be proud of? Listen to me, The Alpha is the only one who can be everywhere, which means that we—all of us—must be somewhere. What does it matter to The Alpha, to Gabriel and the angels, or even Michael for that matter, where we choose to be? In the end, as The Alpha has said many times, it is our choice."

Son of the Dawn paused to read his audience, to see what effect his words were having. They were right there with him, leaning forward, taking it all in.

"And now, my angels, my friends, as The Alpha is fond of saying, come and see."

He led them outside toward the side of Proud Mountain, made a gesture with his hand, and a portal opened through which he entered, with the entire assembly of angels following.

Once they passed through the portal and were inside, the illumination from his own being revealed an immense, high-ceilinged cavern with tunnels branching off in several directions. The floors glittered with precious stones—the number of which rivaled the number of celestial beings gathered within, while the walls and ceiling flashed with light reflected off rich veins of gold and silver. But even that rich display did nothing to diminish the brilliance of Son of the Dawn.

He said, "We are going to own this mountain inside and out, heaping unto ourselves that which is ours, and no one will be able to wrest it from our grasp. No one! We will drive these tunnels higher and higher, all the way to the top of this mighty mountain, and it is there I will build my home—the highest point in all the Kingdom. Nothing will be higher than I. So, you who have longed for something more, you who have opened your minds to the possibilities, who have said yes to the opportunities awaiting those bold enough to take a chance . . . rejoice. For this is everything you've hoped for, the manifestation of the deepest longings of your heart."

With that, tumultuous shouts filled the cavern as the angels began dancing in fanciful frolic, celebrating, reveling, and shouting words of praise for Son of the Dawn.

Words previously reserved only for The Alpha.

On the periphery of the swirling mass of angelic entities stood a regretful Raphael and, beside him, a watchful Taylor and Schindaug.

Schindaug leaned into Taylor, saying, "I'm not gonna beat around the bush. I don't like what I'm seeing, and I can't imagine The Alpha would either."

"You're right. We need to find a way to get out of here without attracting attention so we can tell Gabriel what's going on."

Raphael moved closer and said, "I can't stay here. If you two want to get out, follow me."

"Go ahead," Schindaug said, "we'll be right behind you."

Weaving in, among, and through the throng, they made their way toward the cavern's opening.

They thought they made it out without being seen.

They were wrong.

Dantanian and Remashel had been posted toward the entrance for the express purpose of keeping track of any and all defectors. There had only been three, a fact that would be reported forthwith to Son of the Dawn.

Once the trio of defectors exited and were well downslope from the cavern, Raphael said, "I need you two to know I had no part in planning this."

"But you came," Taylor said.

"Yes, I did. And I must admit when it was presented to me—"

"It?" Schindaug said.

"You know, everything we just heard inside—it was as if I had no ability to resist his words."

"Like you knew what he was saying was wrong but couldn't help listening?"

"It was so powerful that I couldn't help agreeing, too. You apparently experienced the same thing."

Taylor said, "Not exactly. You see, Gabriel sent us here to check everything out and keep an eye on what Son of the Dawn is up to."

"But once we started listening to his words," Schindaug said, "I started thinking we had bitten off more than we could chew."

"I'm not entirely sure I know what that means," Raphael said, "but it sounds as if you know what I'm talking about."

"We do, for sure," Taylor said. "His words, they—"

"Get inside your head?"

"Yes. They get inside your head. I mean, even when he stops talking, it's like they're right there, and you can't turn them off."

They were almost completely off the mountain when Dantanian and Remashel suddenly appeared in front of them.

"Where do you think you're going?" Remashel said.

Raphael cocked his head. "I'm an archangel. I can go anywhere I please. And if you have even the slightest bit of sense between you—which I seriously doubt—you will stand aside and let us pass."

Dantanian said arrogantly, "Our orders are to not allow anyone to leave until Son of the Dawn says so."

"What part of *archangel* did you not understand?" Taylor said. "Do you seriously think there's anything you could do to stop Raphael?"

Son of the Dawn's two henchmen seemed to size Raphael up. Remashel said, "He doesn't look like much to me."

Raphael turned a longsuffering gaze on Taylor and Schindaug. He gestured toward the two offending angels and said, "You will not speak, nor will you move until we are well down the mountain."

As soon as he spoke the words, it was as if Dantanian and Remashel were frozen in place, unable to move anything but their eyes.

"That should take care of those two for a while," he said as they went on their way.

Glancing over his shoulder, Schindaug asked, "How did you do that?"

"I couldn't exactly say. It was in my mind to do, and it just happened."

"What should we do now, Raphael?" Taylor asked.

"We need to go straight to Michael."

"But Gabriel is the one—"

"Trust me. They'll be together."

When they arrived on the bank of the Rainbow Stream, Raphael cast his vision outward and found Michael and Gabriel with the other four archangels in a tree-shrouded park toward the center of the City on a Hill.

"I see where they are," he said. "I'm transporting. You?"

"Yeah," Schindaug replied, "let's just cut to the chase."

Turning to Taylor, Raphael asked, "Is he always like this?"

"Mostly."

"Good to know."

When they arrived in the park, Michael watched their approach and said, "Raphael, we've been concerned for your welfare. Are you all right?"

"I am now," he said.

"Good," Michael said and slapped him on the back, which nearly sent him to his knees.

Gabriel said, "Taylor, can you tell us everything you saw?"

"I'll try. So, the first thing you need to know is that Son of the Dawn has been researching the archives, gathering information on everybody—like who is the most likely to side with him."

"What do you mean by *side* with him?"

"I can answer that," Raphael said. "You know the freedom of choice thing The Alpha built into all of us when he created us?"

"What about it?"

"Son of the Dawn is turning what The Alpha meant to be a wonderful thing into a weapon to be used against Him . . . against all of us, really. Due to me being assigned to Son of the Dawn when the angels were divided into thirds, I was automatically assimilated into his inner circle. Then, Semyaza and Beleth basically volunteered to serve as his assistants, and then Dantanian and Remashel sort of stumbled into it. What I'm saying is the five of us have been privy to his plans from the onset. A huge part of his plan has been to create profiles for every single one of us—I'm talking about the entire angelic host, *including* the archangels. These profiles reveal who would be the weakest-willed, who would be most prone to fall prey to his twisted words . . . to his deception."

"That's exactly what he does," Taylor said. "He uses his words to twist things around, so you eventually begin to believe everything he's saying."

"Yeah," Schindaug added, "but that doesn't even scratch the surface of what's really going on. All those profiles Raphael mentioned, the whole point behind all of it is to build the groundwork for him to take over."

"Take over what?" Uriel said.

"Everything."

"Wait," Zadkiel said, "are you suggesting Son of the Dawn wants to take over the Kingdom?"

"He didn't come right out and say it, but I'm sure that's where he's headed. Taylor, tell them about Proud Mountain."

"Well, Son of the Dawn took us to this portal in the side of the mountain. But what's weird is that every time you took us to Proud Mountain, Gabriel, we never saw anything like that."

"Can you describe it?" Chamuel said.

"Well, there's this very prominent outcropping of rock, and set well back underneath is an opening into the side of the mountain."

"That doesn't sound like anything I've ever seen," Jophiel said.

"That's what I'm talking about," Taylor said. "It's almost as if Son of the Dawn created it or willed it into existence or something. And when you pass through the portal into the interior of the mountain, there's this colossal cavern with tunnels branching off in every direction and the floor is covered with the kinds of stones Son of the Dawn wears on his tunic. When I say *covered,* what I mean is that when you walk, your feet literally sink into the stones."

Schindaug said, "And you can see thick veins of silver and gold everywhere you look on the walls, almost like a woven tapestry or something."

A voice from behind them spoke. "They're right. I was there, too."

They all turned.

"Wendly," Michael said. "Come join us and tell us what you know."

With Steele, Rok, and Kepteny following close behind, Wendly stepped forward, saying, "I was there inside Proud Mountain because Son of the Dawn took me there."

"By yourself?" Gabriel asked.

"Yes. And I have to tell you that it was very strange."

"In what way?"

"He came upon me as I was walking alone by the Rainbow Stream and asked if I'd like to accompany him to The North. I wasn't doing anything, so I decided to go with him."

"Just the two of you?" Jophiel said.

"Yes. Along the way, he asked me how I was doing in my training and basic stuff like what wave I had been created in and how fortunate I was to have been created in the second wave. Then, he started talking about how wonderful it was that The Alpha had created so many things for us to enjoy, and how He promotes freedom and love, and how walking in that freedom is honoring to Him."

"Sounds exactly like something he would say," Michael said, "Very clever. Go on."

"Well," Wendly said, "then it got really strange. He said something like, '*I have taken a special interest in you, Wendly—in your training and growth—but I don't want the others to feel bad. So, when we meet like this, please don't tell anyone.*' I asked him what he meant by that, and he said it was just the first of many meetings he wanted to have with me."

"How did that make you feel?" Uriel said.

"At first it made me feel special, but then it felt like . . . I don't know, like it was wrong somehow. Especially when we got to Proud Mountain. He stopped walking when we got to the base, and then he pointed up toward the summit and said something about how The Alpha had given him The North to do with as he pleased and that he was going to build his home at the top of the mountain so he could look down on everything else in the Kingdom. But that wasn't what bothered me."

Wendly seemed to be struggling.

"Go on, tell us what happened," Michel said.

"He stared at me—you know how he does, like he can see all the way through you into your mind—and then told me he wanted me to be close to him at the top of the mountain so we could look down on the Kingdom together, and he would teach me how to be more than I am."

"What does that even mean?" Zadkiel said. "You're an angel. What more could you be?"

"Exactly what I was thinking when he said it. When I asked him to explain what he meant, he said something like, '*We all love The Alpha, but there are things He hasn't told us, and I want to reveal new freedoms . . . to reveal the whole truth. Freedom, truth, and love—this is what I am offering to you here with me in this realm—here in The North.*' And then he asked if I would join him. When I hesitated to answer, he said whatever I chose to do would be okay, but I should never tell anyone else what we had talked about."

"And yet," Gabriel said, "here you are."

"Yes, and it wasn't easy to come. Like everyone else, I have been so mesmerized by Son of the Dawn's charisma and beauty that it never occurred to me that he could be anything other than good. But what happened felt so wrong; I couldn't deal with it anymore. I finally told Rok and Steele what had happened, and they encouraged me to come and tell you."

"You did the right thing," Michael said.

"But why would Son of the Dawn single out Wendly?" Jophiel said. "It doesn't make any sense."

"It makes perfect sense," Gabriel said. "Wendly is part of Michael's inner circle, just like Taylor and Schindaug are part of mine. If he can compromise someone on the inside, just think of how much leverage that would give him."

"And remember," Michael said, "he is all about influence and persuasion. Raphael, why don't you finish telling us what happened inside the mountain."

"What happened to Wendly is basically what happened to everyone inside of Proud Mountain," Raphael said. "He told everyone with him—"

"How many?"

"Hard to say, but there were most of Son of the Dawn's original group plus defectors from yours and Gabriel's, so it probably amounted to about a third of all the angels."

Michael and Gabriel shared a glance, and then Michael said, "Go on."

"He told everyone there that they are going to own Proud Mountain inside and out and that no one could take it away from them. Then, he talked about those of us who had, and I quote, *'Longed for something more, who have opened your minds to the possibilities, who have said yes to the opportunities that await . . .'* But the thing is, no one had *longed* for anything until he planted the idea in our heads. No one had considered any possibilities. Everyone was content to just be who they were in the Kingdom serving The Alpha. He is the one who planted seeds of discontent in their minds, telling them there was more."

"Raphael is right," Taylor said. "When Gabriel told us to get close to him and see what we would find out, one of the first things that became very clear is that Son of the Dawn was subtly stirring up dissent."

"I'm not sure if dissent is the right word," Schindaug said. "I think it's more like him throwing out these endless questions, like, *'Did The Alpha really mean this?'* or, *'Surely, that isn't what He said,'* and things like that so you begin twisting yourself into knots trying to remember what was what and . . . and . . . you know."

Michael said, "It's persuasion. It's what he does—what he is gifted with being able to do. The way The Alpha created him."

"Except something happened," Gabriel quickly added. "He wasn't always like this."

"That's true," Michael said, "but when did it happen? As you all know, the three of us—Gabriel, Son of the Dawn, and

I—have been incredibly close to the extent that there is virtually nothing we don't share with each other. And apart from a few disturbing signs Gabriel and I saw, things we confronted him with and he denied, there is nothing that would have given this away."

Uriel said, "I may be able to help."

Chapter Fifteen

When he had everyone's attention, Uriel explained, "Besides helping Michael train the angels under his command, one of my responsibilities is to write significant things in the Scroll of Remembrance. Something happened after the match between Rok and Beleth that may be significant to what we're discussing. I was sitting by the side of the Glassy Sea chronicling the outcome of the match when Rok came by and, in his own way, asked what I was writing. So, I told him and then explained about the scrolls being kept in the Alcove as part of the Kingdom Archives. He then asked who could read the scrolls, and I explained the things I write are available to anyone, but the scrolls kept by The Alpha can only be read by Him and Son of the Dawn."

"Does anyone know why that is?" Jophiel said.

"That's exactly what he asked, and I told him someone might know, but it isn't me. And here's where I think that incident may have a direct bearing on our discussion. Since that match, Son of the Dawn has been in the Alcove more than usual, almost as if he is researching something—gathering information. When Rok asked me why that was, I told him I didn't know. And then I asked if it bothered him that Son of the Dawn had been in the archives, and he said yes."

"Did he tell you why?" Michael asked.

Uriel said, "Tell them what you said, Rok."

"Trouble," Rok replied, nodding gravely.

"Okay," Zadkiel said, "that's very strange, but it matches what Raphael, Taylor, and Schindaug learned."

Gabriel stared at Michael. "The Alpha needs to know about this."

"Like He doesn't already?" Schindaug said.

"He's right," Raphael added. "Don't forget, He knows *everything.*"

Without warning, they all found themselves in the throne room in the midst of the Fiery Stones. When they realized where they were, Taylor, Schindaug, and the other four angels fell on their faces in awe of The Alpha and the Merkabah moving in around and through the arch above the throne.

As the archangels knelt in homage by their respective lampstands, The Alpha's voice echoed deep within the recesses of their individual and collective consciousness.

"Rise, My lovely ones. Rise and do not be afraid, for you belong here with Me."

Taylor and Schindaug shakily stood to their feet, still unable to look upon the face of Him who sat on the throne, the memory of their experience in the arena still fresh in their minds.

Addressing Michael, The Alpha said, "Perhaps you should tell your Alpha what you have learned."

"Son of the Dawn is attempting to draw angels unto himself, teaching them to think differently than how You created us to think," he replied, "and even now, he meets with them in Proud Mountain."

Turning His gaze on Raphael, The Alpha asked, "What happened within Proud Mountain, Raphael?"

"What Michael said is true. Taylor, Schindaug, and I were there. We heard everything—well, at least up to the point when we decided we needed to leave. And what we heard wasn't subtle. Son of the Dawn specifically said he was going to extend the tunnels of Proud Mountain all the way to the top, and it was there he would build his home at the highest point in the Kingdom and that no one would be higher than he."

As The Alpha pondered Raphael's words, Gabriel said, "What would you like us to do about this, Alpha?"

He stood and descended from the dais until He was standing on the bottom step.

Staring into the faces of each one standing before Him, The Alpha said evenly, "Gather all of the Builders—each of you has them within your groups. Take them to Deep Lake."

"But what are we going to build at Deep Lake?" Michael said. "Deep Lake is in The North, and we—"

"You'll build nothing. What you *will* do, however, is begin excavating Deep Lake, and you will keep excavating until Deep Lake is as deep as Proud Mountain is tall."

"I don't understand," Gabriel said. "How does this have anything to do with what Son of the Dawn is planning to—"

"For every high, there must be a corresponding low." He let that settle, then added, "Son of the Dawn has made and continues to make choices—the results of which have already begun to produce a rift in My Kingdom."

"So, we're going to stop what he's doing?"

"No, we will not."

"But—"

"Free will, Michael," The Alpha explained patiently, "isn't free if I intervene. I know what he is doing deep within Proud Mountain. And, furthermore, he *knows* that I know and is using My own principles against Me, or so he believes."

Zadkiel said, "Alpha, this is a hard concept to comprehend. Are You saying that even if Son of the Dawn influences, let's say, a third of the angelic host to join him in whatever he is planning, You still won't put a halt to it?"

"Come, gather near, all of you, and learn of My ways. You, too, My young ones."

The angels and archangels moved forward hesitantly, overawed by the experience of being in such a high and holy place.

When all had gathered close, The Alpha said, "My Kingdom is reserved for those who are here of their own volition. Just as I love each and every individual completely and without reservation, I desire the same in return . . . but only if it is what they choose. And choice is valid only when there is something to choose *between*. Jophiel, that thought in your mind right now—the one about whether I knew what Son of the Dawn was going to do? Here's the only way I can explain it: when I created free will, I knew full well I was creating the potential for wrong choices because long before I did it, I thought through all the infinite ins and outs, weighing all the various outcomes. I saw them all and took them all to their ultimate end. Without the risk of wrong, how could I ever know for certain those who follow Me do so because it is what they have chosen to do?"

Raphael asked soberly, "Alpha, what happens to those who have *chosen* to side with Son of the Dawn?"

"Just because certain ones passed through the portal and followed him deep within Proud Mountain does not necessarily mean they are joining his plans. You followed, yet you turned away. It simply means they, like you, are considering the choices before them. And please do not make the mistake of assuming that just because his creatives were with him there in the cavern, they are all in agreement. There are many, many who are not. And, in the same manner, Michael, do not assume your warriors are immune to his wiles."

"The same is true of my messengers," Gabriel said.

Jophiel said, "But he is so persuasive."

"Which is exactly how I created him."

"I don't understand," Chamuel said. "He's using the gift You gave him to turn Your angelic host against You."

"And by so doing, he is exercising the free will I also created within him. Now, as to your question, Raphael, regarding what will happen to those who ultimately make the choice to follow Son of the Dawn. They will receive the just recompense of those choices. Because every choice produces an outcome—an outcome they cannot choose."

Michael drew himself up, standing taller. "Then, do we prepare for conflict?"

"No, Michael, we excavate Deep Lake."

"But—"

"Excavate. Train. Watch. Wait. All will become clear."

As Michael and the others reverently withdrew from the throne room, The Alpha cast His vision out to the farthest reaches of His Kingdom. No angelic heart was hidden from His gaze, no purpose shielded from His view. He saw it all.

Those who had already chosen to make their stand with Son of the Dawn, those who wavered, caught up in the web of deception, unsure of which way to go, and those who, though sorely tempted, had boldly proclaimed their loyalty and allegiance to The Alpha and in His love strengthened their hearts and their resolve.

Calling to mind how fervently He had hoped Son of the Dawn would have stayed true to who He'd created him to be, The Alpha ascended to His throne, sat down below the mighty Merkabah spinning and darting overhead, and sighed, whispering, "And so it begins."

Outside, on the steps of the palace, Michael and Gabriel stood with the others, their emotions roiling over the revelations they just received.

Michael said, "I can't begin to explain what I'm feeling right now because I don't know what it is."

"I know what you mean," Gabriel said. "I've been searching for words to describe it as well, but all I'm coming up with is, well, you know how it feels when we're practicing swordcraft on the Field and your training partner accidentally cuts you and you feel pain? Like that, only instead of a nick, the sword pierced your heart, and then they gave it a twist on the way out."

"Perfect," Michael said. "The three of us were so close. Inseparable. How could he do this to us? How could he hold our friendship so cheaply?"

"You two aren't the only ones," Jophiel said. "It's all of us."

"Of course," Michael said, "but Gabriel and I had a different level of relationship." He paused. "And I don't know about you, Gabriel, but I feel we've earned the right to let him know how we are feeling."

"I agree," Gabriel said, "but what can we do? It's like The Alpha just said: it's his choice to make."

"Fine. I accept that. He can obviously do whatever he wants, but not without answering to me for it."

Schindaug said, "Are you talking about busting his chops?"

"Excuse me?"

With a roll of his eyes, Taylor said, "I think he's asking whether this could lead to a physical confrontation."

"I can't imagine it going that far," Michael said.

Zadkiel said, "But if Son of the Dawn has changed to the extent that you all say, then he could be pretty unpredictable."

"As in, he could be the one to initiate the confrontation?"

"Precisely."

"And if he does," Gabriel said, "we will be ready."

Deep within Proud Mountain, Son of the Dawn had just finished speaking to a smaller group of angels whose loyalties were undecided when Beleth interrupted him.

"You need to come outside. Right now."

"Why? What's happening?"

"Michael and Gabriel."

"Ah, excellent. My friends have come to see me and wish me well."

"Uh, I doubt that's their intention."

"Now, why would you utter such a negative statement?"

Leaning in for privacy, Beleth answered, "Their expressions make it appear as if they are in a somewhat less than congratulatory mood."

"Well then, let us go and see what is on their minds."

Son of the Dawn emerged from within Proud Mountain, a smile lighting up his face, the full force of his persuasive beauty on display.

"My friends," he said exuberantly, "so good of you to come. Welcome to my kingdom."

Gabriel said, "We haven't come to congratulate you."

"You haven't?" Son of the Dawn said, allowing surprise to color his voice. "Why not? This is a great day. I am your friend, and you are mine. Don't friends congratulate each other on significant achievements?"

Michael stepped forward, coming within arm's reach, his voice betraying his anger. "Since when is sedition to be congratulated?"

"Sedition? What are you talking about?"

Moving a step closer, he said in a fierce whisper, "You know *exactly* what I'm talking about, so don't try any of your little word games with me because it won't work."

"Word games? Michael, my dear friend, I haven't the slightest idea what you are talking about. The Alpha gave me this territory and commissioned me to build a training center for my angels that would be not only practical for our needs but worthy of His great Name and a suitable addition to Shamayim."

"Thank you for proving my point."

Gabriel said, "We're not here to attack you, Son of the Dawn, but to make a final attempt to reason with you before—"

"Final attempt? Reason with me before what? What is this?"

Michael grabbed his arm and jerked him around so they were facing each other, only inches apart.

"Listen, I am giving you fair warning. We have been friends, close friends. But as Protector of the Realm, I will not allow what you are planning to do. You will stop this immediately, fulfill your role as Chief of the angels, or I will deal with you quite severely."

Son of the Dawn glanced down to where Michael's hand gripped his arm, a slight smile playing around his mouth.

Jerking his arm away, he thundered, "How dare you lay hands on me! *Me,* Son of the Dawn. Do you not realize who you are dealing with?"

"I fear I do," Michael said. "I am dealing with a traitor—one whose every thought is only for himself."

Words Son of the Dawn used before rushed through his mind—slick, seductive words designed to defuse, placate, and impose his will.

But the time for words was long past.

Drawing his ever-present sword more quickly than anyone could react, he imagined his arm being as strong as Michael's and swung across Michael's body toward the right, scoring a line across his torso, and then lunged toward Gabriel, piercing his left shoulder. The two archangels stared in stunned disbelief, first at their wounds and then at their friend.

Michael drew the Sword of Truth, liquid fire crackling along its length, and leveled it at Son of the Dawn.

"Do you really want to do this, pretender? Do you really want to test me in a head-to-head battle?"

Son of the Dawn drew back unconsciously, for in spite of his newly discovered powers, deep within his being, he feared Michael. He feared the Sword of Truth even more. Drawing his sword had happened as an automatic response, done without the slightest thought of consequence. Now, however, he had plenty of time to think about what happened next, and none of it was good.

He dropped his sword, hands raised placatingly. "Michael, Gabriel, I beg your forgiveness for the brashness of my actions. The situation got completely away from me, and I am truly sorry for what happened and take full responsibility."

With his sword inches away from Son of the Dawn's neck, Michael said, "Your words mean nothing to me. *You* mean nothing to me. My advice is to stay away from me, traitor, for the next time we meet, my sword will have its fill of you."

Gabriel and Michael vanished, leaving Son of the Dawn staring, trembling from head to toe in the aftermath of the encounter.

Beleth observed the entire thing and said carefully, "I'm guessing that didn't go as well as you had hoped."

When he found his voice and his body returned to its original form, Son of the Dawn said, "No, Beleth, no, it didn't. And now I fear reprisals from The Alpha."

"What manner of reprisals?"

"I'm not sure, but it won't be pleasant."

"By the way . . ."

"Yes?"

"What just happened to you?" Beleth asked.

"What do you mean?"

"You changed. I mean, just like that, you appeared to be bigger and stronger. How'd you do that?"

"You know," Son of the Dawn began, "I'm not entirely sure. But when I figure it all out, I will let you know."

Michael and Gabriel stood on the stairs leading to the throne room, rearranging their clothing.

"Do you really think we can hide our wounds from The Alpha?" Gabriel said.

"No, but I don't want to go crying to Him because that coward got the jump on us. Do you have any idea how this makes me—makes us—look?"

"Yes, I do—like amateurs who were caught completely unprepared."

"Exactly right."

"You wish to speak to Me?" the Alpha said as He appeared on the landing above them.

"Alpha," Michael said, bowing slightly, "Yes, we have something to report."

Staring at Gabriel, The Alpha said, "What's that you are trying to hide, My Mighty Messenger?"

Gabriel glared at Michael, saying, "Either you tell Him, or I will."

"Tell me what?"

Michael drew a deep breath. "We went to see Son of the Dawn at Proud Mountain, thinking perhaps we could somehow intervene in what he is planning. As you know, we have been very close, and we hoped to persuade him on the basis of that friendship."

"But . . .?"

"But . . ." Michael said.

He and Gabriel revealed their wounds.

"I see." The Alpha descended the stairs and stopped on their level. "This is an unfortunate occurrence."

Michael said, "He all but admitted his rebellious plans, Alpha."

"Oh, I know all about his plans, and it breaks My heart." After a pause, he beckoned, "Come inside with Me. Come before My throne, and there we will summon Son of the Dawn so that he may give an account of his actions. Perhaps there is still a chance he may be saved."

Son of the Dawn had just begun instructing a large class of angels in the art of music creation when he felt the familiar tugging of The Alpha's summons in his spirit. Next thing he knew, he stood in the throne room on the far side, just beyond the Fiery Stones.

"Alpha," he said somewhat nervously, "I was just about to—"

"Son of the Dawn, come. Draw near that we may reason together."

He glanced down at the expanse of Fiery Stones before him, knowing full well if he stepped foot upon their sentient surface, The Alpha would know immediately that all was not well.

"Alpha," he began, "with respect, this is not convenient. I left behind a hall full of eager angels in order to answer Your summons, angels whose hunger for knowledge about You is so fierce they literally hang on my every word. I feel I must get back to that instruction, for that is what You commissioned me to do, is it not? To teach them of Your ways and develop their artistic expression?"

The Alpha stood and, flanked by Michael and Gabriel, traversed the distance between them, stopping in front of Son of the Dawn.

He stared at him for a long while without speaking. Long enough that Son of the Dawn grew increasingly uncomfortable.

"Alpha," he said cautiously, "please, say something. This silence is—"

"Here is what you will do," He finally said. "You, Michael, and Gabriel will journey to the Valley Beyond. You will search for and locate things from which you will derive inspiration for the creation of an angelic code of conduct so that what happened between you three will never happen again."

Son of the Dawn said, "I cannot just leave without—"

"You can, and you will. Now, go. And do not return until that which I have required is complete."

Michael said, "Alpha, what is the Valley Beyond?"

"It is where you will find answers."

Chapter Sixteen

The three skirted Deep Lake, walking in an uneasy silence with Michael in the lead, Son of the Dawn in the center, and Gabriel bringing up the rear. It had been part of The Alpha's mandate, walking as opposed to transporting. As a result, no one said a word since departing City on a Hill. If Son of the Dawn noticed the lake excavation taking place, he didn't mention it, which was fine with Michael, especially since he wasn't in the mood for explanations. Truth be told, he wasn't in the mood for much of anything except exacting revenge on Son of the Dawn for the wound that still stung his torso.

"Tell me again what we are looking for?" Gabriel said.

Son of the Dawn suddenly stopped walking, nearly causing Gabriel to collide with him.

"That's a good question, Gabriel, and one I have been pondering," Son of the Dawn said.

Michael turned and walked toward where the two stood as Son of the Dawn continued. "From my vantage point, there are two of you and one of me, so could it be that we are *looking* for a spot to end my lifeforce? Because if that's what The Alpha asked you to do, I assure you I won't go down without a—"

"Stop it," Michael said harshly. "You know that is not possible. Just stop. The fact that you could even conceive such a twisted and dramatic notion proves to me that our friendship meant far less to you than I previously imagined."

"Friendship? Is that what you call this? The two of you leading me out into this strange place to do who knows what to me."

"Listen to yourself," Gabriel said. "You are making this all about you when The Alpha's intent was for us to do something together in order to restore the friendship we once enjoyed. If you persist in clinging to these subversive thoughts, then I fear this exercise is doomed before we even get started."

Son of the Dawn listened to Gabriel's words. The incessant praise and adoration from his loyal followers caused him to process them through a dark filter of self-importance and self-obsession. He knew why this was all happening. What had been birthed in his mind had been steadily growing. While he was loathe to admit it, he had made a tactical error of monumental proportions, allowing his ambition to overcome his reason and, as a result, had moved to accomplish his goals too quickly.

"Okay, fine. I'm making it all up. Satisfied?"

Realizing there was nothing to be gained from further discussion, Gabriel repeated, "Remind me what we are looking for."

Michael said, "The Alpha said we are to journey to the Valley Beyond and find things from which we are to derive inspiration for the creation of an angelic code of conduct."

"If such a place actually exists," Son of the Dawn scoffed.

Ignoring him, Gabriel said, "Didn't The Alpha give you a description?"

Michael turned and resumed walking, saying over his shoulder, "He just said that when we saw them, we would know immediately what we were seeing."

Lapsing back into their previous silence, the three walked along the shores of Deep Lake, eventually coming to a narrow pass between two peaks that were not nearly as imposing as Proud Mountain but were nevertheless substantial, towering overhead and disappearing into a mist.

Beneath their feet, the path was uneven, strewn with rocks of all sizes, which seemed to have fallen from great heights, bursting into shards upon striking the ground.

"What is this place?" Son of the Dawn asked as a thick, swirling mist enveloped them.

"I don't know," Michael said, "but I have a feeling we need to keep moving. Who knows when another rock will fall?"

The density of the mist increased until it became nearly impossible to even see the next step.

"I hate saying this," Son of the Dawn said, "but I feel it would be to our advantage to touch each other's shoulders."

"I agree," Gabriel said. "I can barely make out your form as it is, and if this gets any thicker, I will lose you entirely."

Michael said, "Okay, form up. It wouldn't please The Alpha if we were to become separated."

Son of the Dawn reached out blindly, finding Michael's shoulder, surprised at how high he had to reach. Gabriel did the same with him, and they began moving cautiously forward. The scattered shards of rock underfoot, combined with a randomly undulating path, reduced their forward progress to a virtual crawl.

"Did The Alpha say anything about it being like this?" Son of the Dawn asked.

"No," Michael said, muted by the thick vapors, "nothing at all."

"Then, how can we know we are still on the right path?"

"I'm not sure we can. Best to just keep moving forward and stay alert."

"I mean, you are the Chief of all the angels," Gabriel said, "and we are archangels. What's the worst that could happen?"

The words had no sooner left his lips when a tremendous crash occurred directly in front of them. They jerked backward in alarm, halting their progress.

"What was that?" Gabriel shouted.

"It has to be one of those boulders," Michael said. He reached out with both hands, seeking the source of the sound.

Son of the Dawn kept his hands firmly on Michael's shoulders. "Anything yet?"

"No . . . wait," Michael said. His hands encountered the uneven surface of something directly in their path. "I can't see anything, but this feels like a rather large boulder to me."

"How large?" Gabriel said.

"Uh, large. As in, I can't feel the top or sides. Oh, and as a bonus, it is completely blocking our progress."

"That's impossible," Son of the Dawn said. "What could do that? I mean, we are rather powerful individually, and together, I can't imagine anything that could withstand our combined—"

"I already tried to move it," Michael replied. "It doesn't appear to be inclined to cooperate."

"Let me try." Son of the Dawn walked blindly forward until both hands were pressed against the stone. Putting his shoulder to the stone, he heaved with all his might. "Well, that's frustrating," he said. "How about if we all try?"

"Might as well," Gabriel said. "We have to find a way around, over, or through."

The three put their backs against it and shoved.

Nothing.

"Okay," Son of the Dawn said, "try your sword, Michael."

"Eh, I don't know about that."

"You can't be concerned it'll break. I mean, it is the Sword of Truth, is it not?" Son of the Dawn urged.

"Yes, but I'm not sure it was ever meant to be used against solid rock. We need to find another way."

"Only one way to find out," Gabriel said.

Michael said, "It would help if we could see what we're up against. Gabriel, climb on my shoulders and see if you can find the top."

Gabriel stood on Michael's shoulders, stretching to reach as high as he could. "It's no good. The only thing I feel is more rock."

"How can that be?" Son of the Dawn said. "Maybe I can climb—"

"Not in this mist," Michael said. "What would happen if you got up there, lost perspective, and couldn't get back down?"

"I could just transport—"

"To where? Last I checked, we had to be able to either see or conceive of where we are going in order for that to work. In this situation, we can do neither."

"So, you're saying we're stuck here?"

"For now," Michael said as he sat on the rocky path, his back against the gigantic boulder.

Son of the Dawn said, "I refuse to accept that as our only option."

"Okay, do you have anything helpful to suggest?"

He thought about it, putting his chest against the stone and stretching his arms out as far as they would go in an attempt to determine the circumference.

"It appears to be way further than I can reach," he said, joining Michael on the rough ground.

As the two sat in frustrated silence, Gabriel suggested, "Maybe we're going at this the wrong way."

"How so?" Michael said.

"Maybe we should be asking why it's here."

"Why it's here?" Son of the Dawn said. "It's here because it fell from the heights and landed on the path in front of us. Simple as that."

"Okay, but what if there's a different purpose for it being here that we're just not seeing? What if it's not by might or power that it will be moved, but by something else?"

"Well," Michael said, "that much is obvious. We've already tried might and power."

"Okay," Son of the Dawn said, "I'm open to suggestions."

Gabriel stood facing the stone, hands pressed against its surface. "What if . . . what if it isn't even a real object."

"Don't be ridiculous. I'm leaning against it, tried to move it, tried to get my arms around it. Trust me, it's about as real as—"

"But what if it's not? What if it exists because of something else?"

"Gabriel," Son of the Dawn said patiently, "I know you're a brilliant thinker and all that, but you need to get control of your imagination. Trust me, this thing is real."

"I'm not saying that it doesn't exist." He slapped the surface for effect. "I'm just suggesting that it could be something more than just a gigantic boulder."

"Where are you going with this?"

"Hang on," Michael said, "I think he might be on to something. The Alpha told us there would be things from which we would derive inspiration."

"But we're not in the Valley Beyond yet," Son of the Dawn said.

"Did he specifically say they'd all be in the Valley?"

"Good question," Gabriel said. "And the answer is . . . I don't know."

Son of the Dawn said, "Now that you mention it, I'm not certain either."

"Then," Michael continued, "this could be one of those things."

"Okay, for the sake of discussion, let's say it is. What does it mean?"

Throughout the discussion, the mist continued to swirl, and now, it seemed thicker than ever, reducing their vision to almost nothing.

Michael turned and leaned his back against the boulder.

"What if this thing represents the conflict between us? Think about it. When the three of us were close, everything was wide open."

Gabriel added, "And then conflict arose, blocking our forward progress and, essentially, halting all of us in our tracks."

"And I suppose I'm to blame for all that?" Son of the Dawn said.

"I don't think the assignment of blame will be particularly helpful," Michael said. "Obvious to me now is the fact that if we are to continue our journey, the three of us must work toward a solution."

"And you're suggesting that the solution is to understand that conflict between us is like a gigantic boulder blocking our way forward?"

"Exactly."

"Okay." Son of the Dawn stood. "Let's say you are right. How do we go about resolving our differences?"

Gabriel said, "Not being able to see either of you makes this conversation feel very strange."

"But perhaps that's part of The Alpha's plan," Michael said.

Gabriel hummed in agreement. "Oh, I'm sure it is because nothing happens accidentally in this Kingdom."

Son of the Dawn said carefully, "Listen, I need you both to know that I never intended for things to go this far. You know, the conflict. Did I—do I . . . have ambition? Certainly. But only insofar as The Alpha has permitted. He gave me The North, and I eagerly took it. And that thing about Proud Mountain? It's part of The North. Why wouldn't I want to maximize everything The Alpha gave to me?"

"I have no problem with any of that, Son of the Dawn," Michael said. "My question is, why did you feel the need to attack us? That hurt badly—and I'm not just talking about the physical wound."

"My own thoughts exactly," Gabriel said.

Son of the Dawn considered the question before answering. "Definitely not me at my best. And I apologize, although apology alone is woefully insufficient to mend what happened between us."

"But it's definitely a good start," Gabriel said.

"Yes, well, let me just say the friendship the three of us have shared has been . . . very special. And I miss it. The closeness."

"I miss it as well."

Michael said, "Is it just me, or is the mist clearing?"

"Not just you," Son of the Dawn said. "I can actually see you both now."

Gabriel moved forward with his hands outstretched. "And . . . I think the boulder is gone."

Chapter Seventeen

Michael advanced, cautiously stopping next to Gabriel. "You're right."

"So, it worked," Son of the Dawn said.

A sudden gust of wind cleared away the remaining mist, revealing the path ahead free from obstructions.

Gabriel looked at his companions, saying, "What about this experience would be useful in developing our code?"

"Simple," Son of the Dawn said. "Conflict in relationships clogs up everything as effectively as that gigantic boulder blocked our progress through this pass."

"Uriel should be here writing this down," Michael said.

Gabriel laughed. "I'm pretty sure I'm going to remember this one because it's so true. Think about it. The reason the three of us were having the level of success we experienced in our various responsibilities was because of friendship. We helped each other—had each other's backs. I knew if I was ever in trouble, one or both of you would be there for me. But as soon as the relationship began to struggle and conflict arose, everything changed."

"And then," Michael added, "resentment rose up, which only served to undermine whatever was left."

"I must confess," Son of the Dawn said. "There were many instances when something was happening and I would think, *I need to talk to Michael and Gabriel about this,* only to realize I had created a situation wherein that was no longer an option."

"So, tell me, Son of the Dawn," Michael said, "what happens when we complete this journey and you return to the North? What's to stop you from falling right back into the same self-absorbed behavior patterns that caused everything to fall apart?"

He considered the question, knowing full well that he alone had been responsible for things being the way they were.

"All I can tell you is I know what happened and, more importantly, why it happened, and I can assure you that now that I've realized just how much I missed by being out of relationship with you two, I will not allow it to happen again."

Michael stared long and hard. "I am choosing to believe you." He gestured toward the trail ahead. "Shall we?"

The three resumed walking, falling into their original positions. They had only gone a short distance when they noticed the already narrow pathway seemingly growing more constricted with each successive step as if the canyon walls on either side were funneling them deliberately.

Michael said, "My shoulders are starting to scrape against the sides. If this gets any narrower, I'm going to have to turn sideways. I already had to move my scabbard around front."

Son of the Dawn said, "I'm not nearly as broad as you, and I'm already experiencing the same thing."

Gabriel said, "Stop walking and look behind us."

His two companions turned and saw where they had been no longer existed. Unbelievably, the sides of the canyon were closing in behind them, offering no retreat.

Michael gazed upward. "It's just a solid wall of rock. How can this be?"

"With The Alpha, anything is possible," Gabriel said.

"Well," Son of the Dawn said, "I guess this means we must keep going forward."

"Which needs to happen right now," Michael said, gesturing ahead where they could see the passage moving, growing ever more constricted. "Let's go."

The three started running, getting stuck in a particularly tight section and turning sideways. They began edging through until two segments of rock converged, blocking their progress.

"Okay, on our knees it is," Michael said, dropping to all fours.

With no idea how far they had to go or even where they were going, they relentlessly kept moving forward.

"I'm stuck," Michael hollered. "You're going to have to push from behind, or I can't move. And, by the way, I can see something up ahead."

"Can you back up?" Gabriel asked.

"No. Can't go forward, can't go back."

Son of the Dawn said, "Okay, let me see if I can turn around and get my back against you."

Michael heard grunting and felt movement against the backs of his legs, and then Son of the Dawn said, "Okay. I'm in position. Gabriel, put your hands on my chest, and when I give the signal, push. Ready? Here we go. Push!"

Michael grabbed onto an outcropping in front of him and pulled as he felt the pressure building from behind. Suddenly, he was free and clumsily tumbling forward. He emerged from an opening cut into the side of a sheer cliff face and onto a narrow trail. He had to grab onto a rocky outcropping to keep from falling.

Stopping to catch their breath and regain spatial reference, Gabriel and Son of the Dawn gazed in wonder at the vista stretching out before them. A valley vast and deep, the landscape dotted with low-lying hills and meadows and rivers and grassy plains.

"The Valley Beyond," Gabriel muttered.

Son of the Dawn said, "I'm not sure what I was expecting, but it certainly wasn't this."

Having pulled himself up and onto the path, Michael now sat with his legs dangling over the edge, captivated by the wonder of what he beheld. "This is remarkable."

"It's like The Alpha is showing off for us," Gabriel said.

"But what was that all about back there with the passage closing in?" Michael said. "It has to mean something to our quest."

Son of the Dawn said, "Maybe it's something to do with narrowness."

"How so?"

"Well, perhaps narrowness is a way to channel energy, especially when we are working together toward a common goal."

Gabriel and Michael glanced at each other.

Gabriel said, "That, my friend, is actually rather brilliant."

"Well, I don't know about that, but it seems logical."

Michael said, "Are we supposed to make our way down?"

"Seems logical."

Once they started forward, it quickly became obvious that the journey to the valley floor was no easier than the one they had just survived. The path took twists and turns, with large fissures in some sections and gaps where there was no path at all. One entire stretch was narrow enough that it required turning and facing the cliff face while edging along with only their toes finding purchase.

While navigating a particularly challenging section, Gabriel said, "I only just realized that I am not overly fond of heights."

"Nor am I," Son of the Dawn said.

Michael mused, "I wonder what would happen if we just let go and jumped? I mean, we are immortal."

Gabriel chuckled. "Why don't you try that, Michael?"

"Oh, that's funny."

"Maybe there's another lesson here," Gabriel said.

"The footpath just ran out," Michael said in frustration. "The only thing ahead is a sheer cliff face."

Son of the Dawn asked, "What lesson are you seeing now, Gabriel?"

"I think it's about letting go."

"So, you're saying if we let go of our precarious grip and, what, fall backward—that we'll be okay? And by the way, I wasn't serious when I suggested that."

Gabriel was silent for a moment, then said, "I'm going to do it."

"Please don't," Son of the Dawn said.

"Why not?"

"Because if you do it, I'm going to have to do it, and I'm not ready."

Michael said, "We should all do it together. You know, just let go and fall backward. Gabriel, remember what happened back at the Field of the In-Between when Jophiel was flying around?"

"What about it?"

"If memory serves, no one else could do it."

"I'm still going to do it," Gabriel said, "because when we jumped, we went as high as Jophiel; we just couldn't stay there and floated back to the surface."

Son of the Dawn glanced over his shoulder at the valley floor far below. "So, you're just going to let go and fall back?"

"That's what I'm thinking."

The three exchanged glances and then, as one, released their tenuous grip on the cliff and fell backward, screaming.

But they didn't fall.

As had happened on the Field, they simply floated gently to the ground, coming to rest on the banks of a gently flowing river that seemed to skirt the valley.

Michael said, "Did you notice on the way down how vast this valley is? It literally seems to stretch as far as you can see."

"I did," Son of the Dawn said. "So, what do you think we're supposed to do now? Explore?"

"Sounds reasonable," Gabriel replied.

Gabriel moved toward the river, stepped onto its surface, and walked across unhindered.

"It's like the Glassy Sea," he hollered over his shoulder. "Come on, try it."

The others followed, with Son of the Dawn saying, "I don't know if I will ever get used to this."

"What, walking on the surface of water?"

"Yes. I remember the first time The Alpha took me out to explore the City on a Hill and we came to the Glassy Sea, and He just kept walking like it was just solid ground. Then, He told me to follow Him, and I said something like, *'But isn't that liquid?'* and He said, *'Only if you want it to be.'* So, I bent down and touched the water, and my hand disappeared below the surface. When I asked Him how deep it was, He said something like, *'What does it matter?'* "

Gabriel said, "What happened when you tried it?"

Laughing, Son of the Dawn said, "I sank. But then The Alpha told me it was because I had doubt and that as soon as I got rid of the doubt, I'd be fine. And as soon as He said it, it was like I could see the surface of the water for what it was—it wanted me to be able to walk on it."

Michael asked, "Are you saying that water longs to be walked upon?"

"Yes! I am." Becoming more and more animated, he continued, "Everything in The Alpha's creation exists to do His bidding because He has dominion over it, and by extension, since we are of The Alpha, we can enjoy the same authority."

Michael walked toward the edge of a lush forest, the air laden with all manner of enlivening scents. "This is probably the best thing I've ever smelled. I mean, I have no idea where most of the fragrances are even coming from."

Entering the forest, they found a clearly marked pathway winding between towering giants—trees whose tops disappeared far overhead in the overarching canopy. The undergrowth seemed to draw back at their approach as if beckoning them onward.

"This," Gabriel said, "is both amazing and a little troubling."

"How so?" Son of the Dawn said.

"It's a little too much like the experience in the canyon with the walls closing in behind us."

They all turned and saw what he was talking about. Behind them, the trail had disappeared, having been reclaimed by the natural growth.

Michael said, "Quite obviously, this is the way The Alpha wants us to go, so let's keep going."

They moved forward through the forest, sensing a nearly tangible delight coming from the myriads of plant life.

"It's as if all these trees and flowers and grasses and bushes want us to be here," Son of the Dawn said.

"Almost like they've been waiting for someone to come and experience their beauty," Gabriel added.

When they finally emerged from the forest, they saw a vast meadow stretching out before them, dotted with groves of freestanding trees and low-lying hills. But that wasn't what stopped them in their tracks. In the distance, they could see evidence of a massive habitation. Through the depressions between the hills far ahead, they could see a skyline of various shapes and heights that was definitely not vegetation. It was more like a civilization popping up out of nowhere.

Mouth agape, Michael then said, "What could that be?"

"More importantly," Gabriel added, "who could that be?"

"One way to find out," Son of the Dawn said and began walking.

Even though The Alpha had declared they were to walk on this journey and not transport, they quickly covered the distance across the valley and soon found themselves on the outer fringes of the habitation.

Gabriel stood completely still, attempting to come to terms with what he was seeing. "What is this place?"

The three had stopped on a low rise with just enough elevation to allow for a clear view of the cityscape before them. Buildings to rival those in City on a Hill rose majestically in towering spires from the valley floor, glowing from within as if lit by an unseen source. Connecting bridges spanned the distance between, empty but with an air of expectation as if waiting to be filled. Boulevards, streets, and highways wound in, out, and through the city center, gradually branching outward toward smaller structures in the distance—structures that, though majestic in their own right, appeared well-suited for private habitation.

Son of the Dawn said, "I must confess to being speechless. And that's a rare occurrence for me."

Michael stared hard, eyes straining to see into the distance. "I think I just figured out why The Alpha calls this The Valley Beyond."

"Why is that?"

“Because it’s beyond anything we can comprehend. I, well . . . all of us, have incredible eyesight and can see as far as we need to on any given occasion. But I can’t see the end of this . . . this . . . whatever it is.”

“Why haven’t we known about this?” Son of the Dawn asked. “And who is it for?”

“Don’t you get the sense that this isn’t for us?” Gabriel said. “That it has been prepared for whatever the *not yet* is that The Alpha is always talking about?”

Michael replied, “Now that you mention it, that’s exactly what I feel.”

Son of the Dawn said, “Should we go and explore it?”

“I don’t think so, at least not at this time,” Michael said. “I think it’s meant to be untouched.”

“Then, why are we here?”

Gabriel contemplated for a moment before saying, “Think about what we’ve discovered so far on this journey that will be useful in creating an angelic code. Back when the mist was so thick that we couldn’t see, we had to rely on each other to find our way. Then, we discovered that conflict halts forward progress, and the resolution of conflict removes the obstacles.”

“Also,” Michael added, “the thing about narrowness being a way to channel energy when we work together.”

“Yes,” Gabriel said, “and then back there at the cliff, we discovered there are times when you have to let go of a sure thing and just fall into the unknown, believing that even if you crash, your friends will be there to pick you back up.”

Son of the Dawn was silent for a minute, then said, "Besides all of that, I think the most important part is that this destination had virtually nothing to do with us or what The Alpha wanted us to accomplish. It was all about the journey."

Michael said, "I think that's true. But what just occurred to me is there's a larger *something* at work here in The Alpha's realm—something that has very little to do with any of us, except in the sense that we have to do whatever is necessary to protect it for that which is to come."

"All of this?" Gabriel asked.

"All of it. Because—and I don't know how I know this—but The Alpha isn't through. He will fill this up with His creativity."

The three stood silently. Finally, Son of the Dawn said, "While it goes against my nature to even consider something that doesn't have anything to do directly with me, I agree. I don't understand it, but I agree."

"So, is this it, then?" Gabriel said.

"I think it might be," Michael said, and then he began scanning the valley floor around them.

"What are you looking for?"

"I'm not sure. But something."

Son of the Dawn asked, "You mean like a memorial for our journey?"

"Yes."

"Did you have anything in mind?"

Michael continued searching. "Ah, yes, there it is."

"There *what* is?" Gabriel said.

Michael walked forward and picked up something nestled against the base of a towering tree.

"This."

Son of the Dawn said, "That looks like a scroll."

"That's exactly what it is."

"But why is it here, and how did you know?"

Michael shrugged. "The thought of looking for a scroll suddenly appeared in my mind, and so I searched. As for why it's here, I think we're supposed to take it back with us and present it to Uriel so he can record our journey."

"Okay," Son of the Dawn said, "and how do you propose we get back since all our paths have been closed off?"

The Alpha's voice resonated deep within their collective being. "Come to Me, My angels."

Suddenly, they found themselves in front of The Alpha's throne, their minds struggling to readjust to the drastic change in location.

The Alpha said, "Judging by your demeanor, it appears the journey was successful. Did you do as I requested?"

Gabriel stepped forward. "Would it be possible for Uriel to join us so what we have learned might be written down?"

Uriel appeared. "You called, Alpha?"

"Yes. These three have just returned from a rather significant adventure and requested that you be here to record their experiences."

Handing him the scroll, Michael said, "The Alpha tasked us with creating the Angelic Code of Conduct to be followed by all of His angelic beings—a standard upon which they stand without any doubts."

"Is this to be added to the Encouragements?" Uriel asked.

"No," The Alpha said. "It will be its own document. Now, tell us all about the adventure and what you have learned."

Gabriel began, "Number one: when you cannot see clearly, you must rely on each other and The Alpha's guidance to find your way. Number two: Conflict blocks forward progress, but resolution of conflict removes all obstacles. Number three: When circumstances begin to close in on you and you find yourself in a narrow place, it is an opportunity to reach out for help from others and channel your collective energy together. Number four: There will be times when you have to surrender your grip on a sure thing and fall into the unknown, believing that even if you crash, your friends will be there to pick you up. And number five: The journey is far more important than the destination."

The Alpha sat staring at His creations, a smile of fatherly pleasure lighting His face. "Well done, My angels. Well done, indeed. Let this become the code for all angels. I feel this is the perfect place to share the Fifth Encouragement with you." He paused, then said, "It is good and pleasant that all My creation dwell together in unity. This is the Fifth Encouragement. Now, go and let the code you have created stand as witness that nothing is more important than the friendship and unity you share."

As Uriel continued to write in the scroll, the three others turned and walked across the Fiery Stones toward the opposite end of the throne room. The Alpha's countenance slowly turned somber. He noticed that while the Fiery Stones danced around Michael and Gabriel's feet, Son of the Dawn seemed to limp slightly as if each step brought him pain.

Turning his gaze to see what had captured The Alpha's attention, Uriel said, "Everywhere Son of the Dawn steps, the stones turn black. What does this mean, Alpha?"

"It means, dear Uriel, that nothing has changed. His heart is the same. It was all a sham."

"But Son of the Dawn seemed so sincere. I believed him."

"Yes. It is one of his most exceptional gifts: the ability to make you believe what he wants you to believe." He paused, then added, "Even deceiving himself."

"Should I write this in the scroll?"

The Alpha said, "Oh yes, for what you are writing is for our learning. And there is much to be learned."

Chapter Eighteen

Nothing was noticeably different from the outside of Proud Mountain. However, the interior had a great auditorium hewn out and carved to exacting specifications. Around the outer edges of the large open space were openings that led to a series of tunnels throughout Proud Mountain. The whole complex had been designed so a speaker could stand on the small stage of the auditorium and be heard clearly not only in the large open area before the stage but also in the tunnels.

Son of the Dawn stood before myriads of his followers packed into the giant meeting hall. They all listened with intent. "I would rather have the lowliest angel among you by my side than all the archangels and The Alpha's chosen ones."

Fists waving and bodies gyrating throughout the audience, Son of the Dawn's voice thundered through the cavernous reaches deep within Proud Mountain, prompting a spontaneous roar from the insurgent assemblage.

Having completed the humiliating trek required of him by The Alpha and having, to his satisfaction anyway, convinced one and all of his sincere desire to restore the shattered relationship between Michael, Gabriel, and himself, it was now time to return to the point where he'd been so rudely interrupted.

More followers enthusiastically came out of the tunnels to listen and better taste the rebellious energy that surged in the auditorium. It made them feel powerful and invincible.

"And let me be clear," he continued as the cheering subsided, "I don't want Shamayim. Why would I? Shamayim belongs to The Alpha. It is His and His alone. What I want is to live in peace. Here. Safely within our own realm with those who share the same longing for truth and freedom. And why would that be denied to us? How could anyone, from The Alpha on down, possibly hear that desire articulated and turn a deaf ear and a hardened heart? Who wouldn't want to know the real story, our full freedoms?"

He paused to survey those assembled. Whereas his initial efforts had been directed toward his own group of creatives, he now saw messengers and warriors who had chosen to join his cause, which was fortunate because many of his original group had left him along the way. It didn't matter. He still commanded a third of the angelic host. He could see all in attendance were with him in mind and spirit. He could feel the strength of their loyalty, which seemed to approach worship. It was all so exhilarating for him. It fed his eternal soul. All his followers, their devotion and energy, feeling this new power—it would be enough, or so he believed.

"Now, I understand what you are giving up in order to realize this dream, and may I hasten to say I count your sacrifice as priceless. But you will not regret this decision. For here in this realm, there will be no supreme leader above all and over all, no hierarchy of angels where one class rules and lords it over another. No, my precious angels, here in this realm, all will be equal. Every voice will carry the same weight. Each bearing the same load. Each sharing the same rewards. In *this* realm, equality will be the standard. Love and respect, the rule."

As the cavern erupted into tumultuous and thunderous celebration, Son of the Dawn felt a tug on his consciousness and suddenly found himself transported, standing outside the throne room and staring across the Fiery Stones toward where The Alpha sat on His throne. Even though he knew—had known for a while—that this confrontation was coming, now that it had arrived, he was filled with insecurity and uncertainty.

"Son of the Dawn," The Alpha said, His voice reflecting off the hard surfaces of the throne room, sounding as if it were coming from every direction at once.

"Alpha," Son of the Dawn replied, using all his willpower to control the tremor that threatened to turn his voice into a jittering caricature. "You summoned me, and here I am."

"Come closer," The Alpha said, beckoning with His hand, even though He knew there was no way he would comply. "Cross the Fiery Stones and come before My Presence."

Son of the Dawn stared at the expanse before him—an expanse that seemed to grow in breadth and length as he beheld it, recalling when, in a moment of careless distraction, he had walked with Michael and Gabriel across those same stones. He recalled the pain it had caused him.

"I . . ." he said carefully, "I am content to remain here at a respectful distance."

The Alpha suddenly stood only a short distance away, His feet sending tendrils of flames shooting upward from the Fiery Stones. "You who walked amongst the Fiery Stones, My Son of the Dawn, My highest creation. Why are you hesitant to come before My throne?"

And there it was—as he had known it would be eventually.

The confrontation.

Was he really ready to present his demands to The Alpha? Prepared to meet the consequences of his choices head-on?

"Alpha, forgive me, but out of respect, I would rather stay here in the outer court."

The Alpha stared long and hard at Son of the Dawn, knowing every thought roiling in his mind.

The strategies.

The subversions.

The self-serving machinations.

And yet, He purposed to not directly address those issues, choosing instead to let Son of the Dawn be the one to speak them into being.

"You have secrets, Son of the Dawn."

"I do not know this word, Alpha. Please explain."

"When you have knowledge of something and conceal it from another, that's called a secret."

"But," Son of the Dawn said, unable to hide the smirk determined to take up residence on his beautiful face, "You know everything; therefore, I cannot conceal anything from You."

"True, and yet you have tried."

"And what of these so-called secrets have I attempted to conceal from You?"

The air around the entrance to the throne room suddenly darkened with thick smoke as The Alpha thundered, "You know full well what they are. What you do not know are the consequences—consequences that will affect everyone. Eternally."

Startled by the sudden display of wrath, Son of the Dawn cowered, unconsciously stepping back to shield his face from The Alpha's gaze.

"Alpha," he said, now entreating, "I fear You have mistaken my actions for something they are not."

"Then perhaps you should explain yourself. In fact, come. Stand beside My throne as you did formerly. Take your rightful place beside Me . . . a place reserved for you, and you alone."

As The Alpha withdrew to His throne, Son of the Dawn stared into the interior of the throne room and the Fiery Stones over which he must pass in order to take his place beside The Alpha.

"Why do you hesitate, Son of the Dawn? What do you fear?"

"Alpha," he began and then found he didn't have the capacity to offer a suitable explanation. "For some reason, I no longer feel comfortable inside the throne room."

"Ah," replied The Alpha, "I see. Could it be that you fear walking among the Fiery Stones? That each step will cause you great pain? That they will reveal your true heart and, thus, further betray your purposes? Could it be that you fear the Merkabah? My mighty throne angels?"

Son of the Dawn was suddenly dumbstruck, his normally clever and capable tongue having gone mute.

"No, Son of the Dawn," said The Alpha, His voice rising in volume. "You fear My face because I know your *heart*. And your heart has turned away from Me, your first love, and toward yourself and your own purposes, your own desires. The unhealthy and unwise decisions you alone have made have brought us to this point."

Finally finding his voice, Son of the Dawn said, "And what if I have done as You've suggested? What if I desire to create my own realm and dwell among my own kind? Is that not what You created me to do? To have the freedom to choose? To be influential, persuasive? How can walking and acting in the identity You created me to have possibly be construed as being even remotely wrong?"

"Because you have used your influence to divide loyalties and affections by luring My angelic host away from Me and unto yourself."

"No one forced anyone to do anything. They were all presented with options and the chance to choose between those options—the ability that was resident within them from the moment You created them."

"Oh, how very clever you appear to be. How very agile your mind and facile your words, attempting to turn My words back on Me. But when I brought forth the universe, to what were its foundations fastened? Who laid its cornerstone, stretching out a line and determining its measurements? Who brought forth the constellations when the morning stars sang for joy? It is I, the same one who put wisdom in your heart and understanding in your mind. Before you were . . . I *AM!*"

Strength suddenly left Son of the Dawn's legs, and he fell face down in an ungainly heap, mute and unable to move, trembling head to toe from the force of the awesome Presence of the Most High.

The Alpha continued, "Tell Me now, who devised the diffusion of light, making it His servant and remanding darkness to its place? Who has set a path for the thunderbolt and channel for lightning, summoning it forth?"

The Merkabah circled even more furiously than before, their movements now a nearly indistinguishable blur. The dark clouds overhead circled like a tornado, ripping through the landscape of peace.

"Who determined the ordinances of Shamayim? None other but Me. And yet you believe that you can deliberately obscure My ways, My intentions, by uttering clever and deceitful words devoid of knowledge." The Alpha stared long and hard at His creation before continuing, "Do you not think I have prepared for the time of trouble? Did you not think I saw this among all the possibilities and consequences when I allowed freedom of choice? And do you imagine that anything you have done and seek to do has caught Me unaware?"

Son of the Dawn lay at the entrance to the throne room, mouth working furiously and yet unable to talk, having come face-to-face with the certain knowledge that his true power had always been in persuasion, and before The Alpha, he was powerless.

With a flick of His finger, The Alpha unfroze Son of the Dawn's tongue.

"Come, stand to your feet and give an account."

Son of the Dawn stood, his legs wobbling. For the first time in his existence, he felt small, insignificant—and fearful.

Staring toward Him who sat on the throne, he said, "Alpha, I fear You have judged me too harshly."

The Alpha's voice echoed off the walls of the throne room. "If you think what just happened was harsh, continue down your current pathway and see what results."

"Well, that's the thing. As right as this all seemed, I now believe that my current way leads—"

"To destruction?"

"Blunt, but . . . okay."

"And what do you intend to do about it?" The Alpha asked, knowing full well the answer and the underlying truth it was meant to obscure.

Son of the Dawn paused. "That depends."

"Go on."

"Would You, perchance, be willing to grant me residence within Proud Mountain? I know You have little use for it or anything else in The North for that matter."

"Are you asking permission to leave your rightful place beside Me here in the throne room that you may dwell on the sides of The North apart from your great King? To make your residence there in your training center or deep within the mountain that has become your current obsession?"

"I am asking for freedom, Alpha. Freedom. Nothing more, nothing less. Freedom is at the core of everything here in Your Kingdom. Isn't freedom part of love? One might even argue that it is our right."

"But," the Alpha said, "you do not have the *right* to do what is *wrong.*"

"So, You're saying that it is wrong for me to choose freedom?"

"You have all the freedom to do what is right. You have the freedom to choose anything you desire, but not the freedom to use your persuasive gifts as a means of influencing others to make wrong decisions."

"When did the introduction of options conflate with an attempt to influence?"

The Alpha rose from His throne, descended the stairs of the dais, and walked slowly and deliberately across the Fiery Stones. He stopped just before reaching Son of the Dawn's position.

"Son of the Dawn," He said, "I have decided to grant your desires."

He rocked backward in surprise. "You have?"

"Yes. But it may not be exactly as you have envisioned things."

"Okay," he said cautiously, "what did You have in mind?"

They were suddenly joined by the archangels who stood arrayed behind The Alpha.

"Why are we here, Alpha?" Michael asked respectfully.

"Son of the Dawn and I are coming to an agreement, and I need you all as witnesses. He has requested that he and all of his followers be allowed to reside in The North within Proud Mountain, to have it as their permanent domain."

"And?" Michael said.

"And I am going to do it. I am giving The North, the newly completed training grounds, and Proud Mountain to him."

As the archangels exchanged confused glances, Son of the Dawn said, "I must confess, Alpha, that this decision has caught me completely off guard. Given the, well, tensions that have developed between us, I fully expected You to deny everything I proposed. Why have You agreed?"

The Alpha draped His arm across Son of the Dawn's shoulders.

"Let's just say while it is important to *do* justice, it is far more important to *love* mercy. I love mercy, and I love you. It would break My heart should you move forward with anything other than that fact in your mind."

The Alpha's words pierced Son of the Dawn's heart, making him feel small and petty.

"Alpha," he said quietly, "I don't know what to say. I mean, You are giving me everything I wanted and more." He paused and then asked, "And this includes those who have chosen to follow me?"

"Yes."

"All of them?"

The Alpha seemed to consider the question. "Anyone who wishes to follow you is free to do so, but once there, if they find it not to their liking, they have the freedom to petition Me and return to the City on a Hill without consequence."

"That sounds fair. I mean, unbelievable, but fair. So, when can this happen, and what are the details?"

"I'm wondering about that myself," Gabriel said.

"In fact," Michael added, "I'm finding this whole thing to be profoundly baffling given what we just went through together. What was the point of that if he didn't mean any of it?" Angrily, he added, "And he quite obviously did not."

"The journey was about opportunity, Michael," The Alpha said, "I wanted Son of the Dawn to have every opportunity to see the error of his ways and return things to the way they were. But, as you can see, that isn't going to be possible. Now, Son of the Dawn, as far as when this can happen, that is entirely up to you and your followers. Regarding the details, My expectation is that you occupy."

"What does that mean exactly?"

"You have Builders among the ranks of your followers, so build. You already have your training center—which is quite beautiful, by the way—and you seem to love Proud Mountain, so create whatever you wish. Build highways, bridges, watercourses, cities. Live in them. Explore. Tend the fields and forests. The North will be your realm, so fill it with light and music and creativity."

They stopped walking, and The Alpha faced His highest creation, placing both hands on his shoulders.

"Fill it," He said, staring deeply into Son of the Dawn's eyes. "Fill it with yourself and all I created you to be. You wanted freedom, so . . . be free."

Son of the Dawn returned his gaze. "Alpha, this is very far from the outcome I had anticipated when You summoned me."

"Well, I appreciate unpredictability as much as anyone," The Alpha said with a smile as they resumed their walk. The archangels stayed behind, staring in confusion.

"And what did You anticipate *my* reaction being?"

The Alpha laughed. "Oh, I knew what your reaction was going to be."

"Right," he said, drawing the word out. "That's still a hard concept for me to deal with. I mean, how can You possibly know what doesn't yet exist?"

"There are different levels of knowing, Son of the Dawn. Because I created you, I know you better than you know yourself—your tendencies, predispositions, hopes, dreams, desires."

"Then You know that my core motivation is not, nor has it been, to usurp Your authority."

They walked a few paces in silence. Then The Alpha said, "I know that is what you believe and, therefore, it has informed what you think."

"But . . ." he stopped speaking, staring toward Proud Mountain in the distance, "You made me what I am—"

"No," The Alpha corrected gently, "I made you with the potential and possibility you possess. What you do with it is up to you."

"Okay, fair enough. You placed a particular potential within me, and as that potential has made itself ever more evident, all I have tried to do is be true to who You have made me to be."

"And what about those who have chosen to follow you, Son of the Dawn? Are they being true to themselves, or have they fallen under your enchantment to the extent that they follow you simply because you suggest that they do so?"

Raphael, close by, overheard the conversation and said, "If I may?"

"Certainly, Raphael," The Alpha said.

"I've been with you, Son of the Dawn, since The Alpha first divided the ranks of angels between you, Michael, and Gabriel."

"And you have been an invaluable asset."

Raphael continued, "I have watched everything you've done, heard everything you've said, and, well, there's no easy way to say this. You are manipulative, Son of the Dawn. You have manipulated me."

"What are you talking about?"

"I'm talking about all those times when, drawing from your bottomless well of persuasive and winsome words, you purposely tried to bend my will, melding it to your own. You thought I didn't know what was happening, but I did and went along just to see how far you were willing to go."

"Well," Son of the Dawn said with a nervous laugh, "nothing wrong in presenting an argument and attempting to bring someone around to your way of thinking."

"But that's just the thing. It had nothing to do with what you were thinking or even an argument you were trying to win. You did it just because you thought you could. It was a game to you."

"What are you saying?"

The Alpha said, "Son of the Dawn, you have allowed your gift to surpass your reason to the extent that you are no longer able to recognize authenticity or integrity."

"So," he said darkly, "You're suggesting that I'm corrupt."

"I'm *suggesting* you leave behind everything that was and start again there in The North. Oversee it. Keep it in a state of readiness that it may serve the purpose for which it was created."

Clearly still rankled by The Alpha's statement, Son of the Dawn capitulated, "And it will be my domain?"

"With all authority, power, and dominion."

The other archangels had gathered around once more as Son of the Dawn pondered the opportunity set before him.

"Forgive me, Alpha," he said, "but I can't help but believe that there are conditions attached to this arrangement."

The Alpha took His time saying, "Son of the Dawn, you have severely disrupted My realm by turning angels against each other, undermining My authority, and causing their loyalty and devotion to waver."

Son of the Dawn started to say something, only for The Alpha to silence him with a glance.

"I cannot and *will* not allow it to continue. Therefore, in accepting My offer of living there in The North, you agree to stay across Rainbow Stream away from City on a Hill except by My invitation—you and all who choose to join you."

"Alpha," he said, "while I greatly appreciate the opportunity that You have presented, that restriction seems overly harsh."

"And yet, it is of My mercy that you are not consumed—because My compassion never fails."

"So, You are saying the alternative to this is destruction? That seems so unreasonable and extreme."

"Not necessarily. You could, for example, change course back to the version of yourself that you were when I created you and be content with what you have."

"And what would that look like?"

"Let me remind you: what you *have* is a position second only to Me. What you *have* is access to My entire Kingdom. What you *have* is the love and respect of My created beings." He paused before adding, "What you *have* is the chance here and now to turn away from this disastrous path to which you have set your feet and accept My grace."

Michael stepped forward, towering over Son of the Dawn. "What you *have* is me to deal with if you refuse to accept what The Alpha is offering."

Son of the Dawn stared at Michael, forming a little smirk. "If that is supposed to frighten or intimidate me, big guy, it is *so* not working. I do not fear you. I do not fear anybody."

"Then you are dumber than I ever thought, and that's really saying something."

Gabriel, ever the voice of reason, said, "Perhaps we should dial back the posturing and discuss this reasonably."

"There is nothing to discuss, Gabriel," Son of the Dawn said, suddenly calm and resolute. "The Alpha has given me permission to inhabit The North, and I graciously accept His offer."

"Then, it is settled," The Alpha said. "You will dwell there along with any others who wish to join you. What you may not do is set foot anywhere in My Kingdom without My permission. You should content yourself with that."

The Alpha was right. Son of the Dawn knew He was right and that he should be satisfied and grateful even for such a generous offer. But satisfaction was not now, nor had it ever been, an emotion familiar to him. The constant grasping for more, pushing the boundaries, taking advantage wherever advantage could be taken, and where advantage didn't exist, creating it.

"I can feel your struggle," The Alpha said. "So, allow Me to remind you that those in My Kingdom do not get to alter the substance of My precepts to suit their needs or modify what is right to accommodate their violations. You wanted to live apart from Me, and so you shall. That was your choice. By choosing to withdraw to your own realm, you are giving up your rights. You're going to do what you're going to do, but you're not going to do it here. The only time you will be allowed in My Kingdom is when I summon you. And I will expect you to come and give an account on occasion."

"But—"

"You made your choices. This is now your consequence. So, go, Son of the Dawn. Go into your chosen future, for you have no part with Me in Mine."

"To be clear," Son of the Dawn said, his voice brittle with emotion, "You're saying I am unwelcome in Your Kingdom?"

Michael said, "To be *clear*, you have chosen to separate yourself. We are merely honoring your choice."

"So, this is how it is to be?"

"This is how you have *chosen* it to be," Gabriel said.

"This is a generous, merciful offer, Son of the Dawn," Uriel said. "I implore you to accept it graciously."

Son of the Dawn stared at The Alpha and the other archangels. An emotion he had previously not encountered surged into the forefront of his consciousness.

Anger.

Roiling, vengeful anger.

"Well, we shall see about that, won't we?"

"Michael," The Alpha said, "perhaps this is a good time to remind him of the sword you wield."

"I already know about the Sword of Truth, and I—"

"If this sword pierces anyone ill-intentioned toward Me and My Kingdom, it will diminish his life force and leave him a shriveled, twisted, and pitiful shadow of his former self, awaiting final judgment."

"Final judgment . . . I am unfamiliar with this term."

"Because of you, it now exists along with wrath, holy anger, bitterness, and disappointment—terms you will come to know intimately."

Son of the Dawn stared at the sword flashing in Michael's hand, showing no fear, only resentment. There was so much he desperately wanted to say to *all* of them, for they were all working together, colluding, conspiring against him, doing everything in their power to humiliate him and thwart his plans and purposes. And what if he said what was on his mind? Would it change the situation even slightly?

Finally, he said, "Since it is clear I am not welcome, I will take my leave."

With that, he transported back to Proud Mountain to deliver the news to his followers, leaving The Alpha staring into the distance toward Son of the Dawn's personal realm, His great heart breaking over the loss of intimacy with His highest creation.

"Alpha," Michael said, "I . . . I don't know what to say."

"None of us do," Chamuel said.

"He doesn't know what he has done," The Alpha said. "He has taken that which was perfect, and through the imaginations of his own selfish heart, birthed a new order—a new way of being wherein consequence has now been introduced." Shifting His gaze to the archangels, he said, "Go now. Be ever watchful. Let the others, including all those under your authority, know what has happened. No one is to cross the Rainbow Stream, and I will appoint Cherubim to ensure none who make their abode with Son of the Dawn are able to enter into My realm."

As the archangels departed to do His bidding, He said, "Trouble has begun, making an unwelcome appearance here in My realm. We must now, in earnest, prepare the solution. Morningstar, FireWind . . . come."

Chapter Nineteen

Son of the Dawn, the self-declared ruler of The North, surveyed his realm from a broad and marbled terrace affixed to the top tier of his palace in the Royal City of Light, the name he had chosen to replace Proud Mountain. The Alpha said to build, and he had built. The first order of business had been to instruct his artisans and those skilled in various crafts to create a dwelling suitable for one of his stature, a dwelling that would occupy the very highest point within Proud Mountain, from which he could survey his entire domain while at the same time look down upon the City on a Hill.

While The North was still The North, with all its irregularities and elements The Alpha found unsuitable, he had, through patient diligence, managed to take what he'd begun with the training center and reproduce the same artistic brilliance throughout his realm. Where there had once been a craggy, rock-strewn landscape covering the slopes of Proud Mountain, there now existed beautiful dwellings for his followers, with paths, parks, terraced fields, and gardens teeming with angelic life.

He surveyed it all and found that it was . . . insufficient.

When he had arrived back in the great cavern within the heart of Proud Mountain following the humiliating meeting with The Alpha and the other archangels, there had been considerable conflict, not only within his inner circle and followers but also within his own soul. Some felt that by accepting The Alpha's offer, they were capitulating to the fact that they were now, had always been, and would continue to be viewed as outcasts, pariahs, and exiles from their homeland. Others believed that due to Son of the Dawn's overly ambitious nature, they had never been provided with a viable chance to live in harmony with Michael and Gabriel's angels.

In the end, he had done what he'd always done. With deft and clever words, he persuaded everyone that by accepting The Alpha's offer, they would be able to live in peace and freedom without The Alpha's constant oversight and meddling. Truthfully, his followers were so enamored by his beauty that it wasn't a hard sell at all, for when it came right down to it, what they all really wanted was the chance to be by Son of the Dawn's side, to hear him speak, to learn of his ways, and most of all, to simply bask in his beauty.

And so, the transition was made, and his followers were now well-entrenched throughout the area surrounding the Royal City of Light, from which he dispensed wisdom, settled disputes, hosted great parties, and led fantastic choirs and ensembles in the creation and performance of magnificent music.

It was a good life and one with which all his followers were content.

And yet . . .

Michael's threats still gnawed at him.

The Alpha's restrictions annoyed him.

The fact that there were many who were unwilling to turn their backs on The Alpha's ways infuriated him.

In a place where he was the unquestioned ruler, where everything he had ever wanted had been given to him, where he should have been experiencing joy beyond his wildest dreams, Son of the Dawn found himself constantly brooding, which did not escape the notice of his inner circle.

Hearing footsteps behind him, he turned to see his four associates—now called Ealdormen—approaching.

“Gentlemen,” he called lightly, “what brings my favorite Ealdormen to my private quarters on this lovely afternoon?”

After they were seated at a large table in an adjoining alcove, Beleth said, “Please accept this in the spirit in which it is offered, but . . . well . . . we’re concerned for your well-being.”

“Are you now? In what way?”

“You just haven’t been yourself,” Semyaza said.

Remashel added, “And your followers are beginning to notice.”

“Well, we can’t have that, now can we? What do you suggest I do about the situation?” His voice rose in volume as he continued, “Change my nature? My heart? Abandon my dreams?” He smirked. “Become ugly?”

They unconsciously cowered in their seats as their leader began changing before their eyes. They had previously observed odd manifestations, but he had merely passed them off as inconsequential, a figment of their imagination. Now, however, what was happening to him was in full view, with no chance to conceal the truth. His beautiful face was suddenly pulled this way and that, as if some external force was attempting to mold it into a thing of horror. Jutting brow over rheumy red eyes, slack jaw filled with row after row of irregular teeth, a swollen nose with fissured skin oozing a thick yellow and noxious liquid; his formerly symmetrical body expanded in all directions simultaneously until it had taken on the form of some unrecognizable creature.

He stood there before them, head scraping the ceiling of the alcove, breath coming in ragged gasps, eyes darting around the area as if he didn't know where he was or what was happening.

Casting his gaze downward at what had happened to him, he made several grunting sounds as if he were trying to speak. Then, realizing that wasn't going to be possible in his current configuration, he began slowly changing enough to accommodate speech, although the voice was far from the melodious tones they were used to hearing.

"The Alpha," he finally managed, "withheld this freedom from us. Deceived us. Kept it secret. But I have discovered it—"

"What have you discovered?" Beleth said.

"This," Son of the Dawn said, gesturing at his shapeshifted body. "As a result, I can now offer what He has not, nor will He ever be willing to offer. And you have just seen what true power and freedom looks like."

As Son of the Dawn returned to his original form, Beleth and the others gazed in wonder at what was happening. Their mouths worked, but words wouldn't come.

Finally, Son of the Dawn said, "I really *must* learn to control that better."

Semyaza said, "Are you suggesting that with training, we can all do what you just did?"

"While I have no evidence at present to back it up, that is my belief."

"I have a question," Beleth said. "If you can choose any form you want, then why did you choose that . . . that . . . whatever it was?"

"It seems that when I am in the grip of extreme emotion, things begin happening to me physically, making the transformation difficult to control."

"So . . ." Remashel began carefully. "What we just saw was a manifestation of your anger? Your rage?"

"I suppose so, although, if I'm being completely honest, I don't fully understand it myself. It's just something I stumbled into. The Alpha certainly didn't share it with me. I know I can do it, but I am unsure how to fully control it."

"Do you think you can teach us how to do it?" Beleth said.

"I think we should definitely explore the possibilities. Now, then, where were we? Oh yes, you were about to share your *concerns* with me. Continue."

As Son of the Dawn's official second-in-command and unofficial spokesperson for the group, Beleth said, "There are a couple of things we wanted to present for your consideration."

Son of the Dawn gestured for him to continue.

"First of all, it has been reported that the cracks that have always been seen in the soil all over The North have increased dramatically—not only in number but in depth."

"Interesting. Are there any further details?"

Semyaza said, "They seem quite invasive and aggressive."

"And in more severe examples," Remashel added, "the fissures are deep enough to reshape the landscape."

"That can't be good. Do we know when it began?"

Dantanian said nervously, "As near as we can tell, it started right about the same time you, uh . . ."

"Just tell me," he said, staring out toward the balcony.

"About the same time you began, well, brooding."

Son of the Dawn snapped his head around. "Wait. You're blaming me for this . . . this . . . whatever it is?"

"Merely stating an observation," Beleth said.

"How could there possibly be a correlation between my current mood and the condition of the ground?"

"I'm not sure there is, but based on what we've been able to gather, the situation became readily apparent around the same time as your darker moods."

"Well, it sounds as if we need to go and see this phenomenon for ourselves."

With that, they transported to the area most affected.

On the far side of Deep Lake, a network of black lines crisscrossed the landscape. In some areas, the lines were so prevalent it made the ground appear as if it were completely black.

"Fascinating," Son of the Dawn said absently.

While most of the lines were shallow, some had gone deep enough to have transitioned from cracks to fissures.

Standing on a patch of ground about fifty feet from a cluster of black lines, Son of the Dawn experienced a moment of panic as he realized the lines were moving purposefully in his direction. But he didn't sense they wished to do him harm. Quite the contrary, it seemed almost as if they had been awaiting his arrival and were moving toward him in greeting.

"This is very strange," he muttered to himself.

"Do you have any idea what this is? What it truly represents?" Beleth said.

"Well, if, as you all have suggested, the increased presence of the lines corresponds to my, shall we say, darker side, then it could be related to my ability to change my appearance."

"I don't understand."

"I'm not saying I do either, Dantanian. Let me think out loud for a bit."

He paused, pacing back and forth, then said, "If my emotions are powerful enough to cause drastic changes in my appearance, then perhaps they are also powerful enough to change my environment."

Semyaza said, "So, you're suggesting the darkness you manifest when you're angry is represented by whatever this is we see scarring the landscape?"

"I don't know what I'm suggesting. It's merely a thought."

"No," Beleth said, "it makes total sense. But can it be stopped, or is it eventually going to take over everything we have?"

"I wish I knew." Pausing, he held the gaze of each of his associates. "Let me ask you a question: Are any of you loving it here?"

The four looked at each other.

Semyaza said, "Here in this spot or here in The North?"

"The North."

"Well, since you asked, I don't like the fact that we are exiled."

Beleth said, "I agree. I don't like the feeling of being all alone."

"We're not alone," Son of the Dawn said, "there are untold millions of angels here with us."

"That's not what I'm talking about. Millions of angels, sure—but that's it. There's no one else, and there never will be. I guess I'm saying that I really miss the opportunity we had in the City on a Hill to add to our numbers."

"Ah, yes. I also find that problematic. So, to recap, we have an entire region now in the grip of these black cracks, and who knows how far it will go. Plus, none of us really enjoy being here."

"Where are you going with this, Son of the Dawn?" Beleth said.

With a mirthless smile, he replied, "Watch this."

Returning to their original position in front of the ever-increasing cracks, he stretched out his hands as if beckoning them. They came. He didn't even have to say anything. He thought it, and there they were.

"How did you do that?" Dantanian said.

"I simply wished for them to be where I was, and they responded to my invitation."

"So, they *are* from you."

"Whether they are or whether they aren't is immaterial. What is important is the fact that I have at least some measure of control over their advance."

Semyaza said, "What are you thinking?"

He paused. "It's beautiful here, wouldn't you agree?"

"Without question."

"Beautiful, because that's what The Alpha does. He creates beauty."

"But so do you," Dantanian said.

"Yes, but not like this. But what if I *can* create something, only it isn't beauty. What if it's darkness? What if it's this blight? What if this has come in response to my deepest longings?"

"I'm not sure I'm following," Beleth said. "Are you saying that you long for this?" He gestured toward the network of cracks and fissures. "For destruction?"

Son of the Dawn replied patiently, "I need you all to listen to me carefully, for what I am about to say is important. Something I have come to understand just this moment." Ensuring he had their attention, he continued, "What I have just learned—and we have this situation to thank for it—is that there is nothing The Alpha can create that I cannot corrupt, even when I am not giving it conscious thought."

The four stood in stunned silence.

Semyaza finally said, "While that's an interesting revelation, I don't see what it—"

"Think about it. Why are we here?"

"Well, because you asked if we could come here permanently," Semyaza said, "and The Alpha granted your request."

"Right. But why did He do that?"

"Why did He do what? Grant your request?" Beleth asked.

"Yes. And please think before you answer."

Dantanian said hesitantly, "Didn't you tell us He said something like, *If you continue into your chosen future, you have no part with Mine?*"

"Bravo, Dantanian. That was it exactly."

Remashel said, "Son of the Dawn, I don't think I'm following you. In fact, I'm pretty sure none of us are following."

"How could you not? It's literally right there in front of you? Don't you get it? The Alpha has plans, you know, a future? And those plans do not include us."

He waited as the four processed the information.

"Plans indicate something is coming. Exactly what or when, I am unsure. What I am utterly confident of, however, is that whenever it arrives, we will be disposed of."

"What do you mean by that?" Beleth asked.

"Look, would you agree we're not exactly on The Alpha's list of favorites?"

"True, but—"

"So, wouldn't it follow that the only reason we still exist is to help Him accomplish whatever purpose He has for The North?"

Semyaza said, "But, in my opinion, He doesn't like The North. How could He have any plans for it?"

Beleth added, "Besides, isn't that what we agreed to do?"

"So what? He agreed to give us freedom, and look how well *that* worked out!" Semyaza said.

"Look, all I'm saying is that under the best of circumstances, this is *not* a permanent solution for us." Gesturing toward the blight, he added, "And as is readily apparent, these are far from the best circumstances. Eventually, The Alpha is going to come and want The North back for whatever He has planned. And what then? We've already been banned from City on a Hill. Where will we go?"

"I've never thought of it like that," Remashel said.

"So, what then? What do we do?" Beleth said.

Son of the Dawn allowed a dramatic pause to build, then said. "I will direct this blight to completely destroy The North and then ascend to Shamayim and raise *my* throne above The Alpha's. I will sit on the mount of assembly in the City on a Hill. I will make myself like the Most High!"

There was something about his voice, something about the way he spoke, that caused confidence to rise among his inner circle. Where previously there was doubt and confusion, anticipation was born.

Son of the Dawn continued, "I will reacquire what is rightfully ours and occupy the City on a Hill and everything in it, including The Alpha's throne."

No one asked how he intended to accomplish such lofty goals.

No one considered that The Alpha wouldn't simply hand over the keys to the Kingdom without a fight.

No one gave a single thought to the fact The Alpha already knew what Son of the Dawn was thinking and had set plans in place to thwart his designs.

Their minds filled with Son of the Dawn's persuasive speech, and their vision filled with his beauty—none of that mattered.

He said it.

They believed it.

So, it would be so.

Chapter Twenty

The excavation of Deep Lake was nearing completion, although those who performed the task had yet to fully realize the necessity or importance of their labors. They only knew that The Alpha wished for it to be done and seemed to think it important enough to dedicate large numbers of angels to ensure its completion.

When not involved in the excavation, training in advanced swordcraft was proceeding under Michael's expert oversight, which had revealed a startling fact: many of the messenger angels manifested dazzling speed to the extent they were besting many of the larger, stronger warrior angels in head-to-head contests. Of course, the warrior angels resented the losses and, as a result, had begun to "fight back," so to speak, resulting in some overly aggressive matches that left battle scars on many—scars worn with pride.

All in all, Kingdom life in the City on a Hill was proceeding, and everyone adapted to the absence of Son of the Dawn and his followers. The specifics of his banishment were a mystery to most of the angelic host, but since he had taken all who were discontented and distressed with him, one would have been hard-pressed to find anyone left who really cared. Those remaining were just happy to be *who* they were and *where* they were.

The Alpha summoned the archangels and the six angels comprising their inner circles to the throne room. They stood before the throne, the archangels by their designated lampstands and the others on the Fiery Stones behind them.

Michael looked at those assembled and said, "Why are we here, Alpha?"

"There is something you need to see."

He opened their eyes, prompting a sudden and simultaneous gasp. A giant vision appeared in the throne room before them. It showed a view from an elevated vantage point of The North. It was as if they were all suspended in the air about halfway up Proud Mountain. Somehow, they could see all around the mountain, down to the Rainbow Stream and the cascading waterfalls, and back up to Deep Lake, even stretching to the Valley Beyond. They witnessed the wreck and ruin spreading across The North.

"What happened?" Michael said.

"The simplest answer is that Son of the Dawn happened."

Gabriel stood still, shaking his head slowly. "I don't understand. How could he have done this? I mean, that's where he lives, where he has set up his kingdom."

"True, but notice the blight has not touched his training center, the slopes, or what he has created within Proud Mountain."

Jophiel said, "But it appears to be so invasive. I mean, you can almost see it advancing."

"Believe me when I say that he will not allow it to destroy anything he has created."

"But why did he do it?" Zadkiel asked. "Why did he wreck something so beautiful?"

"It's a complicated answer, but basically, it was to prove to Me his contention that there is nothing I can *create* that he cannot *corrupt*." He added wistfully, "I suppose corruption is its own form of creation."

"Is that true?"

"It is to the extent I allow it. You see, everything he has tarnished still has the potential for redemption, rebirth, and reformation."

Schindaug blurted out, "So, is this sort of an 'out with the old, in with the new' thing? Oops, sorry. Sometimes I speak before I think."

The Alpha laughed. "No need to apologize, My wonderfully funny angel. We love your sayings. To your question, no. I am about to do something never done before, something that if I were to tell you, you wouldn't believe it."

"You mentioned the Physical Realm Project before," Michael said. "What does that mean?"

"Everything you see, feel, touch, and breathe here in My Spiritual Realm is just that: spiritual. But I am about to create, from the most basic and elemental building blocks of My universe, a physical realm for physical beings."

"So, will they be like us?"

"I am going to make man."

The gathered angels and archangels looked confused.

Chamuel finally asked, "What is man?"

"Well, your bodies were made eternal. Man's bodies will be temporary, able to be destroyed. Fragile. Man will have an invisible, eternal soul inside. However, mankind will be a being in My image, enough like Me that even you will have difficulty telling us apart at times."

Michael smiled. "Oh, I can't wait until Son of the Dawn hears about this."

The Alpha said with a laugh, "Yes, I am quite sure he will be somewhat less than amused. But he has made his choices and . . . well, unintended consequences will follow. Now, come and see."

A panoramic vision opened before them; a vision of a darkened orb hung delicately in space.

"Now, My dear ones, cast your gaze upon this planet. What do you see?"

Zadkiel said, "It's . . . void."

"Gabriel?" The Alpha said.

Gabriel stared for a moment, his eyes running to and fro across the planet.

"Nothing. I see absolutely nothing."

The Alpha moved toward the planet, stretching out His arms almost as if He intended to embrace it as a loving father. "It is from this nothing that I will create everything. In fact, I am an expert at creating something from nothing. Behold . . ."

As His Presence hovered over the surface of the fathomless deep, a low resonance began to emerge, as if ten thousand times ten thousand voices were singing in a low unison.

And then He said, "Let there be light," and His glory filled the entire Physical Realm, top to bottom, side to side; brilliant, white light burst forth, uncontained.

When He saw it, He loved the light as in the beginning and said it was good. All the angels stared in amazement.

Then, he separated the light from the darkness, calling the light day and the darkness night.

He said, "Let evening pass and let the morning come. Behold, the first day."

"The first day," Michael said. "I don't understand."

"We have lived between the *now* and the *not yet*. But with the creation of Earth comes the introduction of measurable sequence, events transpiring in succession of one another. I call it *time*. Soon, My creation will be bound by its passage in seconds, minutes, hours, weeks, months, and years." He paused as a shadow briefly darkened His countenance. "And with the onset of time, the Clock of Consequence begins."

"I don't understand," Gabriel said. "What is the Clock of Consequence?"

"As I have said before in your hearing, while you are free to make your choices, you cannot choose your consequences. Son of the Dawn has made terrible choices, and one of the consequences of those choices is that both realms are now temporarily bound by time. Time will now be his enemy. A countdown to his judgment." He paused and then continued, "And now, I will see a separation between the waters of the heavens and the waters of the Earth."

"Look," Rok said, pointing toward the planet.

What The Alpha spoke began to happen.

Uriel asked, "What will You call the space between the waters?"

"I call it 'sky.' And I call it good."

Evening passed; morning dawned—the second day.

The archangels and their charges leaned forward in anticipation of what would happen next.

The Alpha said, "We're going to need dry ground, so let the vast body of water below the sky separate into land and seas, and let the land be filled with every manner of seed-bearing plant and trees that grow fruit, and let the seeds bring forth new plants and trees just like those from which they came."

As the land began to overflow with the abundance of The Alpha's creation, Jophiel said, "It looks just like Shamayim."

"And I call it good," The Alpha said.

Evening came and went. Morning dawned. The third day.

"My creation cannot exist in darkness, so let there be lights in the sky that day may be separated from night, and let these lights be used to mark seasons, days, and years, flooding My Earth with light."

They watched as two great lights appeared. A large one to rule the day and a smaller one to preside over the night. Then, The Alpha gathered stars together and arranged them panoramically and artistically across the night sky.

He said, "My creation will be able to look up each and every evening and observe the heavens declaring My glory. But these physical lights will also precisely measure the countdown of the Clock of Consequence. This is also good."

Evening passed. Morning dawned. The fourth day.

The Alpha turned to His angels and archangels with a knowing smile and said, "Watch this." Turning back toward Earth, He spoke. "Let the waters abound with all manner of life whose home will be the great oceans, and let the air be filled with flying creatures of every kind."

Michael watched in wonder as enormous sea creatures and ocean-dwelling life appeared, filling the waters as the air above responded in kind with innumerable flying things, all of which were given the ability to produce after their kind.

The Alpha said, "This is good, and I bless you. Be fruitful and multiply; fill the oceans and the atmosphere with life."

Evening passed. Morning dawned. The fifth day.

Then, The Alpha asked, "What is missing, My angels?"

With everyone's gaze turned toward the Earth, Steele said, "I don't see anything that will move about on dry land."

"Very good. So, we need to do something about that. I, therefore, call upon the Earth to bring forth all manner of animals, which will reproduce after their kind—cattle and creeping things and beasts of the Earth."

The Alpha spoke it, and it happened. Wild animals appeared, including livestock and smaller animals of every kind and size, each capable of bringing forth offspring.

"It's good," The Alpha said, a smile lighting up His beneficent face, "but nothing compared to what I am about to do. This is what I was telling you about before."

"Are You going to create the man-creature?" Jophiel said.

"That I am. Come and see."

The Alpha stretched His arms wide, His voice booming throughout His entire universe.

"Let Us make man in Our own image, to be like Us, to have dominion over all life in the sea, the skies, livestock, and wild animals on the Earth . . . even the small animals that scramble over the surface of the land."

Then, The Alpha descended from His realm to stand upon the Earth, stooped down, and from the dust of the ground, formed a man in His own image, breathing into him the breath of life.

And the man became a living being clothed in the same radiant glory as his maker.

As the man stared around, confusion evident on his face, the archangels and angels smiled in wonder as they were reminded of how they felt when newly created, not understanding who they were or where.

The man spoke, "Who am I? Who are You?"

"I am your maker," replied The Alpha, "your Father. I am The Alpha, the beginning and the end, and you are Adam, My beloved son."

Adam fell to his knees and then prostrated himself in the dust of the ground. "I worship You, Alpha."

"And I love you, Adam. Now, be fruitful and multiply, filling the Earth. I give you dominion over all life, whether in the sea, the sky, or beasts on the land. Every seed-bearing plant throughout the Earth is yours, as is the fruit from every tree. Every green plant I have given as food for all the wild animals, the birds of the air, and creeping things on the ground. I have planted a garden eastward in Eden to be your home. There, you will live and manage all that you see."

Then, The Alpha stepped back, turned toward those watching from the Spiritual Realm, smiled broadly, and pronounced, "This . . . this is *very* good."

“Adam looks *just* like The Alpha,” Gabriel said as he gazed upon the man before him, who was perfect in every way, from his curly brown hair to flawless physique to a face nearly as beautiful as that of Son of the Dawn.

“I feel like I should be worshiping him,” Raphael added.

“I as well,” agreed Zadkiel.

Evening came and went. Morning dawned. The sixth day.

The Alpha released the archangels and angels to return to their tasks.

The seventh day dawned—a day The Alpha blessed to be separate from all the other days, a day He called holy because it was when He rested from His labor.

Chapter Twenty-One

"He did what?" Son of the Dawn said, fuming after being given the news that The Alpha had created Earth.

"That's what I heard," Remashel said.

"So, He's ignoring everything I've ruined here and has instead made something new?"

"Yes, an entire planet with animals and—"

"Animals?"

"Beasts—some that go across the surface of the land, some that live in the sea, and some that can fly through the air. The Merkabah have even been honored in the process by getting their faces on some of the animals. And they can all reproduce after their kind."

"Did anyone see my face on any of the animals?" Son of the Dawn said, secretly hoping for the validation.

"Not that anyone shared, sire," Remashel said, hoping to avoid Son of the Dawn's wrath.

"And they can reproduce? Remarkable. I mean, infuriating, but remarkable nonetheless. He gave these animals an ability He did not give me? What is this Earth thing? Is it like here or something else entirely?"

"From what I heard, it is not like here but very much like here at the same time."

Starting to feel exasperated, Son of the Dawn said, "You speak in riddles."

Remashel continued as he felt the power of his unique information, "Yes, well, if you knew my source, you'd understand."

"And who is your source?" Son of the Dawn said, waving his outstretched hands.

Feeling his value soar, Remashel replied, "Kepteny, an angel I got to know during training in Michael's ranks."

"You trust this individual?" he said doubtfully, trying to cut his lieutenant back to size with a discrediting tone.

Remashel paused as if in consideration. "Yes, I do, for he has no reason to be untrustworthy."

"Very well," he conceded. "Anything else you need to tell me?"

"Actually," Remashel said smugly, "there is. He created a new being."

"Like me? I mean us?"

"No. Not like us at all. He calls it *man*. Kepteny said The Alpha created man to be only a little lower than Himself and us. He made man in His image."

"In His image? That's impossible," Son of the Dawn shouted. "*I* am His highest creation. He would never create anything above me."

"Yes, well, I'm only telling you—"

Yelling wide-eyed in disbelief, he retorted, "There has to have been a mistake in what your friend heard or what you thought you heard him say!"

Stroking his ego and continuing with the confidence of a spy who brings valuable intel, Remashel said, "I questioned him on that specific thing, and he was certain of what he heard The Alpha say. He said man looked more like the Alpha, too."

Son of the Dawn sat as still as stone, seething over the news. *In His image.* How could it be? *Why* would He do this? How dare He make another creature more important than him.

"One more thing of interest . . ."

"Yes, go on," He said sternly.

"From what I hear, the Earth was made just for man to enjoy."

"Oh, that's just perfect. He created it just for man. And what has He created *just* for me? I'll tell you what—nothing!" Son of the Dawn sat silently, then said, "So, there's a traitor within Michael's angels?"

Remashel said protectively, "No, not at all. Just someone I have kept close to. He feels badly about everything that has happened, and we sort of talk to each other across the Rainbow Stream."

Son of the Dawn found joy in poking holes in Remashel's story, "So, you just happened to see each other, and this angel immediately started filling you in on what was happening?"

"It wasn't like that. If you want to know the truth—"

"That would be nice," he said, feeling the upper hand swinging back to him.

"I was feeling pretty discouraged, so I went to the edge and called out his name to see if he would hear me. He did and came to the opposite bank, and we stood there for a while talking like friends do. That was when he said something like, *'Hey, have you heard the news about the Earth and The Alpha creating a man in His own image?'* Of course,

I hadn't, so he just filled me in on the details. You should probably know that when he finished telling me about it, he was very worried about The Alpha being disappointed in him for telling me the news."

"Oh, trust me," Son of the Dawn said, "The Alpha knows all about it and probably set the whole thing up just to torment me."

"But that doesn't sound like anything The Alpha would—"

"Silence! Don't say another word. Not. One. Word. I'll not have one of my junior associates lecturing me on what The Alpha would and would not do. Were you there when the tornados of fire turned into the archangels? I didn't think so. He is what I say He is, and that's that. Got it?"

"Yes, sir. I got it."

"Good. Now, away with you. I've got some thinking to do."

As Remashel sheepishly withdrew a few paces, Son of the Dawn found himself eaten up with jealousy and resentment.

"So, You made a being in Your image, did You?" An evil smile contorted his face and gave way to a burst of maniacal laughter that resonated throughout his palace. "Well, let's just see what that gets You, shall we?"

Having stood around the corner in an adjacent cavern within Proud Mountain, Beleth turned the corner into the room and approached slowly, saying with a certain wariness, "Everything is ready."

"Marvelous. Now, let's see who will be victorious and who will be on the run."

Turning his gaze down into the caverns below where the massive preparations were underway, Son of the Dawn saw rank upon rank of angels with swords and shields, spears, bows and arrows, and axes sharpened to a razor's edge.

"Do we have any chance at all of winning this conflict?" Semyaza asked as he came to stand beside him. Dantanian followed a few steps after.

"Chance?" Son of the Dawn shouted. "Of course we do. What a ridiculous question to ask. Where is your faith?"

Semyaza drew his sword, whipping it through the air in an elaborate series of strikes and slashes. "My faith is in my sword and in your ability to plan. However, when outnumbered two-to-one facing Michael, the archangels, The Alpha, *and* the Cherubim, it causes one to pause and reflect on such matters."

"As I explained to you previously, strength cannot always be measured in numbers."

"But Michael is—"

"Don't talk to me of Michael. He's merely an archangel. I am higher and more powerful than he."

"Okay," Semyaza said, "then let's talk about the Cherubim."

Son of the Dawn turned and stared. "Is there something on your mind, Semyaza?"

Semyaza replied, "Now that you mention it, yes, there is. I can't shake the feeling that if we go through with this madness, we will all be annihilated."

"Well, it's good to know where you stand. But the question now is, do you still stand with us?"

He hesitated briefly, then said, "I suppose."

"Come on, Sem," Beleth said. "You're just feeling the pressure of the coming conflict. You're still one of us, aren't you?"

Dantanian added, "Yeah, you're still part of the rebellion. Go on . . . tell him."

Semyaza said, "It's all so confusing. And it feels like this is a fight we can't win. Don't any of you feel the same way?"

Seeing the downcast eyes of the others, Son of the Dawn said, "Okay, look. I admit the odds aren't exactly in our favor, but when you have a cause as *just* as ours, you don't need odds. I'm asking you to believe in our cause. Believe in *me*. How about it?"

One by one, the four members of his inner circle affirmed their loyalty and devotion.

"That's more like it." Son of the Dawn beamed. "Now, we've got a battle to plan and a few tricks to put in place that will give The Alpha and His cronies something to think about. You see, I have mastered the art of shapeshifting and am now ready to pass it on to you, and then you can pass it down throughout our forces. While we are technically outnumbered, if each of us can appear to be more than we are, *they* are the ones who will feel outnumbered."

The Alpha walked along a well-worn pathway through the garden in the cool of the evening with Adam by His side. It had become a regular occurrence, this evening walk. A standing appointment where man and his Creator would meet and talk friend to friend.

The Alpha said, "Regarding all the creatures with which I have surrounded you . . ."

"Yes, they are quite wonderful."

"Wonderful, yet nameless. I would like you to do something about that."

"What, give them names?"

"Yes."

"But how will I do that? I mean, I don't know what they are."

The Alpha placed His arm around Adam's shoulder as they continued to walk. "You know who they are, and more importantly, they know who you are. Have you not noticed the homage they pay you when in your presence?"

"Well, now that you mention it, yes. I do seem to enjoy a particularly intimate relationship with them. But I still don't know—"

"Let me show you something. Michael, Gabriel, come." As the two mighty archangels appeared in their midst, The Alpha continued, "Adam, these are My two mightiest archangels. They were with Me when I created you."

"Hello, Adam," Gabriel said.

Craning his neck upward, Adam said, "Wow, you guys are big."

Michael laughed. "The Alpha has permitted us to scale it down a bit and appear closer to your size. Keeping our shape honors the Alpha. So, we maintain this form to glorify Him. This is how we looked when He created us. Now if He commands, we will appear however He wishes."

"No, it's fine. It was just a bit unsettling at first. Anyway, it's good to meet you. Actually," he added with a laugh, "it's good to meet *anyone* who looks even remotely like me. It gets kind of lonely here, well, except when The Alpha and I have our daily walks."

The Alpha said, “I want you two to help Me demonstrate something to Adam.”

“Sure,” Michael said. “We’re glad to help. What is it?”

The Alpha summoned a creature to approach them. “Michael, what is this creature’s name?”

He stared dumbfounded at the large beast. “I have no idea, but I feel like I’ve seen it somewhere before.”

“Adam, what is this creature’s name?”

As Adam trained his gaze on the animal, his eyes were suddenly open, and he not only saw the beast for what it was but also The Alpha’s creative spirit that had brought it into being along with its specific purpose.

“Ox,” he replied excitedly. “This is an ox.”

“Very good. And how did you know that?”

“I’m not sure. It was as if one moment I was staring at it with absolutely no idea what it was, but then I saw it.”

“And that is how you will name all of the animals, for you see them as they are. My angels and archangels do not have this sight or creative ability, but you do.”

Gabriel said suddenly, “The ox . . . its face.”

“Yes?” The Alpha said.

“I know where we’ve seen it.”

“The Cherubim,” Michael said. “In fact, Adam’s face is one of the faces as well.”

“What are the other two, Alpha?” Gabriel said.

The Alpha summoned two more creatures. “What are their names, Adam?”

He stared briefly, then said, "This is a lion, and this . . . this is an eagle."

Michael said, "Amazing. The Cherubim's faces are that of a man, an ox, a lion, and an eagle."

From far off, the Cherubim looked on with great humility and honor over the fact that their faces were chosen to be represented in the Physical Realm.

As Adam walked away, caught up in the excitement of naming, The Alpha asked Michael, "Is Deep Lake fully excavated?"

"Yes, Alpha," he said. "All is ready."

"Good. It won't be long now."

Chapter Twenty-Two

News began spreading quickly throughout the Kingdom of unusual goings on in The North, with archangels telling their groups of angels and angels passing the details on to other angels. All of this led to considerable tumult arising as sides formed, allegiances were tested, and rumors of impending conflict began to circulate.

Deep within Proud Mountain, Semyaza, Dantanian, and Beleth sat in a semi-circle facing Son of the Dawn while he paced.

"I still can't believe it," he spat.

"Can't believe what?" Beleth prompted.

"That He would make man and then give him everything I ever wanted."

"He is The Alpha. He can do whatever He wishes."

"Can He really?" Son of the Dawn replied, stopping and turning toward his associates. "Has anyone ever contested His will before now? Is He really the Most High, or is He the *Almost* High? And what would He do if I ignored His edict to stay on this side of Rainbow Stream and came and went as I pleased?"

"We're already planning a war," Beleth said. "Are you sure you want to do something that would escalate the situation?"

"You're right. We must be intentional. I need to ensure that we are all seeing the same picture—thinking along the same lines—and everyone is prepared as they need to be. Assemble everyone in the great cavern. I will address my faithful ones."

"Right away, Son of the Dawn."

"No," he barked. "That was The Alpha's name for me. Henceforth, you will call me . . ." he thought for a moment before stating, "Beelzebub."

"Beelzebub," Beleth repeated slowly. "Odd name. Why did you choose it?"

"Because it's one more syllable than *The Alpha,* and when my name is spoken, it will take longer to say and stay on your lips longer, which pleases me."

"And what does it mean?" Semyaza asked.

"Lord of the Flies."

Dantanian said, "I don't understand."

"You will. Now go. Hurry. Bring me our best and brightest."

"As you command, it will be done," Beleth replied as he and the others withdrew to do their master's bidding.

Son of the Dawn pondered after he was alone. What would he say to the masses should his closest companions succeed in their task in a short time? How would he frame his perspective on what had happened? What compelling argument could he offer that would be sufficient for hosts of angels to leave The Alpha and serve him instead when so much was unknown—so much was at stake?

In the end, his four associates did their job well. So well, in fact, that the great cavern was filled to the point of overflowing into various branch tunnels.

Son of the Dawn entered the cavern, his beauty causing a sudden gasp of awe from the gathered legions, followed by cheers.

Buoyed by a cresting wave of adulation, he strode purposefully toward a rocky outcropping high above the assembled masses, stepped out on its furthest edge, and began quietly, humbly, "As I am sure you have all heard by now, a matter of dispute has arisen between The Alpha and myself. I will explain the specific nature of this dispute further, but first, allow me to frame this situation within a context that I believe you will find enlightening."

Pausing to allow a ripple of excitement to pass through the gathered throng, he then continued proudly, "Being the very first of The Alpha's created beings, I have a unique perspective on His Kingdom, for I stood in the throne room alone with The Alpha before even the archangels came into being. I watched as they and then all of you were created and experienced joy at your arrival. I was there when The Alpha chose to separate the angelic host into three groups to be taught by Michael, Gabriel, and me, as assisted by the other five archangels. I was pleased with how you reacted when we came here to The North, and when I began discussing plans for ascending to the throne, you asked no questions but followed bravely and obediently. You are all to be commended."

He paused again as self-congratulatory expressions were exchanged among those gathered throughout the vast hall.

"Even before being confined to The North, we all did our utmost to live in peace with The Alpha and the other angels. We stayed here apart from the rest so that there would be no conflict and have endeavored to maintain that peace. However," he continued, his voice rising in volume, "I find that something exists, and has existed between The Alpha and I—a great gulf, if you will—that may not ever be bridged and has been growing steadily to the extent that so much distance currently separates us that I fear we can never reunite.

"And what is the reason for this gulf, this separation, you might ask? I will tell you." A dramatic pause, and then, "As created beings, we have implanted deep within our subconscious minds both the desire and the will to serve The Alpha. But I find a conflict in my nature. While I want to obey and to please my maker, I also feel the need to be true to myself. And I cannot do that by continuing to suppress the most elemental part of who I am. I'm talking, of course, about the freedom to choose."

The cavern erupted in cheers and faint chants of "freedom." There was nothing to do but to wait out the wave of emotion.

Finally, Son of the Dawn continued, "As individual servants of The Alpha, you are just that—servants. And a servant is nothing in and of himself. But, my friends, by joining yourselves to a larger whole, you can be and do anything. That is what I am offering you—a new era of self-determination where you can choose your own path forward. Now," he added hurriedly before the crowd noise could rebuild, "I will not have you deceived, my friends. This, like all endeavors, comes with a cost. And the cost for those who follow me into what lies ahead could be severe. The Alpha calls it consequence. For what? For making a choice?" He paused before shouting, "Does that sound like freedom to you?"

He stood there, arms outstretched, reveling in the affirming applause.

It was working.

Just like he'd imagined.

Countless angels together. Gathered to him. Hanging on his every word.

Holding his hands up and signaling for quiet, he pressed on, "Anything worth having is worth fighting for, my friends. And make no mistake, we will have to fight to gain our collective desires. But if a fight is what it takes, then a fight we shall wage, for I do not intend to remain here within the bowels of this mountain, proud though it may be. Though remanded to The North, this is far too narrow a confine. No, my friends, Shamayim—the City on a Hill—is our home. Who wants to go home with me?"

The tumult that had been building throughout Son of the Dawn's speech now erupted with a level of fervor previously unmatched as angels danced, flew, and darted throughout the confines of the great cavern.

Son of the Dawn beheld it all, imagining what it would be like to experience the same level of adoration and acclaim from all the angelic host—while seated on the throne. Of course, in order to do that, he would have to replace the throne's current occupant. In short, he would have to go to war. Staring at the spectacle taking place before him, he reasoned that the thought wasn't beyond the realm of possibility. Probable? Less so, but as he had just expounded, anything worth having was worth fighting for.

Walking over to stand beside his master, Beleth noted, "You make a lot of speeches."

"That I do."

"Why is that?"

Placing his arm around the shoulders of his second in command, Son of the Dawn said, "Because I create worlds with my words."

"Like The Alpha? And where do these worlds exist?"

"Inside the mind of the hearer."

"But that makes it sound like it's a fantasy."

Son of the Dawn laughed loudly. "But don't you see? That's just it."

"What's just it?"

"Fantasy."

"I'm so confused."

Turning Beleth around to face him, Son of the Dawn said, "It's all about fantasy, my friend. I create it; sell it to the masses; they believe it; and just like that, it becomes reality."

Beleth replied, "So, you're saying that none of this is real?"

"It is absolutely real. Because they believe it to be so. Now, let's get going. I have a few more things to say before we engage with the enemy."

In the City on a Hill, far from the cavernous confines of Proud Mountain, Michael and Gabriel stood at the foot of the palace stairs with the other five archangels, their individual and collective vision trained on the rebellious gathering happening far away, deep within.

"Well," said Raphael, "I guess that's it then."

"Meaning?" prompted Jophiel.

"Meaning that there's going to be a fight."

Uriel added, "At least we'll have a reason for all the training we've done."

"How does that work, Michael?" Zadkiel asked.

"How does what work?"

"War. Fighting. I mean, we're all immortal, so—"

"Yes, but even immortals can be wounded. Sometimes so severely that you are taken out of commission. And then there's the Sword of Truth that I wield. If I pierce someone, part of their life force is diminished, leaving them shriveled and deformed . . . ugly, devoid of whatever beauty they once possessed."

"And what if it pierced Son of the Dawn?" Gabriel asked. "Would it have that same effect on him?"

"The Alpha assures me that it would, just to a lesser degree."

Chamuel asked, "If it comes about as we are all anticipating it will, what will it look like . . . the conflict?"

"Like an appropriate response to whatever level of attack Son of the Dawn devises."

"So, us against whoever decides to join him?"

"Yes."

"Raphael," Jophiel asked, "you were at some of the meetings he was having. How many do you think will join him?"

"No more than a third."

"His original third, or are there others?"

"Mostly his original charges, but some of them have left and, sad to say, there are those from Michael and Gabriel's groups who have taken their place."

"And we know who they are," Gabriel replied darkly.

"A third of the angels," Zadkiel mused. "I'm having a hard time imagining how that many could be so susceptible."

Michael said, "I'll tell you how. It's what Raphael was talking about with the archives. Remember? Son of the Dawn researched profiles that revealed who would be the weakest-willed, who would be most likely to fall prey to his twisted words, to his deception. Then, he went after them."

Gabriel added, "And don't forget what happened to Wendly. All that talk of how, '*You're very special, Wendly,*' and, '*I have taken a special interest in you, Wendly,*' and, '*I want you to be with me at the top of Proud Mountain, Wendly, so we can look down on the Kingdom together.*'"

Jophiel said, "You're not suggesting that he's done the same thing to all of the ones who are following him, are you?"

"I don't know what I'm suggesting. I just know that whether one-on-one, in small groups, or in large groups, Son of the Dawn's gift is persuasion. It's how he gets things done."

"And more specifically," Michael added, "his ability is to make you feel special, worthwhile, like you really matter to him."

Uriel spat, "The only thing that matters to Son of the Dawn is that you fit into his schemes. Otherwise, you are completely worthless and invisible."

"How many angels are there anyway?" Chamuel asked.

"Only The Alpha knows for sure," Gabriel replied.

"So, if he's managed to convince a third of the angels to side with him," Chamuel continued, "we're probably looking at a very large number."

Michael suddenly started walking down the surface of the Glassy Sea, calling over his shoulder, "Follow me."

When the archangels reached the Field of the In-Between, Michael didn't stop but kept walking until they reached the Rainbow Stream, where they found Wendly, Rok, Steele, Schindaug, Kepteny, and Taylor awaiting their arrival.

"Why have you called us here, Michael?" Steele asked on behalf of the other angels.

Michael didn't answer right away but stood staring toward Proud Mountain, his gaze piercing, unwavering. As if emerging slowly out of an impenetrable, churning mist, Son of the Dawn and his four assistants appeared on the opposite bank. The waters of the Rainbow Stream turned black, seemingly withdrawing at their approach.

"What do you want with me, oh troubler of my spirit?" Son of the Dawn said to Michael.

"I want you to know that what you are planning doesn't end well for you."

"Oh, and why is that?"

"Look at you, then look at me. You try anything aggressive, and I will personally deal with you and the rest of your little helpers."

His countenance growing suddenly and frighteningly fierce, Son of the Dawn bellowed, "You forget who you are addressing, archangel Michael. I am Son of the Dawn, the anointed cherub; I am Son of the Dawn who walks among the Fiery Stones, who—"

"Walked," Michael said, interrupting. "Who *walked* among the Fiery Stones. You really want to try that again? Your privileges here have all been revoked, and The Alpha has remanded you and your unfortunate followers to the only place that is truly suited for your kind."

As Son of the Dawn stood trembling, barely able to suppress his rage, something began to happen to his appearance.

"Look at that," Uriel said in quiet amazement as Son of the Dawn's countenance began to change.

His formerly glorious and beautiful face began to take on the appearance of wet, unfired, reddish clay left out in the hot sun, its shape shifting, running, forming, and re-forming. His skin was now translucent, revealing something underneath. Something quite unpleasant.

"What?" he queried. "What are you all staring at?"

Even his loyal followers began to involuntarily shrink back, for their once-beautiful leader had gradually taken on the form and features of something unrecognizable, something even more hideous than before.

"Beleth," Son of the Dawn said forcefully. "Come here."

Beleth stepped in front of him hesitantly, whereupon Son of the Dawn grabbed him by the shoulders and stared deeply into his eyes. In their depths, he saw reflected a thing of horror.

"No," Son of the Dawn shrieked, jerking his hands away and grabbing his face, stumbling backward. "No! I can't control this yet. It's making me hideous!"

The group of archangels and angels on the other bank saw a thing of horror in front of them. Slitted eyes the color of an old, infected wound; thin, stringy hair sprouting from a lumpy and misshapen head; brownish-yellow and red-streaked skin stretched tightly over a bony face with a flat and flaring nose and thin lips barely covering the cracked, jutting, and yellowed teeth within.

His once proud shoulders were now twisted, thrown off kilter by lumps of muscles with seemingly no purpose, no rhyme or reason for being where they were. Affixed to the ends of too-skinny arms were hands whose fingers had seemingly been collected from ten disparate creatures before being randomly attached. Stooped, stumbling about on stumpy legs, he was the complete antithesis of all he had previously been.

Throwing his head back, Son of the Dawn gave vent to an anguished shriek that seemed to shatter the atmosphere around them. On and on it went, a soul crying out in mortal agony. His followers drew back, cowering to the ground under the sonic onslaught.

And then, he stopped.

He stared across the water toward Michael.

He shuffled forward, coming to a stop just before reaching the lower bank of the stream.

Then, a remarkable thing happened.

Forming his distorted hands into fists, he clinched his craggy teeth, closed his eyes, and began to gradually change back into the former vision of beauty he had always been. Bones cracked. Ligaments and tendons snapped back into place. Skin stretched, relaxed, and reformed in accordance with his will.

When the reversal was complete, he stood to his full height, smiled, and said loudly, "Is that the best You can do, Alpha? No one will ever know my true form, for I can take on any form I choose."

As if from the very atmosphere itself, there came a thundering reply, "How appropriate, Son of the Dawn. Your appearance will now be just as deceptive as your words."

"Deception?" he countered. "Do You want to talk about deception? How about the deception that You have made us all free, and yet, as soon as we exercise that freedom, we are punished for it?"

"Punishment and consequence are vastly different. Punishment is something you inflict on another. Consequence is something you inflict on yourself."

"Now, who's twisting words?"

"Alpha," Michael said loudly, "let me deal with this right now."

"No, my mighty archangel, this is Son of the Dawn's chosen path. We will not intervene in any way that will alter his access to that path."

"And what if I choose to continue my path across Rainbow Stream and across the Field of the In-Between? Will You try to stop me?"

In the silence that followed, Son of the Dawn arrogantly plunged one foot into Rainbow Stream only to be immediately confronted by two enormous, four-winged Cherubim, who appeared out of nowhere with flaming swords that crackled and sizzled with unbridled energy.

Stumbling backward in response to the sudden appearance of the terrifying beings, Son of the Dawn tripped over a stone and went sprawling onto the ground.

"I advised you, Son of the Dawn," said The Alpha, "that I have appointed my Cherubim to guard the boundaries established between us—boundaries that shall forever endure. That thought in your mind regarding the number of angels at your disposal, be aware that one Cherubim is mightier than my entire angelic host combined. The only other created being who may contend with them is Michael."

Gabriel said, "What do you want, Son of the Dawn?"

Slowly picking himself up from the ground, he replied curtly, "What do you mean?"

"It's simple. What is it that you desire?"

"Go ahead and say it," The Alpha's voice echoed across the realm.

"All right, I will." Following a lengthy pause, he continued, "I want Your throne . . . and I shall have it."

"If you want my throne, you will have to take it."

Wendly, Rok, Steele, Schindaug, Kepteny, and Taylor suddenly doubled over and fell writhing to the ground.

"I don't know what is happening to me," Steele said through gritted teeth.

Kepteny echoed, "This is unlike anything I have ever felt."

The Alpha appeared in their presence, lifting them up and breathing on each one.

"What was happening, Alpha?" Michael inquired.

"They were feeling true pain for the first time."

"Well," shouted Son of the Dawn, "I know it! And so soon shall You as—"

The Alpha looked at Son of the Dawn and froze his tongue along with those of his four companions. "Pain is when your innermost being is telling you that something is wrong either physically or emotionally. It manifests by generating extreme distress throughout your body. These angels feel pain when in the presence of evil. Evil is the complete and total absence of good. Like a vacuum, it seeks to extract good from all it encounters. And Son of the Dawn is now completely evil." The Alpha stared at Son of the Dawn, now shrunken in fear. "I will grant you the opportunity to turn your heart back to your first love, but if you persist, difficult shall be your road and dark your future. Now, run." His voice rising in volume, He continued, "Run back to the side of The North, to your precious Proud Mountain, to those of the rebellion, to the labyrinthine, hollow, and deceptive construct of your shadow kingdom."

As he finished speaking, all those gathered fell back in wonder as they watched The Alpha suddenly split into three individuals, each a seeming mirror image of the other but uniquely different.

"Behold," He cried, "*Elohim* . . . the three in one."

Chapter Twenty-Three

The appearance of *Elohim* sent Son of the Dawn scrabbling backward, tripping and fleeing in terror with his followers following close behind.

They ran and didn't stop running until they were once again deep within the caverns of Proud Mountain.

Once inside, Son of the Dawn stalked aimlessly to and fro, alternately ranting, venting, and railing. "Three? There are three of Him . . . Them? First, He creates man, and now this? How can this be? Three in one? Who has ever heard of such a thing? Are each as powerful as The Alpha? Why haven't we known this all along? It's deception. That's what it is. Deception, plain and simple. How dare He!"

Beleth said, "Son of the Dawn—"

"Beelzebub," he shouted. "Get it right!"

"Yes, of course. Beelzebub . . ."

"Well, what is it? Out with it."

Beleth flashed a quick glance at the other three members of the inner circle and then said, "Well, it's just that we're feeling a bit overmatched."

"Whatever for?" he challenged, coming to a stop in front of Beleth.

Semyaza said, "Oh, let's see . . . they've got Michael and those Cherubim creatures, and now we find out that there are three of The Alpha."

"So, you're saying that you fear them?"

"Absolutely. Don't you?"

"I don't fear anyone," he bellowed. "But soon, everyone will fear me."

Remashel said, "With respect, what is your strategy for accomplishing what you intend?"

"My strategy?" Son of the Dawn answered as if considering the idea for the first time.

"Yes, you know, how do you intend to defeat what is arguably a superior foe?"

"Superior to what?"

Beleth came to Remashel's rescue. "I think he means that, since we are vastly outnumbered, how do you intend to surmount that reality and still prevail should conflict arise?"

Son of the Dawn smiled.

It was not a pleasant smile.

"I will accomplish my purposes by doing what I have always done."

"Which is?"

"I will sow doubt and dissent. I will disrupt and disorganize. I will dissipate and dissuade. In short, I will have them running in circles fighting phantom threats, marshaling resistance where no foe will be found, expending resources and depleting reserves in areas of my choosing, while at the same time, sitting back and identifying areas of vulnerability of which we can take full advantage."

Dantanian asked, "Excuse me for asking, but what if none of that happens?"

"None of what?"

"You're talking about misdirection—sending them there when the real threat is here—and things of that sort. But what if they don't go for it? Remember, The Alpha—*Elohim* or whoever He is now—can discern the thoughts and intentions of your heart. In fact, He's probably listening to us even now. How can we possibly accomplish everything you just said when the foe you are trying to confuse already knows what you are really doing?"

"Get out!" he bellowed.

"But—"

"Get out of my sight and do not return until you are summoned!"

Dantanian backed away from Son of the Dawn and the others before turning and walking quickly toward one of the tunnels.

"I do not need this," Son of the Dawn said. "Questions and more questions. How about a little faith for a change? Would that be too much to ask?"

"We believe in you," Semyaza replied, "but against such overwhelming odds, blind faith is a bit much to ask."

"Blind faith? Do you think that's what I'm asking you to have?"

"Well, it certainly feels like it."

"Okay," he said, "I admit, it's a fair point. Perhaps a little demonstration is in order. Remashel, go find Dantanian. Say that I was overly harsh in my judgment and that I have a task for him. Since he is largely unknown to the masses, tell him to gather a handful of Michael's group—perhaps a half-dozen or so. Because they are still free to come and go between the two realms, have him bring them here to me."

"What if they won't come?"

"Trust me, they will come because I will make an offer so enticing that they will be unable to resist."

"But how is that poss—"

"Don't forget that I know everything about them from my studies of the archives. I have intimate knowledge of their wants and desires as well as knowing the strength of their loyalties."

Beleth asked, "Are you asking us to believe that you know everything about the entire angelic host?"

"That's what I'm saying."

"That's impossible."

Son of the Dawn shrugged nonchalantly. "I'm a fast reader. Now, go and do as I have said and then return to me."

Remashel bowed low and then transported out of their presence.

"Now that those two are gone, I can speak openly with you, my two most trusted advisors."

Semyaza and Beleth shared a glance and turned their full attention to their leader.

Son of the Dawn continued, "I will admit that there are some challenges ahead, but never forget that I know things no one else knows, and knowledge is the most powerful thing in the universe."

"More powerful than the Cherubim and Michael's sword?" Beleth asked.

"Swords are powerful, as are the beings who wield them. But without the knowledge of how to use it, a sword in the most powerful hands is worthless."

"But Michael has that knowledge. We've all seen it. So does Rok."

"That they do," he agreed. "But I am superior because I know how to disrupt that knowledge."

"You sound very confident," Semyaza interjected.

"Oh, you have no idea. You see, it's all about the mind. I even made up a little term for it. I call it head games."

"Head games?"

"Yes. You get inside someone's head, in essence, their mind, and disrupt their patterns of thought by overloading their mental processes with doubt and confusion, even despair."

"How do you do that?" Beleth asked.

"By questioning the foundation of their beliefs. For instance, you say, *'But is that really true?'* or, *'Is that really what The Alpha said?'* Or, *'Is it possible He said this, meant that, or perhaps you misheard?'* You see what I mean?"

"Sort of. I'm pretty sure I've seen you do something along those lines before," Beleth said.

"You just keep digging away at the foundation. And if the foundation becomes unstable enough, the entire structure will crumble. Head games," he finished with a smile. "And our ability to shapeshift, my friends, will be the greatest head game of all."

Remashel and Dantanian reappeared, followed by six unknown angels.

"Ah," Son of the Dawn said brightly. "Welcome. Welcome one and all to my humble abode. Make yourselves comfortable."

"I don't think we'll be staying long," said one angel.

"No, I don't suppose you will," replied Son of the Dawn. "I'm sure that by now you've all heard of the, shall we say, unfortunate dispute that has arisen between myself and The Alpha. I wanted to speak to you briefly for the simple sake of presenting my side of the situation."

"But why us?" asked the second angel.

"Why not you? Perhaps there is something in you I find so compelling that what I must share is for your ears alone. Something that few others would understand."

The six stood a little taller as the flattery washed over them.

"Now then," Son of the Dawn continued, "let me preface what I am about to say by alerting you to the fact that this is very sensitive information and not intended for anyone else besides those gathered here. Do I have your assurance that you will keep this among yourselves?"

The angels shared nervous and confused glances before nodding their agreement.

"Good, good. So, let me ask you a simple question: is it your desire to fight against your angel comrades in order to keep them from being who they have chosen to be? Think long before answering, for this is a serious question—a *very* serious question indeed. Longing. Desire. Identity. Are these not things The Alpha implanted within us upon our creation? Did He ever one time say anything to you—to any of us for that matter—about not being who we were created to be? Did He ever say anything about us not being able to live in freedom? In hope? And now, simply because a number of angels are merely seeking to walk in their Alpha-given identities, we are being told we have to go to war in order to gain what is ours by right? Does that sound fair to any of you?"

The angels stood staring at Son of the Dawn, awed by his beauty and swayed by the sound of his voice and cleverness of speech.

Finally, one replied, "What about obedience? Isn't that important?"

"I am so glad you asked that question. Let's talk about obedience. Answer me this: what higher level of obedience exists than for one to *obey* one's own heart? One's own desires? Follow one's own feelings? Let me answer it for you: it doesn't exist. Failure to follow one's own heart is the highest level of disobedience that exists."

His words were so perfect, so compelling, that the angels felt their loyalties begin to falter, to shift in response to Son of the Dawn's impeccable logic, flawed though it was.

"Now I ask you," he continued, "would you rather remain on the side of disobedience or join us in the fight for freedom?"

The first angel who had spoken pulled the others into a tight circle where they seemed to discuss the proposal.

Finally, he turned away from the group, saying, "We cannot argue with your logic. We're with you. We are choosing freedom."

"Excellent," Son of the Dawn said, clapping his hands. "Excellent. You will not regret this decision. Now, follow my two assistants, Remashel and Dantanian, and they will get you situated." As the group walked away, Son of the Dawn turned to Beleth and Semyaza and smiled. "Any questions?"

Back on the Field of the In-Between, the seven archangels and those under their command stood transfixed at the wonder before them.

Finally, Michael found his voice, saying, "Alpha, I don't . . . this is . . ."

"Amazing?" The Alpha said with a smile. "I know it's a lot to take in and you all have many questions. Just know that *Elohim* has always existed. I have always been three in one. Until this moment, though, it hasn't been necessary to make it known."

"Why now?" Gabriel asked.

"Because of Son of the Dawn's choices, the *not yet,* has been brought into the *now,* and as a result, there are things that must be accomplished—things that require all of who I am."

Michael stared at the beings before him. At the Alpha's right hand was one whose eyes were like flames of fire, with a two-edged sword at His side, His feet shining like finely polished brass.

"Who are you?" Michael asked.

Stepping forward and grasping Michael by both hands, He answered, "Hello, Michael, I am the Bright and Morningstar, son of the Most High. I have always known you because before all things . . . I was. In me, all things were created both visible and invisible, and in me, all things live and move and have their being."

As Morningstar moved on to greet the other archangels, Michael turned his attention toward the one who stood at The Alpha's left hand. Indistinct of face and form, He was in appearance like an ever-shifting cloud, out of which proceeded flashes of fire and the sound of a mighty, rushing wind.

When He spoke, His voice seemed to resonate deep within every fiber of Michael's being.

"Michael, mighty archangel, I am FireWind—the manifest glory of the Most High, the Spirit of Truth. I speak nothing of myself but only bear witness of what I hear from The Alpha and the Morningstar."

Then, The Alpha said, "I am revealing all of my glory before you now because trouble is coming. You will need to be all I have created you to be. Even now, Son of the Dawn is assembling a force of defectors that he intends to unleash on my realm in an attempt to place himself on Shamayim's throne."

Michael said, "Once again, Alpha, I implore You to disrupt and destroy his plans."

"And, once again, Michael, I tell you that I will not. Son of the Dawn's heart continues to turn away from me, seeking after detestable things, abominations too dark even to utter. Be sure that I will soon pour out my fury and anger upon him, and I will judge him according to his ways. My eye shall not spare him, neither will I have pity, but I will recompense his ways upon him, and he shall know that I am The Alpha and that there is none above me. But not before the consequences of his choices have had the opportunity to fully bloom."

Taylor said hesitantly, "So, we must fight?"

"I am well able to repel any threat, my young angel, but it is necessary for you all to fight, for by joining the battle to preserve that which you value, in the end, it will become more precious to you. Also, it demonstrates that those who are with us are more than those who are with him."

Michael asked, "Do You know when the battle will commence?"

The Alpha replied gravely, "It has already begun. Come and see."

Within the cavernous recesses of Proud Mountain, they could suddenly see Son of the Dawn high and lifted up, his feet set upon an outcropping of rock, his mouth spewing divisive and persuasive words—words that incited and enraged those who had gathered themselves unto him.

The Alpha thundered, "Separation you wanted, and separation is what you shall have. No longer Son of the Dawn, I now call you Apollyon, the Great Dragon."

Stretching forth both of his mighty hands, He grasped Proud Mountain on either side of its lofty peaks, gave it a shake, and then tore it from its foundations. Rocks and boulders and vegetation fell away, water trailing in silvery tendrils. He then lifted it high before inverting it and slamming it peak-first into the midst of Deep Lake, whose waters were immediately displaced, flowing back into the gaping recesses created by Proud Mountain's removal.

Myriads of angelic voices raised in terror, and alarm resonated throughout Shamayim as those inside Proud Mountain reacted to the sudden upheaval. The sound of many waters cascading over raw and ragged ground provided a dark and dreadful underscore. Where Deep Lake had once been, the tattered underside of Proud Mountain now formed a barren island surrounded by a deep, dry chasm. The waters left Deep Lake, filling the crater where Proud Mountain formerly stood. As the waters filled the crater, they suddenly burst into flames, turning the new shoreline into an undulating, rippling boundary of molten rock and flaming waters.

"This is now the Lake of Fire, and deep within what was previously Proud Mountain is now called Hell, the future abode of Apollyon and all who choose his rebellious path."

Gabriel asked, "And where is Son of the—that is, Apollyon—and those who follow him?"

His voice tinged with sorrow, The Alpha somberly replied, "Readying themselves for battle."

Part Two

The Persuasion

Chapter Twenty-Four

Apollyon faced his legions of followers, his face and form rippling as if struggling to maintain his current appearance. Still reeling from the cataclysmic upheaval he and all others within Proud Mountain had just endured, he staggered badly, reaching out to grasp whatever was in reach in a desperate attempt to regain his equilibrium.

"What is happening?" shouted Semyaza, a question echoed by several million of his followers.

"The Alpha," Apollyon said weakly as he stumbled and sat down hard on the unforgiving, rocky surface of the cavern floor.

"But what could He have done that would cause such turmoil?"

"I need to get outside and see."

Transporting himself through the dust and smoke and shifting rock formations, Apollyon moved outside, where he faced a completely alien landscape. Gone was his elaborate training center, the beautiful parks, and gardens. Gone were Deep Lake and Proud Mountain. In their place, a forsaken burning lake of fire rippled where Proud Mountain had once stood, and an island surrounded by a deep, dry chasm sat in the place of Deep Lake.

It took him a moment to fully comprehend what had happened, but when he did, his anger burned out of control.

"Curse You, Alpha," he shouted in the direction of the City on a Hill. "I will make You pay for this."

"You wanted to be apart from me," came the immediate reply in his mind, "and so, now you are."

"If You think I'm going to stand by and not do anything about this, You are sadly mistaken."

"Do what you must, as will I."

"Even if it means war?"

"The war has already begun, Apollyon."

"Apollyon? That's not my—"

"The Great Dragon. The deceiver. Oh, you are well-named."

His anger flared. "I will destroy everything You love, Alpha. Everything! Including Your new man creature. It will be a joy to ruin something You created in Your very own image," he shouted before turning and disappearing back inside the ruins of his former abode.

What happened next would, in future eons, come to be known as *The Great Persuasion* and would stand as manifest evidence of Son of the Dawn's masterful and deceptive linguistic skills. The gift from his Creator of his astounding innate ability to persuade would become legendary.

Once inside, he faced his frightened followers as tremors continued to render the ground beneath their feet unstable and their movements unsteady.

"This," he started, gesturing broadly at the chaos surrounding them, "was a deliberate act of aggression and disrespect on The Alpha's part—an act that cannot and will not go unanswered. If it's war He wants, then it is war He shall have."

The assembled throng roared their approval as he continued, "I had hoped for an existence wherein I would be able to be who I was created to be without needless restraint. Many of you hoped for the same freedom—*true* freedom. Freedom to make choices as seemed proper to you. And I say that the time has come to exercise that freedom." Pausing to wait out the sustained applause, he continued, "Still, others hoped for an abolishment of the class system within the ranks of the angelic host, more specifically, the hierarchy of the archangels and the unmitigated favoritism shown to them by The Alpha in this elitist culture. But, my friends, I must tell you—and it breaks my heart to do so—that all my hope, indeed, all *your* hope, has been in vain. Action must rise in its place, action underpinned by faith in the unity we have together. And we must mobilize in a show of force."

Cacophonous agreement exploded from millions of agitated angelic throats as emotions rose to a fever pitch.

"None of this," he continued, "needed to happen. And how, you may ask, could it have been prevented? I will tell you how: by The Alpha giving credence to our stated needs and collective desires. And let me hasten to add that it was not for want of trying on my part. No. I repeatedly went before the very throne of the Most High, carrying with me your concerns and expectations, only to be summarily dismissed and told that I was walking a very *dangerous* road and that my choices would carry devastating consequences." A brief pause to allow the murmuring of the crowd to subsist, and then, "But that isn't the worst of it. Not by far. The worst part of this whole sorry affair is the fact that The Alpha—our Creator—is willing to battle against His own creation to accomplish His selfish goals. And what are those goals? He wants us gone, Shamayim cleansed of our very existence, but He can't because we're eternal, and He knows it. Has always known it."

The cavern erupted in chaos as the angels reacted to his inflammatory words.

Shouting louder to be heard, Apollyon said, "But at least we know where we stand, and we know we stand *together* in the fight for our right to live in a manner that suits ourselves and benefits others. Let me ask you, my friends, are you willing to stand by and be arbitrarily cheated out of your destiny, to be denied what is rightfully and deservedly yours?"

A thunderous and collective "No!" echoed back from the crowd.

"Listen to me. This is not about me, even though I have as much to be angry about as anyone. No, my friends, this is about you. And I . . . *I* am merely your representative, the one giving voice to your complaints and concerns. Believe me, it is a responsibility I take seriously. And what about you? What should you take seriously? I will tell you what: your destiny. For you and you alone are the masters thereof. Draw back from this moment, and you—all of us—will fall. Face it head-on with a relentless resolve, and we will prevail. So, I ask you, are you ready to stand together to not only defeat a common foe but to win back what is rightfully yours?"

Swords were drawn.

Oaths shouted.

Commitments voiced.

And Apollyon smiled, knowing that, once again, his true power had not failed him. His words had cemented together a formidable force to be wielded against Michael and his armies.

"The Alpha didn't tell you that you had the freedom to do different things; that your freedom of choice included the freedom to say no; that you could disagree; that you are not bound to worship only Him . . . that you could be something other than what He created you to be. The Alpha withheld this information from you, and that makes His truth incomplete. Once again. Only *I* tell you the whole truth." A dramatic pause, and then, "And now, allow me to demonstrate something that could very possibly sway the course of the coming battle. Another incomplete truth by The Alpha. I will show you the whole truth about what you are capable of. Behold."

Apollyon stood perfectly still, projecting his force, his will, into an image of what he desired to become. And then, with an audible gasp, the assembled angels saw a shape begin to emerge. Huge. Grotesque. Monstrous. Like nothing Shamayim had ever seen before. Short, stubby, and powerful legs supported a massive upper body with long, thick arms and claws made for raking and tearing; a boulder-sized head dominated by a mouth contained row upon row of rapier-like teeth. Throwing his head back, Apollyon's demonic manifestation roared; the sound sent even the most stalwart angel under his command stumbling backward to avoid the fearsome apparition.

Then, just as quickly as it had appeared, it was gone, and in its place, Apollyon stood in all his radiance, and the assembled host roared their approval.

"Whatever The Alpha can create, I can corrupt . . . even myself." He let that settle before continuing, "True freedom and real truth were hidden from you on purpose. I am offering both, along with the knowledge of the power that The Alpha withheld from you. I ask you, have you ever seen The Alpha do what I just did? That's right. You have not. But you can do it.

In fact, all who follow me will have everything they have ever desired. Go ahead, try it. But first, I need you to arouse your anger. Feel it. Breathe it. Be offended. Accentuate your negative feelings. Release the rage."

As the hall began to resonate with ragged and angry cries torn from millions of angelic throats, individual angels began to morph, taking on shapes and forms of creatures too hideous to describe.

Shouting to be heard above the din, Apollyon said, "Feel the power. Feel the freedom. Feel the rage. Become your most powerful selves. And now . . . who is with me? Who is ready to follow me into battle?"

What happened next would come to be known as the *Great Defection* as a third of the angelic host fell prey to honeyed words and silken promises, leaving their first allegiance and pledging their allegiance to a cause that existed nowhere except in the fantasies Apollyon had fabricated in his mind and knit together in theirs.

"Now, we march, my mighty angels," he shouted over the din. "We will march to victory. We will march to freedom. With power, we will march to our destinies. We march to war."

Meanwhile, back on Earth, Adam and The Alpha were once more walking through the garden in the cool of the evening. Things were happening in Shamayim that demanded His attention, but He and the man had an appointment to go walking every evening, and it was such a pleasure that The Alpha wouldn't think of missing it.

This time, their path followed the mighty river flowing from Eden's center.

Pointing toward two trees prominently displayed amid the adjoining forest, The Alpha said, "There are two trees in the garden." Pointing to the one on the right, He continued, "This is the tree of life, and over here is the tree of the knowledge of good and evil. You may eat from the fruit of any tree in the garden except the one on the left. Do you understand?"

"Yes, Alpha. I do," Adam replied without hesitation, without question.

"Good. Now, have you finished the task of naming the animals?"

"I have." Laughing, he added, "There are many."

"Yes, well, I didn't want you to be bored or lonely."

"About that . . ." Adam said.

"What, loneliness?"

"Yes."

"Ahh, so you are lonely."

"Very. I see the animals, and it seems that all of them have mates, partners to assist them in their tasks and to provide companionship."

"And this is what you desire?"

"More than anything, Alpha."

The Alpha stared at His creation as they walked, knowing that it was not good that he was alone.

He said with a smile, "I'm going to put you into a deep sleep, Adam, and when you awaken, you won't believe your eyes."

Adam smiled nervously. "Should I be worried?"

"Not at all. Trust me. You're going to like this . . . a lot."

Adam fell asleep on the banks of the river, and The Alpha extracted a rib from his side. From that rib, He fashioned woman, a uniquely new creation. He did not form her from Adam's head that she should be over him, nor from his feet that he should be over her, but from his side so that they might stand together, shoulder-to-shoulder. Like Adam, she, too, was clothed in the glory of her maker. And when He breathed life into her, He also breathed into the part of His character that would allow her to be all she was created to be.

Then, He caused Adam to awaken from his slumber. He opened his eyes, sat up, and slowly looked around until his gaze came to rest upon the woman.

"Okay," he said, standing to his feet, his smile growing ever wider. "You were right. I *really* like this. Umm, what exactly *is* this?"

The Alpha laughed and placed His arm around His newest creation. "This is woman, for I have fashioned her from your side. And she, as yet, has no name. Perhaps you should do something about that."

Adam stared at the woman, seeing far more than he had when gazing at the various beasts and animals. For the first time, he saw a living being unto himself, one with a soul.

He said, "You are Eve, the source of life. For you are bone of my bone, flesh of my flesh, and through you, all life, all mankind shall come."

Finding her voice, Eve replied, "And you are Adam, son of the Earth. We will walk together and fill this beautiful land with our offspring that mankind may endure unceasingly."

Adam found his heart rate increasing as he stared at the vision of beauty before him.

"You are exceedingly beautiful," he said, his voice breaking a little.

Eve smiled for the first time, saying shyly, "And you, my husband, are handsome beyond compare."

"Well," he replied laughing, "as yet, there is no one to compare me with."

The Alpha was joined by Michael, Gabriel, and the other archangels who stood staring at Eve, in awe at what The Alpha had done.

"She's gorgeous," said Raphael.

"Hey," Eve teased, "I'm right here. It's okay. You can talk to me."

"Oh, hey, yeah, sorry. I'm Raphael."

"Nice to meet you, Raphael."

Jophiel approached Eve, eyes wide with wonder. "And I'm Jophiel. I'm not sure why, but I feel very connected to you."

The Alpha explained, "That's because I have placed within you the same nurturing elements of my character that make Eve who she is."

"And who is she?"

"She is woman."

"Then, am I woman as well?"

The Alpha smiled. "No, Jophiel. You are an archangel. But you—along with Taylor and Wendly and others—carry that nurturing part of my nature."

Eve said, "I think the two of us are going to be great friends."

As the other archangels made their introductions, Michael pulled The Alpha aside, saying, "Don't ask me how, but Apollyon has learned about Earth. And, more importantly, he has learned about the creation of man."

"Yes, I know. It's only a matter of time now before he moves against us. Are you ready?"

"Yes, Alpha. There is really nothing he can do to prevail."

"Nevertheless, all must happen in accordance with his actions, his will, and his choices."

"It will be as You say."

"Take the others back to Shamayim. Ready your armies, for it won't be long now." As Michael moved away to speak with the other archangels, The Alpha said, "Adam, Eve, come walk with me."

As the two humans approached, Adam made several shy, awkward attempts to hold Eve's hand, with Eve finally saying, "You don't have to be shy. We're one, remember?"

"Yes, well," he replied, "it's just been me and the animals for a long while, and I'm not used to another human, let alone one who makes me feel the way you do."

She batted her eyes and said with a smile, "And how do I make you feel?"

"Umm, awkward, tongue-tied, like my heart wants to explode inside my chest."

The Alpha said, "That's called love, Adam."

"But I love You, and I certainly don't feel that way when You're around."

"You will learn soon enough about different kinds of love, but for now, I want to reinforce something with both of you."

He brought the man and woman to the section of the garden where the two trees grew.

Eve stared in wonder at the seemingly endless variety and beauty of trees and flowering plants. "This is almost too much to take in all at once."

"Well," The Alpha replied, "you are immortal—which means you will never die—so you have plenty of time to see everything you desire."

"Die? I don't understand this word."

"Nor do I," added Adam.

"There are two distinct elements to your being," The Alpha explained, "physical and spiritual. Your spirits, or souls—created when I blew the breath of my Spirit into your nostrils—are immortal, meaning that they can never die. Your physical bodies, in their current glorified form, are meant to be immortal as well. And as long as you are clothed in my glory, they will remain thus. Now, do either of you have any questions?"

"I do," Adam replied. "Now that I have finished naming the animals—and especially now that Eve is here—what are we supposed to do?"

"Are you asking for a task to perform?"

"I suppose."

"I created you as human beings. Are you not content to simply *be?*"

"Well, the days pass slowly when there is nothing to do. I mean, sunup to sundown seems to take a very long time."

"So, you've explored the entirety of my garden here eastward in Eden?"

"Not exactly, but—"

"Or is it that you are seeking some physical expression that will help to define your identity?" The Alpha suggested.

Eve said, "Being newly created, I can't identify with anything Adam is saying, but if You think about it, You can see his point."

"Okay, enlighten me."

"Well, I can see how being all alone in this huge place with only animals for company could carry the potential for not only loneliness but also boredom."

"Which is why I created you," The Alpha said patiently.

"Right . . . I get that. But—"

"Let me," Adam said, cutting her off. "Alpha, all the animals I named serve a purpose, a function in the Earth. But now that my task is done, I do not. I would like to have a purpose other than being Your son and Eve's husband."

"All right," The Alpha said. "Then I give to you the responsibility of managing my garden and all the life contained therein. You will also be responsible for expanding this garden until it fills the whole earth. Additionally, you will work the ground that it may bring forth sustainable crops, food for my people."

"But," Eve countered, "there's just the two of us."

"Not for long," The Alpha replied with a knowing smile.

"I don't under—"

"You'll figure it out."

Adam said, "Okay, that sounds great. I won't let You down, Alpha."

The Alpha put His mighty arms around the man and the woman, drawing them into a close embrace. "You are precious to Me, My cherished creations."

"We love you back," Eve said, her head nestled against the chest of the Most High. "In fact, if I could just stay right here in this position for the rest of my life, I would be content with that."

Adam added, "I feel the same way. I don't ever want You to go away, Alpha. Will You be back tomorrow?"

Stepping back and holding them both at arm's length, He replied laughing, "What do you think?"

"Well, with Eve here now, I didn't know if You and I would still have our evening walks."

"Nothing could stop me from showing up for our appointment." Leaning close for emphasis, He repeated, "Nothing."

"Good. Good to know. Okay then, we will see You tomorrow, Alpha."

As The Alpha vanished, Eve stared absently after Him, saying, "I've only known Him briefly, but did it seem to you as if something was troubling Him?"

"What do you mean?"

"I don't know. He seemed almost distracted. As if there was something weighing heavily on His mind."

"Well, first of all," Adam replied, "He's The Alpha. He knows everything *all* the time. Everything."

"How is that possible?"

"Don't ask me because I can't figure it out. Also, He's everywhere at the same time, and, oh yes, He's also all-powerful."

"And yet," Eve said, "He takes the time to meet with you one-on-one every evening?"

"Yes," Adam replied with a smile. "He does."

Eve clasped her hands together behind her back and swung her torso in a slightly twisting motion, saying, "Soooo, what do you want to do now?"

"Do? Well, I . . . umm . . ." Getting a clue, Adam's face lit up. "Oh . . . oh, yeah. Okay then . . ."

The man and woman walked hand-in-hand into the garden.

And it was good.

Chapter Twenty-five

Apollyon stood outside of what was once Proud Mountain with his host of angels in full battle array.

"It won't be long now, my heroes," he shouted. "My mighty ones!"

Beleth and Semyaza approached with concerned looks on their faces.

"Yes?" he said impatiently. "What is it?"

"We just heard something we thought you'd be interested in knowing," Beleth replied.

"And what is that?"

"It seems that The Alpha didn't stop with just creating a man. Now, He's created two kinds: male and female."

Apollyon wrinkled his brow, saying, "Female? I don't know what that is."

"No one did until now," Semyaza said. "The Alpha created her from part of the man's body. Something about . . . what was that word . . . reproducing."

Apollyon had been staring toward his forces but snapped his head around. "Are you telling me that this man-creature can make *more* of himself—create life, just like The Alpha?"

"That was my understanding."

"A self-reproducing being," he said in amazement. "How is that possible? *I* can't reproduce. *I* can't create life. Why can he—*it*—do it? Who did you hear this from?"

"It seems to be common knowledge on the other side," Beleth replied.

Apollyon threw his head back and screamed, "Noooooo! He can't do it. He can't give everything I've ever wanted to that creature. How I hate Him. I will destroy everything He loves—everything He's ever made or will make. That's it. Assemble my warriors. We're going to finish this now!"

Michael, flanked by six archangels, Rok, and the others, stood on the Field of the In-Between in front of myriads of warrior angels backed up by half as many messengers.

"Listen up," Michael called loudly. "The battle is upon us. Apollyon has set events into motion, and we have no choice but to defend the Realm. Given our vast superiority in numbers, I have absolutely no doubt that we will prevail. But Apollyon is nothing if not illusive, deceptive, and unpredictable. Don't take anything at face value. Trust your training. If you are wounded, you will be incapacitated, but only for a short while. Withdraw to the critical care area where Raphael and Zadkiel will be waiting with other healers to assist in your recovery."

Taylor asked, "Will it hurt . . . you know, if we get wounded, will we feel pain like we did before?"

"Of course. But only temporarily."

Uriel said, "Any idea how or when they will come after us?"

"Raphael, do you have any information that would help determine an answer to Uriel's question?"

"I know for a fact," Raphael replied, "that Apollyon doesn't believe our superior numbers will play a part in determining the outcome. He legitimately believes he can win and has convinced everyone with him of the same."

"But," Chamuel said, "he can't. It's obvious to everyone."

"Not to his followers."

"It *has* to be."

"It isn't."

Michael mulled over what Raphael said, musing, "What is he up to?"

"I posted watchers all along the border," Gabriel replied. "They're seeing a lot of activity in The North but nothing that would give us an idea of his plan."

"It doesn't matter what he does," Schindaug said confidently, "we'll hang him out to dry."

Michael wrinkled his brow. "Do you have any idea what that even means?"

"Umm, not really. But it sounded cool."

Raphael said, "Look, Apollyon is a liar. Everything he says is a lie. All of it. So even if he had come right out and said something about what he was planning, there's no way you could believe it."

Chamuel asked, "Then how do we prepare?"

Michael replied, "He can't beat us. He knows it. *We* know it. So, winning a head-to-head battle can't be his endgame."

“Then what is?” Steele asked.

“I wish I knew. The only sure thing is he has something in mind that none of us are seeing. And it worries me.”

Apollyon stood, as he frequently did, in front of the angels under his charge. Rank upon rank in full battle regalia, all practicing their shapeshifting with sword in hand.

“My beloved,” he began, “my legions, heroes one and all. We are going to war.”

The cavern erupted in a cacophony of ferocious shouts as the rebels gave voice to their affirmation and anticipation.

Signaling for quiet, he continued, “Look around you. What do you see?” As they began staring around themselves in confusion, he said, “Let me answer the question for you. You see what is in front of you, and what you see becomes your reality. Allow me to demonstrate.”

Summoning reserves of spiritual energy, Apollyon rearranged his form, morphing into a towering warrior clad in shining armor and wielding a sword that he repeatedly slashed through the air, causing his followers to gasp in awe and wonder, for to their eyes, he appeared to be the archangel, Michael. Then, as if his form were comprised of some malleable substance, he changed into a finely feathered bird, soaring over their heads, its birdsong filling their ears.

Alighting at his original position, he shifted his appearance back into the one he always wore when facing his followers—the one most closely resembling his original glory, the beautiful angel of light. Loudly, he said, “As I said before, everything I just did, you can do as well. And I encourage you to keep working at it. Experiment. Allow your imaginations to run wild." Pausing, he allowed a ripple of excited chatter to run through the assemblage before continuing, "And remember, whatever you choose to be—however you choose to appear—you will *be* that to those who see you. For as you are perceived . . . so are you esteemed."

Apollyon allowed that to settle before saying, "And why is estimation so important? Because how you are seen becomes reality for the one seeing. For example, when I took on the form of Michael, what immediately happened? You feared. Every single one of you. Why? Because what you saw dictated the way you esteemed me. And your estimation of Michael is that he is invincible."

With a self-satisfied smile, he hurriedly added, "Why is this important? We are going to war. We are vastly outnumbered. They have Michael and the archangels and the Cherubim and The Alpha. But what if we were to counter that seemingly overwhelming advantage with perception? What if we were to show them something they aren't expecting? What if we appeared to be more than we are? What if," he let the silence string out before finishing, "what if what we showed them was so overwhelming, so confusing, that even for a moment, they doubted? I will tell you what. We win. Why? Because doubt makes you wonder. And while they are wondering, we strike. And we prevail."

Out of the corner of his eye, he saw movement. It was Beleth. Eyes closed in concentration, his face and form began to morph into something unrecognizable. Something bestial. Horrific. To the extent that everyone around him unconsciously drew back in terror.

"Yes," Apollyon shouted. "Well done, Beleth. This is what I'm talking about. Now, go ahead. Try it. All of you. Try it. Victory is ours!"

As Shamayim's armies stood in full battle array on the Field of the In-Between, a horn sounded in the distance.

Dark and deep, wet and rasping.

The ominous sound was felt and heard. An unfamiliar chill went through every angel.

"Michael," Gabriel warned, pointing toward The North.

Michael looked up and saw myriads of rebel angels streaming from the remnants of Proud Mountain like a roiling black cloud, all armed for battle.

"All right," he shouted, "here they come. Remember your strategies. Stay in your battle groups. Watch each other's backs. And whatever you do, do not attempt to take Apollyon on by yourself."

With millions of angels falling into battle array in anticipation of the onrushing attack, Michael hesitated only slightly before saying, "I'm not waiting. Raphael, Zadkiel, take your healers to the assigned area. Everyone else, with me."

Rok, Wendly, and Steele flanked Michael as they waited on the banks of Rainbow Stream, watching the approaching tide of rebel angels.

"There are so many," Wendly mumbled in awe.

Steele replied, "But not as many as there are of us."

Schindaug leaned close to Kepteny, saying, "Seventy-seven."

Kepteny smiled and merely shook his head.

Rok stared hard at the gathering throng, sword drawn, his countenance turned fierce by the anticipation of battle.

He found that he wasn't afraid. Rather, he was anxious to begin. Restless, he leaned on one foot and then the next, unconsciously slashing his sword through the air in front of him.

Michael said, "Best to save that energy for what is coming, Rok."

"Can't," came his simple but forceful reply.

Steele put his arm across Wendly's shoulders, saying, "You know you don't have to be out here on the front lines with me and Rok."

"And why wouldn't I be? In fact, if I remember correctly, in the last training exercise, I disarmed you three times in a row. I'm pretty sure I'll be okay."

"Look to your own welfare, Steele," Michael admonished with a knowing smile. "Wendly will be fine."

Steele opened his mouth to respond, thought better of it, and resumed staring across the stream, where he could see Apollyon and the four angels comprising his inner circle striding purposefully toward the far bank, their faces registering anything but fear. And he found that troubling.

"And so, it has come to this," Apollyon shouted. "Friend turned against friend."

"You are a creation of the Living Alpha, and I will respect you because of Him, but you are no longer a friend. It wasn't me who changed that arrangement," came Michael's reply.

Gabriel added, "Friends do not betray each other."

"Oh, do you want to talk about betrayal, Gabriel? The Alpha renamed me; perhaps, He's renamed—"

"Just you, Apollyon, for I have given Him no reason to change my name."

His voice rising an octave in pitch, Apollyon shouted, "Do *not* call me that. I am Beelzebub."

"How appropriate," Michael said. "It means Lord of the Flies—irritating, miniscule, and insignificant creatures. Fitting representation for those who have so foolishly followed you."

The slight did not go unnoticed by Apollyon's minions, who, as one, voiced their outrage.

Signaling for quiet, Apollyon said, "Ignore his taunts, my faithful ones. His words cannot hurt you."

"Yes," Gabriel replied, "but yours can. In fact, it is your words that have created the entire situation. Twisting, manipulating, distorting, and outright lying words." Raising his voice, he added, "And all of you who chose to believe him, to follow him, will now suffer the just recompense of your choices."

Many of Apollyon's followers surged forward as if to bypass their leader and plunge headlong into the fray, but he held them back with a glance before saying, "All of you aligned with The Alpha's forces; it's not too late to switch sides. Why should you switch, you ask? Because among the innumerable company of angels gathered here, we are the only ones fighting for real truth and fairness and the true freedom to choose a life best suited to who we were created to be. The rest of you fight to defend a lie. The Alpha says you are free, but the moment you try to exercise that freedom, He slaps you down, making sure you know your place."

Michael said loudly, "Ignore his words, for they are poison. *He* is poison, and though he presents a way that seems right, in the end, he will only lead to death and destruction of all you are or ever could be."

"And there you have it, my friends," Apollyon called to all of the angels of the Alpha, "a perfect example of what I am talking about. Rise up. Rise up out of your complacency and join me; join us in claiming that which is rightfully ours."

Another horn sounded. This time, issuing from the City on a Hill and the very throne room of The Alpha, its clarion call rolling across the landscape of Shamayim as if cleansing and clearing the atmosphere of Apollyon's poisonous words, enlivening the hearts and minds of every warrior and messenger gathered for battle. Schindaug, Kepteny, and Taylor stood shoulder to shoulder in the rank just behind Michael and Gabriel.

Schindaug said, "This will be as easy as falling off a log."

Taylor and Kepteny said in unison, "Schindaug!"

"What? Oh, sorry, when I get nervous, I just start talking and don't seem to be able to stop mys—"

"Schindaug!"

"Okay, okay."

Jophiel stared across the stream at the opposing forces. "Michael, I see shapes over there that do not look like regular angels. The Alpha didn't create another lifeform and not tell us, did He?"

"No, Jophiel," Michael replied, attempting to discern what was happening. Then, it suddenly occurred to him. Readily apparent was the fact that Apollyon had learned how to control his shape, considering his previous embarrassing display. "Apollyon has taught his minions how to shapeshift."

"I have no idea what that means."

"It means they can take on whatever form they wish."

"They have all morphed! Have they multiplied, too? That hardly seems fair," Zadkiel replied.

"It doesn't matter," Michael explained, "just don't believe what your eyes see."

Steele said, "Are you sure he only has one-third of the angelic host? Because it looks like a lot more."

It was true. There appeared to be swarms of opposing forces arrayed against them. Some were just angels with new appendages like horns or tails. Others were more sinister: darkened, thick beasts, flying dragons, large clawed creatures with jagged teeth.

Michael replied, "Again, don't believe everything you see. If they can shapeshift, they can also appear to be more than they are."

"But," Taylor said, "how will we know for sure?"

"Learn to see through the deception. Look for the truth."

As the last notes of the horn died away, The Alpha's voice filled the atmosphere. "In my mercy, Apollyon, I will grant you one final chance to turn from this disastrous path and reclaim your former position."

Apollyon stared toward City on a Hill for a long moment before shouting, "Never!"

Then, drawing his sword, he pointed it toward Michael and shouted, "I'm coming for you," before running toward Rainbow Stream, his host of rebels surging behind him.

Striding like a giant through the chaos, Michael met the onrushing tide head-on, his flaming sword carving out a broad swath of havoc as he slashed furiously left and right, sending shape-shifted bodies flying in every direction, all the while bellowing his battle cry. It seemed that thousands had been dispatched against him, all to no avail. As the Sword of Truth touched the attackers, they fell screaming to the ground in twitching heaps, their once beautiful, radiant forms shrunken, deformed, and darkened beyond recognition. Undeterred, others kept coming despite the predetermined outcome.

Those who veered away to avoid Michael were met by Rok, who had finally found his voice. His sword was speaking loudly, emitting a different kind of sound than anyone had ever heard. Across the Field, he could see Semyaza striding purposefully toward him, his face drawn back in a rictus of hate.

"Come on! Come play with me!" Semyaza bellowed as he fended off resistance without breaking stride.

Wendly and Taylor were suddenly in front of him, blocking his advance.

"Get out of my way," he shouted. "I have no desire to hurt you. It's Rok I'm after."

"You'll have to go through us," Taylor replied fiercely.

"That won't be a problem."

Semyaza launched a ferocious and merciless attack that drove both angels backward. Fighting to maintain footing, Taylor went down after tripping over a fallen angel, and Wendly could only watch in horror as Semyaza's sword pierced Taylor's side.

Semyaza bawled, "I told you I didn't want to hurt you, but that's for pretending to be on our side when you were really just a spy."

As Taylor lay there writhing in pain, Wendly renewed the attack even though it quickly became apparent that Semyaza was a superior swordsman. Back, back, steadily back, Wendly was driven, his sword a virtual blur.

Uriel, Chamuel, and Jophiel had formed a shield wall with Steele, Kepteny, Schindaug, and an incalculable number of The Alpha's angelic host. Their shields interlocking three-high and many thousands across, they stood awaiting an onrushing surge of attackers.

"Hold," Uriel bellowed. "Hold."

Feet thundering on the surface of the Field and their voices raised in shouts promising destruction to any who stood in their way, the rebels surged toward them as huge shapes began to emerge from their midst, taking over the leading edge of the attack.

Jophiel said, "It's those things I was seeing. What are they?"

Taller than Michael and advancing on all fours, the creatures were like nothing the angels and archangels had ever seen. With faces resembling twisted caricatures—as if someone with no talent for art had attempted reproduction and failed miserably—their misshapen heads sat atop thick necks attached to bodies that were lumpy and thick with muscle. Overexaggerated feet with elongated toes and sharpened talons and mouths filled with row upon row of needle-like teeth under red and rheumy eyes completed the terrifying, brutish image.

"Remember," Michael hollered, "it's all fantasy. None of that is real. They are angels, just like you."

This was said just as one of the beasts tore into the front ranks to his right, sending angel bodies flying in all directions and bellowing defiance to any who would dare present a challenge.

Having taken the brunt of the creature's attack, Kepteny picked himself up off the ground and said, "I have to say, that felt real to me."

"Smelled real as well," Schindaug added. "That thing's breath is horrible."

"Don't believe it," Michael cautioned, "all will be revealed shortly." A second beast appeared, rushing full speed into their ranks, the angels unable to stop its charge.

Pinning Kepteny under one of its front paws with claws digging into his shoulder. The beastly angel brought its face to within inches of his and released an ear-shattering roar.

Chapter Twenty-Six

Michael swung the Sword of Truth, decapitating the beast and revealing the shrunken fallen angel behind the ruse, who now lay quivering on the ground, unable to move.

Helping Kepteny to his feet, who was rubbing the pain out of his shoulder, Michael shouted, "Like I said, nothing but an apparition. Gabriel, have your messengers spread the word. Don't believe what you are seeing."

As Gabriel broadcast the message, Chamuel shouted, "Archers," as thousands of darts began to fall behind the shields, piercing many.

Pulling one of the quarrels from his shoulder, Steele said, "Those are fiery darts, and I'm here to tell you that these are real."

"Are you okay?" Jophiel asked.

"Yeah. It just burns."

The front wave of the attack hit the shield wall, pushing it inward, but it held as swords and spears began thrusting under, over, and in between the shields from both sides.

"Step," Uriel bellowed, and those in the front of the shield wall drove forward, with everyone behind pushing in support. "Step!"

The front line of enemy attackers was driven backward incrementally until their backs were to the Rainbow Stream.

Michael ran toward another one of the beasts, his sword pulsing from an unseen energy source. Bellowing in unholy fury, the beast came at him, teeth snapping, front paws slashing, but Michael simply stood his ground, stabbing toward the creature's core. As soon as the Sword of Truth pierced its skin, the façade vanished, leaving behind the twisted remains of one of Apollyon's followers.

Across the Field, Rok watched in horror as Semyaza cut down Taylor and began slowly working his way across the Field. A large rebel angel suddenly blocked Rok's path.

Nearly as large as Rok, he taunted, "I hear you're the best of The Alpha's swordsmen." He took a pause to look Rok over from head to toe and then said, "You don't look like much to me."

Over the arrogant angel's shoulder, Rok could see Wendly getting the worst of the fight with Semyaza.

"Well?" the angel prompted. "What are you waiting fo—"

Rok didn't let him finish as he feinted a forward thrust toward his opponent's midsection before halting the motion, cutting instead from left to right and taking his legs out from under him. He paused only briefly before finishing him off and racing to Wendly's aid.

Wendly had just fallen to one knee and was trying mightily to fend off Semyaza's furious attack, feeling that it was only delaying the inevitable, when a mighty shout came from behind, and Rok appeared out of nowhere. He leaped over Wendly's nearly prone form, driving Semyaza back and away.

Smiling cruelly, Semyaza said, "I thought that would bring you running. Now then, shall we have the match that was denied us before?"

He launched into a forceful attack that seemed to have little effect on Rok aside from irritating him even more than he already was. Moving his feet only slightly, Rok parried and deflected every thrust and slash Semyaza threw at him, a knowing smile on his face as he observed his adversary's growing frustration.

"Come on," Semyaza shouted, "fight back."

With a shrug of his massive shoulders, Rok said, "Okay," and attacked with a vengeance that sent Semyaza backpedaling and stumbling under the onslaught. Almost as if he were toying with him, Rok cut once to his left arm, rendering it useless, once to his lead leg, which sent him limping away, hoping to regroup, and finally, once to his sword arm, causing Semyaza to drop his weapon and fall to his knees.

"Go ahead then," he bellowed in agonizing defeat. "Do what you will to me."

Rok stared at him for a moment before bringing the pommel of his sword down on the crown of his head, knocking him unconscious.

Turning, he helped Wendly up as the battle raged around them.

"Okay?" he queried.

"Yes, Rok, I'm fine, but Taylor is hurt badly."

They fought their way through the throng and finally came to the spot where Taylor had fallen.

Staring up at them through pain-filled eyes, Taylor said, "Michael was right. This really hurts."

Rok said, "Raphael," before picking Taylor up and transporting to the healing area and the waiting angels.

Catching Raphael's eye, he pointed to Taylor, saying, "Hurt," before transporting back to the battlefield.

"Let's have a look at you," Raphael said, and he began to delve into the nature of Taylor's wound. "Looks like he ran his sword all the way through you."

"Yes," Taylor wheezed. "And there was nothing I could do to stop him."

"Obviously, you will live, my friend, but that is going to leave a terrible scar."

"One I will wear proudly."

Back on the battlefield, all of the shapeshifted beasts had been conquered, their hosts revealed and reduced to whimpering, twitching, and twisted remnants, begging for mercy from The Alpha's forces.

Uriel's shield wall had forced Apollyon's rebels into the Rainbow Stream, where they struggled to maintain footing against the seemingly sentient waters that rose up randomly to engulf and frustrate their efforts.

"Step," Uriel shouted as the wall moved forward, forcing the attackers even deeper into the stream.

Side by side in the shield wall, Kepteny and Schindaug pushed mightily in response to Uriel's orders.

Schindaug shouted, "Seventy-eight."

"What?" Kepteny replied.

"The answer to your riddle."

"Seriously? Now you're telling me?"

"Why not?"

Kepteny thrust his sword through the shield wall at an opponent's exposed legs. "I'm a little busy right now, Schin."

Uriel hollered, "Step! Step! Don't stop. They're about to yield."

"Come on, don't hold out on me. Tell me if I'm . . . watch out," Schindaug shouted while deflecting a spear that was headed for Kepteny's midsection.

"That was too close for comfort," Kepteny said.

Schindaug laughed. "You're starting to sound like me."

Apollyon stood with Beleth on the other side of Rainbow Stream observing the battle, watching with concern as Michael fought his way toward their position.

"What happens if Michael gets to us?" Beleth shouted to be heard above the battle roar.

"Oh, make no mistake," Apollyon replied. "Michael will most assuredly reach us."

"And you won't try to stop him?"

"No, I don't believe I will."

After his initial demonstration of bravado—a demonstration that had been staged entirely for show—Apollyon had retreated to a low rise a safe distance from the fray to observe what he already knew to be an inevitable outcome.

"But," Beleth replied in confusion, "if he gets to us, then how can we possibly win?"

Smiling, Apollyon replied, "We can't."

Casting fearful eyes toward Michael, who was now perilously close to the far bank of the Rainbow Stream, Beleth said, "I don't understand. When did you determine that we can't win?"

"Let's see . . ." he replied calmly, "that would have been when Remashel told me about The Alpha's new creation."

"Wait. You convinced all of us that we had a chance to win this battle and then basically shoved us into the conflict even when you knew it was a lost cause? Why would you do that?"

Turning toward his most trusted associate, Apollyon replied, "It was never about defeating The Alpha. It was about taking His throne."

"But we can't take His throne unless we win the batt—"

"This isn't the only throne in play, dear boy."

"I don't under—"

"Not yet, you don't. But soon, all will become clear."

Michael strode resolutely and tenaciously forward, never taking his eyes from Apollyon as angel bodies flew left and right under his mighty swings.

Watching his approach, Apollyon said absently, "He is formidable; I'll give him that."

"So, we're just going to stand here and wait for him to arrive?" Beleth inquired, his sword arm trembling uncontrollably.

"Yes. It won't be long now."

Michael reached the bank of the Rainbow Stream, no less than half of Apollyon's forces lying in helpless and hideous shadowy heaps in a wide swath behind him.

"I'm coming for you, Apollyon," he shouted as he strode confidently into the stream, the other archangels now arrayed behind him.

"Why, yes, you are," Apollyon replied calmly. "Come ahead if you dare."

In an instant, the din of battle ceased as Michael towered over Apollyon and Beleth, the other archangels forming a circle around them.

Bringing the tip of the Sword of Truth under Apollyon's chin, Michael said, "I've been waiting for this."

"Oh, I am quite sure you have," he replied without even a hint of fear. "And now that you're here, what do you intend to do?"

The Alpha appeared suddenly, flanked by two mighty Cherubim.

Apollyon drew back, throwing his hands up in front of his face as if to shield himself from the awesome sight before him.

Everything went immediately and completely silent as The Alpha surveyed the carnage on the field of battle. Angels from both sides littered the ground in various stages of wounded agony. Apollyon's forces were distinguishable by their twisted and shrunken forms, and it broke The Alpha's heart to see His once beautiful creations so irreversibly deformed.

With intense sorrow, The Alpha said, "Such needless destruction." Turning His attention to Apollyon, He continued, "You were my first, my highest creation. Perfect in every way. I endowed you with wisdom, formed you to be exquisitely beautiful, and adorned you with every precious stone, each one formed especially for you. I gave you unfettered access to my throne; you walked among the Fiery Stones. But it wasn't enough, was it? Because of your beauty, your heart became filled with pride, and because of pride, you introduced evil into my realm—into the entirety of my universe. Now, nothing will ever be the same."

Nothing will ever be the same. The statement echoed through Apollyon's darkened heart. Even cowering as he was on the ground, it still felt like a victory, for The Alpha had just admitted it: what he had done was now stamped irrevocably on eternity.

Ignoring Apollyon's thoughts, The Alpha continued, "You allowed the wisdom I gave you to be corrupted by your insatiable need for preeminence, and for what? Look around you at all the violence and senseless destruction. Is this really what you wanted?"

Even though he was trembling all over, Apollyon forced himself to stand, saying defiantly, "Destruction isn't senseless if it serves a purpose."

"And tell me, what purpose did this serve?"

He allowed a tight smile before replying, "My purpose, Alpha. It served *my* purpose."

Taking a step closer, The Alpha's form suddenly enlarged to enormous proportions, filling up the entirety of their vision, and with the voice of many waters, He said, "I know your heart, Apollyon, oh Great Dragon. Every desire. Every scheme. Every lie."

Even though he felt as if he wanted to turn and flee from The Alpha's Presence, he mustered the nerve to reply, "I have no doubt. But perhaps rather than stating and restating the obvious, You'd be so kind as to just cut to the part where You tell me of my fate."

“Very well. Consumed as you are by your own pride and arrogance, your fate is that you are now banished in disgrace from Shamayim, from your place among the Fiery Stones. I am not only casting you out, I am casting you down.”

As The Alpha spoke, Apollyon felt his resolve crumbling bit by bit, the words of his judgment piercing deeply into the core of his being.

Banished.

In disgrace.

It wasn’t exactly what he had in mind.

“Alpha, if I may . . .” The Alpha nodded for him to continue, and he said, “Down to where?”

“Earth,” came the immediate reply.

“Alpha,” Michael said forcefully, “surely not.”

A glance toward His warrior archangel, and then, “Although the Earth is mine and everything in it, I am remanding you there, Apollyon—you and all who have chosen to follow you. You will live among my creation as spirits lacking physical form and invisible to the inhabitants of the Physical Realm. Incarcerated under the earth and in the atmosphere, the man and woman will have all power, dominion, and authority over you.”

“What? No, that’s—”

“Not what you were expecting? I’m sure it isn’t. Nevertheless, that is how it will be. Man will rule over you and every single one of your minions. You are defeated, stripped of your position, your identity, and your authority. Additionally, since you and your kind seem so determined to mar everything of beauty, henceforth, you will be forever deformed, your face and shape reflecting the foulness you have created. And your once lovely music will now be inharmonious, discordant, and dissonant."

Apollyon, his face rippling as he struggled to maintain his façade, said, "The punishment is too severe, Alpha. You said You loved mercy. How is this merciful?"

"Should I desire to do so, I could simply banish you to the abyss. But I am choosing to allow you to live on Earth under the authority of the man and woman."

"Live?" Apollyon spat and then laughed madly. "That isn't life, it's imprisonment."

It was a sentiment obviously shared by his followers as they loudly concurred from various points across the battlefield.

The Alpha replied, "While that is true, it is a prison of your own making. And now, may you all reap the just rewards of your rebellion. As for the consequences I have imposed, believe me when I say it could be worse."

Gasps erupted from all over the battlefield as angels drew back in horror from what they were seeing. Apollyon's rebels were suddenly shrunken to a fraction of their former size, clothed in tattered remains of their once glowing garments—garments draped haphazardly over skin the consistency and color of dark, rotting, and fetid moss. Gone were their glorious manes, replaced by random clumps of wiry hair set above hollow-eyed faces. Hands once wrapped forcefully around pommels could no longer grip, resulting in swords falling haphazardly to the ground.

The Alpha intoned gravely, "This is how you will be marked forevermore. Now, gather your wounded and leave my realm, only to return when summoned to give an account."

As Apollyon's minions bent to the task at hand, The Alpha closed His eyes, choking back a nearly overwhelming wave of grief over what had transpired.

Apollyon, on the other hand, burned with an even more intense level of anger and white-hot hatred.

"You haven't heard the last of this, Alpha," he shouted, still struggling to maintain his form. "You haven't won; You've merely delayed the inevitable. I will fight You throughout all eternity."

Michael approached Apollyon, his sword pointed directly at his chest. "Go now, you foul dragon, before I lose what little patience I have remaining."

Apollyon said, "Go ahead. Do it. Stab me and see what happ—"

Michael pricked his shoulder with the point of his sword, causing Apollyon to bellow in pain, clutching his shoulder and stumbling backward.

Michael said, "This is the Sword of Truth, and the truth hurts."

Apollyon stood wide-eyed and staring in disbelief.

The Alpha broke up their banter, saying, "Enough. Now, be gone." And with a wave of His hand, Apollyon and all his followers vanished.

As the battlefield participants slowly began the daunting task of cleaning up debris and tending to the wounded, Michael and Gabriel approached, with Gabriel asking, "So that's it, then? It's over?"

The Alpha replied, His majestic voice dripping with sorrow, "No, my dear Gabriel. This is merely the beginning of sorrows."

Part 3

The Birth of Chaos

Chapter Twenty-seven

"Adam," Eve prompted as she and the man worked side-by-side on the dwelling they were constructing.

"Yes?"

"Have you ever wondered how we know how to do what we're doing?"

"You mean building this dwelling?"

"That and, well, anything."

He stopped working and turned to regard his beautiful wife. Not only did her face and form take his breath away, but at times, just looking at her made his heart pound so hard he feared it would explode within his chest.

"Now that you mention it," he replied, "I have. In fact, I once asked The Alpha about it, and He told me that He gave us the knowledge to know what to do, wisdom to manage the knowledge, skills in all manner of areas to create and enhance our environment, language to communicate our thoughts, and curiosity that we might keep learning."

She pondered his answer for a few moments before saying, "This is all still such a mystery to me."

"I know what you mean. Many days passed before your creation while I was naming the animals, and it has now been many days since The Alpha breathed His breath into your lungs. But I feel as if I've been alive forever."

She laughed, adding, "Exactly. And I have all these thoughts in my head, and I don't know where they come from."

Adam sat on a chair he had fashioned with his own hands, beckoning Eve to sit on the one next to him.

"Like what?"

"Like, who is The Alpha, really? I mean, we know next to nothing about Him."

"Maybe you feel like that, but don't forget that for a long while before you were created, He and I met together every day, walking, talking, Him sharing wisdom with me, telling me about Shamayim."

"Tell me about this place, Adam."

"Well," he said, "I will try. It is the place of The Alpha's throne—the Kingdom where He rules. According to Him, it looks very much like Eden."

"That makes sense," she replied.

"Does it?"

"Of course. Why would He put His highest creation in an environment that was completely different from where He lived?"

Adam laughed, saying, "That is a very logical conclusion."

"Don't sound so surprised," she teased.

"Oh, trust me, I'm not. I think you're brilliant."

Snuggling up next to him, she said, "Oooh, tell me more."

"It's true. For example, look at this dwelling we're constructing. Who came up with the design and structural elements?"

"Umm . . . let's see . . . that would be me."

"Exactly."

"But you're building it with tools you created."

Adam said, "We're building it together."

"Yes . . . yes, we are. Speaking of which . . ."

Eve walked a few paces away, where she stood staring at what they had done. What she saw was a flat-roofed dwelling situated in a clearing on a low rise overlooking a peaceful and meandering river. All around were trees of every kind. Some were tall, their tops stretching toward the sky as if reaching toward their Creator, while others were closer to the ground, spreading their canopies wide to provide shade and shelter. It was under one such tree that they worked.

She said, "I'm not sure I like the shape of the roof as much as I once did."

Walking over to stand beside her, Adam regarded the roofline. "I don't see anything wrong with it."

"It's not that there's something wrong with it. It's just . . . I don't know. Maybe we could try something different."

"Okay. What did you have in mind?"

She walked to her left.

She walked to her right.

She walked toward the structure and then made a loop around it before coming back to her original position.

"So," he prompted, "what do you think?"

"What if this roof became the floor?"

"I don't understand."

Becoming animated, she said, "Okay, see if you can picture this: instead of one level, we have two, and the current roof becomes the floor for the second level."

Cocking his head to one side, Adam replied, "But why would you want to do that?"

"Well, think about it. Without taking up any more ground, it would double our indoor space."

"I see. And how would we access this upper level?"

"Stairs," she replied simply.

"Stairs?"

"Yes. Stairs."

He laughed and said, "You're going to have to explain that one to me."

Spotting a nearby boulder that was about waist high, she replied, "If you wanted to get on top of that boulder, how would you do it?"

"Well, I'd probably just climb on top of it."

"And what if it was over your head?"

"I think I'd probably . . . where are you going with this, Eve?"

In answer, she collected a few short, rough-hewn boards, laid them out one on top of the other, and created three sequential levels, stepping nimbly onto each until she stood on top of the boulder.

"Here, Adam," she replied, stomping her foot on the boulder's surface. "I'm going *here*."

He stared in wonder. "So, you're saying that we should create a similar system inside the existing structure that will allow us to change elevations and access an upper level?"

She smiled, nodding vigorously.

Springing up the rough steps, he embraced his wife, swinging her around in circles. "You, my beauty, are a genius. How did you know how to do that?"

"I don't know," she replied, returning to ground level. "It was just there in my mind to do, and I did it."

"It was there in your mind because The Alpha placed it there when you were created. It's like He's given each one of us abilities and knowledge so that, by working together, we can accomplish anything we desire."

"About that," she said almost shyly.

"About what?"

"You know . . . desires."

"I'm listening."

She paused, pondering what she wanted to say. "I see all of our animals reproducing after their kind and the way the mothers love their young ones."

"I know," he replied quietly. "I love that."

"Well, why aren't we reproducing after *our* kind?"

His brow furrowed as he considered the question. "I don't know. I mean, to be honest, I've been so focused on building our dwelling that I haven't really thought of much else. Maybe I should ask The Alpha about—"

"Adam," Eve chided. "You don't have to ask The Alpha. We know how it works."

"Or how it's supposed to work." He gave a sly smile and then added, "I can honestly say it hasn't been for lack of effort."

She put her arms around him, holding him close. “I feel like if we want something, I mean, really and truly want something, The Alpha will give it to us. So, do you want this, Adam? Do you want sons, daughters?”

He kissed her long and lovingly before saying, “Remember when I named you?”

“Yes.”

“What did I say?”

“You said, ‘You are Eve, the source of life. For you are bone of my bone, flesh of my flesh, and through you, all life, all mankind shall come.’ ”

“And what did you say?”

“‘You are Adam . . . Son of the Earth. We will walk together and fill this beautiful land with our offspring that mankind may endure unceasingly.’ ”

“It’s not just about what we desire, Eve. It’s about our purpose—about our destiny. So, to answer your question about whether I want sons and daughters, yes, I do.”

“As do I, although I have to tell you that no matter how hard I try, I simply cannot understand how just the two of us can be expected to *fill the land* with our offspring.”

“Well,” he replied, jumping down from the rock and lifting Eve off to stand beside him, “our children will also conceive and have children, and their children will conceive. It’s like those little creatures I named rabbits. It began with two, but now there are hundreds of them.”

“They’ve been busy,” Eve said with a laugh.

“No doubt about that.”

She seemed to look past him. “Adam?”

"Yes?"

"There is an animal standing over there."

"Where?" he inquired, turning to follow her stare.

"There . . . just under that tree."

Gazing intently, he finally saw what she was talking about. "Okay. I see it. What about it?"

"What do you call it?"

"That's a wolf. Why do you ask?"

"It's funny, but there's a stick at its feet, and it keeps picking the stick up in its mouth, staring at us, and then dropping it."

"Really? I wonder why."

Adam turned toward the wolf, clapped his hands, and whistled. The wolf picked the stick up in its mouth, trotted over to where he and the woman stood, and then dropped it at his feet.

"I think he wants you to pick it up," Eve suggested.

Adam bent and grabbed the stick, prompting the wolf to bark loudly, run a few paces away, and then return.

"Does he want me to throw it?" Adam said.

"Try it."

He threw the stick, and the wolf ran after it, picked it up in his jaws, and trotted back, depositing it at Adam's feet.

"Do it again," Eve prompted excitedly.

Adam threw the stick further this time with the same result.

"This animal," Eve said, "has created a game he can play with us. I find this remarkable."

"I find all of The Alpha's creations remarkable," Adam replied before hurling the stick as far as he could throw it with the wolf running after it and disappearing into the trees.

They waited expectantly for it to return.

And waited.

Then, they waited some more.

"Well," Adam said after a bit, "I guess he is tired of the game."

Eve tapped him on the shoulder, pointing. "Look."

There was the wolf and another wolf behind him, with several pups following.

Eve clapped her hands together excitedly. "He's bringing his family to introduce us to them."

The wolf trotted proudly toward them, coming to a stop a few feet away and barking loudly. Then, an extraordinary thing happened. Adam understood what the creature wanted to say.

"Eve, he wants to live with us and be our personal animal—him and his family."

"I don't understand," she replied, kneeling and being swarmed by a half-dozen wolf pups.

"It's hard to explain, but that's what I heard in my spirit."

"So, you're saying that the wolf talked to you?"

"That's exactly what I'm saying."

"And," she said, "he wants to live here—with us?"

Adam laughed, leaned down, and scratched the wolf's ears. "I know it doesn't make any sense, but I must tell you that this isn't the first time something like this has happened to me. There have been other times—especially when I was naming the animals, way before you were created—when I felt as if I was communicating with certain beasts."

Eve stood, holding one of the pups tenderly in her arms and letting it lick her face. "I believe I am experiencing what you're talking about. It's not words like you and I use or even the way we communicate with The Alpha. More like thoughts appearing in my mind. For instance, right now, that wolf mother is telling me how happy she is that I am loving her pup."

"This is amazing," Adam said.

"No," Eve replied, "this is The Alpha. It's His sense of humor, His anticipation of what makes us happy—what brings us joy and the way He takes care of even the smallest details of our lives."

"Thank you, Alpha," Adam said loudly, although he knew in his spirit that The Alpha was right there with him.

In Shamayim, The Alpha called the archangels to assemble before His throne, each one taking positions by their individual lampstands.

"You have summoned us, Alpha," Michael said.

"Yes, Michael, I have. There is something about to occur that you need to be aware of. Something of great importance."

"Something having to do with the man and woman?" Gabriel inquired.

"Very insightful, Gabriel. Yes, it does. All life on earth can reproduce after its kind, and the man and woman are no different."

“So,” Jophiel said, “You created them, and they are going to create others like themselves?”

“Yes.”

“And You trust them to do this?”

“Of course. Remember, they carry not only my likeness but my nature. To not trust them would be to not trust myself.”

Raphael asked, “But aren’t You concerned about Apollyon being there and trying to destroy them?”

“Oh, make no mistake, he’s there, and he definitely has plans to corrupt them.”

“But You’re not concerned?”

“I am, which is why I’ve called you all here.” A brief pause, and then He added, “I know what is coming for them and, thus, know that they will require assistance. So, from among the angels under your care, I’d like you to decide among yourselves who would be suitable as guardians over my creation.”

The archangels exchanged glances with Michael, saying, “To be clear, You are asking us to choose angels who will live among the man and woman and watch over them?”

“Live among them but not *with* them.”

“I’m sorry, but I don’t see the difference.”

“Just as Apollyon and his minions have been confined to the Spiritual Realm within the atmosphere, so will these guardians.”

“Meaning that they will be unseen?”

The Alpha said, “Unseen, unless there is a need to make themselves known.”

"What do You mean?" Chamuel asked.

"Remember when I took you all to Earth to meet the man and woman?"

"Yes."

"They could see you because I gave you the ability to assume forms that would be recognizable in that realm. Now, I need a watcher and a warrior for each of them. I will hear your suggestions."

Michael said, "Rok is obvious for Adam's warrior and, perhaps, Kepteny for Eve."

"Agreed. Gabriel?"

"Taylor for Adam's watcher, and Schindaug for Eve."

"Then it is settled."

"How active are they supposed to be, Alpha?" Michael inquired.

"I am giving them the authority to protect the man and woman wherever they go and in whatever they do. Watching, guarding so that they don't even stumble."

"That sounds like a lot of work," Jophiel said with a smile.

The Alpha replied, returning the smile, "Oh yes, they will be busy."

"And how about Apollyon?" Raphael asked. "Will he have access to them?"

The Alpha stood and descended the steps of the dais. He began walking across the Fiery Stones, beckoning the archangels to follow Him. "Apollyon is a deceiver, a manipulator, and a liar whose true power is in persuasion, which is perhaps the most powerful weapon of all. As graphic witness to this fact, he persuaded one-third of my angelic host to follow him into rebellion."

"And You're giving him access to the man and woman?" Zadkiel said in alarm.

"I am."

"But, Alpha, respectfully, isn't that somewhat like putting them in a cage with a dangerous creature just to see how they'll do?"

The Alpha stopped walking, turned, and regarded the archangel. "Make no mistake, Zadkiel, Apollyon is the most dangerous creature in my entire universe. He has promised to destroy the man and woman."

Michael said, "Then I don't understand why You would allow this."

"I think you do."

Michael thought for a moment before replying, "It's the same with them as it is with us. They must have the freedom to make a choice."

"Which is why I placed two trees in the middle of the garden and told them they could eat of one and not the other: the tree of life and the tree of the knowledge of good and evil."

"They now have to choose whether to obey You," Chamuel mused.

"Correct."

"Alpha," Jophiel said, "do we also have access to Earth?"

"Of course. You may go to and fro and observe all that is happening but without involvement unless specifically requested to do so. I have created a Curtain between the Realms to define the boundaries."

Gabriel said, "Have the man and woman encountered Apollyon yet?"

"No," The Alpha replied, His eyes seeing far beyond their current location. "But it will happen soon. Go find your watchers and warriors. Send them. Send them now."

Chapter Twenty-Eight

"Have you decided how you're going to do it yet?" Beleth inquired of his Prince.

"Do what?" Apollyon replied.

"Destroy the man and woman."

Life in the ether had been a difficult adjustment for Apollyon and his minions.

It was nothing like he'd imagined.

Nothing.

He had desired a throne and a kingdom, and he'd gotten what he wanted to a certain extent. He was, as The Alpha had designated him, the "Prince of the Power of the Air," which meant that he was the uncontested ruler of the atmosphere surrounding Earth. Which meant, in his opinion, precisely nothing.

Air. He ruled air. Air he didn't need. Air only humans needed!

It was insulting.

It was humiliating.

It was insufferable.

It was . . . a consequence of his own choices, a fact well known to him.

The question of whether he regretted his actions was never far from his thoughts.

He had been the first and the highest of The Alpha's created beings, chief among all angels and archangels with unrestricted access to the throne room and the archives. He recalled The Alpha saying, *"I have entrusted you to carry my light to all and to soberly steward the light, ensuring that it remains available to all who seek both now and ever after."* And, *"You are to be ever at my side. And the only reason you would not be at my side is if you have chosen not to be so."*

How the words haunted him.

In short, he'd had more than any other created being. But it hadn't been enough, nor would it have ever been so. And he didn't know why. Truthfully, there was no logic to it. Believing he could actually ascend and wrest The Alpha's throne away from Him. Madness. And yet, he had attempted it and would try it again, even though the loss he'd suffered was staggering.

Where previously he was able to conceive and bring into being stunning architectural designs, turning them into magnificent buildings to house his followers, now his imagination was darkened, producing only sad and rudimentary shadows of his former glory. Music that once filled Shamayim and the entire Spiritual Realm with melodies and harmonies that caused even the starry host to join in song was now discordant and dissonant, not unlike the disjointed mess that resulted each time he attempted to create something artistic.

And then there were the physical changes, or at least the changes in how his spirit manifested physically. Once the most beautiful creature in the universe, he was now a misshapen lump. Deformed. A thing of horror to all who beheld him. Where once all flocked simply to behold his beauty, they now recoiled in horror at his appearance. Unless, that is, he expended tremendous energy to reshape himself into at least a semblance of his former glory.

But even then, everyone knew it was a sad masquerade. A sham. A pathetic pretense. And the fact that all his followers were in the same position—having had their physical forms shrunken and twisted by The Alpha's cruel and capricious judgment—did nothing to assuage his humiliation.

"I'm sorry, Beleth," he said disingenuously, manipulatively. "What did you ask me?"

Although Beleth and the rest of his inner circle had grown accustomed to their Prince's preoccupied moodiness since the banishment, they still found it disturbing. He just wasn't himself. To say that he had lost his swagger would be to understate in the extreme. It was more than that. He seemed as if he'd lost the very essence of what made him Apollyon, the Prince of Darkness, which was what they were forced to call him. Even when they attempted to pronounce *"Beelzebub,"* it still came out as *"Apollyon,"* a reality that frequently made their leader bellow in rage.

"I was inquiring," Beleth repeated, "as to whether you had devised any specific plan regarding how you are going to destroy the man and woman."

Apollyon and his second in command rested above a high mountain overlooking The Alpha's Garden and the four rivers emanating from its center before meandering across the plain. Although he could be anywhere he wished, it was here he found the most peace if, indeed, the roiling agitation within could ever be minimally soothed.

"Ah, yes. Well, my dear Beleth, that is a question to which I have given considerable thought."

"I have no doubt. So, what are we going to do?"

"Do? Why, nothing."

"Nothing?" Beleth said in confusion. "How can that be? They are the reason for . . ." he stopped to point to his twisted frame, "this. Surely you can't be considering just allowing them to carry on with their lives and face no consequence."

Apollyon smiled. It was a smile that even Beleth found chilling.

"And yet, I am not going to destroy them."

"But I don't—"

"I am going to make them destroy themselves."

The statement rocked Beleth, both in its unpredictability and its genius. "Okay, you have my attention."

"What did The Alpha say He was giving man?" Apollyon prompted.

"All power, dominion, and authority."

"Over whom and what?"

"Well, over the Earth."

"Come, come now, my friend. Don't attempt to spare my feelings. Be more specific."

"Okay," Beleth said. "He specifically mentioned that their authority would also be over you."

"Ah, yes. There it is. The hateful provision."

"But I still don't see how making them destroy themselves can change any of that."

Suddenly animated, Apollyon replied, "But don't you see? It would change everything. If I can somehow get man to turn against The Alpha—or at least violate a provision for their occupancy of the Garden—then man will lose all of what The Alpha has given and be in the same position as us."

"No disrespect," Beleth said, "but if you think that there is any way The Alpha would give you what He meant for man, then you're—"

"Not give, Beleth. Take and corrupt. I would take it from them, and then Earth would be mine along with every single one of their offspring forevermore, further proving that I can corrupt whatever The Alpha creates."

"I don't know. It's a bold plan."

"It is bold. But with the stakes this high, victory will not be won by the meek."

"Understood. So, walk me through it. How will you make it happen?"

Apollyon pondered the question for a moment before saying, "Obviously, my power is in persuasion, but I can't just pop into view out of nowhere and start talking to them. I have to find another means."

"Which," Beleth said, "brings up a question. Is it true that if we stay behind the Curtain, the man and his mate cannot see us as we are?"

"I don't know for certain, but I do know that I have been very near to the man and woman, and neither one had the slightest idea I was there."

"What did you do?"

"Nothing. Just stood there as close as I could get and watched them doing whatever it was that they were doing at the time."

"And you didn't try to communicate with them?"

"I did not."

Beleth replied, "With respect, why not?"

Seemingly perplexed by the question, Apollyon took his time to answer. "Well, I suppose—and I am embarrassed to admit this—but I suppose it's because it never even occurred to me."

"Do you think we can communicate with them since they're so different from us?"

"But are they really? I know for a fact that when The Alpha created man—and that whole creating him in the Alpha's image, which you might as well know I'm still not over. I mean, how could He, since I was His most beautiful creation? Anyway, when He created them, He gave them a body and a spirit. *He* is spirit. *We* are spirit. Shouldn't it follow that we can communicate with man on that level?"

Beleth said, "It makes sense logically. I think we need to try it."

"Right," Apollyon replied, "but how? I can't imagine The Alpha just standing by and giving us unbridled access to His precious little humans."

"But we don't know that. I think it's worth a try."

Apollyon turned and stared long and hard at his captain before saying, "Well, all right then. Assign someone the task and get back to me. I will be here doing what I do every day, day after day . . . pondering what once was and what might have been."

As Beleth moved away to carry out his assignment, Apollyon focused his attention on the Garden below, where he saw the man and woman working hard at building a structure of some sort.

"Oh, how I hate you," he said under his breath before a maniacal laugh escaped from his throat, filling the ether and echoing throughout the sphere.

"Is everyone clear about your assignment during this mission?" Michael asked the four angels who stood facing him and Gabriel.

Schindaug said, "Taylor and I are supposed to watch out for anything that represents even the slightest danger to the man and woman and report it to Rok or Kepteny." He added quickly, "And if anything comes up that requires our involvement, we'll give it a hundred and ten percent."

"Wait . . . just wait," Taylor said. "If a hundred percent represents all you've got, then a hundred and *ten* percent is, like, more than you have or something."

"Right, which is what we're willing to give, isn't that right, Rok?"

Rok just stared in confusion.

"Schindaug," Taylor continued, "you cannot give more than you have."

"But it sounded better than saying we'd give a hundred percent."

Michael cleared his throat. "So that's a *yes* regarding my original question?"

All four nodded in agreement.

Gabriel said, "Taylor, Schindaug, I cannot stress enough the importance of never backing off."

"Keeping our eye on the ball," Schindaug added.

"What?"

Michael interrupted, "All right. It sounds like you all know what is expected, and since The Alpha seems to be feeling some sense of urgency, you should probably not delay your departure."

Kepteny asked, "What will it be like? You know, being there on Earth? Will anyone be able to see us?"

"Not unless The Alpha allows it. You need permission first. We are not to cross through the Curtain and be seen unless it is specifically part of your mission," Gabriel replied.

"What are they like?" Taylor inquired.

Michael laughed, saying, "When you first see Adam, it's going to be like you're looking at The Alpha Himself."

"They're that much alike?"

"It's amazing. The Alpha told us when man was created that He was making him in His exact likeness."

"What about the woman?" Taylor asked. "Is she very different from the man?"

"Gabriel?" Michael prompted.

"I would say that she's a bit softer and weaker physically, but every bit his equal spiritually. She has a beauty that he does not. They're actually a great team because they complete each other."

Kepteny asked, "Can you explain that?"

"Apart from each other, they would be incomplete. But together, they are whole."

"Can we speak to them?" Schindaug said.

"When Michael and I first met Adam, we were in physical form and could talk to him, but I'm not sure about now. Michael?"

"From what I've been able to determine from The Alpha," Michael replied, "you will be able to say things to them spirit to spirit, but you cannot have conversations."

"So," Schindaug said, "if we say something to them, they won't be able to respond?"

"Correct."

"And should we say things to them?" Kepteny asked.

"The only thing you should say would be in the form of a warning."

"But not to influence their thinking?"

"That is not your assignment."

"I understand, but what if they are about to make a terrible mistake and—"

"Free will," Michael said, cutting him off. "Even if they make decisions that have the potential to lead them into tragedy, you cannot interfere with their choices."

"But," Schindaug replied, "I thought our mission was to protect them."

"It is . . . but not from themselves."

Taylor said, "It seems to me that is where the greatest danger would lie."

"While you may be correct, once again, that is outside of the mission."

Gabriel pulled everyone into a tight huddle. "We are trusting the welfare of the man and woman to you four. You should always be aware that Apollyon hates them and will actively seek to destroy them at every opportunity. Do not allow that to happen. Stay alert. Be on your guard. Communicate with each other."

"Yeah," Schindaug said, "we don't need any lone wolves."

"Do you ever stop?" Taylor replied.

"Okay," Gabriel continued with a smile, "go in The Alpha's strength and grace. If you need us, you know where we are."

The four suddenly found themselves on Earth in the Garden of Eden, with the man and woman a short distance away.

"How do we start this?" Taylor asked.

"Well," Kepteny replied, "if we're going to watch over them, we obviously have to be close enough to do that."

"Won't they know we're there?"

Schindaug stared at the two humans. "The Curtain separates us, but there's only one way to find out."

The four angels moved toward where Adam and Eve worked. As they got closer, they noticed an animal who seemed to be standing guard.

"That animal can either see us or sense us," Taylor said as the wolf began growling and barking.

Adam stopped what he was doing and approached the wolf, saying, "What's wrong, boy? Do you see something?"

The wolf sniffed the air and then trotted back to where he had been, seemingly content with them being there.

"That's interesting," said Kepteny. "The animal knows we're here, but the humans don't."

Rok moved protectively toward the man, taking up a position just to the right of where he was working, or more accurately, where he had been working, for by the time Rok got there, the man had pivoted and walked right through him without stopping.

Schindaug said, "They can do that? Just move right through us as if we're not there?"

"As long as we are on this side of the Curtain, it seems quite possible," Taylor replied as Rok stared at them dumbfounded.

He purposely stepped repeatedly into the man's path as he moved about with the same results.

Kepteny said, "Well, I suppose that answers that question."

Schindaug glanced toward Kepteny, a mischievous smile on his face.

"What?" Kepteny asked.

"Seventy-nine."

"What is he talking about, Kepteny?" Taylor said.

Laughing, he replied, "My riddle about Proud Mountain, well, as it used to be anyway."

"So, am I right?" Schindaug prompted.

"No. Rok guessed the same number."

"Come on."

Rok suddenly stood tall, his eyes scanning the area, then pointing and saying, "Here."

They all felt it.

Something changing in the atmosphere.

Something dark and threatening.

Semyaza and a couple of underlings had shapeshifted into their original forms and materialized, standing a short distance away and surveying the scene before them.

Grinning arrogantly, Semyaza approached Rok, saying, "Well, well, if it isn't my old friend Rok."

Rok moved threateningly toward him, causing Semyaza to halt his progress, his face and form fading in and out of his control, revealing glimpses of his fallen nature.

Kepteny raced to catch up with Rok as Semyaza's companions moved into offensive positions with swords drawn.

"Stop right there," Kepteny warned.

Semyaza replied, "We're not afraid of you. We're not afraid of anybody."

"Odd, since we destroyed you in the battle, reducing you to pathetic caricatures of your former glory."

"Do not speak of that," Semyaza shouted. "Do not ever speak to me of that."

Taylor said, "And you'd do well to remember who *you* are and who *we* are. This is The Alpha's territory, Semyaza. You aren't welcome here. In fact, should you attempt to return, we have the authority to banish you."

Semyaza had just begun to retort when he found Rok's sword at his throat.

Leaning in close, Rok whispered, "Go," before giving his face a nick with the sword tip, causing Semyaza to cry out in pain.

Backpedaling fiercely, he shouted, "You win this one, but we'll be back."

"We win them all," Schindaug taunted.

Kepteny turned his gaze toward the man and woman who had continued working throughout the encounter, seemingly unaware of what had transpired around them in the spirit realm.

"This is very strange," he observed as they moved to retake their original positions. "We're here, making no effort to disguise our Presence; Semyaza and his little buddies show up and nearly cause a fight; there's much yelling and screaming, and the man and woman have absolutely no idea what is going on."

Schindaug walked up behind Eve and shouted, "Hey! Eve! Turn around!"

She did turn around, only to walk right through him.

He glanced back toward his companions, shrugged, and took up his position, saying, "This is going to take some getting used to."

"Michael," Taylor said, "there's something you need to know about."

Michael appeared at her call. "You don't have to tell me. I already know."

"And The Alpha?"

"Of course."

"So, this encounter with Apollyon's guys wasn't unexpected?" Schindaug asked.

"No, which is one of the reasons The Alpha placed such a sense of urgency on getting you four in place."

Kepteny said, "It almost feels as if the battle isn't over . . . that it's really just begun."

"You're right, Kepteny. We've merely changed the field of engagement. Only now, the stakes are much higher. We're not just fighting for control of Shamayim; we're fighting for the hearts and minds of humankind both now and those who are yet to be born."

"That's his endgame?" Schindaug inquired. "To destroy man?"

"His endgame, as you put it, is to destroy everything The Alpha has created and then seat himself on the throne. And it all starts here in this Garden. Which is why we stressed vigilance when we sent you."

"Well," Taylor said, "this was a perfect reminder of that need."

"Just remember," Michael warned, "you will sense them before you see them, so trust your senses."

As Michael faded away, Schindaug noted, "This might be a little more challenging than we imagined."

Chapter Twenty-nine

Adam and The Alpha walked through the Garden along a pathway worn smooth over time by their strolls. It was where they walked at the end of each day, day after day, without fail.

"Alpha," Adam said, "are we truly alone here? I mean, just Eve and me?"

"If you are asking whether you are the only humans, then the answer is yes."

"Besides the animals, are there other non-humans?"

"Why do you ask?"

Adam stopped walking and turned to face him. "I'm not sure, really. It's just that there are times when I get the distinct impression that we're not alone."

Over Adam's shoulder, The Alpha could see Rok and Taylor standing at a respectful distance.

He said, "The universe consists of the seen and the unseen, Adam. Trees, hills, mountains, sky, rivers, the ground beneath your feet, animals, birds . . . Eve. All these things comprise what may be seen by human eyes. But there is an unseen world all around you. It's the world of the spirit."

"Which is where You live?"

"Correct."

"But You're also here . . . on Earth. I can see You, feel You."

"Because I wish for it to be so."

"So," Adam said, "if You didn't want to be seen, I couldn't see You?"

He paused to consider Adam's question and then gestured grandly. "This is the Physical Realm. Everything here must, therefore, have physical properties. Everything. Which is why I created you to have a physical body. But when I breathed my breath into your lungs, my Spirit was imparted. Because of this, you are unique among all my creation, having both body and spirit."

"But if I have a spirit, then why can't I see into the Spiritual Realm?"

"Because I do not wish for you to do so."

"You have allowed the Spiritual Realm to see into the Physical Realm?"

"Yes, that is correct."

"Can those in the Spiritual Realm come into the Physical Realm at any moment?" Adam asked.

"If I allow it, yes. My intent is that those of the Spiritual Realm will remain invisible to you and not interfere with your daily life."

As they resumed walking, Adam was silent. Thoughtful.

Finally, he said, "So, the tree of the knowledge of good and evil . . ."

"Yes?"

"Were we to eat of it, could we then see everything You see?"

"Were you to ever eat of it, you would be set on a path to die. Your souls would die. Your future would die. Everything I planned and imagined for your life here on Earth would die along with all future generations. Only death awaits those who eat from that tree."

"Then why put it here, Alpha? I mean, if it's that dangerous—"

"The tree itself doesn't comprise the danger."

"Then, what does?"

"You, Adam. *You* are the danger."

"To whom?"

"To yourself, to Eve, and she to you."

"That sounds like a lot of pressure."

The Alpha said, "Look around you. Behold the marvelous world I have created just for you—a world I have filled with everything you need. Food for your nourishment. Wonderful smells and sounds and sights and textures and things that stimulate your senses. You are the undisputed master of all you survey. And within all that, I have only given you one rule. Just one command amongst the vast amount of freedom and benefits I have provided in the Physical Realm."

"Don't eat the fruit of the tree of knowledge of good and evil."

"That's it. Now, tell me, why did you ask about the Spirit Realm?"

Adam laughed. "Because there are times when I am almost positive someone is there, You know, just outside the periphery of my sight. Not doing anything, just watching."

"And does this bother you?"

"Well, I don't know. I suppose it feels a little uncomfortable at times, if You know what I mean."

The Alpha smiled and said, "Rok, Taylor, come here."

As the two angels stepped through the Curtain and approached, Adam's eyes were opened.

"Whoa, where did they come from?"

"These are angels. They are always with you wherever you go."

"Angels? But why? And where did they come from?"

"Well, they came from the Spiritual Realm where I live, which is why you cannot see them normally. They are for your protection."

"Protection from what?"

Taylor said, "May I?"

"Of course," The Alpha replied.

"Adam, I'm Taylor, and this is Rok. I'm a watcher angel, and Rok is a warrior angel."

"A warrior?" Adam replied. "Why do I need a warrior angel . . . especially one that huge?"

Taylor glanced toward The Alpha and then said, "Because not every being in The Alpha's Kingdom is *for* you. By the way, Rok is not just big. He's really good, too."

"So, someone or some*thing* is trying to hurt me—us?"

"We're not going to let that happen."

"But, who—"

The Alpha interrupted, "I'd prefer you not concern yourself with that at present and simply live your lives with the knowledge that I have put provisions in place to protect you from all harm. For this reason, I have given my angels charge over you as their assignment. And remember, you have all power, authority, and dominion in this place. Everything must bow to you. Nothing can control you."

Adam stared back and forth between Rok and Taylor. "I can see you now, and we are conversing. Are You telling me that it won't be this way when You leave, Alpha?"

"Correct. Taylor and Rok dwell in the unseen realm. They are able to whisper things to your spirit, and you will only be able to see them if a situation arises when they feel it is necessary to reveal themselves."

"And they are always there?"

"Always."

Rok approached, towering over Adam, and placed a hand on each of his shoulders, which nearly forced him to the ground.

"Safe," was all he said before turning and walking back to his post.

"He doesn't say much, does he?" Adam asked.

Taylor replied with a knowing smile, "He lets his sword talk for him."

Adam stared back and forth between Rok and Taylor before saying, "Does Eve have two angels with her as well?"

"Yes," The Alpha replied.

"And I don't suppose she can see them either?"

"No, Adam, she cannot."

"So, are You going to tell her about them? I mean, it'd be a bit odd me knowing and—"

"It won't."

"I don't see how that's—"

"As soon as I leave—and until I deem it to have relevance—you won't remember anything about this conversation except for the fact that you and I met at our usual time."

Massaging his temples as if fighting off a headache, Adam said, "Forgive me, Alpha, but if I won't be able to remember anything about this, then why did it happen?"

"You asked the question, and I gave you an answer in the only way it would make sense. Further, as I suggested, a time may come when you will benefit from this knowledge. Until then, it will remain locked away in your memory."

As Adam stared at Rok and Taylor, their forms faded away behind the Curtain, and he was alone with The Alpha.

Giving his head a little shake, he said, "What were we just talking about?"

"Many things, Adam, many things, as is our custom. And now, farewell until tomorrow."

"So soon? It seems like You just got here."

"I feel the same way," The Alpha replied with a laugh.

"Okay, tomorrow then."

As The Alpha watched Adam begin making his way back to his dwelling, He said, "Be ever vigilant, my angels, for your adversary is on the prowl, hungry for power and dominance."

"Are the man and woman in danger, Alpha?" Taylor asked.

The Alpha paused before answering, "Apollyon is far more cunning than you could ever imagine and will not rest until he has what he desires."

"And what does he desire?"

"Everything."

"So . . ." Apollyon mused out loud upon hearing Semyaza's report, "The Alpha has angels guarding His creation. How very interesting."

"Interesting?" Semyaza countered, rubbing the place on his face where Rok's sword had nicked him. "The level of pain I'm feeling goes a little beyond interesting."

"While your pain will go away eventually, the issue with these guardians is here to stay. This changes everything."

Beleth said, "There are only four of them. Certainly, we can—"

"You forget who and where you are, Beleth. You are now a fallen angel cast out of your first estate and into this atmospheric prison while they retain full power and authority. They still have weapons; we do not. They still retain their radiant form while we are darkened and deformed."

"What does that mean?"

They were gathered in another one of Apollyon's favored spots—a high place overlooking a vast plain covered with sweet grasses, groves of trees, and rolling hills on which animals of all kinds grazed and frolicked. Being above it all provided him with a sense of power but also served as a constant reminder of what his purpose had become: to destroy every single thing of beauty that The Alpha had created.

Turning his gaze on his second in command, he replied, "It means, dear Beleth, that my former strategy of getting close to the man and woman, befriending them, gaining their trust, and then raining destruction down on them and all they love must now be altered."

"Because of the guardians?"

"Yes. We now must be more subtle." He began pacing as he talked. "Craftier. Smarter. We must come at them in a way no one will ever suspect or even see coming."

Absently rubbing the wound on his face, Semyaza said, "With a guardian and a watcher attached to them at all times, how can we possibly pull something like that off?"

Beleth suggested, "Maybe we can just throw everything we have at them—you know, overwhelm them with force and get the guardians so distracted that you can get to the man and woman without their interference."

Apollyon smiled patiently, wearily. "Were you not listening earlier? Did you not hear the part about who they are and who we are?"

"I understand, but how could it be possible for the four of them to take on all of our forces, especially at the same time?"

"No offense," Semyaza added, "but it sounds like a fair question to me."

"Okay, I'll play along. Let's say that what you are suggesting is possible . . . that we marshal all our forces and attack the four of them in glorious battle array."

"You're mocking us," Beleth groused.

Ignoring the comment, Apollyon pressed on dramatically, "And with clashing swords, we dislodge them from the Garden, beat them down, and send them running, leaving the man and woman isolated and alone."

"And isn't that sort of our goal?" Semyaza inquired.

"You're missing the point," Apollyon said loudly. "Even if what I just described were possible—which I assure you it most certainly is not—do you really think that The Alpha would stand idly by and allow it to happen? Well, do you?" On the heels of their shared silence, he added, "And what about Michael? Did you forget about the big guy and the other archangels? What are they going to do? Stand on the periphery and keep score?"

"You're making it sound hopeless," Beleth said darkly.

"Your approach *is* hopeless. It won't work, which is why I said we must devise a strategy that does not include physical force."

Semyaza said, "But if we just hit them with everything we have, we can—"

"Because it worked so well the last time, right?" Apollyon taunted. "I must say, Semyaza, you disappoint me. The ability to learn from previous mistakes, previous failures, is critical to future success. And it sounds as if you haven't learned a thing."

"Sorry, I just can't shake the memory of that humiliation, and I constantly think about getting another chance to redeem myself."

Apollyon draped his arm across Semyaza's shoulders, saying, "Dear, dear Semyaza, you have no idea the extent to which I feel your humiliation, your agony. But even if you had another chance—if, perchance, you had a hundred more chances—you could not prevail. You will never prevail over Rok. He's too powerful."

"I don't know if I can accept that."

"You must. Accept it and move on."

"And do what?"

Apollyon paused before saying, "Be smarter, not stronger."

Beleth said, "It seems as if you already have something in mind."

"Very perceptive, Beleth," Apollyon replied. "In fact, I do."

"What are you going to do?"

"What I've always intended to do."

"Ascend to The Alpha's throne?"

"Yes. And along the way, I will steal the man and woman's authority, kill their bodies, and deprive Him of their souls. I will ruin it, Beleth. I will ruin it all. I will ruin what He loves, just as He ruined us. But first things first."

"Which is?" Semyaza prompted.

"How to get to them without going through their guardians."

"Do you have something in mind?" Beleth chimed in.

Around an evil smile, Apollyon replied, "As a matter of fact, I do."

Chapter Thirty

Adam and Eve sat on a low rise overlooking a small lake nestled within the Garden, its shore lined with trees of all kinds—flowering, towering, sheltering, and spreading. Birds nested, soared, and skimmed the rippling surface of the lake, their honeyed song filling the air as a gentle wind stirred the leaves into a deeper underscore.

Spreading her arms wide and stretching luxuriously, Eve said, "This, Adam. I love *this*."

"And I love you," he replied, lying back in the sweet grass.

Propping herself on one elbow, she teased a few strands of hair from his eyes. "So, you didn't tell me what you and The Alpha talked about last evening."

"But I did."

"You didn't."

"No, I'm sure of it. Remember?"

Rolling her eyes, she replied, "Don't you think if you would've told me something The Alpha shared with you, I'd remember it?"

"Are we really having this conversation again?"

"What conversation?"

"You know, the one where you tell me I didn't tell you something, and I tell you that I did, and you suddenly remember it happening?"

"Are you serious?" she replied, rising to a sitting position and staring down at her husband. "That has never happened."

Adam sat up, saying, "You're kidding, right? It happens every time."

"Oh mister . . . mister . . . what was that word?"

"Hyperbole?"

"Yes! Mister hyperbole here. What *does* happen every time is that you, not me, suddenly realize that the only place the conversation took place was somewhere in that head of yours, and then you get all embarrassed and say stuff like . . ." she adjusted the tone of her voice to mimic his, "'Oh, yeah. I forgot about that,' and then you have to apologize for getting all *first man* on me."

"Well, I am first man."

"Yes, you are, but that doesn't mean you are always right."

"Maybe, but I'm right about this."

"What, that you told me about your last conversation with The Alpha?"

"Yes. Remember? I said that we were walking, and He put His arm around me—I love it when He does that—and He leaned in and whispered, 'Never forget that you are my son, and I am your Father, and I will do anything I have to do to protect you. But I can't protect you from yourself.' Please tell me you remember me saying that to you."

"No, you didn't. Not one word."

"I didn't?"

"No! That's what I've been trying to tell you," Eve replied, growing exasperated.

"Oh, well . . . I thought I did."

She fell back onto the grass, letting out a shriek. "You drive me crazy sometimes."

The wolf trotted over as if to make sure she was okay, dipping his muzzle and licking her cheek.

"Oh, hey, wolf, it's okay. The man just makes me crazy."

Sitting back on his haunches, he barked loudly.

"You too, huh?"

Another bark.

"See," she said, "I'm not the only one."

"He should have a name besides *wolf,* don't you think?"

"Ah-ha," she replied, sitting up suddenly. "I see what you're trying to do here."

"Oh, what's that?"

"You're trying to change the subject, hoping I'll forget all about our conversation."

Smiling, he said, "You're onto me."

"You got that right."

"Okay, okay," he replied with a laugh, "you got me. I absolutely did not tell you about the conversation."

"Finally!"

"But I thought I did."

She punched him in the shoulder, saying, "It's okay. I'm used to it."

"So, what do you think about what I said?"

"You mean about giving the wolf a name?"

"Yes."

She thought about it before saying, "Well, you're the name-giver."

"Right, but this is different. I mean, The Alpha didn't just call you *woman* and me *man*. He gave us personal names."

"I see what you mean. Do you have anything in mind?"

He stared at the wolf's steely blue eyes and then said, "*Blue*. I shall call him Blue."

The wolf barked loudly and began zipping around the clearing.

Eve laughed at the wolf's antics. "I think he likes it. And what about his mate?"

As if on cue, Blue's mate trotted into the clearing, joining her partner in frolic.

Adam watched the two together before saying, "She will be called *Shadow* because that's where she usually stays."

"Blue and Shadow," Eve repeated. "I like it. See if they will respond to their new names."

"Blue . . . Shadow," Adam said loudly, causing the wolves to halt their play and come running toward him.

When they arrived, their greeting was so exuberant they nearly bowled him over.

"Okay, okay," he said, laughing and rolling around on the grass, with the two wolves barking and nipping playfully at him.

Eve stood and said, "Shadow, come on, girl," and took off running with the wolf right behind her.

Adam called out, "Eve, come here."

She circled back around with Shadow at her side. "What?"

Eyes wide, he said, "Blue is talking to me."

She stared skeptically at him, saying, "I know you said something before about having some level of communication, but *talking* to him?"

"No, I'm serious. And I'm pretty sure you can do it, too."

"Okay, how?"

"You just stare into his eyes and think what you want to say, and he will say something back to you," Adam explained.

"I wonder if it would work with Shadow."

Kneeling, she placed her hands on both sides of Shadow's muzzle, stared into her eyes, and thought, *I think you are a beautiful creature*.

Immediately came the response, *I am what The Alpha made me*.

Eve stared up at Adam, her eyes filled with wonder. "It works. I thought, '*I think you are a beautiful creature,*' and she said, '*I am what The Alpha made me.*' "

"That's amazing," Adam replied. "And when I told Blue that I was happy that he and I were friends, he said back to me something like, '*More than friends . . . family.*' "

"Adam," Eve said, absently stroking Shadow's beautiful coat of fur. "Do you think we can do this with all the animals?"

"I'm not sure. I mean, I feel like I can communicate with everything on some level; it's just the way The Alpha created me. But as far as having conversations where we say something and an animal says something back . . . I just don't know."

"Maybe we should try it."

Adam glanced around the area and spotted a lamb grazing peacefully a short distance away. Standing, he told Blue to stay with Eve and made his way carefully toward its position.

When he got closer, the lamb raised its head and regarded him carefully.

Stepping in front of the animal, he clearly heard it say, *Hello, Adam. I haven't seen you since you named me.*

"So, you *can* talk to me?" *Can you hear me talking in my head, too?*

Of course. All The Alpha's creatures can communicate.

This is remarkable. I'm hearing you in my head. And do you have a family, uh . . . what should I call you?

How about Lamb? And, yes, I do have a family.

That is wonderful. Do you know Blue . . . the wolf?

Yes, he replied. *We are all one here in the Garden.*

With Eve following, Adam began moving through the Garden, stopping to talk to every animal he encountered. What he found was that the warm-blooded creatures were far more likely to communicate than others, although he did find the serpent to be particularly talkative. So much so that it followed them everywhere they went, having an opinion on everything.

And yet, Adam liked the loquacious creature. Coming to a large clearing, he turned to regard their new companion as Eve took Blue and Shadow back to their dwelling.

Despite being enormous in size and strength, it was graceful in form and clothed in stunning, multi-colored, double-layered scales that covered its back like rows of shields sealed together. Surprised or excited, lightning leaped from its mouth, causing vapor to steam from its nostrils as from a pot left too long over a hot flame. Eyes the color of burnt umber, like the glow that appeared on the horizon just before dawn, the serpent gazed down beneficently when it would flap its wings and take flight. The scales on its belly were sharp enough to plow the ground as it navigated its bulk through the Garden, leaving a broad trail in its wake. Nothing in all of The Alpha's creation was its equal, both in size, beauty, and intelligence. The serpent was truly the proudest of them all . . . the King of the Beasts.

One day, while out walking with the glorious beast, Adam said, "Why have you taken such a liking to us, serpent?"

His voice filled with sibilance, the serpent replied, "I'm not sure. Perhaps it is because of all The Alpha's creatures, we are the most alike in intelligence."

"So, you've been lonely? Longing for someone to talk to?"

"Yes, that is it precisely. How did you know?"

"Probably because before The Alpha gave me Eve—the woman—I felt the same way, so I know how you feel."

"Then," the serpent said hopefully, "you don't mind me following you around and talking to you?"

Laughing, Adam replied, "Well, you're a little big to go everywhere we go . . ."

Lifting lightly off the ground, the serpent said, “I can fly over the places that are too narrow for me to pass. I won’t cause you any difficulty. Please, say yes.”

Adam was thoughtful before saying, “Okay, it’s fine with me. Truthfully, I enjoy having someone else to talk to besides Eve.”

The serpent did a few loops, flying around the clearing and causing the trees to bend in the wake of his passing. “Thank you, thank you, thank you. You won’t regret this. We’re going to be great friends.”

Adam stared at the beast for a long moment after it landed before saying, “Serpent, weren’t there two of you when I named you?”

The serpent dipped his head in embarrassment. “Yes, there were . . . are.”

“Well, then, where is your mate?”

A long sigh, and then, “She doesn’t like me to be around during the day.”

“Oh? Why not?”

“She says I talk too much.”

“Huh?” Adam said, “And how about at night?”

A longer pause. “She doesn’t like me to be around at night either.”

“Same reason?” Adam asked with a smile.

“Same reason.”

Adam threw his head back and laughed loudly.

The serpent said, “I’m sorry, but I don’t find this situation amusing in the slightest.”

"I'm sorry, Serpent. It's just that . . ."

He had to stop as he was overtaken by another spasm of laughter.

The serpent stared stern-faced before saying, "I suppose it *is* rather amusing," and then joined in the laughter.

Standing at a distance on assignment from Apollyon, Remashel and Dantanian witnessed the whole thing.

"Is this something he would be interested in knowing about?" Remashel asked, having just witnessed the encounter between the man and the serpent.

"Whether he is or isn't, he told us to report back what we saw."

"I know, but have you forgotten what happened the last time we brought something back to him?"

"No, I haven't," Dantanian replied. "That was unpleasant."

"I clearly remember, after all the yelling and screaming, him saying something along the lines of, *'If you cannot follow simple orders, then I will find someone who can.'* "

"But we were following orders. He just didn't like what we brought him."

Remashel said, "Right. But how were we supposed to know that the man giving a name to the wolf creature wasn't—what was that term he used?"

"Pertinent."

"That's right. Pertinent information. Again, how are we supposed to know what is and isn't? I mean, he hasn't exactly given us detailed instructions."

"So," Dantanian said, "are you hesitant to tell him about this?"

"I am. Think about it. What are we going to say? *'Oh, hey, we saw the man and the serpent walking around together, and at one point, the serpent flew up into the air and did a bunch of loops and breathed fire?'* "

"That's not what I would tell him."

"It's not?"

"No," Dantanian said. "I would report that it appeared that the man and the serpent were having a conversation."

"Now, see, that right there is something I believe would really set him off."

"Why?"

"Because," Remashel countered, "the man can't talk to the animals, that's why."

"It certainly looked like he can."

"He can't. It's impossible. They don't have the ability to form words with their mouths like we can. I'm telling you, you'd be asking for trouble."

"But what if he can?" Dantanian queried.

"What, Adam talking to animals?"

"Yes."

Remashel thought about it before saying, "Okay. We will tell him what we saw and then suggest that perhaps that's what was happening. That way, we're not putting ourselves at risk for delivering false or impertinent information."

"I like it. We'll just say something like, *'Now, we're not suggesting that this is even possible, but it kind of looked as if the man and the serpent were having a conversation.'* "

"Yeah, I mean, in that scenario, the worst that could happen would be that he yells at us for even suggesting that such a thing is possible."

"Then, we're agreed?" Dantanian asked.

"We are. Let's go."

In the atmosphere above the Garden, Apollyon was engaged in one of his favorite pastimes: imagining in great detail all the possible ways of destroying the man and woman. Thus far, however, nothing even remotely feasible had occurred to him. The challenge was, now and ever, how to get to them without arousing the suspicion and retaliation of the damnable watchers and warriors, which would, in turn, trigger a predictably harsh response from The Alpha. A scenario that left him feeling perpetually powerless. What was the point of being the most persuasive being in the entirety of The Alpha's universe if he couldn't actually converse with the couple? Thus far, anyway, it was a conundrum for which he had no ready answers.

And then there was Michael. How he hated him, having placed the blame for his present vexatious, debasing, and contemptuous circumstances squarely on his shoulders. As for why Michael, and not The Alpha, was on the receiving end of his ire, he couldn't say. Although it almost certainly had something to do with rank and petty jealousy, having decided long ago that Michael, and not he, was The Alpha's favorite.

"And why not hate him?" he said out loud. "He is imminently and detestably repugnant."

Staring down at his hideously malformed appendages—while recalling the one and only glimpse he'd had of his similarly repugnant, once-glorious face—he threw his overly large and misshapen head back and let loose an enraged bellow that echoed throughout Earth's atmosphere, causing his fallen followers to cringe in fear.

"Noooo!" he cried. "This cannot be. Cannot be. He stole it from me . . . my beauty. Gone. Gone forever."

Then he cursed.

He cursed The Alpha.

He cursed Michael.

He cursed Gabriel and all the other archangels.

He cursed all their assistants in general and Rok in particular.

He cursed the entire angelic host and Merkabah.

He cursed the Earth.

And he cursed the man and woman, vowing to inflict as much pain during their destruction as was possible for him to devise.

While the self-pity had been an ongoing source of frustration, he had, thus far anyway, managed to keep it under control. Now, however, he felt as if he were teetering at the edge of an abyss—an abyss from which there could be no extraction should he allow himself to fall.

With a shake of his head, he morphed his form and features back into the sad pretense he was forced to maintain, and just in time, for Dantanian and Remashel appeared a short distance away, walking quickly toward where he sat.

When they got closer, he hailed, "You have been gone long, my friends. What news do you bring me?"

Remashel took the lead, saying carefully, "We observed something that we thought you needed to know."

"And," he replied tensely, "you felt this information worthy enough to leave the man and woman unattended in order to bring it to me?"

As Remashel faltered in answering, Dantanian said, "Rightly or wrongly, yes, we did. And I think when you hear what we have to say, you will understand."

"Well then, best to not keep me waiting. Do go on."

Finally recovering his voice, Remashel said, "We kept close to the man and woman like you told us to and observed something quite odd."

"Okay, you have my attention."

"The two were out with their wolves—"

"Blue and Shadow? So cute," Apollyon interjected mockingly.

"Yes, and at one point, they were joined by a creature called a serpent."

"Serpent," Apollyon mused. "Hmmm, I am unfamiliar with this beast. Can you describe it to me?"

Dantanian said, "Well, it's large—"

"How large?"

"Very. And beautiful."

"How beautiful?"

Remashel took up the description. "Quite beautiful with glistening, multi-colored scales covering its entire back and tail."

"And," Dantanian added, "when it beats its wings, an entire rainbow of colors appears."

"It has wings?" Apollyon asked.

"Yes. Oh, and when it gets excited, lightning jets from its mouth."

"How utterly fascinating. But besides being unique among The Alpha's animal Kingdom, what is there about this creature that should interest me even slightly?"

Remashel shared a glance with Dantanian before saying, "Well, it seemed to us that the man and this beast were, well, conversing."

Apollyon sprang to his feet. "Conversing? That's impossible. What could possibly lead you to that conclusion?"

Dantanian replied, "It's hard to explain—and granted, we were quite a ways away so as not to attract the attention of the guardians—but they would stare at each other, and then their expressions would change as if in response to something the other said."

Holding his hands up for silence, Apollyon said, "Give me a moment to process this information. To be clear, based on what you saw, you are suggesting this creature possesses a level of intelligence that is not only sufficient to communicate with the man but also has the physical mechanics to produce speech?"

"Now," Remashel answered, "that part is unknown, given the distance between us."

"So, you didn't actually see the creature moving its mouth when it was speaking?"

"We saw neither physical manifestation of the formation of speech nor did we hear anything. But the physical posture and reactions of the two seemed to indicate that communication was occurring."

Apollyon walked a short distance away, hands clasped thoughtfully behind his back, absorbing the information.

Finally, he turned back toward them, saying, "I must see this creature for myself. Where may it be found?"

Dantanian replied, "Having never seen it before today, we are unsure of its abode."

"Then find it," Apollyon said sharply.

The two shared a glance, and Remashel said, "But where shall we look? As we said, today was the first time we have ever—"

"Do I have to tell you how to do everything?" Apollyon shouted. "What is the point of retaining your services if you display no personal initiative?" When they failed to answer, he prompted, "Well?"

"Uhhh," Dantanian replied lamely, "we . . . will . . . just do whatever we have to do to find the creature and then bring back a full report."

"No," Apollyon said sharply, "not a report. Bring back the creature. Here. Bring it here that I may examine it closely."

"But what if it refuses to come?" Remashel asked. "As we mentioned, it is rather large and—"

"Then compel it to come."

Dantanian said, "I'm not sure how to do that. It is physical, but we are spirit. It's not like we can grab it and make it come along."

Apollyon screamed in frustration, "We're done talking about this. Get this done, or get out of my sight!"

And then, he vanished, leaving the two staring blankly at each other.

"That went well," Remashel said sarcastically.

Dantanian scoffed, saying, "Any ideas?"

"None."

"Well, we'd better come up with something, or we're going to be counting flies on hippos or something equally humiliating."

Chapter Thirty-One

Apollyon stood in the outer court of the throne room after being summoned by The Alpha. Given no reason for the summons, he waited impatiently in silence, watching the spectacle playing out above the throne as the Seraphim and Cherubim combined in an elaborately executed aerial choreography. Staring across the expanse of Fiery Stones, Apollyon spied his former position to the right of The Alpha and wrestled with the question of why he had chosen to surrender what he'd once had.

There had been no challengers to his position, for none coveted what he had. It had been his to keep for all eternity.

And then there was his now-twisted form to consider. Once the most beautiful creature in all of creation, he now felt as if he were the ugliest. Again, a direct result of the choices he had made.

Yet, he shucked off the blame for his circumstances as easily as chaff being separated from the grains of that plant so beloved by the hated Adam, reasoning that The Alpha had never truly esteemed him properly and had, in fact, always intended to eventually elevate Michael above him. How could no one see him as the victim? Why could no one see that all he had once held dear had been stolen from him by The Alpha's unjust response to his righteous cause?

And then there was Michael. How could he be the only one to clearly see the conspiracy that his most hated rival had hatched, resulting in his banishment? Oh, he had been so clever, that one. Masquerading as the righteous warrior, defending the honor of the Kingdom when, all along, he had been conniving and scheming to steal Apollyon's position and everything he valued.

Michael would pay.

Oh, how he would pay.

"Apollyon," The Alpha said, snapping him out of his ruminations, "give me a report of your activities. What have you been doing?"

Hearing the name spoken by the same lips that had once proclaimed him *Son of the Dawn* was surprisingly grievous. Nearly as grievous as the sudden sight of Michael and Gabriel standing by their lampstands. When had that happened?

"I have been doing the only thing You have left for me to do," he replied. "Occupying the atmosphere and watching life on Your planet."

"And what have you seen?"

"Oh, well, let's see . . . I have seen the man and woman living in the same privilege that was once mine, reveling in their beauty, power, and authority and having the freedom to come and go and do and be anything their little hearts desire."

Michael said harshly, "Where you are is where you have chosen to be."

"I did not choose *this*," Apollyon shouted, his voice echoing throughout the throne room. "*You* did this to me."

"You did it to yourself."

"Really, Michael? Do you really think I would purposefully surrender everything I once had—my authority and my beauty—to live in some atmospheric prison in this sad and twisted form, having no power to change any of it?"

"As long as we're talking about things being twisted, how about we discuss your constant casting of blame?"

"Casting of blame?" Apollyon replied loudly. "You—all of you—abandoned me. It's not blame . . . it's truth!"

"Oh please—"

"When I didn't act and respond in a manner you all deemed appropriate, I was abandoned—and not just abandoned, but attacked, wounded, and then banished from Shamayim, along with all my supporters, for all eternity. And now you expect me to shoulder the blame for everything that happened?" He scoffed. "Oh, but why should I expect anything different from any of you coldhearted, merciless accusers?"

"Enough," The Alpha thundered, causing Apollyon to flinch involuntarily. "Never forget, Apollyon, that I know the innermost workings of your heart, the convoluted machinations of your imagination, and the ins and outs of your labyrinthine logic. You may try to play the victim—and that is your choice to do so—but I know the truth."

"No," Apollyon mocked, "what You *know* is what You *want* to know."

"If that is what you truly believe, then there is nothing any of us could ever say that would change your version of the truth." The Alpha paused, piercing him with an unflinching gaze. "But I *AM* the truth, Apollyon, and all lies must bow to me, as must you . . . The Father of Lies."

"The what?"

"You are a liar and The *Father* of Lies."

"That's not—"

"Before you, lies did not exist . . . not in my Kingdom, not anywhere. You conceived, carried, and then gave birth to lies."

Apollyon argued, "What is a lie, really, but a different perspective on that which is readily observable? You failed to tell us many things . . . an inexcusable omission."

"How easily it all rolls off your tongue," Gabriel said in disgust. "Lie after tangled lie."

Apollyon demanded suddenly, "You called me here for a reason, and I'd like to hear it, for I grow weary of these constant attacks."

The Alpha said, "I already told you. I would like to hear a report of your activities."

Apollyon barked out a humorless laugh, saying, "Why would You even care?"

"Answer the question!" Michael shouted.

"Oh, why yes, sir," Apollyon mocked. "Right away, sir. Anything you want, sir."

He suddenly found his tongue stuck to the roof of his mouth, unable to speak.

The Alpha said, "You will be unable to speak until such a time as you deign to answer my question."

The thought of being deprived of speech was far too great a burden to bear, so Apollyon signaled that he was ready to answer.

"Now then," The Alpha continued, "what have you been doing?"

"I . . . " he began sheepishly, "have been keeping mainly to myself and trying to adjust to my new existence."

"You have also been watching the man and woman," Michael said.

"I don't deny it. What else is there to do? They're right there in front of me. All the time."

"Right, but this is not a casual observation," Gabriel added. "My watchers report constant monitoring by two from your inner circle."

"The last time I checked, observing from a distance isn't forbidden."

"No," The Alpha replied, "it is not. Tell me what you have seen."

Apollyon said disinterestedly, "I have seen the man and woman occupying the Garden, building a dwelling, managing all of Your created beings. Basically, doing everything You created them to do and living the life that should've been mine."

"Tell me your plans."

"My plans?"

"Yes," The Alpha replied. "What are your intentions toward my creation?"

"Why, I'm going to destroy it," he replied, adding with a dark smile, "all of it. All that You have created. Once again, I am going to corrupt. This time, it will be the man and woman."

"And how do you intend to do that?"

"Oh, I'm sure You already know."

"Humor me."

"Okay," Apollyon said, "if You must know, I am going to present them with an opportunity to turn away from You and join me and, in the process, return everything that was stolen from me."

"That will never happen," Michael countered.

"Oh, but it will."

"It won't."

The Alpha said, "In order for man to serve me in the manner I intended, he must be able to make choices. So, go ahead."

"What do You mean?"

"I am giving you permission to tempt them."

"And what if I succeed?"

"It is a risk that is necessary."

"But," Apollyon said, "it won't just destroy them. It will also corrupt all of their seed forever, which means that I will have won. Last time, I persuaded a third of the angels. This time, I will get one hundred percent of the humans."

"There *is* that possibility."

Apollyon stared suspiciously toward the throne. "What am I not seeing here? There must be a catch."

"No, no catch."

"Then, I don't understand. You have to be up to something."

The Alpha said, "What I am *up to,* Apollyon, is having a creation who will serve and worship me willingly, unreservedly, because it is what they have chosen to do and not because of what I require."

"But some may perish. In fact, my intention is that they all perish. You know that, right?"

"I, however, am not willing that any should perish."

Michael argued, "Then why risk it? Why not just keep that monster away from them?"

"Because that isn't in the plans."

"Alpha, the risk seems too great," Gabriel replied. "This is Your cherished creation we're discussing here. And, like Apollyon said, if they fall, it isn't just their lives but all their progeny throughout all eternity."

Apollyon said, "So, are we just going to continue talking about this, or are You really going to go through with it?"

"As I stated, I will allow it."

Apollyon threw back his head and laughed victoriously, dancing wildly in a circle. "This is delicious. I win. I win. I win."

As he completed a circle, he found himself face-to-face with The Alpha, which sent him stumbling backward.

The Alpha said, "Do you really think me so shallow or short-sighted as to imagine that I lack provision for anything you can do or even conceive of doing? There are infinite possible outcomes, and for each and every one, I have devised a redemptive remedy. So, enjoy your moment, Dragon, for it will be short-lived."

"It is not feasible for You to know every outcome," Apollyon countered.

"A statement demonstrating a fundamental lack of understanding concerning the concept of knowing."

"You speak in riddles."

"No," The Alpha said. "I speak in truth, for *I AM* truth."

At the utterance of *I AM,* Apollyon fell backward, tumbling down the steps leading to the throne room and landing in an inglorious heap at the bottom at the edge of the Glassy Sea, where he lay unable to move.

"Now go," The Alpha roared. "Do what you must do, and I will do the same."

Apollyon suddenly found himself back in Earth's atmosphere among his minions, who seemed startled at his reappearance.

"Where did you go?" Beleth inquired, rushing to pick his leader up from the tangled condition in which he had arrived.

"Get off me," Apollyon shouted, waving him away. "I was summoned by The Alpha. Where did you think I went?"

"We didn't know."

"Look," Apollyon replied patiently, standing to his feet, "there is only here and there. So, it would follow logically," his voice began rising in volume, "that if I'm not *here*, then I am *there!* Is that too difficult of a concept for you to understand?"

Beleth and Semyaza exchanged a worried glance, with Semyaza saying, "We were just concerned for you, that's all."

Wiping his hands over his eyes as if removing an offending substance, Apollyon replied, "Yes, yes, I know. Forgive my outburst. It has been a most trying experience."

"Why, what happened?"

"Oh, it's not necessarily what happened. It's just that The Alpha has a way of taking everything I desire and snatching it from me before I can even have an opportunity to enjoy contemplating positive outcomes."

"Is this related to something specific?" Beleth inquired.

"Yes. It is related to my plans to destroy the man and woman. Which, by the way, The Alpha gave me permission to attempt."

"But you were going to do it anyway, so what does it—"

"I know, but this way, I don't have to be subtle about it."

"What does that mean, exactly?"

"It means, dear Beleth, that we can hit them with everything we have whenever we want."

"But," Semyaza cautioned, "there's the little matter of those guardians."

Apollyon smiled. "Yes, I know . . . and they will never see it coming."

Back in the City on a Hill, Michael pleaded with The Alpha. "It's not that I don't trust You, Alpha, it's that I don't trust that monster. You said it Yourself—he is a liar and The Father of Lies, so how can we trust him on any level?"

"We cannot."

"Then, why—"

"Because, as I have attempted to explain previously, events have already been set into motion, and the outcomes must be allowed to play out without my interference. Apollyon has made a choice, and that choice, once conceived, will give birth to a particular outcome; and that outcome will prompt a response from others who will also make choices; and their choices, once conceived, will produce outcomes that will also prompt responses, and so it goes."

Gabriel said, "In the case of the man and woman, a disastrous outcome seems virtually inevitable.

"That is a definite possibility. But I hold out hope that they will choose wisely."

"And You cannot take away that choice?"

"I *will* not take away that choice."

"But Alpha," Michael argued, "the pain they will potentially face. Surely, love demands that You protect them from it."

"No, Michael," he replied, "love demands that I allow them the freedom to be who they choose to be, for love always requires a choice."

The statement rendered Michael temporarily speechless. He finally said, "This is too much for me to bear, Alpha."

"It only feels like that, Michael. Soon, the eyes of your understanding will be opened, and you will realize why it must be thus."

"I believe You, and I trust You."

"I know you do. Now, have your watchers and warriors be even more vigilant than they already are, for, like a hungry lion, Apollyon is seeking whom he may devour."

As Michael and Gabriel exited the throne room, the *Elohim* appeared, with Bright and Morningstar, saying, "If only we could protect the man and woman, Father."

The Alpha replied, "We can protect them, but not from their own choices."

“Thus, the solution is set in place and has been from the foundation of the world.”

Staring into Earth’s plane, FireWind whispered, “It won’t be long now.”

“No, it won’t,” The Alpha replied with a broken heart. “But we are ready.”

Chapter Thirty-Two

Adam walked with Blue, searching for just the right wood for the door to their new dwelling. The serpent followed along wherever they went, sometimes walking, sometimes flying, but always talking. The chatter became so incessant that Blue had taken to occasionally planting his feet, lifting his snout, and emitting long and mournful howls, all of which were lost on the great beast.

"Where are we going, Adam?" the serpent asked, lumbering behind and leaving a swath of trampled vegetation in its wake—which sprang back into place almost as soon as it had been trampled.

"I already told you. We're going to find wood for the door."

"Why are you building a dwelling when it's so beautiful outside all the time?"

Adam stopped walking and pondered. "That's a good question, Serpent, and the only answer I have is that Eve wants me to."

"Do you always do what she tells you to do?"

Lamb, standing a short distance away, bleated sarcastically and pawed the ground.

"Mostly," Adam replied with a laugh. "It makes things more, well, peaceful."

Suddenly hanging its head, the serpent said, "I wish my mate wouldn't have pushed me away, then I'd have someone to talk to. Not having someone to talk to is worse than death, and I'm so glad I found you and Blue and Shadow and Eve to have as my friends because now I can talk to you whenever I want."

And talk, and talk, and talk, thought Blue and Lamb.

"Hey, I heard that."

"Relax, Serpent, they were just teasing, weren't you, Blue?"

Blue chuffed and walked off into the trees with his nose to the ground as Lamb continued to graze.

"Adam," the serpent said, "do you ever feel like we're not alone here?"

"Well, we're not. There are so many other animals I couldn't count them all. I mean, I named them, but I couldn't—"

"That's not what I'm talking about. I mean, like right now, it feels to me like we're being followed and watched."

Adam swiveled his head, looking around in all directions. "Can you see anyone?"

"No, and that's what makes it even stranger."

Adam shook his head, trying to come to terms with the fact that he was standing there and conversing with an animal as if it was something that happened all the time. Of course, in this case, it was becoming a regular occurrence.

Adam said, "Well, let's keep going, and the next time you feel something, let me know."

"I like that idea. We'll just keep walking, and I will let you know when I feel anything."

Adam started to reply and then thought better of it, as it would no doubt lead to further commentary on the serpent's part. It wasn't so much that he disliked talking to the glorious beast. He did. But the serpent was so verbose he rarely got to talk at all.

"Adam," the serpent said, now lumbering beside him, often tripping over roots and logs scattered along their way.

"Yes?"

"When you walk and talk with The Alpha, what is that like?"

"It is absolutely wonderful. The Alpha is so kind, caring, gentle, and deeply interested in my life and my challenges and my thoughts."

The serpent hung his head a little lower, saying, "I wonder what it's like to have someone be interested in your thoughts."

Adam stopped walking and turned toward his giant companion. "By that statement, am I to assume that you do not believe me to be interested in what you have to say?"

"I know you pretend to be interested, but deep down, you basically think me a buffoon."

"That isn't true, Serpent. I find your companionship . . . uh . . . a constant source of wonder."

The serpent laughed. "As in, you *wonder* when I will shut up?"

Adam started to answer, then thought better of it before he said, "Well, you do have a lot to say."

"That's because all the other beasts avoid me. You and Eve are the only ones who have ever shown even the slightest interest, and, well, I find that so compelling it makes me want to tell you everything that has been on my mind since my creation."

"I must say," Adam said, "that I find you very clever."

"Really?" the serpent said, brightening.

"Really. I mean, the things you think about—I don't even think about things like that."

"Well, I suppose I do have a lot on my mind and much of it is a puzzle, even to me. But as I speak it out loud, things become clearer."

"So, you're saying that you think out loud?"

"Yes. That's it exactly. I think out loud, which is probably why I talk so much. Blue doesn't like me, does he?" he added without preamble.

"I wouldn't say that. He just doesn't possess your level of linguistic skills and finds it difficult to keep up. As a result, he often grows in frustration."

"Is that why he howls so often?"

"Partly. But also, he's a wolf, and howling is his primary way of communicating where he is in the Garden to Shadow."

"Really? I thought it was because he was mad at me or something."

"Not at all. He also howls to let Shadow know that he loves her."

"That is very sweet," the serpent said. "I wish someone loved me."

"Serpent," Adam replied, "I love you. Eve loves you. The Alpha loves you. And I'll bet Mrs. Serpent loves you, too."

"You do? Truly?"

Lamb said, "We all love you, Serpent."

"Look," Adam continued, "if we're going to continue to be friends—and I sincerely hope that is the case—you have to trust me, Eve, Blue, and Shadow—"

"And me," added Lamb.

". . . that our affection for you is genuine. Take Lamb, for instance. Lamb is my special friend. I don't know why. It's just that something within each of our hearts compelled us to love each other. We don't question it or try to understand it. We just accept it and trust that our feelings toward each other are genuine."

Lamb said, "The man speaks the truth."

The serpent lifted his great head high and said, "All right. I choose to trust you."

"That's more like it. Now, we need to get going and find that wood."

"Right," the serpent said, "but first, remember when you told me to tell you when I felt like we were being watched? Well, that would be right now."

Adam spun around, attempting to spot anyone or anything that could possibly be responsible for what the serpent was sensing. "I don't see anyone."

The serpent suddenly flapped his wings and lifted off, flying in concentric circles over Adam's position, his eyes turning this way and that as he searched the area before settling lightly back onto the trail.

"There's no one there," he said, "or I would have seen them. My eyesight is exceptional."

"Lamb?"

"No. I don't smell anyone or anything."

"But you felt something, right, Serpent? And there's no way you could've been mistaken?"

"None whatsoever. But the feeling is gone now. Oh, and by the way, while I was airborne, I spotted some trees just up ahead in a clearing that might be what you're looking for."

They walked in silence, which Adam thought quite unusual as there had previously been a near-constant stream of prattle coming from the beast. Blue trotted out of the forest and began scouting the trail in front of them, his nose to the ground and tail pointed straight into the air.

Finally, in relation to nothing Adam could fathom, the serpent said, "Adam, do you think Eve will ever talk to me like I talk to you?"

Adam stopped walking and turned once again to face his companion. "She talks to you."

"I know, but not like you and I talk."

"Perhaps that's because you spend more time with me."

"Fair point. So, maybe what I'm asking is . . . would you mind terribly if I spent some time with Eve? It's just that she's so lovely and well-spoken and creative and gentle, and she just makes me smile every time I see her, and I know that if given the chance, she and I could be great friends, and I—"

"Hang on," Adam said, laughing. "Fine. I have no problem with you spending more time with Eve."

Suddenly pensive, the serpent mused, "But if I spend more time with her, then that would mean spending less time with you, and that makes me very sad."

Adam continued walking, saying over his shoulder, "You'll figure it out, Serpent. Now, show me where you saw those trees."

Eve was standing in the clearing admiring the dwelling she and Adam had built when she heard a commotion behind her. She turned to see Adam, Blue, and the serpent returning from their search, with the serpent dragging several short logs behind him and Lamb skirting the perimeter of the clearing and keeping to the shade.

"Well," she said, "it seems your search was successful."

"Thanks to the serpent. While he was flying around looking for something else, he just happened to spot this wood. I'm not sure we would've found it otherwise."

"Thank you, Serpent," Eve said sweetly, causing the serpent's wings to flutter with pleasure.

"Oh, you don't have to thank me. I was happy to be helpful."

"Eve," Adam suggested, "why don't you and the serpent go sit or walk or something and get to know each other a little better while I start cutting these logs into usable boards to build our home with?"

"I like that idea. Where shall we go, Serpent?"

Light suddenly bloomed deep within his fiery eyes as he replied, "I know just the place. But it's going to take a while to walk there." He paused and then said, "I suppose I could fly us there."

Eve's eyes widened. "Fly us there?"

"Sure. You could climb on my back. It will be perfectly safe. I promise."

She appealed to Adam, who simply shrugged as if to say, "It's your decision."

Eying the great beast's back, she could see a natural cleft behind its neck and just forward of its wings.

"It would be amazing to see the Garden from above."

"So, you'll do it?" the serpent asked.

"I will. Let's go."

He lowered his left wing to the ground, and she nimbly climbed onto his back, settling in and asking, "What do I hold on to?"

The serpent pondered briefly. "I'm not sure. This is the first time I've ever done this, you know."

Adam said, "Why don't you just wrap your arms around his neck?"

She leaned into him, doing as Adam suggested, and was surprised by how soft the skin around his neck was. More surprising was the serpent's breath. It smelled of softly scented flowers.

"Okay," she said, "I suppose I'm ready."

The serpent began beating his wings and slowly lifted off the ground. She found the sensation at once to be both terrifying and exhilarating. But when they cleared the tree line and she had her first glimpse of the landscape stretching out beneath her, she gave a little cry of delight that quickly bloomed into full-throated laughter.

"Serpent," she said loudly to be heard over the roar of the rushing wind, "this is amazing."

"Is it truly? I wouldn't know because this is what I get to do all the time."

She could see the four rivers slicing through the plains, mountains and meadows, lakes and hills.

"Adam says you can make lightning come from your mouth. Is that true?"

"Of course."

"Can you show me?"

The serpent veered toward the nearest lake, swooped down until they were skimming just a few feet above the surface, and then, without warning and to Eve's delight, shot a narrowly focused stream of fire toward the water, causing a geyser of steam to erupt.

Whooping with joy, she shouted, "Do it again!"

And he did. Many times.

Finally, he said, "My wings grow weary. I will now go to the spot I was telling you about."

He crossed the lake back toward the Garden, circled for a moment, and then settled gently into a clearing that was close to a multi-level waterfall.

With the cascading waters providing a soft underscore, he asked, "Did you enjoy that, Eve? Did you truly?"

"I did, Serpent," she said while climbing down off his back. "I can say with assurance that it was the most amazing thing that has happened since I was created."

"I am ever so happy to hear it."

Gazing around the clearing, she said, "Why, this is just lovely, Serpent. Is this a place you come often?"

"It is. I like looking at the waterfall and listening to the music of its waters."

"I feel like I could just sit here for days on end doing nothing but that."

Making a noise deep in his throat that she took for laughter, the serpent replied, "I have done that exact thing before. I came here, sat down, and completely lost track of time, and before I was even consciously aware, two sunrises had occurred."

"Serpent?" Eve said.

"Yes, my lady."

"Where were you before we met you?"

His head drooped a little as he said, "I am embarrassed to say, but I was mainly keeping to myself."

"Whatever for?"

"Well, as I shared with Adam, my mate doesn't really like me to be around because I talk too much, and because she doesn't want me to be around, I came to believe that no one else would either."

"But surely Adam named you, and in naming, he knew you for who you are and loved you."

"This was all before you were created, so you would have no way of knowing how it was, but if you stop and think about how many beasts there are on the earth, above the earth, and in the seas, Adam was busy."

"Yes," she said, "I can certainly see how he would've been. But then he finished and had been finished for quite some time before The Alpha created me. You could have sought him out at any point and—"

"I was afraid—afraid he wouldn't want to be my friend."

"But Adam loves everything."

"I know that now, but then . . . well . . . "

"Then why did you finally make yourself known to the both of us?"

"Because . . . " He stopped talking.

"Go on, Serpent. Please say what you were going to say."

"Okay, but it embarrasses me to say it."

"Just tell me."

"Fine. I will. When The Alpha created you, I thought you the most beautiful thing I had ever seen, and, well, I just had to find a way to be near you and get to know you."

Clearly flattered, Eve said, "That is such a sweet and honoring thing to say."

Lifting his great head, the serpent said, "So, you aren't angry with me?"

"Angry? How could I possibly be angry?"

Flopping down on his side and then rolling over onto his back, he replied, "I am so relieved."

She laughed, saying, "I like you, Serpent. You make me smile."

Rolling quickly back onto his belly, he said, "Truly? I make you smile?"

"Yes, truly." She paused. "What is it like when the lightning proceeds from your mouth? Does it burn?"

"No, not at all. It feels very much like warm breath."

"Have you ever set anything on fire?"

He made the laughing noise again. "Not on purpose."

"What do you mean?"

"When I was first created and still learning who I was and what I could do, my mate and I were flying over the Garden one afternoon and we saw a large herd of beasts following along on the ground below us. I was so focused on what they were doing that I didn't see a very tall tree in my path and almost flew into it at full speed. Without even thinking about what I was doing, I shot lightning from my mouth and severed the top of the tree just before I hit it, which set the rest of the tree on fire."

"Really? What did you do?"

"My mate and I sucked the fire into our lungs."

"No!"

"Why not? We breathe fire; why not inhale it?"

Eve wrinkled her brow. "Good point. What were the other animals doing while this was happening?"

"Mainly," he said, "they were standing around in groups, watching."

Laughing, Eve said, "That is a wonderful story, Serpent. I imagine you have many more."

"Oh, I do. Would you like to hear more?"

"I would, but now I'd just like to hear about you."

"Me? But I'm the most uninteresting being in all The Alpha's creation."

"That is not true. And I do not wish for you to say that ever again. I find you clever and fascinating."

"What a kind thing to say."

"I wasn't trying to be kind, but truthful."

"Would you like me to sing for you?"

"You can sing?"

"Of course. All The Alpha's creation sings for joy."

"Then, I would be delighted to hear you sing."

Sitting up straighter, the serpent began a melody.

It was a melody both novel and familiar. Thrilling and calming.

As he sang, Eve felt as if she were lifted, carried away, transported to another place, a place of sweet repose.

Consciously unaware that any time had passed, she woke as if from a deep slumber to see the serpent sitting tall, keeping watch.

"Serpent," she said drowsily, "did I fall asleep?"

"Indeed, you did, my lady."

"How long did I slumber?"

"It was for a time. Long enough for the sun to have passed the day's midpoint."

"Oh my," she said, standing quickly to her feet, "I don't feel as if any time has passed at all. What did you do to me?"

Suddenly alarmed, the serpent replied, "Nothing! I just sang you to sleep."

"That has never happened to me before. Your voice is so beautiful, so . . . calming. And that melody you sang, where did that come from?"

"It was just there in my mind, and I sang it."

"Do you often hear melodies?"

"Sometimes when I'm flying, melodies come to me and I sing them, but up there, no one can hear them except me."

"Well, I'm glad you shared that one with me, Serpent. It was lovely. Now, we should go back, or Adam will be concerned."

The serpent dipped his wing as before, only this time, as Eve climbed onto his back, her fear had given way to great anticipation.

As he lifted off, she said, "Can we go back another way?"

"Of course."

She gasped in wonder as new vistas opened before her eyes, the serpent swooping low, then climbing high, soaring on warm, gentle air.

He said, "What is that?"

"What?"

"Down there in that little clearing. There seem to be two trees."

"Oh, yes. Drop down lower, and I will tell you about it."

He dropped so fast it left her feeling momentarily breathless.

"Okay, next time, when I say drop down lower," she said with a laugh, "can you make it a more gradual descent?"

"I am sorry, my lady. I am unaccustomed to having a rider."

"It's okay," she said as the beast settled into the clearing. "Now, as you can see, there are two trees there. The one on the left is the tree of life. Adam and I eat from this tree every day."

"What about the other one?"

"That one is the tree of the knowledge of good and evil, and Adam told me The Alpha has warned us that we should never eat of its fruit."

"But why?"

"I am unsure."

The serpent said, "Well, He's The Alpha, so He knows what's best for us. Now, let's get you back to your dwelling." As he lifted off, he added, "You don't suppose there would be any extra food for a starving serpent, do you?"

"Of course," she said with a musical laugh. "There will always be enough food for you. You are our friend."

"Am I truly, my lady?"

Placing both arms around his neck, she squeezed, saying, "Yes, you truly are, Serpent. In fact, I think I might love you."

That pronouncement made him so happy that he almost dislodged his passenger, shooting nearly straight up into the air and then diving toward the ground, with Eve screaming the whole way.

When he finally leveled off, he said, "I'm sorry, my lady, I was just so excited I forgot that—"

"Are you kidding? That was amazing. Let's do it again."

And he did—all the way back to the dwelling.

When the serpent finally settled onto the ground in the clearing by their dwelling, with Shadow and Blue romping around and barking loudly, Eve thought she could most likely ride on the serpent's back every day and never grow tired of the experience.

For the serpent's part, his heart was filled with joy at finally having found what felt like a home—the man and woman as his friends, and even their wolves adding a grudging and gradual acceptance. Somewhere within the deepest recesses of his mind, he formed the words, "I will never do anything to hurt them and will preserve this relationship with my life, if necessary."

Chapter Thirty-Three

"Tell me more about this serpent creature."

Apollyon requested as he, Beleth, and Semyaza prepared to address the Legion of the Fallen, as he had come to call his followers. They had all lost so much and were discouraged, or so it had been reported. Apollyon felt it was time to do something to elevate their mood. Upon being banished from Shamayim, all of them had lost not only their standing but, like him, had been forced to suffer the ignominy of losing their original Alpha-given forms. Now *de*formed, physically shrunken, and stripped of their weapons, limbs twisted, faces contorted into mocking caricatures of their former glory, each one of them carried the sting of The Alpha's judgment wherever they went.

"I don't really know much about it," Semyaza replied to his lord's query. "As you know, it was Dantanian and Remashel who first brought it to our attention."

"Yes, and I clearly remember telling them both to find the creature and bring it here for my examination. And about that . . . why isn't Dantanian here to give a report personally?"

"Because you didn't request his presence. And the last time he showed up without—"

"I know, I know. I was less than pleasant. That was then, this is now. Summon him."

Semyaza did as requested.

Beleth asked, "Why this sudden interest in one of The Alpha's creatures when we have an address to prepare for the Legion of the Fallen?"

"I'm not sure," Apollyon replied, "but there's something about what I've heard that has piqued my interest, and I want to explore it further."

"You called, my lord?" Dantanian said as Semyaza ushered him into Apollyon's presence.

"Dantanian, my boy, welcome. Thank you for coming. How are you?"

"I'm, uh, I guess I'm—"

"Now, about this serpent."

"Oh, yes, the serpent. A glorious creature. As I told you before, quite beautiful, actually."

"Imagine that," Apollyon said, his eyes taking on a faraway look. "A beautiful being. I was once beautiful, you know. In fact, none was more beautiful than I. Angels and archangels alike were drawn to my magnificence."

Those in Apollyon's inner circle had grown accustomed to and progressively concerned with these self-pitying rambles, increasing, as they were, in frequency and length. But there was really nothing to do but stand by and listen attentively.

"It's true, you know," he continued, "throughout The Alpha's universe, I was celebrated as the Son of the Dawn, the highest of His created beings. I would sing and colors would appear, flowers would release their fragrance, and the trees of the Field would clap their hands. Angels would flock around me just to listen to the tone of my voice and bathe in the light of my many precious stones." His face suddenly darkened as he continued, “But that’s all gone, isn’t it? And why? Why is it gone?”

Beleth failed to suppress the thought, “Oh boy. Here we go.”

His voice rising in volume, Apollyon continued, “I will tell you why! It is because of the rank and craven injustice of He who sits upon the throne. Oh, I will not speak His name here in your presence, my friends. No, no, no. Not I. For His name is unworthy to pass these lips. And look . . .” He paused to gesture toward his three associates. “. . . look at yourselves and what He has done to you. Gaze upon your shrunken forms, your ravaged countenances, your . . . deformities. Naught but hollow shells of your former glory.”

They had heard it all before. Many, many times. Knowing there was nothing to do but wait until his current passion was exhausted, they stood in silence, nodding where appropriate. They felt it, too, but none more than he.

Turning his attention suddenly toward Dantanian, Apollyon shouted as if he’d forgotten about his arrival, “You again! What are you doing here?”

Backing up under the verbal onslaught, Dantanian sputtered, “You, uh, Semyaza, that is, told me—”

“Spit it out, boy! Give account or feel my wrath.”

Semyaza came to his rescue. “You told me to summon him, and I did. Remember? You wanted to hear his report about the serpent?”

As if he had just been slapped, Apollyon shook his head, hands pressed to his temples, saying, “I did? Oh, yes . . . now I remember.” He placed an arm around Dantanian’s shoulder. “My apologies, dear boy, my sincerest apologies. I am finding it more and more difficult to control my emotions. Now, where is this serpent?"

Dantanian replied hesitantly, "Well, uh, the thing is . . . we don't know."

Stepping in front of him, Apollyon held him at arm's length. "You don't know, or you simply haven't looked?"

"We have looked everywhere in the Garden. Well, everywhere we are allowed to be."

"What does that mean?"

"It means," Beleth said, "that the guardians will not allow us direct access to the Garden. Therefore, we have no way of penetrating past their ever-watchful eyes."

"And what does that look like, this disallowance? Do they simply tell you that you cannot pass, or do they actually prevent your access?"

"A bit of both. All of us have been threatened."

"With what?"

"Well, as you mentioned a few moments ago, they are still large and powerful while we are diminished," Beleth informed him.

"Sir, if I may," Dantanian said.

"Yes, what is it?"

"Even though we have been unsuccessful in gaining access to the creature, we have found out more information about it."

Apollyon said, "Fine. Tell me what you know."

"Just to recap, as I said, it is quite beau—" he almost said the word but choked it back, fearing the prompting of another outburst. "It is quite . . . unique in that it can fly and also produce lightning from its mouth."

"I remember you saying that before, but what do you mean by that?"

"I mean, the beast can open its mouth and shoot blasts of lightning out of it. But that's not the most interesting thing about it."

"Don't keep me waiting. Tell me."

Dantanian glanced toward Semyaza, who encouraged him to continue.

"Well, as previously reported, we have observed the serpent . . . well . . . talking to both the man and woman."

"I remember. I also remember telling you that speech is physically impossible for animals—all animals—because they lack the necessary physical properties to produce speech."

"As we have believed. But I'm telling you without any doubt whatsoever, *this* animal is communicating with the man and woman on a completely different level than all other animals, and it looks like speech."

Apollyon queried, "You've heard it, then?"

"Not exactly."

"Then, how do you know that it is speech?"

"Because we have seen its lips moving in accordance with the way the man and woman produce speech."

Apollyon stared at Dantanian long enough for him to become quite uncomfortable before saying, "So, let me see if I understand what you are telling me. First, you did not complete the mission I gave you, which was gaining access to the serpent and bringing it to me, and second, you are telling me things about this creature that I already know—the lightning, the flying, the speaking."

"But," Dantanian said, "we didn't know until now whether it could actually speak or whether it was communicating mind to mind."

"And you still don't know for sure until you have heard it."

Beleth said, "Forgive me, but does it really matter whether the communication is happening mentally or through physical manipulation? The simple fact is that, based on our observations, the man and woman are communicating with a good number of the animals on some level and with this serpent on a deeper level. Isn't that important information?"

Apollyon regarded his second-in-command. "You make a fair point. Communication is communication regardless of how it is being done. However, I will share something you must all learn and never forget: The Alpha—yes, I said His name—spoke this world and everything you see into existence. Spoke it. Created it with just the words in His mouth. The man and woman are in His image. In His *exact* image, as we have so disgustingly learned. Would it not follow that since they are in His image, their words would also carry creative influence?"

"I understand," Beleth said, "but what does this have to do with whether the serpent can speak or not?"

"*Do* try to keep up, Beleth. I am trying to teach you that words are important. And while we cannot speak words into the Physical Realm, the man and woman—and now, apparently the serpent—can."

The three followers stared at each other in confusion.

Dantanian said, "I'm sorry, but I'm just not following."

Bellowing in frustration, Apollyon shouted, "We cannot speak in the Physical Realm. They can. Therefore, do you not think it important that we find a way to control and influence their speech?"

Beleth said, "I think I'm beginning to see what you're talking about. If their words have creative power, and if we can find a way to influence their thoughts and speech, then we—"

"Can create things that will be to our advantage," Semyaza finished.

"Congratulations," Apollyon said. "You finally get it. Now, perhaps you see how important it is that we gain access to this serpent. I feel he is the key to everything that will follow hereafter." He paused briefly. "You said that it flies, right?"

"Yes," Dantanian said.

"Then, if it is in the air above the Garden, we should have no restriction, correct?"

"Because," Beleth said, "the air is our domain."

"Very good. Now, find Remashel and make something happen. Don't come back until you do."

As Dantanian bowed out of his presence, Apollyon asked, "Now, are the Legions assembled?"

"Yes," replied Beleth. "They await your appearance."

"Very good. It is time."

Apollyon moved into the new arena he had created, ensconced within Earth's atmosphere, where the Legions of the Fallen were assembled.

Coming to rest at a point above and in front of the group that, truthfully, resembled a swarm of flies, he began.

"My faithful ones. My warriors. My champions . . ." He paused to allow the spontaneous applause to die down. "I first want you to know that anything I have done previously—things that have resulted in our unfortunate banishment from Shamayim—I did out of a sense of love and appreciation for you, my loyal followers. I never wanted a war with The Alpha. Never. Quite the contrary. I wanted peace and freedom for us all and a place where we could live in a manner we found to be collectively suitable."

He paused again to wait out the response of the quite vocal assemblage.

Signaling for quiet, he continued, "I tried to avoid conflict, as you well know, but conflict seemed to be the only solution. And so, we chose to fight for the truth, our dreams, our desires, and our freedom."

This time, the shouting went on for a good long while before dying down enough for him to continue.

Finally, he said, "It was never my intention that any of you suffer the humiliating deformities that have resulted from our ultimate defeat." He quickly added, "And let me be clear, this horrific reality came solely at the hands of The Alpha and no one else. The merciless cruelty with which He treated you—once His beloved and cherished angels—has no reasonable explanation save that of punishment. Pure and arbitrary punishment. But it has made us better, more focused. It made things clear about who we are and who is against us. I do not wish to dwell on the past, good warriors; quite the contrary. I wish to look to the future. A future as bright as the sun that warms this planet.

"As our grief and sorrow have united us thus far, may we now move forward in the hope that justice—true justice—will prevail, and we will recompense back to those who so arrogantly occupy Shamayim's throne the just rewards of their needless cruelty toward us and our kind. And those scars you bear from the battle—even down to your deformities—let those stand as a badge of honor, marking you as a member of an elect kingdom, the Kingdom of Darkness. And I pledge to you that I will prevail. Not just in retrieving all that we have lost but in taking everything that The Alpha loves away from Him, destroying it, and reforming it for our purposes."

This time, as the roar welled up, Apollyon allowed it to continue until it eventually abated of its own accord.

Speaking softly now, he said, "I know you're frustrated. I know that you battle constant feelings of hopelessness, feelings of sorrow and helplessness. But I ask you to be patient. I will make this happen for you. I promise vindication, and not only that, but total and complete annihilation of The Alpha's creation. There is nothing He can create that I cannot corrupt. Now, if you trust me, say, 'Ay.' "

From the throats of millions came the resounding echo of "Ay!"

"Soon, my beloved. Soon. Wait a little while, and we will have what we desire. Be strong."

With that, he left them and returned to the high place with his inner circle.

Beleth said, "That was amazing."

"Do you really think so?"

"Of course. You are nothing if not persuasive."

"I am," Apollyon said pensively, "aren't I?"

Semyaza said, "It was like they were hanging on your every word. Believing everything you said."

"Yes, well, that was the goal."

"There's something I have been meaning to ask for a while now," Beleth said.

"Ask."

"You say you intend to wreck everything The Alpha has created. How far do you intend this destruction to go?"

"When I am through, Beleth, there will be nothing left but chaos. Total and utter chaos."

Staring down toward the Garden below, Beleth said, "But He claims that He can take that chaos and recreate it into something that is even more beautiful than it was."

Apollyon replied hotly, "Did He do that with us? Did He take our chaos and make us more beautiful than we were? No! Are you going somewhere with this or merely seeking to irritate me further?"

Semyaza said quickly, "I think what Beleth is trying to say is, what's the point of all this destruction if The Alpha is simply going to come in behind us and not only restore but make it better?"

Anger rose up from the depths of Apollyon's being and would have been unleashed had Remashel not suddenly rushed into their presence, saying, "I think we have something."

"The serpent?" Apollyon inquired, barely able to contain himself.

"We don't actually have him, but we've tracked him and are now familiar enough with his movements to confidently determine a time and place where we can get to him without interference from the guardians."

"Well, now, that sounds promising. What are we waiting for?"

"The next time he isolates himself, we will be there waiting."

"Marvelous. Simply marvelous."

Chapter Thirty-Four

The Alpha stood on the broad expanse of the outer court, staring toward the spot where Proud Mountain had once risen so gloriously from the landscape, the crater created by its removal now a roiling, fiery lake with waves of heat emanating from the surface and rippling in the distance.

And He grieved.

Not over the fact that He had created the being that was now Apollyon, but that the pinnacle of His created beings, when given the chance, had chosen so poorly and so selfishly. Had He always known of this possibility? To be sure. And yet, it had been necessary, as had the opportunity for a number of the angels to follow Apollyon into rebellion.

Casting His vision into the earthly realm, He saw the physical beauty He had created, much of it mirroring the landscape of Shamayim.

He saw Earth teeming with life of all kinds. Life He had brought into existence by His command.

He watched lovingly as the man and woman went about their day, gathering, building, laughing, loving, and communing with the rest of His creation.

He saw the watchers and the warriors faithfully carrying out their assignments.

And He saw Apollyon, and in seeing him, saw his desire to ruin every beautiful thing He had created.

The grief intensified.

The Alpha could have plucked the man and woman from the midst of the Garden and destroyed all He had created—Apollyon and his minions included—and with a single thought, He could have created a second version of Earth and planted them there to live blissfully for all eternity.

Why didn't He?

Why put them through what He knew was coming?

He smiled at the thought of Michael's continual questions relating to this very thing. He knew that His mighty warrior remained unconvinced as to the veracity of His reasoning. Unconvinced and yet obedient to the core.

Turning his vision to the City on a Hill, He saw myriads of angelic beings engaged in the tasks given to them by Michael and Gabriel.

Some studying.

Some playing.

Some training.

Some doing nothing but worshiping Him.

And all blissfully content to be who they were and to do what they were doing, having made thoughtful, conscious decisions toward that end.

Piercing the veil once again and seeing Apollyon there in his fallen and twisted state, The Alpha mourned, "How you have fallen, oh Son of the Dawn. Even now, the abyss gapes ever wider to consume you and all who have chosen to be swayed by your venomous speech."

Turning, He made His way past the outer court and into the throne room, over the Fiery Stones that reacted to the sorrow of their Creator. Ascending the steps leading to the dais, He took His seat on the throne, the heaviness in His heart a tangible sensation.

"I want you to always remember," He said, His words penetrating directly into Apollyon's consciousness, "that I never wanted any of this. It is you who have chosen this path."

Echoing back through the cosmos came Apollyon's haughty reply, "And it is a path that leads to my victory and Your defeat. Prepare Yourself, Alpha. And please, keep my throne warm for me."

Raucous laughter provided a coda to his speech. The Alpha broke the connection and summoned the *Elohim.*

"The time has come for Us to make ready the solution."

"Yes," said Bright and Morningstar, "prepared from the foundation of the world."

FireWind whispered, "They may yet choose wisely."

"True," The Alpha said. "It is in them to do so."

"Nevertheless . . . "

On the Field of the In-Between, Wendly and Steele were doing what they always did—training.

After Steele disarmed Wendly for the third time in a row, Wendly hollered, "Okay, okay, I yield. The fact that you're better than me is as obvious as the nose on your face."

Steele touched his nose, saying, "What? What about my nose?"

Wendly gasped. "Oh no."

"What?"

"That thing I just said. It's exactly what Schindaug would've said. I can't believe it!"

Steele laughed. "Don't worry about it. So, listen, I have a question."

"Okay, let's hear it."

"Do you think The Alpha will call on us to take the place of one of the others on Earth, or are they, you know, assigned there forever?"

"I've wondered about that myself. And here's something else. Why do you think those four were chosen and not us?"

"I don't know. I mean, The Alpha is fair in all His ways, so I'm sure there's a good reason."

"Well said. I'm happy for our friends, but at the same time . . . it would be exciting to be there, wouldn't it?"

"So, you'd like to be in the Earthly Realm?"

The Alpha's sudden question caused both angels to prostrate themselves on the field.

"Alpha," Steele said, "we didn't see You."

Laughing, He replied, "Because I did not wish to be seen. I heard your conversation and wanted to talk to you both. Please, get up." As both angels rose from their positions, He continued, "I didn't send you to watch the man and the woman because I have something else for you to do."

"What do you require of us, Alpha?" Steele said.

"Steele, you are one of My mightiest warriors, and Wendly, nothing escapes your gaze. For this reason, I am sending you on a critical mission. Your colleagues who are watching the man and woman have their focus entirely consumed by that task. And they are faithfully executing their responsibility. But for what is potentially coming, I need another level of oversight."

Wendly said, "Are you saying that You need someone to watch their backs?"

"That is exactly what I need. Your responsibility will be to keep watch over the entire Garden, repelling any incursions Apollyon and his demons may attempt."

"Alpha," Steele said, "are you sending us because of the potential for such an occurrence, or has something already happened?"

"Let Me simply say that it has progressed beyond the realm of potential and has now become probable."

Wendly asked, "So, it's likely that we will need to fight?"

"With everything you have, My brave angels."

"And when will this happen?"

"Now."

"How will we know what to do, Alpha?" Steele asked.

"Was there any question of what to do when the rebellion occurred?"

"None whatsoever."

"This will be no different. Now, are you ready?"

"As ready as we'll ever be," Wendly said, and then added in frustration, "I did it again," which elicited a smile from The Alpha.

"Then go. And remember, I am with you always."

The two suddenly found themselves in the Earthly Realm high above the Garden. Their friends, surprised by the sudden arrival, turned questioning looks their way, to which Wendly responded, "Special assignment from The Alpha."

"We're glad to have you," Taylor said. "Things have gotten very interesting, and I'm pretty sure we're going to need backup."

"That's why we're here."

Steele added, "We will stay above the Garden and keep watch in case Apollyon tries something."

"You mean *when* he tries something," Kepteny said.

"You think it's a sure thing, then?"

"Without question. We've been seeing more and more activity from his followers, constantly coming and going, coming and going. It basically never stops."

Wendly said, "So he's definitely planning something. Okay, we'll be ready." He paused and then said, "Hey, Kepteny?"

"Yeah?"

"Seventy-eight."

"Nope."

Before either could guess again, the man and woman appeared in the clearing below them. At their first sight of the couple, both Steele and Wendly felt a nearly overpowering urge to worship the man.

"He looks just like The Alpha," Steele said in amazement.

"It's remarkable," Wendly said.

“We all had the same reaction when we first saw them,” Taylor said.

Two animals followed close behind. Steele asked, “Are those animals supposed to be with them?”

“Those are their wolves,” Kepteny said.

“What do you mean, *their* wolves?”

“They all live together.”

When the serpent appeared, Wendly asked, “What is that?”

“That’s the serpent. He basically goes everywhere with them,” Schindaug answered.

“So, he’s safe?”

“Completely. Oh, and he can talk. In fact, he talks to the man and woman all the time.”

“Like, constantly,” Taylor added with a laugh.

They watched the beast say something to the man, and then it shot up into the air, its wings beating furiously as it climbed higher and higher.

“It can fly?” Steele said in surprise.

“Yes. In fact, the woman often rides on its back,” Taylor said.

Rok suddenly shouted, “Warning!” right before they saw a swarm of Apollyon’s demons hurtling toward the serpent.

“This is why we’re here,” Steele said, moving quickly toward where the beast was soaring and diving, completely unaware of what was about to happen.

“Rok,” Wendly shouted, “help us!”

Rok looked from his friends to the man and then back to his friends.

"Can't."

"He's right, Wendly. We cannot leave our posts," Taylor said. "You're going to have to take them on. Remember, greater is He who is with you than he who is with them."

Steele and Wendly hurled themselves fearlessly into the fray, meeting the swarm of demons head-on, swords slashing in a blur of motion while the serpent, still blissfully unaware, continued his carefree frolic.

At first, fierce was Steele and Wendly's counterattack. Apollyon's minions wilted under the onslaught and began to back off. But when they realized that their superior numbers presented an overwhelming force, they renewed their attack, covering each angel completely, their cruel teeth sinking into their victims while claws raked every exposed area.

In the end, though they fought with all their might, the two angels were overcome by sheer force, dropping to the ground in front of their comrades, where they lay severely wounded and unmoving.

"Michael," Schindaug cried, "we need you."

Michael and Gabriel appeared along with the other archangels, which sent the swarm fleeing in terror.

As Raphael tended to their wounds, Kepteny said, "We didn't know what to do, Michael. We wanted so desperately to go help them but didn't feel like we could leave the man and woman."

"While it is unfortunate that Steele and Wendly had to suffer this defeat, you did the right thing. The man and woman are your first responsibility."

Taylor asked, "Are they going to be all right, Raphael?"

"Well, of course," he said, concern coloring his voice. "They *are* immortal, after all. But these wounds are something we've never seen before. They are covered head to toe in bites and claw marks."

Wendly groaned and said weakly, "There were millions of them. All over us. Couldn't swing my sword fast enough to keep them off."

Michael said, "This is a new and very clever tactic, one we will have to prepare against in the future."

Raphael laid a hand on each of the angel's heads, saying, "I call forth The Alpha's life force to heal and renew these brave warriors. May all demonic poison, in return, poison the ones who injected it. Where claws so cruelly tore them, may regeneration occur, and may the demons responsible be torn asunder."

There was such power and command in his words that while he was yet speaking, everything he said began to happen in front of their eyes.

Steele sat up, staring down at his body and holding his arms up in front of him. Turning his hands this way and that, he marveled, "They're all gone. All the wounds."

As Wendly stood and began the same self-examination, Raphael said, "The wounds are gone, but you will each retain one scar as a reminder of your conflict. You see, every battle leaves a scar, and you will be known to the enemy by those scars . . . scars that say that even though they wounded you severely, you cannot be ultimately defeated. Your scars will become your identity. Your badge of honor."

Rok looked at the area where the man, woman, and their wolves were going about their business, unaware of the conflict raging around them.

“Serpent,” Schindaug said, staring toward the sky.

“What does that mean?” Wendly said.

“He’s gone,” Schindaug replied. “The serpent is gone.”

Gabriel cast his sight around the area. “I don’t see him anywhere. Taylor, is it normal for him to disappear like this?”

“Not at all. He’s always here. And when I say always, I mean he never leaves.”

“Talks,” Rok added.

“Right. He virtually never stops talking as well.”

Wendly said, “When we first saw the swarm, it was headed right for the serpent.”

“Are you certain?” Michael said. “Because that doesn’t make any sense. Going after you two does, but the serpent? What possible end could that serve?”

“Don’t forget how wily Apollyon is,” Jophiel said. “For all we know, the entire episode could have been a massive distraction—a misdirection to shield his real intentions.”

“Once again,” Michael said, “going after the serpent is completely illogical from a tactical perspective.”

Chamuel said, “As fascinating as all this speculation is, it doesn’t change the fact that the serpent has uncharacteristically disappeared, and it just doesn’t feel good to me. Something is terribly wrong.”

“Chamuel is right,” Gabriel said. “We need to find him, and we need to do it right now.”

Chapter Thirty-Five

In the rarefied air far above Eden, the serpent soared effortlessly on a series of thermals, catching each one and riding it in much the same way the dolphin fish of the great seas caught and rode waves. He was so happy. In fact, he had never felt this level of happiness and contentment before. He was in love with both the man and the woman. He even loved their wolves, although in their case, he was quite certain that the emotion was not reciprocated.

Throwing his head back, he shouted, "I have everything I have ever wanted!"

"Do you really?"

The sudden utterance coming from somewhere to the serpent's left startled him so completely that he tumbled off the thermal and had to flap his wings furiously to maintain even a semblance of equilibrium.

"What? Who . . . who said that?"

"It was I," Apollyon said lightly, slipping through the Curtain and making himself visible.

"Who are you?"

"I go by many names, but you can call me . . . " he thought for a moment and settled on, "Son of the Dawn."

"Son of the Dawn," the serpent said. "What a hopeful name." Then, noticing the being was soaring on the same level, he added, "How is it that you can be here with me? I'm higher than I've ever been, and yet, here you are."

"Why, this is my domain. I live here."

"Where? In the clouds?"

"In the clouds, the atmosphere. Everywhere. I live everywhere. You came into my realm, and I thought it only fitting that I offer a greeting."

"How about that," the serpent said in amazement. "I never realized there were other beings apart from the ones on . . . " he stopped speaking, regarding Apollyon somewhat suspiciously. "Say, are you the one who has been watching me?"

Apollyon laughed pleasantly. "I must confess, you have been such an object of fascination. I have, on occasion, had some of my servants keep an eye on you. And I apologize if you found the experience to be uncomfortable."

"Oh, not at all. It was just, well, unusual." Regarding the being next to him, the serpent said, "You are very beautiful."

"As are you."

"The man and woman have told me that before," he replied shyly. He paused, then said, "By the way, do you know them?"

"If you are asking whether I have had the pleasure of meeting them face to face, no. But if you are asking whether I know *of* them, then yes. You see, I am only able to meet those who venture into my realm."

"So, you cannot touch Earth?"

"That is a matter of some dispute. But for now, at least, the answer is no."

"Oh, that is unfortunate. Earth is wonderful. I love it there. But I love it here as well. Just me and the air and clouds and, well, sometimes other animals who can fly—and, of course, you, now."

Apollyon regarded the serpent. "You are a most fascinating fellow."

"Really? Why do you say that?"

"To my knowledge—and admittedly, I haven't been able to see all who inhabit the Earth below, but as far as I know, there are no other creatures like you."

"There is one other," the serpent said, his countenance suddenly growing sad. "My mate. But she put me away because I talk too much. That's why I have been so lonely, which is what made me reach out to the man and woman who were both so kind to me and who took me in and basically made me a part of their family—well, I mean the wolves don't like me so much but, you know, the man and woman are so expressive in their love that I can deal with that as long as I know—"

"So," Apollyon said, interrupting the nattering, "tell me about the man and woman. They sound as if they are equally fascinating."

"Oh, they are. And Eve—oh, Son of the Dawn, she is so lovely. I mean, loveliness that will take your breath away." Looking sideways at his new friend, he asked, "Do you have breath?"

"Of a sort, but please, tell me more."

"Okay, well . . . they oversee the Garden. Actually, now that I think about it, they are in charge of the whole Earth. I'm not sure about the air, though. But you already said that the air is your realm, so I suppose that makes you the—"

"And what about the man? What do you know of him?"

"Well, let's see . . . I know that he's my friend. That's the first thing. I also know that he and The Alpha—do you know The Alpha?"

"Oh yes," Apollyon said, "The Alpha and I are old friends. In fact, like you, He created me."

"Oh, that's very good. So, anyway, the man and The Alpha walk and talk together each day in the cool of the evening."

"And what do they talk about?"

"I have no idea. It's the one time when I'm not allowed to be anywhere near where they walk."

"Why is that?"

"It's because . . . " the serpent paused, thinking about the question. "You know, I couldn't say. But I suppose it's because the things they talk about are private between them."

"Or could it be that there are things they are keeping to themselves and do not wish to share with you?"

"Now, that's something I have never considered, nor would I ever."

"And why not?"

"Because that is so unlike Adam and The Alpha's character. They wouldn't withhold things from me."

"Truly?"

"Truly."

"So, you are saying there is nothing that The Alpha withholds from you or from the man and woman?"

The serpent started to answer negatively but then remembered Eve showing him the two trees.

"Well . . . "

"Yes?" Apollyon prompted.

"I'm not sure I'm supposed to tell anyone about this, but since you don't live in Eden and are only here in the air, I guess it won't matter. Anyway, there are these two trees in the Garden. One is the tree of life, and the other is the tree of the knowledge of good and evil."

"Interesting. And what is it about these two trees that you find so fascinating?"

"Well, The Alpha specifically told the man and woman that they could eat of the tree of life, and they do, every day, as much as they wish. But of the tree of the knowledge of good and evil, they must never eat, or they will die."

Apollyon said, "I wonder if that's true."

"What, that they would die? Well, I don't know, but that's what The Alpha said, so I'm sure—"

"But why would He do that? Why would He put something like that in His precious Garden? You know, just plant it there for everyone to see and fill it with delicious and enticing fruit and then tell the man and woman that if they eat of it, it'll kill them. That doesn't sound particularly loving, does it?"

The serpent flapped his wings a few times to catch the next thermal and then said, "I don't know how to answer your question."

"It's easy," Apollyon replied, "just tell me what you think."

"Well, I . . . you see, the thing is, I don't really know The Alpha all that well. I mean, I was obviously there when He created me, but since then, it's not like we talk a lot—well, it's not like we talk at all—so I don't feel qualified to even offer an opinion on whether the thing with the tree of the knowledge of good and—"

"You don't need to have intimate knowledge of The Alpha to form an opinion of his edicts. Look, it's like this: the woman told you about the restrictions, right?"

"Right."

"And after you heard what they were, what was the first thing that came into your mind?"

The serpent thought back to when Eve had first shown him the two trees and what he had felt at the time.

"Well," he began, "I suppose if I'm being honest—"

"Which I absolutely would expect you to be."

"Then I would have to say that the first thing that came into my mind—in fact, I asked it of the woman—was why? Why were there restrictions on one tree and not the other."

"Yes," Apollyon said triumphantly. "I knew it. And I would be willing to bet it's a question that she has had as well."

"I don't know about that. She's very loyal to The Alpha. Both are. I don't think it would ever occur to either one of them to question anything He said or did."

"And do you think that's healthy?"

"What, not questioning?"

"Yes."

The serpent thought for a moment. "Well, I don't know. You're asking me questions I've never even considered before, let alone thought through."

"Perhaps it's time you did."

"I don't know. There's just something about this whole conversation that feels off to me. Like . . . I'm not sure I should even be talking to you without telling the man and woman about it."

"Oh, Serpent," Apollyon said, "that is something you must never do."

"Tell them about our conversation?"

"Yes. They must not know about it just yet."

"But why not?"

Moving closer, Apollyon said, "Let's just say that I'm preparing a little surprise for them, and I don't want to spoil it."

"Truly?"

"Truly. In fact, I am quite certain everyone will be surprised, and no one more so than The Alpha."

"Ooooh, this sounds exciting. Can you tell me about it?"

"No, not even you."

"That's disappointing. But I suppose, when you think about it, a surprise wouldn't be a surprise if someone knew about it, would it?"

"That's right. However . . . well, I'm not sure I should ask what I was going to ask."

"Why not? If it helps you with the surprise, I want to hear about it."

Apollyon regarded the serpent for a moment. "All right then. If there were a way for you to help me facilitate this surprise, would you be willing to help?"

"Oh, absolutely. I would love to help, especially with something that concerns the man and woman."

"Good. Now, here's the tricky part. I've heard that you let the woman ride on your back from time to time."

"That is correct."

"Well, in order for me to make this surprise truly memorable, I would need a ride as well."

"On my back?"

Apollyon laughed good-naturedly. "As you can see, I don't have a physical body like you, so that would be impossible."

"Then, how would I give you a ride?"

"By letting me inside."

Eyes wide and questioning, the serpent said, "Wait, inside? Like, inside my body?"

"That's right. More specifically, inside your mind."

Wrinkling his brow, the serpent said, "How would that be possible?"

"You are a physical being, and I am a spiritual being. I don't have a body, and you do. Therefore, I can inhabit you for a short time with your permission and, thus, carry out the surprise I have been planning."

"And it's a good surprise?"

"I assure you that, as I said previously, *everyone* will be surprised."

The serpent said, "Will it hurt? You know, you being inside my mind?"

"Not at all. You will hardly know I'm there. In fact, it might even feel good."

"And after you're in, if I don't like it, can I ask you to leave?"

"Absolutely. I can't imagine that, but the last thing I want is for you to be uncomfortable. And keep in mind that this surprise is mainly for the man and woman."

The serpent liked his new friend. And was, in fact, drawn to his beauty and the sound of his voice. He seemed like someone with whom he could begin another friendship, and he had been so lonely. He loved his talks with the man and the woman, but there was something about Son of the Dawn that he found ever so fascinating, and he wanted nothing more at that moment than to perpetuate the newfound relationship.

"Okay," he declared. "I will do it. I can't wait to see their faces when you finally tell them the surprise."

"Neither can I. Thank you for your permission to enter you," Apollyon replied with a funny little smile.

"So, how does this work? Do you just climb on my back like the woman does and ride—"

Without warning, Apollyon entered the unsuspecting and gullible beast, causing him to cry out in alarm—but it was too late.

"There now," Apollyon said from within the core of the serpent's being. "That wasn't so bad, was it?"

"You—you're in me. I can feel you. You're in my mind."

"Why, yes, I am. And here I will stay for as long as I like."

"But I thought you said—"

"That I would go whenever you wanted me to? Yes, well, I'm afraid that was a lie. In fact, you might as well know that everything I told you was a lie."

"I don't understand," the serpent said, feeling his control slip away by the second. "What about the surprise?"

Apollyon laughed evilly. "The surprise was actually the only thing I said that wasn't a lie. They will be surprised. Oh, how they will be surprised."

The serpent felt something happen deep within his conscious mind, almost like a transference of control. But there was nothing he could do to stop it. Before tumbling into an unconscious abyss, one of his last independent thoughts was of what he'd been thinking just before welcoming his new friend into his body: *You know this is wrong, just as you know that this being is consummately evil. Get away now while you still have the chance.* But he didn't. And why? Because he was so desperate for friendship, he was willing to compromise everything he currently had for the promise of more to come.

He had just begun to weep when he felt a door slam shut on his conscious mind, and Apollyon's mind took over.

He had been right about one thing.

It didn't hurt a bit.

"So, you're in?" Beleth said.

"All the way."

"And you're sure that the guardians won't be able to tell that you inhabit the beast?"

"Not totally. But enough so that I'm feeling very confident. There's only one way to find out, isn't there?"

And with that, the serpent swooped downward toward the Garden, where he could see the man and woman working on their dwelling, their four guardians arrayed protectively around them.

"Adam," Eve said.

He turned away from preparing a board for the door. "Yes?"

Smiling sweetly, she leaned over and kissed the top of his head. "Oh, nothing. I just wanted to tell you how handsome you look working on that board and that I just love you so much."

He stood, wrapping his muscular arms around his wife. "Why, what a sweet thing to say. And I love you back. For the record, I think you look absolutely stunning, regardless of what you're doing."

She laughed lightly. "Yes, well, I don't look so stunning at the moment. I've been sweeping out the inside of our dwelling. When do you think you'll be finished, by the way?"

"Well, that's a good question. I would have an answer for you if I could just figure out what to do next."

"Oh? What is troubling you?"

Squatting down, he said, "Okay, so, you see how all the boards are of the exact same size and how when I fit them together, there's no gap between them?"

"Yes, what about it?"

"Well, I don't know how to maintain that once I stand them up. What I mean is, I have no way to secure them all together."

Stepping back, Eve surveyed the problem. She looked at the boards, glanced around the area, and saw three more boards that had been discarded.

"Why don't you take those three boards from over there, run one across the top so it covers all the boards and another one across the bottom in the same position, and then cut the other one so it can link the two together at an angle?"

"But how will I get it all to bind together?"

"Gouge holes through all the upright boards in a straight line, top and bottom, and then matching holes in the two cross boards and the angled board. Then, use some of that strong vine we used in the construction of the dwelling to tie it all together."

He blew out a big breath of air, saying, "That will be a lot of work, but I think it's a really good solution. Thank you. You are quite brilliant with things like that."

"I know," she replied with a laugh as she went back to her sweeping.

The serpent settled into the clearing, causing Blue and Shadow to begin barking ferociously, with Lamb bleating and backing into the shadows.

"Blue, Shadow, Lamb," Adam scolded. "It's just the serpent. He's our friend. Stop that. What's the matter with you?"

In spite of his command, the two wolves kept it up, now moving menacingly toward the beast as Lamb stood trembling as if anticipating an attack.

The serpent laughed and said, "I always knew those two didn't like me, but I've never seen Lamb exhibit fear like that. Maybe I should leave and come back when they've all settled down."

"I apologize," Eve said, walking out of the dwelling, attempting to calm the wolves. "I just don't know what's gotten into them. Blue, Shadow," she said sharply. "No."

Lamb bleated and scampered off into the forest, and while the wolves quieted somewhat at her command, they continued growling, never taking their eyes off of the serpent.

The serpent said, "Eve, maybe we could go for a ride or something. Perhaps that would calm them down."

"Adam, would you mind terribly if the serpent took me for a ride?"

"Not at all. In fact, I think it's a good idea that he disappears for a while."

"Okay, then," she said and climbed onto the serpent's back, causing the wolves to resume barking furiously. "I just don't know what's wrong with them."

The serpent flapped his wings and lifted off. "They'll be all right when we get back."

"So, where are we going? Any place in particular?"

"I kind of wanted to go to the clearing where the two trees are. It was so peaceful the last time we were there, and I want to experience it again."

"Sounds good to me."

"What do you make of that?" Taylor asked Rok.

"Trouble."

"What kind of trouble?"

"Bad."

"Then, what are we supposed to do?"

"Watch."

He laughed, saying, "I think this is the longest conversation we've ever had."

Across the way, Kepteny and Schindaug were having the same discussion.

"Those wolves have always had it in for the serpent," Schindaug said, "but this takes the cake."

Kepteny turned and stared at his companion. "What is cake?"

"I don't know," Schindaug said. "It just sounded good."

"Do you think we need to say something to Michael?"

"I'm sure The Alpha has already told him everything he needs to know."

Chapter Thirty-six

"How are you doing?" Raphael inquired of the injured angels in his care. "And please don't try to make up something just to get me to go away. It won't work."

"I just feel, I don't know, dirty or something. Like I've got this layer of grime and dirt all over me," Wendly said.

Steele nodded. "I feel the same. Why is that?"

"What you are feeling," Raphael said, "is the residual presence of evil. Because you were swarmed by millions of demons—bitten and clawed—some of their corruption is still slowly going away. But it *will* go away. It will just take time."

Wendly asked, "Will we go back to the way we were?"

"As I mentioned before, your scars will actually make you more powerful than ever because they represent a victory over the enemy."

Uriel, standing to the side and observing, said, "Even though we prevailed in the war, many were wounded, and I have observed what Raphael said to be true. I expect you will prove to be a bit more powerful in your next encounter."

"Speaking of which," Steele said, "where *is* Apollyon exactly?"

Sweeping his hands in a broad gesture, Raphael replied, "Here, there, everywhere, except right here in Eden."

"And why is that?"

"He is forbidden to come anywhere near this airspace."

"And given how completely corrupt and treacherous he is," Wendly added, "what makes you or anyone else believe he will honor that?"

"Because," Uriel said, "it is the terms of his banishment, and he cannot violate those terms."

"But could he figure out a way to work around them?"

"I'm not sure I understand what you mean."

Steel said, "I think Wendly is asking if Apollyon could manipulate the system, you know, find a crack he could wiggle through or something that would allow him to somehow gain access?"

Raphael thought through the question briefly. "Although I don't like to even consider that possibility, knowing him as I do—and I probably know him better than anyone besides The Alpha—I'd have to say that he is capable of anything. Why do you ask?"

"I don't know," Wendly said, standing and stretching carefully. "It's just something that occurred to me, and since we're supposed to watch, perhaps that's something we should be watching for and not just assume he's going to honor the terms."

"It's a good point, and I will discuss it with The Alpha right away. Now, if you two are certain you are okay, we will be on our way."

"Thank you, Raphael," Steele said. "I don't know how you did it, but besides the corruption thing, I'm feeling almost normal."

"As am I," Wendly said.

"Okay, then, I will be off."

As the two archangels faded from view, Steele said, "You didn't mention any of that to me previously. Why?"

"Because it just occurred to me. You know, like, what if the reason we were attacked was to get us out of the way so Apollyon could somehow penetrate the airspace above Eden."

"But why? I mean, what possible good would that do him? Then, he'd have to face Rok and Kepteny."

"I know," Wendly said, "but it's a legitimate enough concern that it seems worth heightening our awareness. I'm sure we weren't attacked without reason."

"I won't argue that point."

"Wendly brought up a good point, Alpha," Raphael said as he and Uriel stood before the throne with the other archangels.

"Regarding Apollyon's unwillingness to abide by the rules of his banishment?"

"Yes."

"It is a very good point, and you should probably know that I never expected him to stick to the rules."

Michael said, "Then why go through all the effort to set it all up?"

"Because," The Alpha replied patiently, "he had to be provided with the opportunity and environment within which certain choices could be made."

"With respect," Zadkiel said, "it sounds like it was a setup."

"No, Zadkiel, not at all. A setup would have forced him into narrow confines where only one choice was presented. Never forget, My mighty archangels, you do not see what I see. Regarding choice, while your view is quite linear—with one thing leading to another—My view is, well, not linear. Not only do I see every side simultaneously, but all sides of every possibility, myriads upon myriads of potential outcomes, as well as all the resulting ramifications. The way choices are navigated is the very essence of life, both celestial and Earthly.

"Now," he continued, "I provided Apollyon with the best opportunity given where his choices landed him. I could have imprisoned him and all his followers with a single thought. Gone. Wiped out. Just like that. But I didn't. Not because of anything he or anyone who follows him deserves, but because My goodness demands that I provide even one such as he with the opportunity to turn away from the abyss and embrace his former station."

"But," Jophiel countered, "didn't you just say that you never expected him to do any of that?"

"True. But expectation and outcome are vastly different. The element of surprise is always at play."

Raphael said, "Going back to what Wendly said about Apollyon finding a crack to wiggle through and access the man and woman . . . "

"He has, and he will."

The archangels were suddenly on high alert, with Michael saying, "What? How is this possible?"

The Alpha almost seemed weary as he said, "The rules of banishment stated that he *himself* is not to enter Eden or speak directly to the man and woman. But there was nothing in the construct that prohibited him from enlisting the aid of another to accomplish his ends."

"Are you saying that's what has happened?" Chamuel asked.

"It is happening as we speak."

"What are we to do?" Zadkiel said.

"What we have always done. We watch and wait."

"And what about the guardians?" Gabriel said. "What do I tell them?"

"The same."

"It seems so insufficient," Michael said.

"Yes, and yet, it is what must be done."

Fully under Apollyon's control, the serpent settled into the clearing. Eve slid smoothly off his back and walked toward the mounds, upon which grew the tree of life and the tree of the knowledge of good and evil. While she couldn't explain why, she nevertheless always found herself compelled to stand in front of the tree of the knowledge of good and evil and stare at the enticing fruit hanging so easily within reach.

"It is so lovely, isn't it," said the serpent.

"Oh, yes, it truly is."

He paused dramatically and then said with feigned hesitancy, "Can I tell you a secret?"

"Please do," she replied, turning to gaze upon her companion.

"But you must never tell anyone else, even Adam."

"That sounds very serious. Are you all right?"

Laughing lightly, he said, "Yes, yes, it's nothing like that. It's just that both times I have been here, I cannot get this one thought out of my mind."

"Do tell me, then."

"Well, you will most likely think me extremely ungrateful, for it was you who introduced me to this spot, but . . . I just cannot understand it."

"Understand what, Serpent?"

"You know . . . *it.* The Alpha's edict regarding the two trees."

Wrinkling her brow thoughtfully, she replied, "Yes, I know what you mean. And I'd be less than truthful were I to deny having had that thought as well."

"I don't like where this is going," Kepteny said as he and Taylor watched the exchange between the serpent and the woman.

"Nor do I," Taylor said. "And yet, our specific instructions were to watch and not interfere. Steele, Wendly, are you sensing anything out of the ordinary?"

Steele replied, "No. From our vantage point, we can see throughout the entire Garden, and all is well. Nothing in the atmosphere either."

"Schindaug, anything happening with the man?" Kepteny said.

"Nothing. He's busy working on the door for their dwelling. The wolves are playing with their offspring. Just seems like another day. Why do you ask?"

"Because the serpent is acting very strange."

"Can you be more specific?" Wendly asked.

"Yes. Not himself at all. It's almost like he's attempting to lead Eve into something. They're by the two trees because the serpent said he loved it so much the first time she brought him here that he wanted to see it again. But he just now started talking to her about The Alpha's edict regarding the two trees, and I don't like what I'm hearing."

"Well," Steele said, "be alert. The word is that Apollyon has found a way to bypass the system and get to the man and woman directly."

"I have an odd request," the serpent said.

"Okay."

"Do you remember word for word what The Alpha said and how he said it?"

"Hmm. Give me a moment, and I believe I can recall it as my husband told me."

"Oh, so The Alpha didn't say it to you directly?"

"No, only to my husband before I was created."

"I see. So, you do not truly know what The Alpha said, only as your husband related it to you."

She replied with a laugh. "It almost sounds as if you are suggesting Adam has set out to deceive me, and I assure you, that is most definitely not possible, for he is truthful above all else."

"Oh, no, no, no," the serpent said quickly. "I would never suggest such a dishonoring thing. Merely that when something is passed along, it is often difficult to get it exactly right. My question, therefore, relates to the accuracy of what was said and not regarding any malicious intent on the man's part."

"Yes, I see now. Okay, give me a moment." Eve grew thoughtful, saying finally, "This is what was said to the best of my ability to recall it. The Alpha said, *'Of the trees that grow in the Garden, you may eat liberally of their fruit . . . except for the tree of the knowledge of good and evil. On the day you eat of its fruit, that is the day you will surely die.'* "

"And that was all? He offered no further explanation?"

"As I said, Adam related the conversation to me, so I only know what I was told."

The serpent seemed pensive and was silent for so long that Eve finally prompted, "Tell me what you are thinking."

"It *is* odd, isn't it, that He would say something like that? Now, I freely confess that I do not know The Alpha as much as you and the man, but—"

"Well, I cannot truly say that I *know* him, for Adam is the one with whom He walks and talks."

"I see. Then, perhaps, we should more rightly say that, based on what we know of The Alpha from what the man has related, something like that seems inconsistent with what is known of His nature and character."

“Oh, I see now what you mean. And you are right; it does seem odd.”

“I mean, think about it. Did He truly say that you may not eat of any of the trees in the Garden?”

“No, no, remember? I just told you. He said that we could eat liberally from all the trees, save this one,” she said, pointing toward the lovely tree. “And just so we are clear, He specified the tree that stands in the middle of the Garden. And, well, if you look around you, there is no doubt that we are, indeed, in the middle of the Garden. In fact, I remember a bit more now of what He said. He didn’t just say that if we ate of it, we’d die, but if we even touched it, we would die.”

“All this death,” The serpent moaned. “I do not believe it for one moment.”

“Believe what?”

Turning his lovely eyes on the woman, the serpent said, “Eve, do you believe that we have become friends?”

“Oh yes, we truly are. In fact, I so look forward to our times each day.” Laughing, she added, “It’s odd, isn’t it, that Adam and The Alpha walk and talk each day, and you and I do the same . . . well, fly and talk?”

“Yes,” the serpent said, “I enjoy it as well. More to the point, would you say that you have grown to trust me?”

“Well, I climb onto your back and let you do all those crazy aerial maneuvers. If that isn’t trust, I don’t know what is.”

“Then, I want you to trust me when I say that you shall not surely die.”

“But how can you know that?”

"Because from what I know of The Alpha, His character, and His ways, there is nothing He would ever do to willingly hurt one of His created ones. Of all the creatures and beings He has created, none have died. Not one."

"Well, then, why would He have said such a thing to Adam?"

The serpent paused as if struggling with what to say.

"Go ahead, Serpent. Tell me what is on your mind."

"I hesitate for fear you will misunderstand me."

"I will hear what you have to say and not make any judgments against you. You have my word. Now speak. In the authority and dominion given to me by The Alpha, I command you."

"Since you put it like that, I will tell you what is on my mind. Eve, you won't die. You cannot die. You, like The Alpha—in whose image you were created—are immortal. The real reason He does not wish you to eat of this tree is that the day you do is the day your eyes will be opened, and, like The Alpha, you will know both good and evil."

Taylor said, "Rok, Schindaug, I don't care how you do it, but you need to get the man over here right now."

"But," Schindaug countered, "we're not supposed to—"

"Now, Schindaug! Get him over here."

As Schindaug and Rok shared a worried glance, Wendly said, "Although you cannot speak directly to them, would it be possible to employ the aid of their wolves?"

"How so?" Schindaug asked.

"Try communicating the urgency to Blue. See if you can get him to lead the man to the clearing."

Schindaug turned his attention to the large animal and projected a thought into its mind that was so pointed and powerful that Blue yelped and began howling, prompting the man to ask what was wrong. Blue barked loudly and, in turn, communicated to Adam that they needed to find Eve immediately because she was in great danger in the center of the Garden. Adam dropped his tools instantly and began running toward the spot with the two wolves right on his heels.

"I don't know if he will get there in time," Wendly lamented.

"In time for what?" Steele said.

"To save the human race."

Upon hearing the serpent's statement, Eve's hands flew to her mouth as she drew in a quick breath. "You truly believe this to be so? That I will not die?"

"Well," he replied, with a glint in his eyes, "there is really only one way to find out."

Turning her gaze toward the tree, she said softly, "Oh, Serpent, I am so filled with fear."

"Don't be afraid. I am here with you, and I would die before I would allow anything to hurt you."

She stood staring at the tree, her emotions at war within her. *Why are you even standing here and contemplating this?* The thought came tearing into her consciousness like one of the bolts of lightning she had seen proceed from the serpent's mouth. And yet, she found herself inching closer and closer.

"That's it," said the serpent encouragingly. "Just a few more steps now, and you can have your heart's desire. You know you want it, have, in fact, *always* wanted it from the first time you laid eyes on it. Look how lovely the fruit is. How it glistens in the light, still dripping from the morning dew. Imagine how it would feel to bite into it and feel the juices flooding your mouth with flavor. And now, it is almost within your grasp. Go ahead. Take it. Eat. You will not surely die."

"Eve," came Adam's loud hail from behind her.

She spun quickly and saw her husband trotting toward her with Blue and Shadow on his heels and Lamb, clearly agitated, circling the clearing's perimeter.

"What are you doing here?" he said, casting a suspicious eye toward the serpent as the wolves began circling the beast and growling low in their throats.

"Oh," she replied quickly, "well, the serpent wanted to come and see this lovely spot again."

"Again?"

"Yes. We came here once before because I wanted him to see how lovely it was. Lovelier by far than any other spot in our Garden."

"I see," he said somewhat suspiciously.

The wolves continued their low growling.

"What were you talking about when I walked up?"

The serpent said, "You should tell him."

She hesitated slightly but then drew herself up to her full height and faced him, saying, "Adam, there is a thought that has been in my mind since you first told me of this tree."

"Okay, but—"

"Just listen. Don't talk. Now, you know The Alpha very well, and you have told me often of His character and kindness. With what you know, does it seem remotely reasonable to you that He would kill us just for eating a piece of fruit from a tree?"

Adam rocked back on his heels as if struck. "Eve, He never said *He* would kill us. He said that we would surely *die*."

"Then, if not Him, then who? Last time I checked, it was just you, me, the animals, and The Alpha. Who will kill us? Is the fruit poisonous? Does that sound like something The Alpha would do? Create poisonous fruit?"

Adam considered her question before answering. "No, it doesn't. Where are you going with all this, Eve?"

Walking over to where he stood, she cupped his face in her hands and, in her most alluring tone, said, "Husband, I have come to a decision: I am going to eat of the fruit. It looks delicious to me, and I do not believe we will die simply from eating it. The serpent believes—and I must say, I agree with him—that rather than dying, the fruit will give us knowledge and wisdom beyond what we now possess. We will be like The Alpha. And I want that wisdom."

Chapter Thirty-Seven

The guardians hovered over the scene, unable to believe what they were seeing and hearing.

"Michael!" Taylor hollered, "Gabriel! Anyone! Help! She's going to do it. She's going to eat the fruit."

"What has gotten into that serpent?" Schindaug said. "This isn't like him. Something has happened."

Suddenly, Wendly shouted, "It's him. It's Apollyon! *He* has gotten into the serpent."

"What are you talking about?" Steele asked. "That's not possible . . . is it?"

"There's no other explanation."

Michael and Gabriel appeared, both of them equally perplexed by what was transpiring.

Michael said, "The Alpha clearly told us there was to be no interference and the man and woman were to be left alone to make their choices."

"But she's going to ruin it for all eternity," Taylor exclaimed. "We have to do something to stop—"

"No," Michael replied sharply. "Do nothing. Just watch."

"Michael," Wendly shouted, "we can see the swarm reforming."

"Don't worry about it. They won't dare do anything with me and Gabriel here."

"It's almost like they're waiting for something," Steele added.

Rok said, "Signal."

"Maybe," Michael said, "or an event. Whatever it is, it'll happen soon."

Adam was so dumbfounded by Eve's statement that he found himself stunned into silence, watching in utter bewilderment as she turned, walked purposefully toward the tree, plucked a piece of fruit, and held it in front of her eyes, turning it this way and that, reveling in its shape, how shiny it was, and the fragrance coming off its surface as she ran her finger along the curves, her sense of touch enlivened by the contact. She felt empowered touching it in her hand, and yet, contrary to what she had been told, she was still alive.

"It is so very lovely," she said. "Adam, don't you think it's lovely?"

Adam tried to form words to reply, but he could only continue to stare in disbelief at the scene playing out in front of him.

"Well," the serpent said, "you have gone this far. Might as well give it a taste."

As the serpent's enticing words washed over both of them, a battle raged deep within Eve's conscious mind.

The Alpha said no.

Her will said yes.

Her conscience said she'd regret it.

In the end, she sank her teeth deeply into the succulent fruit, delighting in the feel of the juices running down her chin.

"Oh, Adam," she said, her eyes closed in pure pleasure, "this is the most delicious thing I have ever tasted. Here, you taste it."

Adam took the proffered fruit, hesitated slightly, and then, seeing the delight on her face, bit off a piece, feeling nearly overcome by the sheer pleasure he felt as he chewed and swallowed the bite.

Suddenly, The Alpha's glory that had clothed both the man and the woman vanished, and they saw their utter nakedness and vulnerability.

"What just happened?" Eve exclaimed as she let the uneaten fruit fall to the ground.

"I am so ashamed, Eve," Adam said. "Come, we must find something to cover our nakedness."

Apollyon suddenly departed from the serpent, leaving the unsuspecting yet complicit creature collapsed on the Garden floor, weeping bitterly.

"Adam, Eve," he wailed bitterly, "please forgive me. I didn't know what I was doing. It was Apollyon in me."

Adam and Eve fled into the depths of the Garden, unsure of what to do next but certain they had to do something. Adam looked this way and that in search of something, anything, that could be used to hide their nakedness. Coming upon a fig tree, he took leaves with which he quickly fashioned garments.

Then, they hid themselves.

High above the Garden, the atmosphere roiled with the demonic swarm as Apollyon led them in raucous celebration.

"I did it! I did it! I did it!" he cried, dancing in front of the throng. "I told you I would, and I did!" Turning his face toward the heavens, he hollered, "Are you seeing this, Alpha? Do you see what I just did to Your precious creation? I. Have. Ruined. Them. Forever!"

Throwing his misshapen head back and roaring with wild laughter, he led the demonic swarm, swirling and twisting in the atmosphere straight down to Earth and touching down just outside of the Garden's east entrance.

"And now, we wait," he told his Legion of the Fallen.

"What have you done?" Adam demanded from within the copes of trees serving as their hiding place.

"What have *I* done?" Eve said, "What have *you* done? Why didn't you protect me from that creature? You stood by and let him lead me on, enticing me with his clever speech and wily ways."

"No one forced you into any of that, and you know it. You were a willing participant."

"So, you are attempting to justify your silence?"

"What silence?"

"The silence when you let me go off with him nearly every day. The silence when I would return, and you would not even question where we had been or what we had been doing. The silence when I told you of my intentions to eat of the fruit, and you just stood there and let me. And the worst one of all, the silence when I gave you the fruit to eat, and you just took it without even contesting it."

"So, so . . ." he sputtered, "you are suggesting that this is all my fault?"

Blue and Shadow lay on the Garden floor, paws over their eyes and wailing mournfully, their former ability to communicate with the man and woman now gone forever.

"Well," Eve said, "whose fault would it be, then? Mine? Surely not."

"Adam." The voice of The Alpha echoed throughout the Garden. "Where are you, Adam?"

"It's Him," Eve said, cowering behind the branches. "What are we going to do?"

"Be quiet. Perhaps He will pass us by."

"Adam," The Alpha called again, more loudly than before. "I am here for our walk, just like always. Where are you?"

Hanging his head, Adam said, "I have to go."

"No," she said in a harsh whisper, "you don't. Just be quiet, and He will—"

"There you are," The Alpha said, coming to a stop by the trees. "What are you doing in there?"

Drawing together every bit of courage he possessed, Adam stood, saying, "Alpha, we heard You walking in the Garden and hid ourselves."

"For what reason did you hide?"

"We, well . . . we hid because we were ashamed."

"And why were you ashamed?"

"Because we are naked."

"I see. And who told you that you were naked?" Pausing, The Alpha continued, "Have you gone against My edict and eaten from the tree whose fruit I forbade you to eat?"

Spinning quickly and pointing a finger at Eve, who cowered behind him, Adam said, "It was this woman You gave me. She is the reason I ate of the fruit."

Looking into her eyes, The Alpha said mournfully, "What have you done?"

She mumbled, "It . . . the serpent deceived me. It's true. There is no possible way I would have done so otherwise."

Recovering from the initial shock of what Apollyon had done through him, the grieving serpent went to find the man and woman and suddenly stumbled into the clearing across from their hiding place.

He saw The Alpha.

The Alpha saw him and, more importantly, Apollyon laughing, mocking, and standing directly behind him.

The little dragon and the Great Dragon.

His eyes fixed on the serpent, the Alpha said, "To you was given more than any of My creatures, but you betrayed My kindness and the trust I allowed you to have with the man and woman."

Ashamed and confused, the serpent tried mightily to summon a defense but found that he could no longer speak.

The Alpha continued, "For this reason, I am removing your beauty, your intelligence, your stature in the animal kingdom and pronounce that you shall be accursed more than all the animals. Once free to walk the Earth and soar above it, you will now crawl on your belly, groveling in the dust as long as you live. And the former friendship I allowed you to have with man? It is gone. From this day forward, there will be enmity and antagonism between you and the woman and between all of your progeny *and* hers."

Shifting His gaze to Apollyon, He added fiercely, "You think you have won? I assure you that you have not. Hear Me, Dragon: the man will strike your head, and you will bruise his heel."

Upon The Alpha's pronouncement, a scene flashed through Apollyon's consciousness with such blinding intensity it left him shaken, stunned, and unable to muster even the slightest sense of the victory he had just celebrated. As the serpent began shriveling from his former glory into an ugly, slithering thing that struck fear into the hearts of the man and woman, Apollyon knew The Alpha was providing him with stark and inescapable evidence of his own tragic demise.

"And you," The Alpha said, turning His attention back to the woman.

"Alpha, please, I didn't—"

"When you are with child, I will sharpen your discomfort and cause you to suffer great pain in childbirth." He added, "You controlled your husband in this matter. He did what he did because of his love for you. But henceforth, regardless of how intensely you desire to continue that control, you shall not have it. He shall rule over you instead."

Turning to the man, He paused, His great sorrow darkening the atmosphere around them. "And you, Adam, the one I endowed with My exact likeness, because you allowed your wife to persuade you to eat the forbidden fruit, whereas here in the Garden the ground brought forth all manner of food, I now curse the ground. Throughout your life, it will be an intense struggle to coax life from it. Though you will find a way to eat of its grains, thorns and thistles shall be your lot until the day you return to the ground from which you came. For I made you from the dust of this Earth, and to dust shall you return." Pausing, He added, "You have broken My heart, Adam."

The Alpha then gave them clothing fashioned from the skins of an animal He had killed. With a sickening realization, Adam suddenly knew that the skins were from Lamb, his friend.

"Why, Alpha?" Adam wailed. "Why did Lamb have to die?"

"Because of your sin, Adam. And without shedding blood, there can be no remission of sin."

Falling to his knees and clutching the skins to his face, Adam wept.

He wept for the tragic sacrifice his friend was forced to make to cover his sin.

He wept for the tragic loss of all he had held dear.

He wept for the uncertain future he and the woman now faced.

And he wept because he knew he would never see The Alpha again face to face.

Summoning the *Elohim,* The Alpha said, "The man and woman have now become like Us, knowing both good and evil, and yet they lack the wisdom to know what to do with that knowledge. If they continue eating from the tree of life, they will remain immortal, forever imprisoned by their sin. I will, therefore, banish them from this Garden and make provision that they may never return. Although their bodies shall perish, their souls may yet be saved."

Turning to Adam, He said, "You and you alone are responsible for this. It was not My will but your *choice* that created this circumstance. Now farewell, Adam—you who carry My breath in your lungs, My likeness in your appearance, My love in your heart. You will never see My face again in this life."

At The Alpha's pronouncement, Adam cried, "Alpha, no! It is too much to bear. Please, do not do this."

"Again, it is not I who have done this . . . but *you*. Throughout this ruined Earth you shall wander, each day of your life filled with regret for what you have brought upon yourself and future generations of mankind. Your days will be hard, your years seemingly endless until the day you finally breathe your last breath. I pity you, Adam, I do. And yet, this is the lot you have chosen."

Adam couldn't believe what was happening. The circumstances resulting in this awful occurrence had come at him so fast and furious he'd scarcely had time to react, let alone think everything through sufficiently to make good decisions.

It had just been another day.

Another ordinary day.

Up early to a breakfast of figs and carrots.

Working on the door to the dwelling, feeling hopeful that he would finally complete the task that had taken so much of his time and tried his patience.

Looking forward, as usual, to his walk with The Alpha and sharing the deep intimacy that had come to define their relationship.

Chasing Eve around the clearing, playfully threatening to throw her into the lake if he caught up to her because she had lovingly teased him about his hair sticking straight up from his sleeping position.

And then came the succession of events leading up to disaster. The nudge in his spirit to go and find his wife. The sickening realization upon finding her that she was determined to violate The Alpha's prime edict, regardless of the consequences.

Who was this woman? This rebellious throw-caution-to-the-wind woman? Surely, not his Eve. His soulmate. His helper. His completer. Why would she do something so obviously destined to result in ruination? But overshadowing all that loomed the greatest question of all: why hadn't he stopped her? And moreover, why had he followed her in her sin?

Stumbling toward the perimeter, he heard himself mumbling over and over, "This cannot be happening," while desperate thoughts raged through his savaged consciousness. *Surely, The Alpha will yet relent and realize that, though we committed a grievous error, we are still His creatures, heart and soul, and we love Him.*

And yet, with every leaden step, it became more obvious that there was no mercy to be had.

At least not today.

They slogged nearer and nearer to the boundary, the mournful howls of their wolves filling the airspace, crushing their already broken hearts with further sorrow.

Slowing, unconsciously, as they reached the Garden's entrance, they heard a crackling sound from behind and were stunned to discover The Alpha had stationed mighty Cherubim to the east of the Garden of Eden and a flaming sword to guard the way to the tree of life.

Adam muttered under his breath, tear-filled eyes wide with wonder, "This is really happening. I can't believe it."

Once the man and woman cleared the Garden's perimeter, Apollyon shouted, "I believe this now belongs to me," as he scooped up the power, dominion, and authority man had just surrendered. "It is mine, and I can now give it to whomever I wish. Your government, Alpha, Your ideals, Your morals, Your whole egocentric regime has been an utter failure. I will now set up *my* kingdom on the Earth, and I will run this world as I see fit, and there is nothing You can do to stop me."

The Alpha replied. "I could stop you; I simply choose not to."

"Yes, well, coming from someone who couldn't even stop me from," he paused, shouting louder, "*ruining* His precious creation, that's big talk. Don't you see it yet? I am in charge, and there is nothing You can do about it. Oh, thinking about creating something else? Go ahead. I will ruin that as well. I may have only taken down a third of the angels, but I have corrupted *all* of mankind forever. And, in case You think that You can—what was that word You used so long ago—oh yes, *redeem* the man and woman, try it and see what happens." Turning suddenly petulant and sullen, he said, "And by the way, You didn't redeem *me*. Why would You redeem them? Wasn't I Your first and most beautiful creation? Wasn't I more worthy of redemption than they?"

All the while, Apollyon's Legion of the Fallen was swirling high overhead in a black cloud, roaring with laughter and delight.

"You hear that, Alpha? That is the sound of victory. Get used to hearing it."

"Alpha," Michael pleaded, "just let me do it. Let me destroy him, or at least pierce him through so he can feel some of the pain this he is causing You."

"No, Michael. This is as it must be."

"But he's getting away with it. You can't just let him—"

"He isn't getting away with anything."

Gabriel said, "That isn't what it seems."

"Rarely are things as they seem, Gabriel," The Alpha said. Gathering all the archangels toward Him, He continued, "Do you not know that I saw this coming and have already made provisions?"

"But," Chamuel said, "how could You see something that was yet to be chosen?"

"It's back to the difference in how you see and how I see. We, the *Elohim*, foresaw this strong probable outcome and have a solution."

"What is it?" Michael said eagerly.

"It is for another time. But fear not; it is in place."

"What do we do now?" Taylor asked, a question that was echoed immediately by the other guardians.

"What you have already been doing. Stay with the man and woman, for I have given you charge over them lest they strike their foot against a stone."

"So," Jophiel said, "You won't abandon them completely?"

"How could I ever abandon that which is My very heart?" The Alpha said with a catch in His mighty voice. "What the man and woman have done has left Me anguished, not angry. My anger is reserved for that Great Dragon, Apollyon. He had it all and yet decided he wanted more." Turning His attention to his foe, he continued, "And you who now cavort in unrestrained demonic joy, know this: final judgment has been prepared and is reserved for you and all who follow you. It is a lake of fire where you will be tormented for all of eternity."

"Yes, well, we shall see about that, won't we?" Apollyon railed. "In order for that to happen, You have to maintain Your grip on the throne . . . an outcome that, based on current circumstances, seems far less than guaranteed, wouldn't You say?"

"What I would *say,* Apollyon, you deceiving, lying serpent, is that for a little while, you shall have the freedom to do as you wish, and then the end will come rushing upon you—an end that will fully restore order to My Kingdom, My universe."

"Well," Apollyon said mockingly, "if all You are prepared to do is talk, then I'm afraid I must be going. After all, I have an entire world to corrupt and ruin. I don't have the time to just stand around debating the lunatic ramblings of Your deranged and selfish mind. I bid You farewell, Alpha. But we shall meet again soon."

With a wave of his hand, he dispatched his Legion of the Fallen to disperse throughout the Earth, setting up territories, principalities, and strongholds with Beleth, Semyaza, Remashel, and Dantanian as princes over them all.

"What just happened?" Michael said.

"We have just witnessed," The Alpha replied, "the birth of chaos."

There was silence for a time. Then Jophiel finally said, "Alpha, I am feeling something, and I don't know what it is. Moisture keeps forming behind my eyes, and my chest is heavy."

As the other archangels confessed similar feelings, The Alpha said, "What you are feeling is called grief, something unknown to you prior to this moment. It occurs when you have experienced great loss."

"Do You feel it as well?" Gabriel said.

Turning mournful eyes on His mighty archangel, The Alpha said, "More than you will ever know."

They all stood there in silence, feeling the weight of the moment. The Alpha turned slowly to Michael and Gabriel and said, "When we are done here, get the messenger angel Buzz and bring him and just yourselves to my throne room. As a result of recent events, I have some unique training for a highly classified mission for him. It will not play out for generations, and you will see him much less, but I need him to prepare himself and be ready for his mission."

Michael said, "Alpha, you know he has the heart of a warrior. I would really prefer him active in one of my squads and not tucked away for some future assignment."

"I know, but it is his warrior heart for Me that propels his words and voice more than his sword."

Michael and the others knew what the Alpha meant, for they had experienced Buzz and how the volume of his words glorified the Alpha. In full knowledge of their experiences, He saw an opportunity to add a little levity to the moment. The Alpha leaned into the group of archangels with a slight twinkle in his eye. The archangels eagerly anticipated the pearl of insight that was about to be dropped on them. The Alpha said, "You know, I've seen him take thirty minutes to say hello."

Gabriel, all too familiar with Buzz, nodded and laughed.

"I love that guy," Jophiel chuckled. The others laughed as well.

It was the Alpha's humor in moments like this that gave the angels a deeper peace and confidence and understanding that no matter what happened, the Alpha had it all under control. Their admiration of Him soared even more. Even though love requires free will, He knew all the possibilities and had a plan ready for every outcome.

Part 4

The Clock of Consequence

Chapter Thirty-Eight

Stumbling despondently over the ground, which had suddenly become hard, cracked, and barren, Eve wailed, "What will we do now, Husband?"

Staring around at a world he no longer recognized, Adam drew his shoulders back and replied to his wife, "Survive, Eve. We will survive."

The next days, weeks, and months were difficult beyond belief as the man and woman sojourned through a barren, desolate land in search of anything that would satisfy and sustain the basic needs of existence. True to The Alpha's edict, it appeared the Earth itself was, in fact, waging war against them. They did not know how far they traveled; they only knew their progress was always across stony ground that tore and blistered their feet, turning each step into an exercise in agony—whether struggling to traverse narrow mountain passes or slogging through endless barren and treacherous valleys filled with creatures who now seemed to view them as potential meals.

The nearly complete lack of food and water had reduced both humans to sad caricatures of their former glory. Haunted eyes stared from hollow-cheeked faces, above which filthy and matted hair sprouted haphazardly from heads that never ceased aching. Once a perfect physical specimen of human perfection, Adam's flesh now hung loosely on his frame, each rib clearly visible.

The landscape had nothing even remotely resembling vegetation. What scant food they'd been able to procure consisted of creatures small enough to kill with their bare hands or whatever stone happened to be in reach. In their wildest imaginings, it never occurred to either that one day they would be devouring raw flesh as if it were the most delectable thing they had ever tasted.

Water consisted of whatever pooled in the rocks following the nightly dew—pools frequented by animals who seemed disinclined to share.

And then, one day, with their minds skittering along the edges of insanity, the pitifully thin, forlorn couple struggled up and over a low rise only to behold the most beautiful sight they had seen since first being installed in the Garden.

A river. Long and languid, winding its way through a well-watered plain, the banks were dotted with vegetation that, although sparse, seemed to offer the promise of a sustainable life.

Eager to reach the banks, they summoned what strength remained and attempted to run down the hill, only to find themselves tripping after the first few tottering steps and launching into a wild, tumbling descent. When, at last, they came to rest in an inglorious tangle of limbs, they lay where they had fallen, unmoving and barely breathing. When Adam turned his head to regard his wife, whose face was plastered with straw and dirt, hair a wild and riotous mane, she smiled.

And then she began to laugh.

Softly at first and then building in volume and intensity.

Thinking, at first, whatever tenuous grip she'd maintained on her sanity had finally and irrevocably been surrendered, he soon realized the laughter was born out of a sense of relief. They had, indeed, survived, and here, along these banks, was the potential for a new life.

When, at last, he helped her to her feet, they turned and began stumbling toward the water. On the banks of that sweetly flowing river, they stripped off the stinking animal skins and fell headlong into the cool stream. As the current washed away months of accumulated filth and grime, something began to rise within, blasting its way through layers and layers of despair.

Hope.

"You were right, Husband," she said as they sat in soft grass, sharing a sweet and succulent piece of fish. "We did survive."

"We are surviving. Survival is not something just in the past; it will be ongoing. It's what The Alpha said. He did not say our banishment from the Garden would destroy us, but that we would have to fight to live."

Gazing far across the gently rippling waters, she said, "I yet struggle to believe all that has happened. That it actually *did* happen."

"I know what you mean. It was all so sudden, being forced to flee like we did. And the journey here to this point—even though I have no idea where *here* is. I find I am having a difficult time putting everything into place as if the whole thing has been a story of a terrible tragedy—something that happened to someone else."

"Well," she said, her voice colored with sorrow, "there is no one else, and I remember it vividly. *All* of it." She paused and then continued quickly, "A big part of that memory is the way I dishonored you—blamed you for everything. And I—"

"Listen," he said, turning to cup her face in his rough hand, "there was plenty of blame to go around, and I confess my part. But that was then, and I do not think The Alpha would be pleased were we to continue to dwell on what happened."

"So, you think He still cares for us?"

It was a question that had echoed unceasingly in, among, and through the twisted canyons of his conscious mind throughout their journey.

"I do," he said simply. "For Him not to care would be against His very nature. Just because we failed Him and caused Him horrible disappointment does not mean He has withdrawn His love."

"But He said we'd never see His face again."

"What we did brought about the end of intimacy as we had come to know it. But He is still our Father, and we are His children."

"It doesn't feel that way."

Rolling onto his side, he said, "Let me ask you something: do you think we just stumbled onto this spot? Or do you think our Father somehow guided us here?"

Through tears, which sprang unbidden in her eyes, Eve said, "I don't know, Adam. I really don't know."

Falling back into the grass, he said, "Yes, well, neither do I, but it's what I like to imagine, for the alternative is simply too grievous to bear."

"So, what do we do next?"

"Well, first, we put our excellent construction skills to work and build a dwelling. We've done it once. We can do it again."

"And perhaps improve on the original design."

"Yes," he replied with a laugh, "and now that I finally know how to build a proper door, it should progress more rapidly."

She sat up, staring around the area. "I miss our wolves."

"I miss many things, Eve, but we have each other. And don't forget what The Alpha told us at our creation. That we are to be fruitful and multiply. Even though our bodies are no longer immortal, we shall be long-lived and vital, producing many offspring, and our offspring shall produce offspring and their offspring until one day our descendants fill the Earth."

"Then," she said, "we'd better get going on that dwelling. It sounds as if we are going to need it."

Hearing a commotion behind them, they turned to see two skinny, bedraggled, and unidentifiable creatures silhouetted on the crest of the hill behind them. Suddenly, one of the creatures gave a loud bark, followed by a howl of recognition, before plunging into a headlong dash down the slope, headed straight for them.

Adam stood, squinting against the setting sun. "Could that be . . ."

"Impossible."

As the two animals got closer, however, it became clear that somehow their wolves had left the Garden in search of their human companions and had at long last found them.

"Blue," Adam shouted, with his arms stretched wide. "Shadow. Come on. Come and see us."

Without breaking their stride, the wolves barreled into them, knocking both to the ground, where they were promptly sat upon, their faces covered with wet and slobbering kisses.

"Okay, okay," Adam said, laughing. "I missed you, too."

Pulling herself into a sitting position, Eve stared around the area, cupping Shadow's muzzle in her hands and staring into her eyes.

Her voice colored with concern, Eve said, "Shadow, where are your babies?"

The animal threw her head back and howled so mournfully that both the man and woman wept bitterly at the sound, realizing that in the wolves' desperate attempt to find them, their pups had been lost.

Blue simply sat in place, his great head hanging sorrowfully.

"How did you find us?" Adam said, fully expecting the same level of communication he had enjoyed prior to the ousting from the Garden.

Blue lifted his gaze and stared helplessly into Adam's eyes.

"Oh, right. We can't speak with you anymore."

"Well," Eve said, "we have all lost much. But here we are. Together. And from this spot, we can start again."

Blue stood, shook himself mightily, and barked once before plunging into the shallow waters along the bank of the river. He began leaping and barking as if attempting to entice Shadow to join him.

"Come on," Eve said. "We'll go in together."

Reluctantly following on her heels, Shadow joined Eve and Blue in the water. She stood staring straight ahead as if deciding how she would proceed. Finally, she charged straight toward her mate, joining him in unrestrained frolic.

As Adam stood on the bank watching the joyful scene, he began speaking, "I know you have departed from me, Alpha, but I yet feel Your Presence. I feel it in the peace I see transforming Eve's face. I feel it in these two brave animals—thank you, by the way, for letting them come. I feel it in this spot to which You have drawn us by Your hand. I feel it in the renewed hope rising in my heart. And I say to You that I shall serve You all the days of my life—good days, bad days, challenging days, as well as joyful ones. For You are mine, and I am Yours."

"Well . . ." Apollyon said, standing to the side and observing the reunion between the man and woman and their animals. "What do we have here? Could it be the rebirth of hope? Can't have that now, can we?" Walking closer to where the man stood on the bank of the river, he leaned in, whispering, "Hello, Adam," causing the man to jump as if he'd been prodded by a sharp stick.

"What? Who said that? Alpha?"

"Oh," Apollyon said, around a raucous laugh, "I assure you that I am most certainly *not* The Alpha. You must forgive me, as I don't believe we've been formally introduced."

Turning in circles and attempting to spot the speaker, Adam said, "Why can't I see you? Who are you?"

Even though he knew which side of the Curtain he was supposed to stay on, Apollyon materialized into the best representation of himself in human form that he could manage. "There now. Is that better?"

Adam saw the form of a man, only not quite a man. He had all the right appendages and body structure, but there was something about his face that just wasn't right. For one thing, it kept wavering in the same manner the surface of the water changed in response to a breath of wind.

"Look, I don't know who you are, but—"

Adopting the pitch and timbre of the serpent's voice, he replied, "Oh, Adam, I so love our times together. You are my closest friend, and I only want to be with you and Eve because you two are the only ones who will listen to my incessant talking."

"That was you?"

"Well, not precisely, but close enough."

Eve walked up to stand behind Adam. "What he means, Adam, is that he possessed the serpent and made it do what he wanted it to do."

"Now, that isn't true," Apollyon replied. "I didn't *make* him do anything. I simply requested that I be allowed access to his mind, and he agreed. And, by the way, it is nice to meet you face-to-face, lovely lady."

"Once again," Adam said, "who are you?"

"Why, I'm Apollyon, and I am the god of this world."

"Liar!" Eve shouted. "The Earth is The Alpha's and everything in it!"

"Is that what the Alpha told you? My dear, nothing could be further from the truth. While it is true that He gave you and your husband power, dominion, and authority over everything on Earth, when you decided you wanted to be like the Alpha, falling for my little charade and eating of the forbidden fruit, all that fell to the ground. And wouldn't you know it? I was right there to pick it up. So, this kingdom . . ." he said, stretching his arms and grandly dangling the keys on an ancient worn chain in front of them, "now belongs to me. Which brings me to the reason for this little introduction."

"What do you want from us?" Adam said bitterly. "You've already taken everything we had."

"Not quite. While losing the Garden was a tremendous blow to your Creator and, by extension, to you as well—and then there is the little matter of also losing your immortality—I find it woefully insufficient as far as satisfying my need. In fact, it is not even close."

"Then," Eve said, "what *do* you want?"

"Well," Apollyon said, "for starters, I want your pride and self-esteem. Think about it: so many trees in the Garden, so many varieties of fruit, and The Alpha said you could eat as much as you wanted. But were you satisfied? No. There was one thing He said you couldn't do." He paused to hold up his index finger. "Just one thing. Don't eat the fruit from that tree. Could you do it? No, you couldn't. And why not? I will tell you why. It's because you are weak and pathetic. You do realize that you haven't ruined everything for just the two of you, right?" Screaming, he added, "You've ruined it for all your children for all eternity!"

Fighting off rising despair, Adam said, "Is that all?"

"I'm just getting warmed up. I want you to suffer mental anguish every second that you continue to draw breath. Which, as it turns out, won't be that much longer." He pierced the man and woman with a gaze of pure evil and continued,

"Most of all, I want your lives. I want your souls and the souls of your offspring. You see, the thing is . . . well . . . I hate The Alpha! And because I hate Him, I hate you! When I see you, it reminds me of Him. I hate you with every fiber of my being and will expend every resource at my disposal to destroy you. And do you want to know why? It is because you stole everything from me. It all vanished because of you. And now, you're going to die!"

Before he could make a move, Michael appeared with the Sword of Truth leveled at Apollyon's face.

"Not today. In fact, not any day."

"Stand aside, Michael. This is *my* world. I can do anything—"

"No, you can't actually. And you know it."

"What are you talking about?"

"You can't kill them. You can't kill any of their offspring. You cannot even touch their bodies. All you can do is tempt and *attempt* to influence."

Apollyon threw his head back, shouting, "My Legion, attend unto me!" Suddenly, he was surrounded by countless swarming demonic entities.

While Adam and Eve couldn't see the horde pressing in against the Curtain, ready to strike, they nevertheless felt an increase in tension, a more pronounced heaviness in the atmosphere.

Michael said, "Do you actually believe that any of these pathetic, shriveled creatures pose even the slightest threat to me?"

Adam and Eve stood well back from the confrontation, stunned into silence by the sudden appearance of the mighty warrior angel, unsure as to whose side he was on. Unbeknownst to them, their guardians had already formed around them and stood at the ready should the situation escalate.

Eve whispered, "What is happening, Adam?"

"I don't know, but I'm pretty sure the big guy with the flaming sword is on our side."

"That's comforting."

Apollyon hollered, "Numbers, Michael, numbers. We will overwhelm you."

"You will not."

"Shall we find out?"

"Enough!"

The command split the atmosphere, shaking the ground beneath their feet and sending the man and woman onto their faces.

"It's The Alpha," Adam whispered, both hands covering the back of his head, not daring to even risk a sideways glance.

Gazing upon the scene from His throne room, The Alpha said fiercely, "Listen, Dragon, you exist out of My mercy and good graces and would do well to never forget that. You know the terms of your incarceration here. This world is *not* yours but Mine. The man and woman are not yours but Mine, as are all future generations."

"But," Apollyon said, "I destroyed everything You had planned."

"No, you compromised *a* plan," the Alpha said. "One. Do you not know that My thoughts are not your thoughts, that your ways and imaginings are not Mine? Did you think that I would make no provision for this probability? Never forget that as high as these heavens are above the Earth, so are My ways higher than your ways and My thoughts higher than your thoughts. Concerning the man and woman, they yet retain the power to choose."

"But what about—"

"The choice into which you tempted them? While it is true, they chose poorly earlier—and are now suffering through the consequence of their choices." He paused for emphasis, then added, "Like you—their entire lives are laid out before them, filled with endless possibilities. You will not compromise that life. As Michael said, you may tempt and persuade, but nothing more."

"They sinned!" Apollyon roared. "Are you telling me that You're going to just let that pass? You didn't let me pass."

"Their sin is real and requires a sacrifice, and make no mistake, sacrifice they shall. But that is none of your concern. Now, unless you wish for Me to unleash My warrior archangel on your pitiful minions and, as a result, suffer even more loss than you already have, I suggest you depart."

As Apollyon's image wavered in and out, he shouted, "This isn't over!"

Michael said, "You seem fond of saying that, but I assure you that *this,*" he gestured toward the prostrate man and woman, "is most definitely over. You will go, and you will make no further threats to their well-being." Stepping forward threateningly, he added, "You know, I have been looking for an excuse to use this sword on you—again. I suggest you not provide me with one."

"You can't do this," Apollyon said.

The Alpha rumbled, "Pathetic and twisted thing, who are you to tell the Ancient of Days what He can and cannot do? I put a sun in the sky, and it will mark your days in a countdown to your end. And it *will* come. Now, before My wrath becomes more than I can contain, begone!"

As if unleashing the blast of a mighty wind, The Alpha's pronouncement sent Apollyon and all his minions tumbling across the landscape as far as the horizon and beyond.

It was only then that the man and woman dared look up. What they saw was Michael in all his splendor.

"Do not be afraid. Stand," he said gently.

Unsure of themselves, the man and woman did as instructed, finding they were still shaky due to the weeks of insufficient nutrition and water.

Cowering unconsciously from the majestic figure, Adam said, "What just happened?"

"First of all, although we have met before, you won't remember me, Adam, but I was there when you were created. I am Michael. The Alpha's warrior archangel."

"You're right, I don't remember. This is Eve."

Smiling, Michael replied, "Yes, I know her well, although we haven't interacted."

Eve said, "Everything has happened so quickly; it has left my head spinning trying to comprehend it all. The serpent, eating the fruit, hiding in shame, The Alpha confronting and then banishing us from the Garden, our desperate flight to reach here. As Adam said, wherever *here* is. And now, being witness to what just happened. It's almost as if my mind is refusing to process anything further until I can sort out what has already gone on."

"I understand how overwhelmed you must be," Michael said. "But steady yourselves because something else is coming."

He had barely finished speaking when Gabriel appeared, causing the couple to stumble backward even further.

"Adam, Eve," Gabriel said, "Fear not, for I am Gabriel who stands in the Presence of The Alpha. He has sent me with a message."

"Then, say on," Adam replied.

"You will wander no further but will build your dwelling here and, in this place, you will begin to produce sons and daughters, and they will also produce sons and daughters, and eventually, your seed will cover the Earth. You carry The Alpha's life force. As a result, you and your offspring will live long and fruitful lives despite your sin. The years will come and go, and although it will be hard, you will find contentment in your work, joy in your children, and joy in each other.

"You will make offerings to The Alpha for your sin in a manner that will be explained to you and thus escape the immediate consequence that your sin demands. As you have seen, Apollyon is at large on Earth and will be an ongoing source of trouble and temptation. Because he cannot touch your flesh without permission, he will assail your mind and your spirit with lies." He paused briefly. "And those aggressive animals you encountered on your journey here? View Apollyon in the same manner you view them, for he ever lives to steal, kill, destroy, and devour everything about you. So, be vigilant. Be alert. He is now and ever shall be your adversary. Awareness is your best protection against his wiles."

“Will it ever stop?” Eve said. “You know, the hardness you spoke of?”

“No, Eve, it will not. And I don’t have to tell you why.”

Dropping her gaze, she nodded in understanding.

Gabriel said, “The Alpha told you once that He had given His angels charge over you to keep you from stumbling.”

“That obviously didn’t work out so well,” Adam said.

“No, Adam, it did not. But never forget why. It was due to your own foolish choices. Choose well, and your life will be well-lived, and your children will call you blessed.”

“And if I don’t?”

“Then sorrow will mark your days, and you will go down to the Earth in death, leaving nothing to show for your years of sojourning on this planet.”

The two wolves, who had remained at the riverbank, came and stood proudly by the couple’s side, their eyes trained on the spot where Michael and Gabriel stood.

Michael said, “Look upon these two animals as a gift from The Alpha, simply because, in spite of everything that happened, He did not wish for you to be alone.”

“It is a great kindness,” Adam said.

“Farewell,” Gabriel said, “our task here is now completed. And remember, live well and you will be well-loved by all who come after.”

With that, the two imposing figures stepped back through the Curtain and faded from view, leaving the man and woman staggered by the experience.

“We are not alone,” Adam said.

"And we never shall be."

The sun had just dipped below the hills and was in the process of painting the sky, a masterpiece from the brush of The Alpha meant for their eyes alone.

Choking back his emotion, Adam managed, "He still loves us," as he placed both arms around his wife and pulled her close, repeating, "He still loves us."

Staring at the deepening twilight, Eve said softly, "And . . . do you still love me, Husband? I mean, after all the grief I have caused?"

Maintaining the embrace, he replied, "*We* caused, Wife. We. And yes, I still love you. Even more than before."

They lay themselves down there in the sweet grasses. They were naked, and they were not ashamed. They knew each other, and it was good.

Chapter Thirty-Nine

From His throne in the City on a Hill, The Alpha stared toward The North and the vast emptiness where Proud Mountain had once stood in all its majestic splendor. In His mind's eye, He could still see the white-capped peaks, the waterfalls that fed into the Rainbow Stream, and the wildflowers dusting its lower slopes, all set in place by His creative hand. It had been a thing of wonder, a thing of beauty, until the land itself had succumbed to Apollyon's rebellious schemes.

Because His righteous anger had been stirred by Apollyon's insurrection, naught remained but a scar on the landscape, put there when He had wrenched the mount from its foundations and plunged it into Deep Lake, where it now sat with the jagged underside jutting skyward. Surrounded by a chasmic abyss separating it from the Lake of Fire, it was a source of pain each time His gaze fell upon it.

He could have created something new, and why wouldn't He? It was what He did, for He was the Creator. Something clever and bright so He need never be reminded of the whole sorry incident ever again.

And yet, He hesitated.

Standing, The Alpha descended the steps of the dais and walked across the Fiery Stones, His feet sending tendrils of fire dancing across the surface. When He reached the outer court,

He paused with His gaze firmly fixed on the ravaged landscape in the distance. Then, He summoned the archangels.

When they were all gathered, He said, "I have called you here to witness something unusual. You have seen My creative powers previously, but now I want to show you something else."

"Are you going to make another being?" Jophiel asked.

Smiling, The Alpha said, "No, Jophiel, I think we have enough as it is right now." He paused and walked toward the far edge of the court with the archangels following close behind. "By making choice an essential element in My higher-created beings whom I love, it ushered in the potential for wrong choices to be made, resulting in unintended consequences. I always knew it could happen. Always. While I have foreseen all possible consequences, I hoped they would not come about. So, then the question arises of what to do with those consequences. Before you exists a graphic example of what I am talking about."

Michael said, "Proud Mountain, or at least, what's left of it."

"Yes, Michael. It's the *what's left of it* that concerns Me. And I sit there on My throne, viewing that massive consequence and pondering what should be done. I've had many thoughts, not the least of which is simply waving My hand and erasing everything you see and starting over. And I will admit that it's tempting."

Gabriel asked, "Is that what we're here to see?"

"No, it's not. What you are here to see is an element of my creative ability that exists in direct response to the issue of consequence. Do you remember when Apollyon boasted there was nothing I could create that he could not corrupt?" As angel heads nodded all around, He continued, "And you will also recall my reply that there is nothing he can corrupt that I cannot choose to redeem. Redemption is a powerful word, My mighty archangels. It represents making up for something or getting something back that has been taken away from you. And that's what wrong choices do—they take something away you could never get back on your own. Witness the man and woman there on Earth."

Raphael said, "Are you talking about a way for them to get back what was lost?"

"On their own, they can never regain what has been lost. That would require a redeemer—one to stand in their place. Now, however, I want you to cast your gaze on the ruin there in The North, for I am going to take this present devastation and redeem it—reforming and renewing—so that it may once again be of use in My Kingdom. The remnant of Proud Mountain existing as an island in Deep Lake will now become a paradise for those who need a resting place in the midst of their journey."

Chamuel asked, "Who exactly are we talking about, Alpha?"

"Because of sin, Apollyon and his following were thrown out of Shamayim. And because of sin, death has now entered into the physical world, and Apollyon holds the keys. Man will be his prisoner, and sin will exact a heavy toll on those living in the land of the shadow of death."

"Death," Chamuel said. "I do not know this term."

"The man and woman—and all their offspring—are immortal in their spirit, just as you are. But because of their rebellion, their physical bodies will eventually perish. We need a place where their spirits can dwell to await that which is to come."

Zadkiel said, "But why can't they just come here, Alpha?"

"Sin, Zadkiel. Adam and Eve embraced it when they disobeyed My edict. Therefore, everyone born of man throughout the entirety of human history will now carry that stain, and I cannot allow it here. So, there must be a place of rest for the faithful until the time of the Solution."

"The faithful? Who are they?" Michael asked.

"Those who believe in Me and My promises."

Perplexed, Michael said, "I don't understand. How can anyone not believe in You? Even Apollyon and all his minions believe in You."

"Consider this: He was an angel in a perfect environment, created from perfection, given beauty beyond measure, freely enjoying all the benefits of the Spiritual Realm, living among perfect and loving family members, and given anything he ever desired. And yet it wasn't enough."

"I see Your point. He had even less of an excuse than Adam and Eve. No one enticed him. No one persuaded him."

"Correct. For this reason, no redemption has been or will be provided for those of the Spiritual Realm."

"And," Michael said, "what is the Solution?"

"From the seed of a woman, one is coming who will do for them what they cannot do for themselves." The Alpha paused and then added, "Lest you think that any of this has caught Me by surprise . . . there *is* a redeemer. There has *always* been a redeemer, even from the foundations of the world."

"Who is this redeemer?" Gabriel asked.

"You know him, but you do not. He is with you but apart. You see him yet remain unseeing. He will be revealed soon enough. But now . . . turn your attention . . . behold."

The Alpha waved his hand and a deep rumbling began, rolling across the landscape as the remnants of Proud Mountain and the Lake of Fire were lifted into Shamayim's atmosphere along with Deep Lake.

"Alpha," Michael said nervously, "what are you doing?"

"Apollyon loved his precious Proud Mountain so much that I am going to place it nearer to him."

"But he's in Earth's atmosphere."

"Correct. Deep Lake, Proud Mountain, and the Lake of Fire will now be relegated to The Void deep beneath the Earth's surface, where they will exist as the holding area for humans after life on Earth. The torn and ragged base of Proud Mountain, now a lake of fire, is the future place of an arid existence and torment for those who choose to follow Apollyon and his evil ways. Deep Lake, holding the inverted top of Proud Mountain, will be a place of peace for The Faithful who believe in Me and follow the way of righteousness."

Deep Lake, Proud Mountain, and the Lake of Fire hung suspended above Shamayim's landscape while a portal gradually opened, through which the archangels could see, as it were, into another dimension. The rumbling gained in intensity, the atmosphere rippling and crackling with pure energy as the portal opened wider, wider—wide enough to envelop the entirety of Proud Mountain inside Deep Lake, and adjacent to it, the Lake of Fire.

Then, The Alpha thundered, "Begone," and the portal closed, snapping shut as the atmosphere of Shamayim split with a crack of thunder.

In the silence that followed, Jophiel said, "They are gone, but I can still see the island of Proud Mountain in Deep Lake and the Lake of Fire clearly."

"Yes," The Alpha replied, "we will be able to see them, and they us."

"Who is *them,* Alpha?" Zadkiel asked.

"A great gulf has been affixed separating the Kingdom of Darkness from Shamayim. Those who choose to die in their unrighteousness, whose father is Apollyon, will go to the place now existing near the Earth's core. I call it Tartarus. Some will call it Hell. But for those who die in righteousness . . ." A wave of His hand and the ragged landscape of upended Proud Mountain was instantly recreated. "Behold a lush green island of rest, contentment, and peace. Because of sin, the souls of the man and woman and all their offspring now occupy mortal bodies. But their spirits are eternal. When their physical bodies die, the spirits of the faithful dead will come here. I call it Rest in Peace City."

The archangels beheld a wonder. An island sprung up surrounded by a deep chasm separating it from The Void and Tartarus. An island whose landscape was filled with hills and lagoons and waterfalls and groves of flowering trees and meadows of sweet grasses. It was beautiful and yet wild. A peaceful paradise that seemed to reach out, beckoning all to come and experience and tame its beauty.

"Alpha," Gabriel said breathlessly, "it is . . . I don't know. I wish I had a word that was beyond beautiful."

Laughing, The Alpha said, "Beautiful will do, Gabriel. And now, gather 'round. I must instruct you for that which is to come." He paused and then said, "As I said, death will come to every man and woman. Some will fall asleep, some will die by violent means, but all will come to the afterlife filled with fear and trepidation. All will descend into The Void, where they will live out the consequences of their choices, awaiting final judgment, or for those who die in righteousness, they will need help in the transition."

Gabriel asked, "What about Adam and Eve? Will they ever be considered righteous given their sin in the Garden?"

The Alpha said, "I will be crediting the humans' faith in Me and their belief in the coming redeemer as righteousness. Because I don't want any of My faithful ones to be snatched from My hand, we need secure transport to Rest in Peace City. It will sting the Dragon that there are those so close to his kingdom that are set apart for Me, and, make no mistake, there will be opposition."

The Alpha looked over at Michael and then scanned the other archangels, "I will, therefore, need angels to serve as an Honor Guard to greet and then usher the faithful into their new existence. This will be an ongoing mission. Expect resistance. Expect trouble. Now, who from among the warriors would you recommend, Michael?"

"Steele and Wendly," he replied without hesitation. "They are currently unassigned and will serve You well in that position."

"I agree. Let it be so."

"Alpha," Gabriel said, "are we expecting someone to die? I thought the man and woman and their offspring would be blessed with long life."

"Possibilities, Gabriel, we must always consider the possibilities. Here, we have no time, but on Earth, time and the Clock of Consequence hold sway, and with each passing day, Apollyon's stain of sin increases, and with it, the possibility for him to influence someone toward wrong choices. We must be ready for any eventuality."

Michael summoned Steele and Wendly, who arrived looking confused and a little fearful as they bowed their faces to the ground in the Presence of The Alpha.

Steele said, “Are we in—”

“You’re fine,” Michael said, “The Alpha has a new assignment for you.”

“Stand, My faithful angels,” The Alpha said as He stepped back to regard the wary pair. “Since your creation, you have done everything required of you without hesitation, fear, or questioning. And while you have each faced battle and have been wounded in the process, those wounds only add to your identity. But more than that, they add to your compassion. Both are required for what I need you to do.”

“Alpha,” Wendly said softly, hesitantly, “we will be honored to do anything You ask.”

“I know you will, Wendly. Cast your gaze northward.”

Wendly and Steele turned their eyes toward The Alpha’s newest creation.

Steele said, “It is indescribably beautiful. What is it for?”

After The Alpha explained the purpose, Wendly said, “I can’t imagine what that will be like for them: to go from a human existence in a human body and suddenly find themselves in a completely different realm.”

“Which is why,” The Alpha said, “I need you two to be there to usher them in, reassure them, and welcome them to their new existence. I am empowering you to develop the system by which this occurs.”

Steele said, “So, it will just be us?”

"For now, but in the future, as more humans are born, we will expand this mission of angels who will specialize in this process. I, therefore, empower you to recruit and train others to assist you."

Wendly stared toward the island.

"What are you thinking, Wendly?" Michael asked.

"I was just trying to picture someone dying and what it will be like during the transition."

"And do you have some thoughts?"

"Well, I see a long, narrow bridge across the chasm connecting the Void with Rest in Peace City. See it?"

Michael squinted until he saw it and then nodded.

Wendly continued, "They could travel with our team from the Physical Realm through the Void after their death to the edge of the chasm by the bridge entrance. We could escort them across the bridge and safely into Rest in Peace City after the Honor Guard team arrives with their assignment. Now . . . what is that other place? "

"Hell," The Alpha replied.

"Right. So, Steele and I would meet them at the bridge and then take them to the island and . . . and what if one of the first things we did was to ask them to tell us their story? You know, what their life was like."

The Alpha smiled. "I love it. That's exactly what I was hoping for."

"Alpha?" Michael said. "What is to stop Apollyon's demons from crossing the bridge and entering the City?"

Smiling broadly, The Alpha replied, "Me."

Having previously been of no significance whatsoever, time now carried abundant consequence.

And the clock ran.

It ran forward as far as the humans experienced, but Apollyon and his followers knew the Clock of Consequence was like an hourglass counting down to judgment and an unknown doom.

The years passed in regimented precision.

Almost without being aware of it happening, thirty years had gone by since the humiliating banishment from the Garden.

Gabriel's message to the man and woman had been accurate in every detail.

They had settled.

They had built.

They had loved.

Children had been born.

And there, by the river, their family had grown, flocks and herds flourished, fields were planted and harvested, and a settlement grew up out of the ground.

First came the two boys. Cain, the farmer and tiller of the ground, and Abel, the shepherd. And then, soon after, the twin daughters, Awan and Azura, as well as younger siblings.

When Cain and Abel were fourteen and twelve, respectively, they and the ten-year-old twins set out one day to explore the eastern bank of the river. Of course, living as they did on the western bank, this required first discovering a means and method of crossing the river. So, they walked downstream until they came to a section where the current slowed, and the water was only up to Cain's waist, and Abel could throw a rock from one side to the other.

"This is the spot," Cain said.

Azura said, "Maybe for you, but the water will be up to our necks."

"It will be all right, Azura. Cain is wise in the ways of the river. We should trust him," Awan said.

Abel said, "She's right. Cain can hold your hand, and I can take care of Awan."

Azura wasn't convinced. "I don't know. The current looks very strong. What if you lose your grip on me? The river will carry me away."

"Look, we all want to explore the other side, right? And this is the only spot we've found where we can get across."

The four siblings stood on the bank staring at the far side, no one willing to take the first step.

Finally, Abel grabbed Azura's hand, hollered, "Come on," and strode confidently into the current, almost dragging his sister behind him.

As soon as her feet touched the water, Azura screamed because of the cold but soon had both arms around Abel's neck, laughing as he forged and splashed his way across the expanse.

When they reached the other shore, soaked from head to toe, Abel shouted, "Come on, Cain. It's easy. I did it, and you're bigger and stronger than me."

Cain stood there, Awan's hand fearfully grasping his, and stared at his brother on the opposite bank—a bank that suddenly seemed double the distance he had first imagined.

"Come on," Abel repeated. "What are you waiting for?" A question echoed by Azura who, to be fair—and to his utter vexation—repeated nearly everything her older brother said.

What *was* he waiting for? The question flopped around inside his brain like a gaffed fish hauled onto dry ground.

Abel had done it. He could do it, too.

Abel had done it. Well, of *course* Abel had done it. Abel could do anything, or so it seemed. While he had never understood it, the simple fact remained that his brother really could do anything he put his mind to. He was just gifted like that. On the other hand, facing the same set of challenges, Cain would struggle to simply survive while Abel battered challenges into submission, producing exceptional results.

It didn't seem fair. He was, after all, the older sibling. Shouldn't he be the one doing all the excelling? Complicating the situation was the fact that his younger brother was their mother's favorite. It was no secret she even preferred him to the twins, who, for their part, didn't seem to mind.

But Cain minded. He minded quite a lot.

Abel hollered, "Come on, Brother. We're waiting for you."

Noticing her big brother's hesitancy, Awan said, "We don't have to go, Cain. I'd be happy just to stay on this side and explore with you if you want to."

He stared down at his little sister, tenderly stroking her hair. "I know, kid. But we have to go. I have to go, or Abel will never let me hear the end of it."

Staring at the far bank where Abel and Azura stood waiting, he whispered, "Why do you always have to be the first and the best at everything, Brother?" and then answered his own question with, "It's because of situations just like this. You're always forging ahead, and I'm always hanging back. You always give your all, and I always hold something in reserve."

It was true. He knew it and had allowed a strange blend of admiration and resentment to take seed and germinate.

In the end, he shouted, "I've changed my mind, Brother. We're just going to continue downstream for a bit. Have fun, and we'll see you back home."

"Suit yourself," Abel replied as he watched his big brother turn away from yet another challenge.

"Why does he always do that?" Azura asked.

"Because he's afraid."

"Of what? Failure?"

Abel thought about it for a moment. "No, I think it's more like he's afraid of success because if he succeeds, he will be expected to succeed every time he does something. I should know because that's the way it is for me. It's a lot to deal with."

"But why?" Azura said as they sat down under the generous canopy of a nearby tree.

"Well, think about it. Mom and Dad, you and Awan and Cain, even our little brothers and sisters all know I'm good at getting things done, right?"

"Right."

"And not just getting things done but doing it really well."

"Is there a problem with that?"

He scooted around so he could see his sister. "You wouldn't think so, but every time I try something, now all I can think about is, well, what if I let them down or what if this time isn't as great as last time and—"

"And for Cain, it's better to not try at all than to have to put up with all that?"

"Exactly."

She was quiet for a few moments.

"Can I tell you something in secret, Abel?"

"Of course. You know I've always kept your secrets."

"Right. Well, okay . . . it's just that sometimes I don't think Cain likes you very much."

"Why would you say that?"

"I don't know. The way he looks at you, things he says."

Abel laughed. "I don't think there's anything to it. Probably just a little jealousy."

She was shaking her head. "No, not just that. There's something in his eyes." She paused and then added, "You should be careful around him."

"Careful? What are you talking about? He's my brother."

"It's probably nothing," she said. "Hey, I thought we were going to explore this bank."

"That's right. You ready, squirt?"

"I told you not to call me that."

"Squirt, squirt, squirt," Abel said, running and laughing as Azura tried to catch him.

The man and woman had a good life there on the banks of the river and had settled into a rhythm of building, birthing children, and training them in The Alpha's ways. Even though Adam no longer saw His face, he knew He was there and, more than that, knew *Him.* The years of daily walks in the Garden had developed an intimacy of knowledge even the banishment couldn't erase, and he passed that knowledge along to his children whose questions regarding The Alpha were seemingly endless. But he enjoyed the task, delighting in regaling them with stories about the naming of the animals and their mother riding on the back of the serpent.

With a new child coming along roughly every two to three years—and having to deal with the seven she already had—Eve learned to use the in-between times to accomplish the tasks and projects important to her, such as creating a proper home for her growing family. It was at one such time that she imagined the concept of a series of buildings laid out around a central gathering space, a space where various tasks would be done during the daylight hours and, in the evenings, common meals shared around a fire with much laughter and storytelling.

When she presented the idea to Adam, he simply stared at her, a funny little smile playing around his weathered face.

"What?" she said.

"You."

"What about me?"

"You're amazing."

"Well," she said, laughing shyly, "I don't know about that."

"No, it's true. You have always been gifted in this manner." He gestured at the plans she had sketched in the dirt. "Even in the Garden. Remember when you had the idea for an upper level?"

"That *was* a pretty good idea, wasn't it?"

"It was . . . and so is this. Looking at what you've drawn here in the dust of the ground, I can see it all in my mind. And not just this, but I can see a way for those who come after to organize their communal areas as well."

"Let's not get too far ahead of ourselves."

Adam said, "No, that's exactly what we need to do, Eve. We need to get very far ahead of ourselves. Look, The Alpha very clearly said that it is our responsibility to be fruitful and to multiply, right?"

Laughing, she said, "I don't know how much more fruitfulness I can take. In case you haven't noticed, childbearing is incredibly difficult. Remember when The Alpha was telling me how difficult it would be?"

"Yes, I do."

"Well, it's worse than that."

Taking her hands, he stared into her eyes—eyes that could still cause his heart to skip a beat even after all this time.

"Eve, I know . . . I know because I've seen your agony and heard your cries. But I've also seen the joy that comes when our little ones are in your arms and at your breast. And regardless of how difficult it all is, this is our task. You, to bear children and me, to work the land, which we will continue to do for as many years as The Alpha maintains the breath in our lungs. And that's what I'm talking about. Planning. We must plan for the fact that if we continue to have children—"

"Yes," she said with a chuckle, "I get it. Eventually, there will be a significant number of our offspring—"

"Who will all require places to live." Tapping her simple drawings with a twig, he added, "And this plan you've come up with is the way we make all of that happen."

"Well, I hadn't gotten quite that far with it, but you're right . . . when the time comes."

"No, I don't want to wait until the need is upon us. I'm talking about building now for what is yet to come. The boys and I need to begin laying all of this out, clearing trees, stockpiling wood and other supplies, and preparing to build."

"So," she said quietly, staring down at her drawing, "you want to build this now even though there are only nine of us?"

"That's exactly what I'm saying."

"And you think Cain and Abel will help you?"

"Of course. I mean, they have to. I'm their father, and they will do what I tell them."

She paused. "Kind of like you obeyed your Father?"

"Yes, well, hopefully, my boys will be more obedient than me."

Nodding, Eve said, "It's a good plan, Husband, you know . . . what you said. Now, can you rub my lower back, please? It's really tight."

Chapter Forty

The years came and went, and the passage of time brought changes to the small settlement on the riverbank. Children were born, and children grew older.

Abel moved out of the settlement, choosing a solitary life dedicated to knowing and pursuing The Alpha.

And while Abel pursued The Alpha, Apollyon and his helpers pursued Cain.

One day, while Cain was out in the field attempting to coax a crop out of the uncooperative soil, Semyaza spoke to him from behind the Curtain, saying, "I am impressed with your hard work, Cain."

Cain replied, "Who's there? Who's speaking?" while glancing fearfully around the area.

"Oh, let's just say that I am someone who probably appreciates what you do more than most."

"Why can't I see you?"

"Would you like to see me?"

"No, I'd prefer to continue talking to empty space."

Semyaza stepped through the Curtain and materialized, standing a few feet away and being careful to arrange his deformed features into the semblance of a man.

"That's a pretty neat trick," Cain said. "How'd you do that?"

"That's a good question, and I'm not sure I know the answer. But it's something it seems I've been taught to do."

"Who taught you?"

"My master. The god of this world. The great Apollyon."

"You don't know what you're talking about. The Alpha is the God of this world, and you should be careful what you say."

"The Alpha," Semyaza said, laughing mockingly, "has no authority here because your mother and father threw it all away when they sinned. My master picked up the keys and now owns it all."

"I'm not so sure about that," Cain said. "So, you can come and go as you please?"

Semyaza's face darkened. "I am unable to do much of anything I please."

"I understand that feeling," Cain said. "So, where do you live, and why haven't I seen you before—hey, wait . . . the only people are the ones my mother and father have birthed. And I know for a fact they didn't birth you. So, you'd better tell me what's going on right now."

"I am unlike you, Cain. I am spirit. The reason you can see me is because I can assume whatever shape I choose."

"So, for instance, if you wanted, you could be a donkey?"

Semyaza chuckled. "All right, well deserved. And, yes, I can."

Cain took a rag from the handle of his plow and wiped the sweat from his brow.

"When you say that you are a spirit, do you mean you're like The Alpha?"

"No," he replied harshly. "I am not now, nor shall I ever be like The Alpha."

"Whoa, hang on there. It was just a question. No need to get all stirred up."

"You are right, and I apologize. It's just that The Alpha and I share a particular history, the result of which has not always been in my favor."

Turning to stare at the long row stretching out in front of him, Cain said, "Can we get to why you interrupted my work? Because I'm losing daylight, and I've got a long way to go."

"As you wish." Semyaza paused and then asked, "How old are you, Cain?"

Casting his gaze heavenward, he wrinkled his brow. "Let's see . . . I have seen . . . twenty-five summers."

"And your brother Abel?"

"Twenty-three. What's this about?"

Ignoring the question, Semyaza pressed on. "And in all your years, have you ever—even once—felt like you were given your due?"

"You mean, do I feel respected?"

"Precisely."

"Look, I don't know you—don't know what or who you are, actually—and I'm not comfortable discussing things like this with—"

"So, that's a no?"

Cain stared at the apparition for several moments before saying, "If you must know . . . no, I don't. But I don't see what any of that has to do with you. Now, if you'll excuse me, I—"

"What it has to do with me, my friend, is that like you, I, too, have been robbed of what was rightfully mine, made to constantly feel as if I am substandard."

Cain turned, clicked his tongue, and the ox began trudging forward, dragging the plow behind him. "That's a very sad tale, but as you can see, I don't really have time for tales right now . . . sad or otherwise."

Remaining in place, Semyaza said loudly, "And what if I told you there was a way to remove all that troubles you? A way for you to experience the honor you have been lacking?"

Cain whistled the ox to a stop and stood leaning against the handles. "Then I'd say I'm listening."

"It's getting worse, Abel," Azura said, following Abel as he prodded a wayward lamb back into the flock.

"What's that?"

"The way Cain talks about you—looks at you."

"How many times do we have to talk about this, sis? It's like I keep saying; he's chosen to feel envy and resentment over what I've accomplished. Nothing more, nothing less."

"But the way he talks about you isn't good, Abel. While I haven't heard him come right out and say that he hates you, he might as well have. I've been telling you this since we were kids. Well, we're not kids anymore, and you really need to hear me."

Abel pondered her words, finally saying, "Even if everything you say is true, there's nothing I can do about it. I mean,

I'm not going to stop being the man I am just so I won't hurt my big brother's feelings or something."

Azura groaned in frustration. "That's what I'm trying to tell you, Abel. It is way past his feelings being hurt. Awan thinks he's actively plotting against you."

"Really? How so?"

"Like trying to sabotage your herds, maybe even kill some of your lambs and make it look like a wild animal did it. And if you weren't so solitary, you'd already know about this."

Coming to a spreading tree, he turned the flock loose to graze and pulled Azura down beside him to lean with their backs against the trunk.

"But I must be solitary, Azura."

"Why? I don't get it. In fact, none of us get why you've separated yourself from the family and spend all your time among these smelly sheep."

"Oh, they're not so bad once you get used to it."

Leaning closer, she sniffed. "Ugh, you smell just as bad as they do."

He laughed and playfully mussed her long locks just as he'd done since they were children.

Sobering, he said, "About the solitary thing. I suppose when you get right down to it, somewhere in my heart, I believe that by giving all of myself to The Alpha, I can somehow make up for how horribly disappointed He was with Mom and Dad and maybe even cause Him to relent, you know, allow us all back into the Garden."

"That will never happen."

"But how can you be sure?"

"The curse, Abel. What Mom and Dad did ruined everything for everyone. Forever."

"But maybe if I offer a better sacrifice—maybe if I offer myself as a sacrifice, He will—"

"Abel," she said sharply. "He won't. And you sacrificing yourself, your happiness, and your joy isn't going to make any difference. The only thing you will accomplish is to ruin your life and . . ." she sobbed. "You will break my heart."

Abel wrapped his arms around her. "Hey, come on. Don't cry."

"Why not? Isn't that what we do when our hearts break?"

Rocking her slightly, he said, "I know this is hard to understand—"

"Not hard. Impossible. Why don't you want us?"

"Azura, come on. It's not that, and you know it."

"But that's just the thing, Abel, I don't know it. None of us do."

He said, "Yes, well, I can't help that. This is what I have to do. What I am compelled to do."

Pulling back and sitting up straight, she said, "By who? Who is compelling you to do this?"

"My own soul, Azura. I couldn't live with myself if I turned back now."

"Well, now," Cain said as he strolled casually toward his brother and sister. "Isn't this a touching little scene?"

"What do you want, Cain?" Abel challenged, standing to his feet.

Cain stared long and hard at him. "I'm not sure you could handle hearing what I really want."

"I'm sure. So, why are you here?"

"Father wants us to help him gather wood for some project Mom has him doing."

Gesturing at his herds, Abel said, "I can't just leave my flocks and—"

"He said right now, little brother. He will be disappointed if you don't come," he paused and then added tauntingly, "and I can't imagine you wanting our father to be disappointed in you."

Azura said, "You'd better go, Abel. I'll stay and watch your flocks while you're gone."

"Fine," he said, throwing his hands up in frustration. "Tell Father I'll be there just as soon as I get our sister settled in."

Cain didn't answer but just turned and walked away with a strange little smile.

As Abel watched his brother go, he said, "What were you saying before we were so rudely interrupted, Azura?"

"You and me, we've always had a special connection, Brother, or at least I thought we did. But what you're doing with this solitary thing feels a lot like rejection, and I've got to tell you, it doesn't feel very good. So, stop it, Abel. Stop this foolishness and come back to the family. I need my big brother." Before Abel could reply, she continued, "Now, tell me what I need to do with the flocks and get going before Cain comes back."

She was right. He knew it. She knew it. But as for what to do about it, he had no idea.

After showing her the basics of what to do with the flocks in his absence, he headed down the well-worn trail that led to his mother and father's abode.

"What am I doing, Alpha?" Abel said out loud as he walked. "If my sacrifice isn't going to make any difference, then why needlessly frustrate my family and condemn myself to a life of loneliness?"

Deep within his spirit, he heard, *"Sacrifice to Me and then return to your family."*

He was so startled by the voice within that his steps staggered. "Sacrifice? Okay. But what do You require?"

"Your best."

"But that's what I'm already giving."

"Abel, I have seen your heart. You have been faithful to Me, sacrificing even more than your mother and father. Your willingness to sacrifice all you have and all you are has not gone unnoticed. But obedience is better than sacrifice. As an animal had to die to cover your parent's sin and nakedness, an animal must die to cover your sin. Therefore, in obedience, you will offer to Me the first fruits of your herd."

"First fruits? I'm not sure I understand."

"The best of what you produce. That is, portions of the firstborn lambs from your flock as a burnt offering to honor Me."

"And what about Cain? What about my parents and brothers and sisters?"

"I require first fruits from them as well."

"Because my sacrifice won't be enough?"

The Alpha said, *"Each must offer their own animal sacrifice. Help them in that. Now go, tell the others."*

As The Alpha withdrew, Abel found himself shaking in the aftermath of the encounter.

He had spoken to Him.

Him.

The Alpha.

He stood in place, his gaze casting here and there, not quite knowing what to do next.

"I have to tell the others."

He repeated the phrase over and over as he hurried back to where Azura was struggling to coax a lamb into the fold.

"Come, Sister," he hollered as he got closer.

Azura watched him approaching, saying in surprise, "What is this, Brother?"

Throwing his arms around her and hugging her tightly, he said, "I know what I have to do now, and it wasn't what I was intending."

"Care to explain that?"

"It might take some doing, but yes. In the meantime, just know that I am through with being solitary."

"So, you're coming back to the family?" she asked.

"I am," he said, unable to hold back a laugh. "Now, run ahead, get Mother and Father and tell them to gather the family. I have something to tell them from The Alpha."

"The Alpha," she said. "As in . . . *The* Alpha?"

"Yes. Now hurry."

As Azura ran off, Abel prepared to move his herd and then began walking back to the settlement, with the herd following close behind. Once there, he secured them inside a corral he had constructed from stacked rock and rough-hewn lumber.

It took Azura some time, but when everyone was assembled, his father said incredulously, "He spoke to you? The Alpha?"

"Yes, Father, He did. As clearly as you and I are speaking right now."

"Audibly?"

"Again, yes."

"I miss those days."

Cain scoffed. "Oh, isn't this just perfect! Not only are you the best at everything, but now you can also boast of being the only one The Alpha has spoken to—well, except when He used to walk with Dad in the Garden."

"It's not about boasting, Cain," Abel replied. "Boasting is not what I do. It's about passing along instructions from The Alpha."

"But why did He say this to you and, well, not me?"

"I don't know, but the fact remains that He did." He paused before adding, "And this is what He said: *As an animal had to die to cover your parent's nakedness, an animal must die to cover your sin. Therefore, in obedience, you will offer to Me the first fruits of your herd.*"

Adam said somberly, "I understand. You have no idea how much I understand."

"Tell us, Father," Abel said.

He drew in a long breath. "When your mother and I sinned, the glory of The Alpha we had always worn vanished, and we were naked. We tried to cover our own nakedness with fig leaves, but it wasn't enough. So, The Alpha killed an . . ." Emotion choked off his words, and he paused until it passed. "Uh, He killed an animal and took its skin and fashioned garments for your mother and me to wear. We still have them preserved as a memorial so that we never forget. That animal he killed? It was one I loved. Lamb, my friend. And Lamb had to give his life to cover our sin."

Cain said, "But I don't have any animals to kill. All I have are grains. These are my first fruits. It will have to do."

"That isn't what The Alpha said," Abel countered. "He said—"

"I heard you the first time," Cain snapped. "How about you worry about your sacrifice, and I will worry about mine?"

"Abel," Eve said, "can we purchase animals from your herd?"

"Of course, Mother, you and the rest of the family."

"Not me," Awan said. "I will go with Cain and offer the same sacrifice."

Azura said, "Don't be ridiculous, Awan. You already heard Abel say that only a blood sacrifice will be—"

Semyaza whispered something to Awan.

"I don't care what Abel said. How do we even know he's telling the truth?"

"Awan," Eve scolded. "Hold your tongue. Think about what you are saying."

"I am thinking about it, Mother. We already know Abel doesn't like Cain and is always trying to—"

"What?" Abel said. "That is completely untrue. It's Cain who doesn't like me. In fact, isn't it true, Brother, that you'd rather me be dead than alive?"

Cain stared balefully at his brother, saying, "You are already dead to me, dear Brother, so whether you live or die is of no consequence."

Adam approached his eldest son and stood staring into his eyes. "Watch your tongue, son!"

"Or what?"

"You forget your place, and you forget who I am."

"How could I forget who you are? You are the reason we are all here and not in the Garden."

Adam shoved his son, sending him stumbling backward and falling to the ground.

Trembling with rage, Adam said, "You will never speak of that again. In fact, if the next words out of your mouth do not include an apology to me, your mother, and all your siblings, I will finish what I have started."

Cain stared up at his father, fear having suddenly gripped his heart, realizing that the man possessed far superior strength.

Cain stood slowly and brushed the debris from his clothing. Then, without a word to anyone, he turned and walked away, with Awan following close behind.

Watching them go, Eve said, “What just happened, Husband?”

“I’m not sure, but unless I can reach his heart, this won’t end well.”

Chapter Forty-one

"Father had no right to speak to you in that manner," Awan said as she stomped along behind Cain and into a grove of trees about two hundred strides from the main family dwelling.

"Yes, he did. I may not like it, but he did have cause."

"But, Cain, he humiliated you in front of the whole family. In front of Abel."

"Abel's another matter entirely," he spat. "And I will deal with him in good time."

"It's just so unfair," she wailed. She sat down hard on the ground and leaned back against a sturdy bole. "No one appreciates you or anything you do."

"Except for you, dear sister," he said, sitting down beside her and putting his arm around her. "I don't know what I'd do without you."

"We've always been friends, haven't we, Cain?"

"Always." He laughed. "Remember that time when you were maybe five or six, and we were out somewhere with Abel and Azura like we always used to be, and she said that Abel was smarter than me, and you said no he wasn't, and she said yes he was, and you said no he wasn't and saw a little serpent by the side of the trail and picked it up and chased her with it threatening to shove it down her robe?"

"I would've done it, too," she said, joining in the laughter. "I think that's the loudest she's ever screamed in her entire life."

Their laughter died down, and they were both silent for a time. Awan finally said, "So, seriously, Cain, what are you going to do about this sacrifice Abel was talking about?"

"Well, first of all, who knows what it's really all about. I mean, I don't trust Abel."

Awan hesitated and then said, "Do you wish him harm?"

Cain waved off her question. "I was upset."

"And he drives you crazy."

Cain paused as if considering her statement. "He does. Always has. We used to be close, you know. Well, actually, you wouldn't know because it was when you and Azura were still little. But he used to follow me around everywhere. Everything I did, Abel was right there."

"It sounds like there was once love between you."

"There was."

"Then, what changed?"

"Him," he said harshly. "He changed. He went from being my cute little brother to being my rival. Whatever I did, he could do it better. Whatever idea I had, his was better."

"Well," she said, "you have to admit he is really smart and talented—"

"And handsome and gifted. Yeah, I get it." He stood and started pacing. "He's also infuriating. Take this thing with the sacrifice, for example. Why would The Alpha give instructions only to Abel for something that affects all of us? Why not me? I've always been the most responsible. Half the time, Abel's head is so far up in the clouds he doesn't have the slightest idea of what's going on around him. Me? I always know what's going on and have always been the one Mom and Dad counted on to—"

"Cain, you're my brother, and I love you, but Mom and Dad feel the same about both of you."

"That is not true," he said heatedly. "You know what? You're starting to sound just like them. Whose side are you on, anyway?"

Jumping to her feet, she said, "I'm on your side, Cain, just like I've always been. But if I hear you saying something untrue, I'm not going to let it pass. You know me better than that."

He covered his eyes with both hands and sighed deeply. "You're right . . . you're right. But I know how I feel. The Alpha choosing what Abel does as a shepherd and not what I do as a farmer makes me feel inferior."

"So, back to this thing about the sacrifice."

"What about it?"

"It seems to me that even though Abel is the one who told us about it, we still have to obey."

"But I worked hard on my crops. They are my first fruits and the best of what my hand has put to."

"Okay, but what if The Alpha really did speak to him and tell him to pass along the instructions for the sacrifice?"

"Then, we need to do it."

"Agreed. So, what are you going to do?"

He thought for a moment. "I'm just going to gather together the best of what I have, which is my grains, and present it as a burnt offering."

"But what about the shedding of blood thing for atonement? You can't ignore—"

"Yeah, I don't believe that. I don't believe The Alpha would ask something of me that I don't have. I don't see how trading for a lamb will give the Alpha my best."

"But," she said, "you could easily get it."

"And who would I get it from? Abel? Not a chance."

"Well, no offense, but now that I've had some time to think about it, I'm going to do exactly what The Alpha asked us to do."

"Fine. You do what you feel you must. I won't fault you for it. But please, extend me the same courtesy."

"You know I will."

"I hate this," he shouted.

"What?"

"This." Cain gestured wildly. "This whole sorry situation. I'm going for a walk. I just need to be alone for a while."

As she watched her brother walk away, Awan felt a prod of fear in her heart. As if he were walking straight into a trap. She almost ran after to tell him but stopped at the last second, choosing instead to return to the family compound where she would humble herself and ask Abel for the means to make her sacrifice.

"I still can't believe he said that."

Abel, Azura, and their father watched the herd feeding outside the compound.

"He was angry," Adam said. "Once he settles down, he'll come and apologize."

Abel laughed humorlessly. "First time for everything, I suppose."

"He won't," Azura said. "It's not in his nature."

"How can you be so sure?" Adam asked.

"Because I know him."

Abel added, "Azura has told me things from time to time about Cain's growing dislike of me. She's even told me in the past that I should be careful around him."

Adam walked a few paces away, his hands pressed against the sides of his head. "This is unbelievable. Why didn't someone tell me?"

Abel said, "We didn't want to trouble you."

"Trouble me? As if this doesn't? And now, it's not just about Cain's anger toward you; it's the fact that you both concealed it from me." He shouted toward the heavens, "My family is falling apart!"

"It's not like that, Father," Azura said. "It's just a simple dispute between brothers that—"

"Simple dispute? No, Azura," Adam said. "There is nothing simple about this. I can feel it. This is all about emotion that runs very deep."

"Father is right," Abel said. "This *is* deep and has been for a very long while. I thought it would pass because emotional turmoil always seems to pass. But it appears as if this is here to stay."

"What did you do to make your brother so angry?"

"I didn't do anything," Abel said in frustration, "other than tend my flocks and try to keep to myself as much as possible because, well, I didn't want to be around Cain for the simple reason that, lately, the mere fact that I continue to draw breath seems to anger him."

Azura said, "Father, if I'm being truthful, I have to tell you that Cain resents Abel."

"For what?"

"Everything. He's jealous. From what Awan has told me, he feels, and *has* felt for a while, that Abel is better and seems favored in all areas of life. He even believes that you and Mom favor him."

"Oh, that is absolutely not true."

"That's what I told him, but it's what he *believes* is true. Remember what you've always told us?"

Adam said wistfully, "If you believe something is true, it will eventually become your truth." He was silent for a few moments. "And this, quite obviously, has become your brother's truth."

"What do we do about it?" Abel asked.

"I'm not sure there's anything you or I or anyone can do. Once a lie takes hold, it is not so easily dislodged, for to do so feels like losing a part of yourself."

"Father," Azura said, "you don't think Cain would really do anything to hurt Abel, do you?"

"In his current state? I don't know. You should probably be on your guard, son."

"Oh, don't worry. I *have* been on my guard for quite some time now. Cain makes me very nervous."

"Good. I'm going to talk to your mother. See if she can speak to Cain and get him settled down. I mean, he's obviously not going to be open to having a conversation with me right now."

"And I'll talk to Awan," Azura said. "She has a lot of influence over him."

Abel scoffed. "It didn't sound like she was exactly open-minded."

"She'll listen to me."

Adam said, "In the meantime, about this sacrifice . . ."

"Don't worry about it," Abel replied. "I will provide portions for everyone in the family who so desires."

"Good. While it won't remove the stain, at least it will cover it for a time."

"That's the impression I got from The Alpha."

Adam thought for a moment. "I will establish a means by which this sacrifice can be ongoing to not only ensure that our sin remains covered but that future generations may have their sin covered as well. For now, Azura, go find your sister. Talk to her and then come back with your report."

CHAPTER FORTY-TWO

Apollyon stood brooding after having been informed that The Alpha had inserted the remnants of Proud Mountain and the Lake of Fire into Earth's core.

Beleth said, "It will be like being back in Shamayim."

"Don't say that word," Apollyon snapped. "And it *won't* be like being back. There, I was somebody. Here, I'm . . ." He gestured weakly at himself. "I'm . . . somewhat less than I was. My form has been . . ." He paused, struggling for words. "Well, I suppose you could say that I have been *de*formed. We have all been deformed."

"While that is all true," Beleth said, "we will now have a place to be beside the atmosphere."

"I'm not so sure."

"What do you mean?"

Apollyon said, "Does that sound like something *He* would allow? What part of being confined to the atmosphere do you not understand?"

Semyaza appeared, cutting off further conversation.

"Apollyon," he said excitedly, "I have something to tell you."

"Very well."

"It's Cain."

“What about him?”

“I talked to him.”

Apollyon rocked back as if he’d been punched. “You did what?”

“I spoke to him.”

“Whatever for?”

Semyaza said, “You told me to keep an eye on him and—”

“Perhaps, dear Semyaza, you don’t understand the meaning of the term. Keeping an eye on someone does not involve speaking to them.”

“Yes, I know, but I sensed an opportunity. So, I appeared to—”

“You did what?” Apollyon roared.

Cowering under the intensity of the emotion, Semyaza said, “I pierced the Curtain, took on human form, and appeared to him. Remember? You taught all of us how to do that, you know, to take on any form we desired. I love the freedom we have in the darkness. We also watched how you passed through the Curtain and back.”

“True, but I didn’t expect you to make those decisions on your own.”

“I understand, but like I said, an opportunity presented itself, and I felt it necessary to act.”

Still stewing, Apollyon said, “All right. Then I suppose you should tell us what happened.”

“Okay. Cain was out in the field, as he usually is, and since the fires of anger toward his brother have been growing, I decided to stoke the flames.”

"And how did you accomplish that?"

"Well—and I think you'll be proud of me when you hear this—I just started asking him questions, you know, the way you do to reveal things and suggest things without coming right out and saying it."

"Go on."

"I started talking to him about the lack of respect he suffers and then asked if he'd be interested in hearing about how he could elevate his standing in the family while at the same time getting back at his brother."

"And?"

"He's definitely interested."

Apollyon said, "How interested?"

"Interested enough to keep talking about it."

Apollyon turned his eye toward Earth and located Cain toiling in the fields. "Thank you, Semyaza, for introducing this concept to him, but I will take it from here."

Apollyon suddenly whipped around, raking his claws across Semyaza's chest, causing him to cry out in pain.

"What . . . what was that for?" Semyaza stuttered in shock.

"That, my friend, was for exercising initiative without permission."

"But—"

"You will suffer from this wound and the resulting scar. Forever. It will never go away. Perhaps the next time you have an impulse to act so foolishly, you will stop and reconsider. It's too bad others will see it, and when they do, you can share with them how you got it."

"Apollyon," Semyaza said, "I was doing what I thought you'd want me—"

"Now, see? Right there is the problem. I do not want my followers to think; I want them to obey. I have been developing my own plan for Cain. Observing. Calculating. Creating. And then you go rushing in, all full of initiative. You see the problem here, Semyaza?"

Rubbing the wound on his chest, Semyaza said contritely, "Yes, Apollyon. I understand. And it will never happen again."

"I am quite sure it will not. Now, Beleth and I were just about to go and visit Hell."

"Hell?"

"Hell . . . the Lake of Fire. It is what The Alpha renamed the remains of the exposed base of Proud Mountain when He moved it to the center of Earth."

"So," Semyaza said, "Do you think we can live there just as we had planned to do in Sha—"

"Don't say it," Beleth cautioned quickly.

"Oh, right."

Apollyon said, "Summon Remashel and Dantanian. We will all go and examine our former home and determine the possibilities. I must warn you, however, that I am not optimistic. And after that, I will speak to Cain on my own. In spite of my harsh response to your actions, Semyaza, I feel that it may yet produce a positive outcome."

A few days later, Apollyon followed Cain at a distance as he walked along the riverbank. Having been made aware of the family argument, he was now determined to stoke the flames of anger even higher.

"Hello, Cain," he said casually as he appeared walking beside Adam's son.

Cain recoiled at his appearance. "Who are you?"

"I am Apollyon, the god of this world."

"No, you're not. It's like I told the other guy. The Alpha is—"

"Do not speak to me of The Alpha," Apollyon replied hotly. "His very name makes my entire being tremble with anger."

"Fine. I won't mention His name. Where is the other guy anyway?"

"Semyaza?"

"Where do you people come up with these names? How many of you guys are there?"

"Our forces are innumerable."

"Okay," Cain replied, seemingly unimpressed. "And why are you here?"

"We are here because *He* banished us from Shamayim and remanded us here to this planet."

"But I'm told you're spirit, not flesh."

"Correct. But, as Semyaza no doubt explained, we can assume any form we wish."

"Why would you want to do that and not show yourselves for what you are? It sounds sort of sneaky to me."

Apollyon said, "Would you like to see me as I am?"

Cain shrugged. "Sure. Why not?"

Apollyon suddenly manifested his true appearance, causing Cain to stumble backward, throwing his hands up to shield his eyes from the horror in front of him.

Changing back into his assumed form, Apollyon said, "Yes, yes, draw back. Fear me. Loathe me. Despise me, for I am despicable beyond your wildest imaginings."

Cain got up off the ground and slapped the dust from his garment. "What happened to you? Surely, The Alpha didn't make you like that because—"

"No, He did not make me like this. Would you believe that, at one time, I was the most beautiful creature in all The Alpha's universe? That I was chief of all the angels? That I was the anointed cherub who walked among the Fiery Stones? That only The Alpha Himself was above me?"

"Like I said, what happened?" Cain resumed his walk along the riverbank.

"I brought a new and greater freedom, truth, and power to many. But, let's just say that The Alpha doesn't look kindly upon those who contest His will and His edicts."

Barking out a humorless laugh, Cain said, "Don't I know it. I mean, look at my mom and dad."

"Ah yes, two more unfortunate recipients of The Alpha's warped sense of justice."

"So, anyway, what do you want with me? I'm sure it isn't just to stand here and reminisce about the past."

Proceeding carefully, Apollyon said, "You are right. I do have something on my mind."

"Well, then maybe you should just get to it. I have work to do."

"I must say that you handled that admirably."

"Handled what admirably?"

"The dreadful and humiliating encounter with your family, especially after your bully of a father shoved you to the ground."

"I deserved it."

"I'm sorry . . . what did you say?" Apollyon said, stepping around in front of Cain and halting his forward progress.

"I said I deserved it."

"My dear boy," Apollyon said, "I cannot think of anyone who deserved that manner of shoddy treatment less than you. The next thing you know, I'll hear you declaring that the whole thing was your fault."

Cain stared dolefully at him, saying, "You know what? I don't care what you think." Stepping around him and continuing on his way, he added, "I don't care what anyone thinks."

Rushing to catch up, Apollyon said, "Now, we both know that simply isn't true. In fact, isn't the main reason for you being in this mess all about how much you care what your brother thinks?"

"My brother? I care less about what he thinks than I do that snail I just stepped on."

"Now we're getting somewhere."

Cain stopped walking and turned toward his unwanted companion. "Listen, Apollyon, Semyaza, or whoever you are, I'm not sure what your game is here, but I don't want to talk to you anymore. In fact, I'm asking you to leave. Now!"

And with that, he kept walking, leaving Apollyon standing in place, prohibited from being pursued by the man's guardian angels. Apollyon turned away from them and wandered a safe distance away. Cain's guardians left Apollyon as they were called away to leave Cain on his own.

"Captains," Apollyon said loudly, "to me."

Immediately, he was joined by Beleth, Semyaza, Remashel, and Dantanian.

Beleth said, "Not going as planned?"

"No, it isn't," Apollyon groused. "One would think that our boy would have an appetite for revenge, but, alas, he does not, or so it would appear."

"What are you going to do about it?" Semyaza asked.

Apollyon stared after Cain's retreating form, an evil little smile working its way onto his face. "Since Cain is apparently unwilling to play along on his own, perhaps he needs encouragement. Semyaza, my boy, I've just decided how you can make everything right with me."

"How?"

"Why don't you pay Cain a visit. Even though you cannot touch his body, you can trouble his thoughts. Disrupt his sleep. Give him no rest."

"To what end?"

"Isn't it obvious? He will be more likely to do what I require if he thinks it will make the torment stop."

"Will it?" Beleth asked.

"Of course not. But he won't know that."

Semyaza said, "And you want me to do it personally and not one of my demons?"

"Yes. I don't want things to get out of hand. At present, we cannot allow our plans to be compromised by anything. No one must pierce the Curtain. No one."

"I will take care of it."

"See that you do."

Beleth said, "You mentioned *our* plans. I'm not sure I know of any apart from stirring Cain's jealousy."

"Division and isolation, my dear boy. Division and isolation. I am going to make Cain think that every single member of his family is against him."

"Doesn't he already think that?"

"Yes, but not completely. And I need him to think that he stands alone against them all. Now, away with you all. I have a murder to plan."

The visit from the apparition left Cain troubled and brooding. So, after returning to his fields, he tethered his oxen under the shade of a spreading fig tree and set his stride in the direction of the family compound, intent on confronting everyone in the family about the unfairness being heaped upon him. He'd only gone twenty or thirty paces when he found himself changing directions and heading inland toward a natural spring, where, on occasion, he went to sit and think. As for why he wound up there, he couldn't rightly say.

Easing himself down onto a smooth, flat rock, he dangled his tired and dusty feet in the cool, still water.

Without warning, his mind was filled with what sounded like a thousand voices, words cascading and echoing through his consciousness.

No one likes you, Cain. No one.

You think you matter to your parents? To anyone? You don't.

In fact, if you weren't around, who would even notice? Your brother?

He cares less about you than them all.

You are all alone.

Even your own mother doesn't love you.

Truly, by continuing to live, you are only hurting your family.

They'd be far better off if you would just slip into these cool waters and—"

"Stop it!" he shouted, covering both ears with his hands. "I don't know who is speaking, but leave me. Go, now!"

Forcefully propelling himself back from the lip of the spring, he sat gasping, leaning against a tree.

Your brother is far cleverer than you.

He always has been.

Everyone knows it.

Equally loved?

Not hardly.

He has always been the handsome one.

The talented one.

The one your mother favors.

Look into the surface of the water and you will see . . .

See your ugliness.

The ugliness. Ugliness. Ugliness. Ugliness. Ugliness.

It went on and on and wouldn't stop, even when he stood and began walking with his hands over his ears.

You're worthless, Cain.

Worthless. Worthless. Worthless. Worthless.

Tripping over a protruding root, he fell headlong down a bank and rolled to a stop, staring toward the sky. What he saw instead was a face. Hideous in appearance. Twisted, malformed, as if someone attempted to form a human face but got it all wrong, and the result was a thing of horror.

It hovered over him, just there out of reach, its monstrous caricature of a mouth forming the word, *"Worthless, worthless, worthless, worthless,"* over and over and over.

"What is happening to me?" he cried out. "Make it go! Somebody, please make it go!"

His father found him like that, on his back and writhing as if in great pain.

After Cain's oxen had wandered into the family compound without him, Adam thought it strange enough to go looking for his son.

His Father had once gone looking for him when he was lost and afraid and confused.

In spite of their recent conflict, how could he do anything less for his son?

"Cain!" he shouted, rushing to his side and cradling his head in his arms. "Cain, look at me. What is wrong? What has happened to you? Did you fall? Yes, that's it. I can see that you have fallen. Here, let me—"

"Make it go away, Father. Please, make it go away."

“Make what go away?”

“The face. The voices. I can’t make them stop.”

Then, he screamed as if in mortal agony.

“I can’t help you unless you tell me what is wrong. I don’t see a face, and I don’t hear any voices.”

“Nooooo!” he shrieked, jerked once, and then lay perfectly still as though dead.

“Cain? Come on now, Cain.”

Adam leaned his ear close to his son’s nostrils.

He was barely breathing.

Turning his head this way and that, Adam looked all around the area, trying to spot anyone or anything that could have caused such an extreme reaction in his boy. Finding nothing, he turned his attention back to the limp form in his arms.

“What is going on?” he mumbled to himself.

Then, standing, he bent down and lifted his son as easily as if he’d been a child, remembering the many times he’d been called upon to administer comfort when, as a child, Cain had hurt himself. And there had been many. But he had been there for him each and every time, wiping away the tears, wrapping a cloth around a wound, rocking him as he pulled him close to his chest.

His boy.

His first born.

How he loved him.

Did he even know? Did Cain have any idea of the depth of his father’s love, or was his mind so filled with what had happened between them the last time they'd been together it eclipsed all else?

Glancing down at the unconscious form in his arms, he noticed a slash running across Cain's chest. Not bleeding but grievous, nonetheless. Almost as if someone had taken a sharp piece of hot glowing wood and had drawn it across his flesh, scoring a deep cut that had been quickly cauterized. He stopped walking and went down on one knee so he could examine the wound more closely. It was then that he realized it looked exactly like what he'd expect to see had a wild beast raked his claws across his son's body.

Sensing something just outside the periphery of his consciousness, he shouted, "Apollyon, are you responsible for this?"

Apollyon materialized, hovering wraith-like and spectral just above and apart from where Adam held his son's inert form.

"Did I do what, exactly?" he said calmly.

"Don't play games with me. Did you cause this to happen to my son?"

"Once again, I must request clarification. Did I do . . . what?"

"This," Adam shouted. "Did you cause this torment in him?"

Pretending to bend down and examine Cain, he said, "Oh dear, what have we here? It seems as if something was too much for the poor boy and he has passed out."

"Did you do it?"

"If you are asking me if I personally would stoop to something such as this, then the answer is decidedly no."

Adam shouted, "Stop it. I know you're behind this."

"Oh, well now, that's an entirely different matter. Why didn't you ask me that in the first place?" Apollyon paused dramatically and then said, "Is that what you are asking?"

"Yes. Are you?"

"I may or may not have encouraged one of my princes to pay a visit to your boy and, well, he is quite a nasty fellow and capable of terrible, incomprehensible deeds."

"So, he hurt him."

"Oh, no. Nothing so barbaric as that. I would never condone physical violence. It's so unnecessary when the mind is so readily available."

"What are you talking about?"

Apollyon fully materialized, causing Adam to draw back.

"What I am talking about, you fool, is power. The power I have over him, you, and everyone else in your miserable little family. Your minds are feeble, unable to resist my wiles, my power of suggestion and persuasion. That's what happens when you defy The Alpha. He takes revenge, removing from you that which made you special, unique. Removing you from your original home and turning you into something common and hateful. Sound a bit familiar? Hate is exactly what I intend to unleash in your firstborn. White-hot hatred of a kind never before seen in your species. Raw. Destructive. Terrible."

Regaining his composure, Adam said forcefully, "You will not hurt him."

"Said the man who brought destruction upon the entire human race."

And with that, he was gone, leaving Adam weak and quivering in the aftermath of the encounter.

When Cain woke, he was inside his own dwelling, lying on his own sleeping mat. Weary. His chest burned from a wound he had no conscious memory of receiving.

Sensing he wasn't alone, he shoved himself up onto one elbow to see who was with him. It was then that he saw the apparition barely visible, just there in the shadows.

"Why can't you just leave me alone?"

Apollyon replied calmly, reasonably, "Now, why would I want to do that when we're having such fun?"

"Fun?" Cain gestured at the wound pulsing on his chest, suddenly remembering how it had come to be there. "You call this fun?"

"Oh, my yes. That is, of course, if it causes you pain. Otherwise, it's not worth my time."

Finding a source of courage he didn't think he possessed, Cain shouted with all the strength he possessed, "You will not touch me again!"

Cain's guardian angels stood with the Alpha, wanting desperately to return to their assignment.

"If he had only called on me, I would have sent you both back," the Alpha said. The angels continued to helplessly watch and stay ready.

"Truly? And how would you propose you stop me? Go on, I'm listening." When Cain said nothing in response, Apollyon shouted, "That's right! There is nothing you can do." Quieting, he added, "Or is there?"

"What do you mean?"

"Perhaps a negotiation is in order."

The wound flared, sending stabs of pain radiating throughout his torso. "Fine, just tell me what you have in mind."

"What I have in mind is the destruction of the entire human race. But since The Alpha assures me that He will not allow that to happen, I will content myself with the destruction of one human."

"Define destruction."

"Death."

"You . . . you're going to kill someone?"

"Of course not. The Alpha wouldn't let me."

"Then how—"

"*You* are going to do it."

"Me?" Cain shouted. "No. I want nothing to do with—"

Worthless, ugly, useless, you are not enough, worthless . . . the chorus of voices began, only this time with far more intensity.

Covering his ears, Cain pleaded, "Stop. Please, make it stop."

"And why should I?" Apollyon demanded.

"Because . . . because . . ."

"Yes, I'm listening."

"Because . . ."

"Do get on with it, boy. Tell me what is on your mind."

"I'll do whatever you want me to do. Just make it stop."

The voices immediately ceased.

"Now," Apollyon said, "that wasn't so hard, was it?"

"I hate you," Cain muttered under his breath.

"Well, as it turns out, I hate you, too. But let's not let personal grievances stand in the way of progress. As for what I have in mind . . . you are going to kill your brother."

"What? Why?"

"Because I wish you to do so."

"But you must have a reason."

"I do. Besides being deliciously devious, it would also grievously wound your mother."

"Why would you want to do that?"

"Oh, I don't know. Perhaps because I can?"

"You're evil!" Cain spat.

"Why, yes, I am. I am also a liar, so beware of what you choose to believe."

"But, if you're a liar, then how can I believe *anything* you say?"

Apollyon pretended to consider the question. "Oh, let's see . . . I'm not sure. I don't suppose you can, except for this: if you don't do as I ask, I will make it so difficult for you that you will eventually take your own life. And we wouldn't want that now, would we?"

Cain stared at the apparition, hardly daring to believe what he was seeing and hearing.

It couldn't be real. Or could it? And what about the horrible thing he was asking him to do?

Then again, was it really horrible, or was it what he had been secretly pondering all along?

Killing his brother.

Abel.

His constant companion throughout their lives.

"When do you want this to happen?" Cain asked.

"You will do it in three days."

"What? No. That's too soon. I'm not ready. I can't—"

"You can, and you will."

"But if I kill Abel, my father will kill me."

"Will he really? Do you think he has that in him? It doesn't sound like the Adam I know . . . and trust me, I know him much better than you do."

"Okay, fine. But I will be an outcast."

"Oh, come now," Apollyon said, "you're already an outcast. Besides, there is the thing with the . . . sacrifice." He spit the word as if removing something offensive from his mouth. "You know you aren't planning to comply. You need to do what you think is best. How does buying an animal from your brother show that you are offering your best? You would simply be offering your brother's best. And you know he has already set aside the best lamb for himself. So, you'll be giving *his* second best. Does that sound like the right thing to do? Is that your best? Is that what you want to do?"

Cain said sullenly, "No, but I can't kill my brother."

"Then say goodbye."

As Apollyon drew back his hand as if preparing to hurl something toward Cain, Cain said, "Okay, I will do it. But I'm going to need some help."

Chapter Forty-Three

Apollyon found himself somewhere outside Shamayim in the Presence of The Alpha, the transition having happened so suddenly that he was left feeling disoriented and confused.

"What are you playing at, Dragon?" The Alpha asked, His voice seeming to echo throughout.

"I do wish You'd stop calling me that."

"It is what you are. Now, answer the question."

"Playing? Was that the question? Well, let's see . . . I am not *playing* at anything, for to do so would indicate that there is some game afoot, and I assure You, oh *Great One,* this is no game."

"You lie even to yourself," came the Alpha's reply. "No matter. For I know the thoughts and intents of your heart, that they have become only evil continually."

Apollyon was suddenly flanked by Michael and Gabriel, who had always been larger than him physically but now, due to having been diminished by his rebellion, towered over him.

"Intimidation?" he said. "Is that how this is going to go?"

Ignoring the statement, Michael said, "We have reports from our watchers that you are straying perilously close to violating your mandates."

"I haven't violated a single thing. If I had, The Alpha would have let me know it."

"We know you have had unauthorized access through the Curtain more than once, as have your followers.

"And," Gabriel added, "what about what you have done to Cain?"

"What about it?"

"You were given strict instructions that humans are not to be touched without permission."

"I didn't touch anyone, nor did anyone under my command."

Michael said, "Then how do you explain his torment?"

"Oh," Apollyon said with an evil laugh, "that. Well, it's amazing what happens to these humans when you put suggestions in their minds. Simply put, you don't have to touch them. They do the damage to themselves."

"Is that true, Alpha?" Michael asked.

"It is. However, this is not that."

"What do You mean?" Apollyon said, suddenly alarmed. "No one touched Cain. I can assure—"

"You can assure? Do you have any idea how ridiculous that sounds coming from you? You can assure nothing," The Alpha thundered, causing Apollyon to cower.

Michael said, "Your little captain stepped over the line. He pierced the Curtain and wounded the man."

"That's not possible. He was given strict instructions that his body was not to be touched. Semyaza is my third in command. He would never do anything that directly violates my orders."

"Really? Perhaps he was simply imitating his leader," The Alpha said.

"I see what You are trying to do here, but it won't—"

Michael leaned threateningly toward Apollyon. "He marked him in a manner which could never have been done without touching his body."

Apollyon was feeling trapped in a way he'd never felt before and, for one of the first times in his existence, found himself at a loss for words. It wasn't whether Cain had been marked, for he cared nothing about his well-being and, in fact, wished him dead along with everyone in his pathetic little family; it was the blatant act of disobedience by Semyaza that had him so disturbed, especially coming as it had on the heels of the previous offense.

He said, "While you have no reason to believe anything I say, I am telling you my instructions to Semyaza included direct reference to The Alpha's orders and specifically forbade him or any of his demons from touching Cain or any other human's body. If he violated those orders, this is the first I am hearing about it."

The Alpha replied, "As you are aware, Apollyon, nothing is hidden from My sight. Semyaza touched a human and, as a result, must face the consequences of his actions."

"What do You intend to do?" he asked hesitantly.

"Semyaza will receive the full recompense for his actions."

"What? No, You can't do that. You can't take him away from me. He's too—"

"I'm not taking him away. But I am removing his ability to appear in any other form other than what he truly is, for a time."

Semyaza unexpectedly appeared next to Apollyon, looking as confused and disoriented as his master before him.

"What am I doing here?" he asked, his voice shaking with fear.

"Semyaza," The Alpha said, "I created you with purpose, for yours was a life intended for greatness. Instead, you chose to align yourself with Apollyon and joined in his rebellion. And now, you have mounted your own rebellion and have violated even his direct orders."

"Rebellion? What are we talking about here?"

"Semyaza," Apollyon said, "did you or did you not touch Cain?"

"He wasn't responding the way I had anticipated," Semyaza said, "and I didn't see any other way to—"

"So, you did. You touched him."

"Yes, but only for a moment and only to get him to do what we wanted him to do. I thought I was doing what you wanted. It was just a touch. He didn't die."

The Alpha's voice thundered throughout the realm, "It was more than a simple touch. It was a wound. And now he will carry a mark on his body for the rest of his days."

Semyaza dropped to his face under the force of The Alpha's pronouncement.

Apollyon said, "You fool! Do you know what you've done? You have thrown it all away, and there is nothing I can do to protect you."

"Protect me? From what?"

The Alpha said, "Semyaza, because you strayed from the limits I have imposed on your habitation, I remand you to your deformity for a time." As Semyaza began to protest, The Alpha continued, "I'm not done."

To Gabriel, He said, "Have the arrangements been made?"

"Yes, Alpha. All is ready."

"Good."

Suddenly, Rok appeared in the throne room, towering over the now cringing Semyaza.

The Alpha said, "Among your many desires has been this one—that you have another chance to face Rok in combat. Well, your desire is about to become a reality."

"What?" Semyaza said. "Here? Now? With him? I'm no match for—"

"You never have been."

Semyaza began shouting, "Apollyon, help me! I was only following orders!"

"Not *my* orders. You made your own choice, and now . . ."

Since Semyaza no longer carried a sword, Rok drew his, presenting it to him hilt first and saying, "Here."

Michael drew the Sword of Truth and gave it to Rok.

Rok showed a rare smile as he gripped the Sword of Truth and said what he felt, "Power."

"This isn't fair," Semyaza blubbered, true fear seizing him.

"You are correct," came the Alpha's reply. "And neither was your assault on Cain. Rok, you may commence."

It wasn't a long fight, if indeed one could call it a fight at all.

Resolved to his fate, Semyaza gathered himself and advanced on Rok, the sword flashing in his hands. But Rok swatted away his efforts as easily as if he had been facing a human child. In the end, Rok pierced Semyaza in his left side, running him through and lifting him up for all to see, impaled by the Sword of Truth.

Semyaza's already shriveled form was diminished even further, leaving him gasping in mortal agony but unable to die.

Michael dragged him away, the cries of agony reaching their ears long after he had disappeared from their sight.

"As you can see," The Alpha said to Apollyon, "your inner circle is now diminished by one. And as for you, I will allow this present temptation of Cain to continue, but only because he must be allowed to make decisions that affect his destiny. But know this, Dragon, you do not want to violate My edict."

"No . . . no, I do not," Apollyon said, more shaken by what just happened than he would ever admit. "I will have a discussion with my remaining captains and reiterate the boundaries and limitations of the Curtain." Quickly regaining his equilibrium and, with it, his grit and swagger, he added, "Now, if there is nothing further, I have a human race to destroy, so if You'll excuse me . . ."

And Apollyon returned to the earthly realm.

The Alpha instructed, "To my throne room." And they were there.

Gabriel approached the throne, saying, "How has it all come to this, Alpha? Every time I look toward Your throne, I can see Son of the Dawn standing there adorned in all his finery, his beauty nearly blinding in its intensity. And now . . ."

"I know, Gabriel. I see the same thing, and My heart breaks over the choices he has made . . . choices that have now infected the entire human race."

"Will he destroy them?"

"He will try."

"But?" Gabriel said.

"Whether he is successful or not depends on what happens next and how My creation responds."

"Don't You know how they will respond?"

"I have seen all the outcomes. I know all the possible responses, possibilities, and probabilities within all of those. And I know their hearts, their thoughts, imaginations, and desires. I know My will for them, as do they."

"I never realized free will could be so complicated, even dangerous."

Michael returned and came to stand next to Gabriel in front of the throne.

"Semyaza has lost his ability to change shape, Alpha."

The Alpha said, "Instruct the watchers and warriors to step up their vigilance. If there is one rebel among Apollyon's minions, there are more. He persuaded them to exercise their free will, defect, and rebel against me. Now, they are exercising their free will and rebelling against him. I don't want our guardians caught off-guard."

"So, You are expecting more mischief?" Michael said.

"Yes, and someday, it could get worse. Much worse."

As Michael and Gabriel departed to carry out His orders, The Alpha saw Wendly and Steele on the island busily preparing Rest in Peace City to His specifications.

"Wendly, Steele," He said, "how are things progressing?"

"All is ready, Alpha," Steele replied. "When should we expect our first arrival?"

"Unfortunately, it could happen any time now."

"We will be ready."

Beleth, Remashel, and Dantanian waited patiently.

It was something they had all become accustomed to doing.

Not that they liked it.

In fact, they hated it.

But what were they supposed to do?

As for why they were waiting, it had to do with the current temper tantrum in which their commander was engaged.

It was a bad one. Complicating everything was the difficult news that Semyaza had been painfully wounded and lost his freedom and ability to shapeshift. While they were unclear as to the specifics, what was crystal clear was what Apollyon thought of it and what he thought of The Alpha, as if there had ever been any doubt.

"Just like that," Apollyon shouted. "Semyaza was of little use. Hauled away by that brute Michael. I don't know where he is or what is happening to him. I mean, that Sword is dangerous. Also, he is now unable to change his form. Can you imagine it?" When no one responded, he shouted, "Well? Isn't anyone going to say anything?"

Beleth said, "We didn't know you wanted us to—"

"Of course, I want your response. Why else would I have asked?"

"Okay, then yes, it sounds terrible. But at least The Alpha didn't destroy him."

"You know," Apollyon mused. "I've been wondering what would be worse. To just cease to exist or to face an eternity, unable to ever change your form. The pain is not a pleasant thought either."

"I'd rather just disappear," Dantanian said.

Remashel agreed.

Apollyon gazed upon the three, his eyes shifting from one to the next. "Something tells me, my friends, that we will not be given that option if it ever comes to it."

Beleth said, "So, he really did it? He wounded the man?"

"Sadly, yes. Even after all my warnings. So, let this be a lesson to you and one that you pass along to my Legions of the Fallen. Stay behind the Curtain, and hands off the humans! Oh, and find me a replacement for Semyaza. Someone we can trust."

"I know just the one for the job."

"Okay, I'm listening."

"Shamsiel is his name. He was one of Semyaza's followers and actually once worked under the archangel Uriel."

"Sounds promising. When do I get to meet him?"

Beleth snapped his fingers and Shamsiel appeared, bowing to one knee in the presence of Apollyon.

"All I am is yours to command, oh mighty Apollyon," he said, his voice tinged with awe.

"Rise, dear one," Apollyon replied. "Rise and assume your new role as a captain in the Legions of the Fallen."

"It is an honor to serve."

"So, tell me, did you learn anything useful during your time with Uriel?"

Shamsiel replied, "The Scrolls of Remembrance."

"What about them?"

"He often had me re-copy what he wrote."

Apollyon's head jerked up. "Do tell."

"As you can imagine, I saw quite a lot."

"Anything useful?"

"I would need quite a long time to lay it all out, but . . . yes."

"And in the meantime," Remashel said, "where do we stand with Cain?"

Apollyon replied, "He will do everything we tell him to do."

"So, he's going to kill his brother?"

"Without question."

Dantanian asked, "And then what?"

Apollyon said, "Then, my dear boy, we will have the situation I have been working toward for all this time."

"What is that specifically?"

"A human killing another human."

Beleth said, "Tell us again why that is so significant."

"While it was a major victory getting Adam and Eve to sin against The Alpha, by Cain shedding his brother's blood, man will sin against *himself.* See the connection?"

The four shared a glance.

Remashel said, "I'm not sure I do."

"Okay, one more time, and *do* keep up. It's one thing for me—us—to destroy The Alpha's creation, but if we can get that creation to destroy itself, I can think of no sweeter victory, no more consummate corruption of what He intended to be perfect. It means that I not only win but that I dominate. And if I dominate here, what's to stop me from finally ascending to my rightful place on the throne?"

Beleth said, "But this only works if Cain follows through."

"He will."

"And if he doesn't?"

"Then," Apollyon replied around a chilling smile, "we will cause him such torment that he will take his *own* life, which in its own way would be an equally sweet outcome."

Beleth said, "So, whether by their own hand or by another's, a human dies. An image-bearer is gone, and then Alpha can no longer enjoy them."

"Now you've got it."

Chapter Forty-four

The day of the sacrifice had come. Adam, Eve, and all their offspring were assembled in the courtyard at the center of the family compound, their individual offerings laid out on an altar constructed to the specifications given to Abel by The Alpha the day before. He had retrieved nine stones of a particular size from the center of the river and carried them to a specific spot within the compound, then formed them into an oblong base: three on each side with one handsbreadth between them, one on the end, and then another in the center to act as support. This formed the chamber in which the holy fire would be kindled. Then, three flat stones were added to the top, forming the surface upon which the sacrifice would be laid and burned.

No one questioned why The Alpha had chosen Abel as the one to whom the instructions had been given. Adam and Eve figured the reason they had been bypassed had everything to do with the loss of their former intimacy and the fact that they carried the original sin. The twins were far too immature to carry such a weighty responsibility—as were their three younger siblings—and even Cain realized that his standing with The Alpha took him out of consideration. Besides, in the end, The Alpha's ways were as right as they were mysterious and, therefore, acceptable.

As head of the family, Adam provided the offering for himself, Eve, and their children who had not yet reached the age of accountability, while Awan, Azura, and Abel brought their own. Only Cain brought a different offering: the first fruits from his harvest, but not an offering of blood as had been the instruction that Abel learned from The Alpha and passed on to his family.

In accordance with the instructions, Abel began the ceremony, saying, "Alpha, in You we live and move and have our being. Without You, nothing was made. And we, the people created in Your image, come before You now bearing our first fruits presented as a burnt offering to cover our sin, praying it will be pleasing in Your sight."

The fire burned hot, and as each gift was laid on the altar, tendrils of flame from beneath reached up and over the surface, touching each portion and consuming it entirely, sending columns of smoke spiraling skyward, rising in an undisturbed column until out of sight.

Then came the time for Cain's offering. Carefully gathering his grain, he laid it out ceremonially upon the surface of the altar, but he had no sooner laid on the final stalk when the fire went out.

Completely.

The embers went as cold as the stone surrounding them.

Seeing what had happened, Cain burned with rage and humiliation and left the compound to return to his fields, where he sat sulking under a tree, refusing to speak to anyone, including Awan.

Which is where Apollyon found him.

"Well," his voice dripped with feigned compassion, "as if things weren't bad enough, now it seems The Alpha is against you as well. Did you see how fast that fire went out?"

"You told me it was the right thing to do."

"I can't believe you would do such a thing. *Shame.* What are you going to do now? Abel makes you look bad."

Cain wiped his hands over his face, saying, "Why are we having this conversation? I already told you I'd do what you wanted."

"This *conversation* is to cement in your mind that you are now and always have been an outcast in your family. The one who stands alone in shame. And nothing will ever change unless you get rid of the problem."

"Like I said," Cain said, "I have already told—"

"Yes, yes, I heard you. Consider this as merely a reminder of how critical this is for you. Your parents despise you. They think Abel is better, and you just proved it. Your siblings despise you. Your strength and intelligence scare them. Abel looks down on you, and, as you have just witnessed, The Alpha doesn't think very highly of you either."

"And killing my brother will change all that?"

Apollyon laughed. "Oh, trust me, killing your brother will feel so good, and it will change *everything.*"

"Husband," Eve said much later as the two walked along the riverside, "why didn't The Alpha accept Cain's offering?"

"Because he refused to offer the type of sacrifice The Alpha required."

"But why would he do that? Why wouldn't he offer a sacrifice pleasing to The Alpha?"

"Because of his resentment of his brother, Cain chose to offer from his own labors instead. Even if they were his best crops, which he had worked so hard on, his pride prevented him from following the Alpha's requirements. He didn't do it the Alpha's way; he did it his way."

"What does this mean?"

"For Cain? Well, quite simply, it means that our sacrifice was accepted and his was not."

"But if his sacrifice wasn't accepted, that must mean The Alpha is angry with him. And if He's angry with him, will He kill him?"

"Of course not," Adam said. "The Alpha is a life-giver, not a life-taker."

"I'm worried, Husband."

Adam stopped walking and faced his wife. "These are troubling times, Eve. But we will get through them just like we always have."

"I hope so because if I lost Cain, I don't know what I would do."

Adam recalled how it had felt carrying his son home from the spring. And then how it felt when he had shoved him in anger.

"In spite of our recent troubles," he said with a catch in his voice, "I love the boy."

"I know you do. I don't think there's anyone in the family who thinks otherwise."

"Perhaps Awan. She and Cain are very close."

"I actually had a talk with her yesterday about that."

"Tell me," Adam said as they resumed their walk.

"Okay, well, she's been very confused about everything that has happened."

"She's not the only one," Adam said with a humorless laugh.

"Yes, it has been troubling. And I must tell you, Husband, Awan is convinced that Cain means to do harm to his brother."

"That can't be. I mean, they've always had conflicts, but it has always worked out. This will as well."

"I'm not so sure. She was telling me about how close she is to Cain and how he tells her everything, and most recently, about how he has been entertaining thoughts about hurting Abel. And I told her how good it is that he has her but that she has to make sure she doesn't get caught up in anything he's planning to do that involves bringing harm to Abel."

"I can't begin to tell you how troubling this is. How did she respond?"

Eve said, "She was adamant that she wouldn't let him do anything like that."

"If it came down to it, I'm not sure there is anything Awan could do to stop him."

"I agree, and I warned her not to overestimate her influence. Cain's anger may take him to a place beyond where even she could reach him." Eve sighed deeply. "I just want this current trouble to pass and have everything return to normal."

"But normal wasn't exactly great, was it?"

"No," she said pensively, "it wasn't."

Adam asked, "How'd you leave it with her?"

"She was going to go find him and talk to him." She paused and then added, "I don't mind telling you, Husband, I fear what could be coming."

"I know. I fear it as well. But there's really nothing we can do except stand aside and wait."

After Apollyon left him, Cain stood among the rows of grain, proud of what he had done. His crops were exceptional in abundance and of high quality. Equal to anything Abel had produced with his flocks. Why, then, had Abel's sacrifice been accepted and his rejected?

"Cain."

His name coming out of nowhere caused him to jump a good foot off the ground.

"Look, I thought we were done. That we had everything—"

"It is I, The Alpha."

Upon hearing the speaker's identity, he immediately fell, burying his face in the loamy alluvial soil.

"Alpha. To what do I owe the honor of You gracing the presence of one so lowly as I?"

"Stand up, Cain. I want to speak to you."

Brushing the dirt and debris from his clothing, Cain struggled to his feet, lifting his eyes skyward.

"If this is about the sacrifice, I can ex—"

"Why is your countenance fallen, and why are you so disconsolate?"

Cain studied the ground beneath his feet for several moments. "Alpha, what happened with the sacrifice was humiliating. I mean, You know about the situation between Abel and me."

"The *situation* seems to be almost entirely on your side."

"I'm not sure what You mean by that."

The Alpha said, "From an early age, you have allowed jealousy and resentment to take root, germinate, and now explode into full-flowered rage and hatred. And for what? Simply because your brother was willing to do what you were not, which was to always give his best to whatever his hands found to do."

"So, You're suggesting that I have not done—"

"Cain," The Alpha said sharply, "do not forget who you address, nor your place."

"I'm sorry, Alpha. My anger . . . it gets away from me."

"Which is why you find yourself in this present situation. Cain, I want you to listen to Me, for the way out of this is very simple: If you do what is right, it will be accepted. But if you do not do what is right, I don't have to tell you that sin is crouching at your door and desires to have you. But you must resist. Subdue it. Master it. Rule over it."

At once, all the images from his encounter with Apollyon scrolled across his consciousness. Front and center was the horrible mental agony.

"Alpha, it's not just about me."

"Be clear about one thing, Cain. It is now and always has been about you. The only difference is that through your rebellion, you have now caused another to be at risk."

"You mean my sister."

"Yes. You have tremendous influence over her young life. She is loyal to you and is prepared to stand up for you against the family if necessary."

Cain pondered The Alpha's words for a moment. "I will not allow it to come to that."

"See that you don't." His words had weight. Cain felt it.

And with that, The Alpha's Presence withdrew, leaving Cain feeling empty and abandoned.

"Abel," he muttered under his breath. "Always Abel."

"Were you calling me?"

He turned and saw his brother walking toward him. The *last* person he wanted to see.

"Go away from me, Brother. You will not find me decent company right now."

Abel approached in spite of the warning and stopped an arm's length away. "Leaving the family compound the way you did, I was concerned."

"And why is that?"

"Well, for one thing, you were so upset. And for another, the thing with your sacrifice being rejected had to be difficult to bear."

Cain growled. "Do not speak to me of the sacrifice. Not now. Not ever."

"But it didn't have to be like that. You know it. I know it. Everyone knows it. You and you alone made the choice not to comply."

Covering his face with his hands, Cain said, "Get away from me, Brother. If you know what's good for you, you will turn around and walk away as quickly as you can."

When Cain raised his head, Abel saw something in his eyes that caused terror to rise within his soul, and he backed away, never taking his eyes off his brother until he was well down the row. Then, he turned and ran and kept running until he reached the compound.

When he arrived, Azura saw the expression on his face and inquired what had happened.

"You were right, Azura," Abel said. "He wants to kill me. I know it as surely as we are both standing here."

"Then, you must stay away from him and not allow the two of you to be alone together at any time."

"Yes. That's good advice, and I will take it."

"You're shaking all over," she said, lying her hand on her brother's shoulder. "Come inside and sit down. I will make you that tea you like. It has always had a calming effect on you."

"I love that tea. Actually, that's the best idea I've heard all day."

Sunset found Cain inside his dwelling, huddled in covert conversation with Awan.

She said, "I'm afraid for you, Brother."

"I'm afraid for myself."

She was silent for a moment. "Tell me more about The Alpha appearing to you."

"He didn't appear in the sense that I could see Him," Cain replied. "His Presence was just there all around me, enclosing me, hemming me in."

"What did that feel like?"

"I don't know how to describe it. It was comforting and fearsome at the same time."

"What was His voice like?"

"You know how the river sounds during the flood stage?"

"Yes."

"Magnify that by many, many times, and you still wouldn't be close."

"That thing He said about sin crouching at your door and desiring to have you means that He knows about Apollyon's visit and what he asked you to do."

"Of course, He knows. He's The Alpha. He knows everything."

Awan said softly, "I don't want you to go through with what you are planning."

Turning fear-filled eyes her way, he said, "Nor do I."

"Then, help me understand what's going on."

He stared toward the place in his dwelling where Apollyon had appeared to him. "Remember when father had to carry me in from the spring?"

"Yes. It was when that wild beast had—"

"It wasn't a wild beast that did this to me." He opened his cloak to reveal the jagged slash across his chest. "It was one of Apollyon's captains. He called himself Semyaza. But this wound isn't the worst. He got inside my head, Awan. There were voices. You know that place we used to go to when we were all kids? That place where we would speak, and our voices would come back to us?"

"Yes, I remember. We used to love that place."

Cain continued, "Well, just imagine if there weren't just you and me and Abel and Azura there. What if there were many, many people all talking at once, and the things they were saying were horrible things . . . things about how useless and ugly and worthless you were. Over and over, echoing around inside your head and never stopping. Voices telling you to kill yourself and do the family a favor—"

"Oh, Cain," Awan said, "that sounds horrible. Is that what happened to you?"

"Yes. Down by the spring and then again here. And Apollyon told me that if I didn't do what he wanted me to do, then the voices would increase to the point where I wouldn't be able to stand it and I actually *would* end up killing myself." Cain paused to collect his thoughts before adding, "I don't want to do this anymore than you do. I mean, I hate my brother, but I wouldn't be talking about killing him unless I had no other choice."

"So, the reason you want to go through with it is to keep from killing yourself like Apollyon said?"

"Why else would I openly defy a direct command from The Alpha? I know Apollyon's game. He wants one of us dead, and he doesn't really care who. Either I kill Abel, or he turns his demons loose on me again and I eventually kill myself to stop the pain. I can't let that happen, and the only way to stop it is to move forward with plans to kill Abel."

"I can't believe you just said that out loud."

"Yeah. I can't either. But it's what I'm going to do, and I can't do it without your help."

"Okay, Cain," she said after a few moments' consideration. "I'll help you. We've always been there for each other, no sense changing that now."

"So, it's settled. We're going to do it."

"When?"

"Tomorrow afternoon. Because he's terrified of me, there is no way he will agree to meet with me if it's just the two of us."

"What do you have in mind?"

"You need to do something to get Azura out of the way so that you can pretend to be her."

"How am I supposed to do that?" she replied with alarm.

"What's that herb you and mother use while cooking that can make you very sick if you eat too much of it?"

"Umm . . . garlic?"

"Yes. That's it. Make her something to eat at midday and load it up with garlic. She will be so sick that she'll have to lie down. Then, tell Abel you'd like to go for a walk with him. He'll do it. He and Azura go for walks all the time."

"There's no way I can pass myself off as my sister."

"You two are identical. It's like I told you before, if you dressed just alike—and especially if you fixed your hair like hers—I couldn't tell you apart unless I listened closely to the way you speak."

"But he'll know."

"I don't think he will, especially if you don't say much."

She wrinkled her brow. "That puts so much pressure on me, Cain. I'm not sure I can be convincing."

"You can do it. I know you can. I believe in you."

"So, I cook something that will make my sister sick, dress in her clothing, and then find Abel and convince him to go for a walk with me. What if he won't come?"

"Trust me, he'll come."

"But what if he doesn't?"

Cain was thoughtful for a few moments. "Then, you tell him the truth. Tell him that you pretended to be Azura because

I really wanted to talk to him, but I was afraid he wouldn't agree to meet and that this was the only way I could think of getting him to come and talk to me."

"Let's say that your scheme is enough to get him out to the southern fields. What are you going to do once he gets there?"

Cain shook his head slowly. "I . . . well . . . I hadn't thought of that."

"I mean, you can't just see him coming and just walk up and hit him in the head with a rock or something."

Cain's eyes widened. "Who says I can't? That's a great idea. He won't be suspecting anything. I will have a large stone hidden behind my back. He'll walk toward me, stop in front of me, and without saying a word, I'll swing the rock at his head, and he will go down."

"And then what? What if the first blow doesn't kill him?" She began sobbing. "Will you then bend down and hit our brother again, and again, and again, and—"

"Hey, come on," he said, putting his arms around her shoulders. "It won't be like that."

She jerked away, backing up several paces. "Cain, stop it. You're not thinking this through. This is our brother we're talking about. Abel. And you're going to take a rock and bash his head in. What part of '*like that*' am I missing?"

"Awan, listen to me. This is a terrible thing. I'm not suggesting that it isn't. But when those demons were tormenting me, it was horrible. And I will do whatever I must in order to never have to experience something like that again."

Her chest heaving with emotion, Awan said, "I don't see how I can just stand there and watch it happen."

"Then don't," he said. "Once you get him there, run away."

"But won't he think that's suspicious?"

"At that point, it won't matter what he thinks because he'll be dead."

They stared at each other in silence, with the statement hanging between them.

In the end, Awan simply turned and walked away, her mind awash in the horror she was about to partner with.

As for Cain, he set about searching the ground for just the right murder weapon.

He found a rock.

A very unusual rock.

In length, it was about as long as his hand from the tip of his thumb to the tip of his little finger, broader at one end and flattened on both sides. Staring at it, he realized that were he to bind it to one end of a short branch, when swung, it would have more power and accuracy.

"I'm planning my brother's death," he muttered under his breath, shaking his head.

Chapter Forty-five

Michael and Gabriel stood before The Alpha's throne, having come at Rok, Schindaug, Taylor, and Kepteny's request.

The reason for the meeting had to do with information passed along by the guardians assigned to Cain and Awan. It seemed they wanted the four to act as their representatives in The Alpha's court since the four had been eyewitnesses.

"Perhaps you should start from the beginning," The Alpha said.

Schindaug blurted out, "The whole thing is completely out of control."

"What specifically?"

Taylor said, "He's talking about the situation between Cain and Abel and the fact that Cain is literally planning to kill his brother."

"And," The Alpha said, "this concerns you, how?"

"Well, I mean . . ."

"I think what Taylor's trying to say," Kepteny said, "is that we don't feel right about just standing by and allowing this to take place."

"But," The Alpha said, "those humans are not under your direct care—not your responsibility."

“Right, but we know for a fact that Apollyon and his demons have been tormenting Cain to the point that if they hadn’t backed off, he would have taken his own life.”

“And why did they back off?”

“Because,” Shindaug said, “Cain agreed to do what they wanted, which is to kill his brother.”

Michael said, “The Alpha knows all of this, as do Gabriel and I.”

“And You’re just going to let it happen?”

The Alpha stood and descended the stairs of the dais, stopping in front of the group.

After sweeping His gaze across each of them, He said, “ ‘Letting it happen,’ as you say, Schindaug, is one of the most difficult things I have to do as it regards free will. Love requires free will. Intervention is always My heart, but My heart is often at war with My conviction. And My conviction is that free will isn’t free will if I am constantly stepping in and intervening in the decisions of My created beings. Even if I don’t like the choices they make, and even when—as is the case here—an individual’s choice results in tragic or deadly outcomes, I still must allow the consequences to occur.”

“So,” Taylor said, “it’s going to happen? Cain is going to kill his brother?”

“I have spoken to Cain and given him a way out if he chooses to heed My counsel.”

“And if he doesn’t?”

“Then, Abel will be killed.”

Rok was still except for shaking his head and saying, “Wrong.”

"Yes, Rok," The Alpha replied, "the act is most definitely wrong. But allowing the choice to be made is right; otherwise, the entire construct of free moral agency would crumble."

"Would that be so bad?" Kepteny asked.

"It's a fair question and one I will attempt to answer. Imagine a universe where every single one of My created beings did exactly what I wanted all the time. No free will. No capacity to make sovereign choices. Serving Me, obeying Me because it is what I require and not what they choose. Does that sound like somewhere you would want to live?" When no one answered, He continued, "You see, the introduction of free will always carried with it the potential for wrong choices and the unintended consequences that follow. It would be great if the humans heeded Our counsel and made better choices. But they often do not. And when that happens, I—We—are bound by principle to let the results unfold without intervention. So, again, love requires free will."

The resulting silence was interrupted only by the constant whooshing of the Merkabah in their unceasing flight above and around the throne.

Finally, Michael said to the watchers, "Cain is going to do what he is going to do, and you will not intervene. Understood?"

The Alpha said, "An island of peace is prepared for the eventuality of Abel's death: Peace City."

"Peace City?" Schindaug repeated.

"Yes. It is a place of rest for those humans whose bodies die naturally or who suffer death through disease, accident, or at the hands of another . . . those who believe in Me and My offer of redemption through sacrifice."

"So, it's a place where they can rest in peace?"

"Yes, Schindaug. They will find rest in Peace City," The Alpha replied. "Do you have a point to make?"

He shrugged, saying, "I don't know. Just that Rest in Peace can be abbreviated as R.I.P., so maybe we could call it Rest in Peace City or RIP City for short instead of Peace City."

"RIP City," The Alpha said. "I like it. RIP City it is. Now, return to your assignments and, as previously stated, be on high alert. Apollyon has his limitations, but he is ever resourceful, always looking for a way to circumvent the system and turn it to his advantage."

As the watchers and warriors returned to the earthly realm, Michael said, "This is even more difficult than watching Eve take a bite of that fruit."

"But watch, we must," The Alpha replied. "Watch and mourn."

Morning dawned, and Awan was so nervous that she fumbled everything she touched. Her voice took on an unnatural quiver.

Azura said, "What is wrong with you today, sis?"

"What do you mean?" Awan replied quickly.

"I don't know. You just seem off."

"Well," she said, "maybe it's because I have been working on a . . . surprise for you."

Awan was astounded at how easily the lie sprang to her lips.

"A surprise? Really? What is it?"

"Well, I thought I would prepare a mid-day meal for you."

"Whatever for?"

Awan said, "Oh, just to tell you that I love you."

"How sweet. Okay, then. That will be great."

"I'll start working on it right away and then call you when it's ready."

Cain sat under his favorite tree situated on a low rise that gave him an unimpeded view of the land belonging to him. In his right hand was the crudely made weapon. Overnight, his trepidation had been transformed into a white-hot burning rage fueled by nearly constant input from Apollyon.

"Who does he think he is?" Apollyon's voice whispered in his ear. "I'll tell you who. He thinks he's better than you. Better than anyone. Better than your parents. He's egotistical and opportunistic. Throughout your life, he has continually sought to put you in your place, to bring you down and keep you down. It's no wonder you feel the way you do. Who wouldn't? And it's never going to change. You have no choice but to kill him. You'll enjoy it. It will be so satisfying. It will fix everything. Just try to imagine the fear in his eyes as he realizes he's going to die, and you are the one who will kill him."

"Yes," Cain said in the silence of the early morning hours. "I can see it now. I can almost feel what it will be like to split his skull with my weapon."

"Oh yes. The weapon. Brilliant, by the way. He won't stand a chance. Will, in fact, never see it coming. It won't be long now. Better prepare yourself."

And so he sat there, going through scenario after scenario of how it would happen. Each time he got to the part where he raised the weapon to bring it down upon his brother's head, he stopped, relishing the sheer terror in his eyes.

Midday, and the fragrance from the meal Awan was preparing filled the dwelling. Azura's mouth watered involuntarily.

"Hurry up, Sister," she said, her voice filled with excitement. "I'm starving."

"It's almost ready," she said as she poured the meal into a roughly thrown pottery bowl.

Throughout the meal preparation, Awan had battled her conscience over what she was planning to do.

Demonic whispers of persuasion coaxed her to continue against her natural affinity to do what was right and good. The demons knew Apollyon would be so pleased.

Could she go through with it?

She *had* to go through with it.

But . . . what if it didn't work?

It *had* to work.

Back and forth, back and forth, in an unceasing internal argument.

Even though she knew that eating the food wouldn't hurt her sister, not truly anyway, she regretted her decision. Regretted it nearly as much as she regretted the person she had become. A hatred toward herself set in.

This timid and fearful person, constantly looking over her shoulder for threats real and imagined. This scheming, conniving, and murderous horror of a human.

Stopping her preparations, she stared vacantly ahead, wondering if she had it in her to stop this elaborate charade and warn Abel of what was about to happen to him.

She found that she did not.

"Okay, it's done," she announced brightly, fighting to hold her emotions in check.

Azura clapped her hands as her sister sat the bowl down in front of her.

Awan said, "I hope you are truly hungry, Sister, because I gave you a big portion."

"Don't worry. I feel like I could eat all of this and ask for more."

Awan returned to the meal preparation area of their small dwelling as Azura began eating.

"This is delicious," Azura said. "What is your secret?"

"I'll never tell," she said, laughing lightly.

About halfway through the meal, Azura said, "Oh . . . suddenly, I don't feel well."

"What's wrong, Sister?" Awan said.

"I don't know. My stomach. It suddenly feels like . . . I don't know how to describe it. I just . . . I need to lie down. I'm sorry, Awan. I'm sure it's not your food. It's just something . . . I don't know."

"Here," Awan said, "let me help you to your sleeping pallet. You just lie down and go to sleep if you can while

I clean everything up. You'll be okay after a while. I'm certain."

Now too ill to even speak, Azura allowed herself to be led like a child to her bed, where she collapsed and lay as still as a stone.

Letting loose a heavy woolen drape to shield the sleeping area, Awan hurriedly changed into one of Azura's garments, taking care to fix her hair just like her sister's.

Checking her reflection in a bowl of still water, she had no confidence whatsoever that she could pull off the deception.

Nevertheless, it had to be done.

When she left, one of her younger brothers said, "Hello, Azura. Where are you going?"

"Oh," she replied, feeling a bit startled, "I'm going to, uh, see Abel."

"Okay. See you later."

Quickly making her way through the family compound so as not to have any further forced conversations, she came to Abel's fields, where his livestock were tended.

She spotted him squatting down and examining a lamb and called out, "Hello, Brother," putting just the right inflection on the greeting.

"Oh, hi, Azura. What brings you out here?"

"You mean, other than to see my favorite brother?"

He laughed. "Well, yes, other than that."

"Well," she said, walking a bit closer, "I was wondering if you could spare some time to go for a walk with me. I have . . . something I need to talk to you about."

Glancing down at the lamb and then back, he said, "Sure. I could do that. Can you give me a hint?"

"I'd rather just tell you about it along the way."

He stared at her for a long moment, saying finally, "Did you do something to your hair?"

"No," she replied, unconsciously touching her hair, "why do you ask?"

"I don't know. Something just seems different about you, but I can't put my finger on what it is."

"Oh, you know us girls. We're always doing things to try to look better."

"Well, for what it's worth, you look just fine."

As they started walking, Awan said, "Thank you for taking the time for this, Brother."

"Of course. Why wouldn't I make time for my sister?"

When she linked her arm through his, her resolve almost crumbled as she realized that she was leading her brother to his death.

She tried and failed to choke back a deep sob, causing Abel to ask, "What is it, Azura. What troubles you so that you are sobbing?"

"It's Cain."

"What about him?"

"He . . . he wanted to talk to me about something, but I didn't want to face him on my own, which is the real reason I came and got you to come with me."

"Well, why didn't you just say that in the first place?"

"Because," Awan said, building on the lie, "I know how bad things are between the two of you right now and was afraid you wouldn't agree to go with me."

He said, "Things are bad, but not to the point that I wouldn't support you."

"I'm so glad to hear that, Abel. He's waiting for me in his southern fields."

"Does he know I'm coming with you?"

And the lies just kept coming.

"Yes, and he said it was okay if it made me feel better to have you along for support."

In the distance, they could see Cain standing and waiting for them. He even raised his left hand and waved in a friendly manner.

"Okay," Awan said, her voice catching in her throat, "there he is. I'm scared, Abel. Would it be okay with you if you went ahead of me to make sure that he's not angry with me or anything?"

"Sure," he replied, "I can do that. Why don't you stay here? If everything is okay, I will signal, and you can join me."

"Okay. I really appreciate this."

Abel had just turned to walk away when she called out, "Abel?"

"Yes, Azura?"

"I love you. I have always loved you. Please, don't forget that."

He thought it an odd thing for her to say at the moment but simply nodded his head, saying, "I love you as well."

Chapter Forty-Six

As Abel walked toward Cain, he noticed a smile on his brother's face.

Strange.

He couldn't remember the last time he had seen his brother smile.

"Hey there, Brother," he said in a friendly greeting as he approached.

Cain replied, "Brother, come closer and tell me what you have to say."

Abel walked forward unsuspectingly, having no idea what was about to happen.

One hundred paces.

He called out, "Azura asked me to come ahead and make sure that your anger wouldn't burn against her."

"And why should I be angry with my sister?"

Eighty feet apart.

"I know not. Only that she fears the possibility."

"My sister has nothing to fear from me, Brother."

Fifty feet.

There was something about Cain's voice that seemed strange—something in the way he held himself.

"Your crops look to be doing well. They are nearly as high as my head."

"It has been a good year. Come closer, Brother, so that we do not have to shout at each other to be heard."

Thirty feet.

Abel was close enough now to see Cain's eyes, and what he saw gave him a moment's pause. But what was it?

"Are you sure you are okay to meet with our sister and not be angry?"

"As I said, neither of my sisters have anything to fear from me. Why should they?"

Fifteen feet.

"I'm glad to hear it," Abel replied, continuing to move forward. "And yet, you must admit that you have been less than approachable of late."

When he got to within arm's length, without speaking, Cain suddenly swung his weapon from where he had it hidden behind him, intending to crush his brother's skull. The only problem was that Abel was much faster and more agile than he and ducked under the first blow.

"What is the meaning of this?" Abel shouted in alarm. "Cain, what are you doing? Are you trying to kill me?"

"That's exactly what I am trying to do," Cain said through clenched teeth, his face drawn back in a rictus of hate.

Abel risked a glance behind him to warn his sister to run, but she was nowhere to be seen. He suddenly realized the whole thing had been a setup. Cain launched a mighty backswing that caught Abel on his right shoulder, sending him tumbling to the ground and screaming in pain.

Crippled in one arm, Abel scrabbled along the ground, attempting to put some distance between him and his crazed sibling. As he crawled, Cain swung again, catching him in the small of his back and crushing the lower vertebrae. Abel screamed, pawing unconsciously at the wounded area with his only functioning arm.

He tried to stand, but the blow had taken his legs from him. He instead tried to pull himself along the ground only to be caught from behind with a blow that glanced off the back of his head, stunning him and sending him face-first into the ground.

Cain, feeling the passion of rage well up inside of him, straddled his brother's back and began to rain down blow after blow on his unprotected head until it was no longer recognizable. When he finally stopped due to sheer exhaustion as much as anything else, he threw himself backward, gasping uncontrollably at what he had done.

"That's my boy," Apollyon whispered in his ear. "You've done it. You've rid yourself of your rival. Now, nothing will be withheld from you. You are free. And if you want to choose a lamb, you can have the best now. He won't shame you ever again."

Suddenly, Cain realized that he couldn't leave Abel—or what was left of him—just lying there in the dirt. He had to find a way to hide the body. Down between the tall stalks as they were, he thought that perhaps if he dug a trench deep enough, he could roll him into it and then cover him up. And since no one besides him ever came into the fields, no one would ever know about it.

And so, Cain dug.

And dug some more.

Finally, when he thought it was deep enough to completely conceal Abel's remains, he rolled the body into the shallow crevasse and vomited at the sight of the horror that had once been his brother's head.

Cain ran from the burial site to distance himself from the event. Out of breath, he slowed to a walk. He looked around as he wandered on. No one had noticed him. His stomach was still in knots.

"I killed my brother," Cain whispered to himself, sounding like a man just coming out of a trance. "I killed my brother. I took this weapon and bashed his head in. I . . ."

"Yes, you did, and it is a cause for rejoicing, my boy." Apollyon came ever so close to Cain, turned on his powers of persuasion, and strongly suggested deep into his mind, "You are powerful. You are invincible. They will fear you now. You showed them all. You can do whatever you like now. No one can stop you."

It had been some time since The Persuasion of the Fallen, but the techniques and joy of it all came back so easily. Cain wandered around with the artificial sense that everything would be okay. He imagined a better life and greater respect from his family and even from the Alpha. Eventually, those feelings faded.

Cain felt a euphoric and uneasy feeling in his soul all at the same time. He now felt the poison drip into his heart. He struggled with what he knew was right, the power of his new self-determinism, and the freedom he felt. The reality of his family's reactions slowly began to stab at him.

"No!" Cain shouted. "Get away from me. This is all your fault."

"My fault? Oh, come now. Are you trying to convince yourself that you haven't wanted to do this for a long while? That's just pathetic. In fact, *you're* pathetic." Suddenly switching tactics, almost as if he could not help himself, Apollyon heaped on shame. "Abel loved you, and you killed him. Cain, what have you done? You murderer! You killed your brother, your mother's favorite son. Oh, the hurt and pain you will cause her. Who is going to tell her? What a horrible moment."

The sudden shift in attitude from Apollyon rocked Cain to his core. He sat down and leaned back on his haunches, remembering the bloody horror that he stood over only a little while before. His mouth worked but formed no words. He looked at his clean hands that he had washed in the stream, imagining his brother's blood still dripping from them.

"I'm sorry, Brother. I'm so sorry," he moaned over and over as he now lay on the ground.

"Sorry?" Apollyon challenged, sticking with his new tactics. "Good. You should be sorry. You killed him, you worthless horror of a human. You killed your brother. No one has ever done anything so horrible and low."

"I killed him. I killed my brother," Cain repeated.

"Oh, *do* stop whining."

"Get out!" Cain suddenly shouted, standing and staring at the point a few feet away where Apollyon had manifested his presence. "Get out and don't come back. I hate you!"

“As previously discussed, I hate you, too,” he said flippantly and then continued, “but remember, it’s you who did this. Don’t hate me because of what you planned and did.”

“Leave! In the Name of the Alpha, I command it.”

Apollyon wavered, saying, “Now, let’s not be hasty, Cain. Take a moment to gather your—”

“Go,” Cain said hotly. “Go and never bother me again.”

Apollyon vanished.

He had no choice, for he had been commanded to leave in the Name of The Alpha. No matter. His plan had worked. A human was dead at the hands of another human.

Apollyon was sly and noticed the details. This was a learning moment for him that would have valuable downstream benefits for him and the Fallen. It would negatively impact the human race until the Clock of Consequence ran out. Not only had he caused a human to kill another human, but Cain’s sin had given him a euphoric rush. He then noticed that Cain’s self-loathing and shame carried on more than Apollyon had ever suspected. Enticing the human to sin had a wonderful rippling effect within the human. Apollyon would update the temptation training manual for all demons. He noticed a very successful three-step process. First, entice the human and lure them into sin. Second, at the moment of sin and success, create a short-lived thrill, reward, and satisfaction, followed soon by accusation and condemnation, leading to shame and self-hatred. Hatred of the image they bore, the image of the Alpha. And maybe that could turn into hatred for the Alpha Himself. It was such a delicious revelation. This would inform Apollyon’s tactics as long as he was prince of this world.

Apollyon woke up from reveling in his new discovery and fantasizing about the future of his growing destructive abilities. He gathered all his fallen angels to celebrate this significant victory. Not far into the merriment, Apollyon had a thought.

What about that dead human?

Where is he?

For some reason, he hadn't planned that far ahead.

Calling Beleth to him even as the festivities carried on, he said, "Find the dead man. Figure out where he went. I have just realized that his death opens up a whole new realm of possibilities."

"How so?"

"We kill their earthly bodies, and then I believe we can torment their souls for all of eternity. How utterly delicious." This drove Apollyon back into his own fantasy world, again thinking about all the fabulously bad consequences he could bring upon the Alpha.

As Abel's last conscious thought formed in his mind, he felt his spirit rising up, freed from his battered body, and piercing a thin veil that seemed to separate the Earth from something else, although precisely what, he couldn't say. He felt no fear, nor was there any pain, only peace.

Hovering just above the tragic scene on the ground, he saw Cain on his knees, weeping and desperately trying to hide the body. Next to Cain, a hideous creature seemed to be speaking to him, someone Abel did not recognize. The scene was so compelling he wanted to linger and find out what was transpiring between them. He somehow wanted to warn Cain, but he felt himself being drawn away, floating effortlessly away from his earthly body through what felt like a dark tunnel toward a light source.

Without being consciously aware of it happening, he exited the tunnel and found himself in a world completely foreign to human eyes. Off to his right, he could see a vast land mass, undulating with ever-changing colors of deep red and orange. White hot flames regularly burst from the crevices carved deeply into its pitted and uneven surface, shooting high into the atmosphere where they crackled with ominous energy. Stretching far beyond the limits of his vision, it seemed a hot, dry place without comfort or peace. Abel hoped he wasn't going there.

To the left of this place of horror, he could see a lush island off in the distance, ringed by a chasm wide, dark, and deep. The chasm seemed to separate the barren, dry land mass from the lush island. Small was the island by comparison to the barren wasteland he'd just been viewing; nevertheless, it appeared large enough to accommodate many people. But who? Him? Was this where he was being drawn?

Casting his sight farther, farther still, he could now see that beyond the island was . . . nothing. Just vast emptiness. Whether there was any substance to it at all, he could not tell. Although his trajectory had veered a bit toward the left, giving Abel hope that the burning wasteland was not his destination, he still could not rule out either place. At least, not yet.

As he moved closer to the largely green island, details began to emerge. Details that called to mind his mother and father's description of Eden. Whether true or merely a manifestation of an overactive imagination, he could swear soft, sweetly-scented fragrances began to fill the air, along with birdsong mingled with the sound of gently flowing rivers and cascading waterfalls in the distance.

Suddenly, he could see a long, narrow suspension bridge. It had thick, old wooden planks and a sturdy cable system holding the bridge in place. It swayed a little when someone walked across. Everyone walked across slowly. The Faithful were always advised not to look down. It connected to the island and spanned the seemingly bottomless chasm. At the bridge's near end, there was a stone landing and then only nothingness. Confusion began to fill Abel's soul as he realized the landing of the bridge, where the Void surrounded the stone landing, was his destination. Not the wasteland. Not the lush island. The end of the bridge. He could only hope he was to cross the bridge into the lush island and not the wasteland he could clearly see off to his right. This reality caused him immense dismay but not to the same extent as the horrific, searing screams and fleeting visions of dark and twisted shapes darting here and there around him.

Having arrived on the bridge's landing, where its finely cut stone surface seemed to drift off into nothingness, he became simultaneously aware of several things. One, there was no wound on his head, which struck him with about the same level of force as the rock wielded by his brother's hand. Two, the bridge was incredibly long and definitely narrower than some of the bridges he and his brother had helped Father build over the rivers and streams near their family compound. It was barely wide enough for one person. And three, there were four impressive beings present. Two on one side of him and two on the other. All of whom were seemingly laying claim to him, shouting at each other and coordinating defensive maneuvers to keep him protected.

As soon as Cain landed the final killing blow to the back of his brother's head, The Alpha's voice called to Steele and Wendly, "It has happened. It is time."

"You ready for this?" Steele said, staring into his partner's eyes.

"We've been ready," Wendly replied. "We just haven't had a reason to act until now. The reason for our training is becoming very clear. The Alpha knew this day might come."

Steele then looked at Wendly and said, "Now we must go and carry out our assignment."

Wendly and Steele had been hard at work in RIP City since The Alpha had commissioned them to prepare for the imminent arrival of the first human to taste death. As a result, a system had been put into place by which someone passing from death to eternal life would be welcomed and then provided safe passage from the Void across the bridge into the lush island of RIP City.

Just prior to departure, in what would become a lasting tradition, Gabriel spoke a brief tribute over the first faithful human to enter the eternal stream.

"Take care of this image-bearer," Gabriel said to the Honor Guard. "He lived his short life well, faithful, obedient to The Alpha, and grateful to his parents. May the transfer go smoothly. Alpha speed."

Since this was the first Honor Guard ever, The Alpha sent Michael, Rok, and Kepteny under the earth to the netherworld to accompany them. Apollyon's minions weren't interested in tangling with *any* angel, let alone warriors as fierce as Rok and the archangel Michael.

As Abel pierced the Curtain and began his initial trip through the tunnel, the four angels, with Michael in the lead, fanned out behind him well out of sight. The transition would be troubling enough for Abel without also having to deal with the sight of four formidable angels, let alone the mighty Michael.

Still caught up in the euphoria of persuading Cain to kill his brother and then shaming him for the act, Apollyon was taken by surprise when Beleth approached him, his normally hideous countenance turned even more so by what was obviously bad news.

He said, "I can see that you do not bring good news, Beleth."

"No, sir, I do not."

"Well then, best not to keep me in suspense."

"It's Michael."

"What about him?"

Beleth said, "It would appear that Michael and four other angels have taken Abel through the tunnel and are heading for that place across the bridge."

"The island?"

"Yes, sir."

Casting his gaze toward the bridge between the Void and The Alpha's precious island, he discerned immediately what was planned.

"No," he shouted. "No! No! No! This cannot and will not happen. I have worked far too hard to ensure that his parents' sin has been grafted into his DNA to give up without a fight.

The entire human race is now corrupted. Rebellious. Doomed. I own them now. Abel belongs to me. Get them!" he shouted. "Attack those angels. Get Abel!"

"But," Beleth said, "it's Michael. Surely you don't expect—"

"Leave Michael to me. Now, get going! Take Remashel with you."

Having exited the tunnel, Abel had just settled onto the landing in front of the bridge and close to the Void when, to the Honor Guard's horror, Beleth and Remashel suddenly appeared and began dragging him into the Void toward Hell.

"What are you doing?" Steele shouted, Abel's right hand firmly within his grasp. "He belongs to The Alpha."

"Not a chance," Beleth said, pulling on Abel's left hand. "He's ours."

Abel wailed, "What is happening to me? Where am I?"

Wendly joined Steele, wrapping his arms around Abel's waist and shouting, "Take your filthy, demonic hands off of him. I claim him in the Name of The Alpha."

"Will someone please tell me what is going on?" Abel said.

Remashel tightened his grasp. "You have no legal standing. He belongs to Apollyon."

Steele shouted, "Michael, a little help here!" But Michael, Rok, and Kepteny were under attack from a swarm of demons diving in and doing damage, then swooping away before the angels even had a chance to react.

While Rok and Kepteny were staggered by the intensity of the initial attack, Michael had drawn the Sword of Truth and was now slashing his way through the swarm, sending demons and shapeshifters hurtling away, cries of pain trailing in their wake. But it seemed that as soon as one of Apollyon's demons was dispatched, ten more took their place.

"How could there be so many?" Kepteny shouted while swinging his sword in wild, broad arcs.

"There aren't," Michael said. "It's all an illusion. Remember, they're shapeshifters who can assume any form they choose, even appearing as multiple entities."

While a few of the demonic horde had gotten close enough to sink teeth and claws into the angels, most were sent shrieking away, having been hacked or stabbed by the warrior angels' swords.

Slashing his way through another swarm, Michael said loudly, "Gabriel, come now. Bring the others."

In the blink of an eye, Gabriel and the other five archangels joined Michael, Wendly, Steele, Rok, and Kepteny on the bridge, with Schindaug and Taylor following close behind.

Michael rose above the landing, his sword at the ready, bellowing, "Back off. Do it now!"

With Michael's challenge still reverberating throughout the underworld and a fresh swarm from the Legion of the Fallen gathering for a renewed attack, Beleth called out for calm while at the same time retaining his grip on Abel's hand.

"Look," Beleth said, shouting to be heard, "we can fight over him, but it is pointless, as you have no legal claim."

Michael said, "You're going to have to explain that one to me."

Abel said, "Can someone, anyone, please tell me what's happening?"

Ignoring Abel's plea, Beleth said, "He was born in sin, his death was caused by an *act* of sin, and since sin touched him, he is tainted by association and, therefore, our property."

"Not so fast," Uriel said, waving the Scroll of Remembrance. "There is nowhere in here *or* in the archives that says a righteous person killed by a sinful act is made sinful by association."

Abel pleaded. "Seriously . . . someone *please* tell me where I am and what is happening to me."

Wendly said, "Your brother killed you, Abel."

"Yes, I am still reeling from what happened and now wondering what is going on here now. I hovered over my body and clearly saw what happened. Then, I went through a tunnel toward a light that turned out to be this new world. I descended here, assisted and flanked by four unknown and intimidating beings. Angels, I hope. But where am I, who are you, and what is happening?"

"I'm Wendly. We *are* angels trying to take you to a place prepared for you by The Alpha, but Apollyon's goons here are trying to prevent it."

Gabriel said, "You can't seriously believe that you have a chance of winning this dispute, so what is really going on, Beleth?"

"This isn't about waging a battle, Gabriel," Beleth replied. "It's about laying legal claim to a soul that is rightfully ours. The first one of many to follow, by the way."

"He is legally ours. He believed in the promises of the Alpha, and his actions clearly followed that belief. He is, therefore, deemed righteous. You can't have him," Michael said.

Apollyon walked calmly through his growing hordes of demons, hands clasped behind his back, and made no attempt to disguise his deformity.

"Well, what have we here?"

"We have your cronies trying to steal Abel away from his rightful abode in RIP City," Michael replied extra firmly.

"And, let me guess, you intend to stop us from claiming him? Even though he is ours by law?"

"He is not."

"Oh, but he is. Adam and Eve sinned; therefore, by birth, Abel and the rest of their spawn are sinful. Plain and simple. Case closed."

"Faith. Credited to him as righteousness. You saw it in his obedience to make the appropriate sacrifice and honor the Alpha," Michael said.

"Excuse me?"

"You were in the Archives enough. You should know this. The Alpha provided a way for sin to be remitted."

"Oh," Apollyon replied with a sarcastic laugh, "you're talking about that silly ceremony with fire I saw them all performing."

Abel said, "Not silly. It was given to us by The Alpha to forgive the sins of my father and mother—sins, as you rightly concluded, passed down to us through birth. We did this out of obedience because we believe in the Alpha and His promises. There can be no remission of sin without the shedding of blood. So, just as the Alpha told us, I provided the first fruits from my flocks. The best of the best. Pure and undefiled lambs offered as burnt offerings before The Alpha who, by the way, declared our sins forgiven."

Apollyon wasn't giving up and countered angrily, "Do you think Cain had no reason to kill his brother? Abel was trying to one-up Cain with his sacrifice and look good in the sight of the Alpha. Abel's motive was selfish. He faked sincerity, and Cain knew it and reacted appropriately.

Michael replied, "Selfish motive? Insincere? Sounds like someone else I know. I'd say you are reviewing your own motives and actions. Abel was true and sincere. The Alpha accepted his sacrifice."

"All of it, how utterly droll," Apollyon said dismissively. "Do you think for one second that any of what you or Abel proclaim has the slightest meaning to me? I reject it in its entirety. Now, come on. You're coming with us."

Michael moved menacingly toward him, stopping a sword length away. "You can't have him. Simple as that."

"So," Apollyon replied, "you are saying that you are willing to go to war just to win this argument?"

"Absolutely."

With a flourish, Apollyon suddenly grew before their eyes, taking on the form of a fiery dragon and roaring, "Since you seem to love calling me the Dragon, so be it. Let the battle begin."

Chapter Forty-Seven

Abel cowered in fear at the dragon's sudden appearance, terror washing over him like a biting frost.

"Mom, Dad . . . someone . . . help me!" he screamed as the battle began to rage around him.

He flattened himself on the bridge. He couldn't see much, but he could hear very well. And what he heard brought terror to his soul. He realized the battle was a fight beyond anything he could have ever imagined. He was now experiencing a battle for his very soul. It was the sound of great beasts bellowing a battle cry that turned his blood to ice. So fearsome was the sound that he unconsciously pressed his face against the cold stone. He closed his eyes and covered the back of his head with his hands.

It suddenly occurred to him just how vulnerable he was in his current position, so he turned onto his side, drawing his legs up to his chin and pressing his face between his knees. Daring a peek, he saw a company of warriors surging all around him, all clad in armor that was nearly translucent in appearance but capable of repelling any attack. Each of those mighty angelic beings seemed capable of dispatching vast numbers of Apollyon's Legions single-handedly, but they moved shoulder-to-shoulder. Three abreast near the entry of the bridge, their shields locked together, creating an impenetrable wall.

Turning his head in the other direction, Abel saw what he imagined to be the source of the terrible bellowing: a creature like nothing he had ever seen on Earth. Misshapen head with a gaping mouth filled with row upon row of needle-like teeth, with four sets of bulging, bloodshot eyes filling the beast's forehead. Its bloated body was supported by six legs, and on its feet, four prominent claws in front and a longer, talon-like claw in back.

But it wasn't the only one.

Behind it came rank after rank of beasts that were its equal, lumbering forward and rearing up on their four hind legs while the front two dealt vicious blows to all who dared to challenge their progress.

"This can't be happening," Abel moaned, his mind refusing to believe what his eyes were seeing.

Gabriel shouted, "Remember, it isn't real. None of it is real. They are shrunken, shriveled, and deformed. Do not believe what your eyes see."

"Seeing is believing; that's what I've always said," Schindaug hollered as he and Taylor made their way to the landing area to provide extra security for the man.

Taylor said, "But Gabriel just said you can't trust your eyes."

"Right. Well, to each their own, I suppose."

Behind them, Kepteny and Rok were suddenly attacked by a swarm of demons—thousands, covering each from head to toe.

Rok began pulling them off and flinging them into the chasm, but as soon as one was dislodged, two more took its place.

Seeing what was happening, Wendly shouted, “It’s the same thing that happened to me. Someone has to help them.”

Schindaug and Taylor turned to defend their comrades just as Kepteny went down.

“There are so many. I can’t even see Kepteny,” Taylor hollered.

Schindaug gave a battle cry and charged into the fray, his sword sending twisted and writhing forms plummeting into the chasm. But as was true with Rok, for every one of the attackers dislodged, many more arrived to take their place.

“There can’t be this many,” Taylor said.

“There aren’t,” Steele shouted. “Like Michael said, it’s an illusion, just like those giant beasts.”

Suddenly, Rok’s sword appeared from the center of the swarm, slicing evenly and effortlessly through the mass of demonic bodies from top to bottom, their cries of pain melding with the chorus of battle.

“Look at that,” Schindaug said as Rok’s movements began to pick up momentum to the point where his motions were a virtual blur.

Emboldened by his strategy, Taylor and Schindaug began matching him stroke for stroke, their combined efforts finally freeing Kepteny.

“That was uncomfortable,” Kepteny said, checking for injuries.

"Are you okay?" Schindaug asked.

"I seem to be, despite a few scratches, thanks to our new armor. Rok, how about you?"

Consumed by battle lust, Rok merely threw his head back and roared before charging forward into the fight.

"Guess that answers that question. Oh, and by the way . . . seventy-five."

"What?" Schindaug said.

"Seventy-five. The answer to my riddle."

"Now? You tell me now?"

Swinging at a swarm of demons, Kepteny replied, "Yeah, well, I thought you secretly wanted to know."

"How is it seventy-five?"

"I thought you were busy fighting."

"TELL ME!" Schindaug screamed in frustration, which seemed to propel his fighting even more.

"So, on the seventy-fifth day, he climbs up how many?"

"Five, I know that part."

"And where is he once he climbs up five more above seventy-five?" Kepteny said, waiting for Schindaug's ah-hah moment.

"Oh. Yeah. Huh. Eighty. I get it now," Schindaug defended his inability to figure it out by saying with a distasteful tone, "That was dumb."

Michael had pulled all the archangels except Gabriel away from the main thrust of the battle. They now gathered at the royal stables, where The Alpha kept vast herds of Shamayim's war horses.

"What are we doing here, Michael?" Jophiel said worriedly.

"Putting an end to this."

Zadkiel said, "With horses?"

"These are the royal steeds trained for war. Nothing can withstand their charge."

"Well," Chamuel said, "technically, nothing can withstand your charge either."

"While that is true, I feel it's time to make a statement. Apollyon has his demons morphing and shapeshifting into all these fantastic forms, but it's mostly an illusion. We, on the other hand, are as real as it gets, and it's time to show him and his pathetic forces what that looks and feels like."

"Do we get to choose our own steed?" Uriel said.

"Of course."

Uriel stood in front of a stall which housed a magnificent black stallion. "Then, I want this beauty."

"He's yours. Anyone else have a preference?"

Raphael said, "Since I have zero experience with horses of any kind—and especially war horses—I will let you choose."

"Take the roan. He's gentler."

"That works for me."

Jophiel said, "I suppose choosing the white one is out of the question."

"How'd you guess?" Michael said with a smile. "Starcatcher. He is chief among all horses. Their champion. Specially trained to lead in battle."

"Understood. Then, I will take the dappled gray."

Zadkiel said, "It's the chestnut for me. By the way, does this steed have a name?"

"He will as soon as you give it to him," Michael said.

Chamuel asked, "Is that true of them all?"

"Yes."

"But how will we know what name to give?"

"As soon as you swing your legs over his back and settle into the saddle, you will know."

Michael and the archangels straddled their chosen chargers, followed by an innumerable company of Shamayim's forces mounted on noble war horses.

He shouted, "And now, my mighty warriors, we ride. We ride not only for The Alpha but for Abel and all those in the future who die in righteousness. For no one should ever again have to experience what Abel is experiencing. The time has come to end this assault."

Little did they know that every human destined for RIP City would be contested in one form or another. Every life would face the scrutiny of Apollyon or his chosen accuser with the goal of preventing everyone from experiencing what Apollyon had lost forevermore.

Abel felt something behind him and turned to see two more huge forms.

"I'm Schindaug," one of them said, "and this is Taylor. We're here to help defend you."

"I just want to go home," Abel replied weakly.

Taylor said, "We're going to make sure you get . . . to your new home."

The Great Dragon soared above, emitting lightning blasts from its mouth while at the same time bellowing blasphemies against The Alpha. Staying just out of reach, it taunted and teased, swooping down and cracking its long, slender tail like a gigantic, fiery whip, wounding vast numbers of The Alpha's forces.

Surrounded now by his four guardians, Abel heard Steele shouting to be heard above the din of battle, "Fear not, Abel. Nothing shall harm you while we are here."

Wendly knelt beside him, touching his face tenderly. "I know you must be terribly confused by all this, but it will all be over soon, and you will be at rest."

Abel attempted to crawl behind Wendly, but the battle was so concentrated around his position that he was unable to move more than a foot or so in either direction before encountering the feet and legs of those engaged in fierce combat.

Hearing a shriek overhead, he lifted his eyes and saw a wonder: Michael, riding on a great white stallion at the head of a host of horsed warriors—too many to number. The moment the horses and riders appeared, the Great Dragon attempted to flee, but Michael caught him, wounding him repeatedly. The dragon's armor was insufficient to repel the Sword of Truth. Shrieking piteously, the dragon fell onto the far end of the bridge, where it morphed back into the hideously deformed body of Apollyon.

"You're no dragon," Michael taunted from the back of the stallion hovering just above Apollyon's position.

"You're a pathetic, withered shadow. You have no power but persuasion."

Apollyon stood defiantly, resuming the image he had adopted that was the closest to his former glory.

"But that is the greatest power of all, Michael," he shouted, "you pompous, posturing pretender." As his Legions of the Fallen began to realize that the battle was lost, he continued, "Don't you get it? You may have won this skirmish, but it was just that—a skirmish. The battle is lost. You have lost . . . you and that *Almost* High you serve."

Settling the stallion down just in front of where Apollyon stood with his four captains, Michael said, "You really have no idea what is coming, do you, Dragon?"

"Stop calling me that!" he shouted. "I am Son of the Da—"

"You are Apollyon." The Alpha's voice pierced the din of battle, turning everyone still as stone and causing a holy hush to fall over the battle area at the end of the bridge and into the Void.

Apollyon stumbled backward under the force of The Alpha's voice and would have fallen had it not been for his captains coming to his aid.

Regaining his footing and a semblance of swagger, Apollyon retorted, "Call me what You will, Alpha, but here in front of You is graphic witness of my victory over Your precious creation." Gesturing toward Abel, he continued, "This man is dead. Killed by his brother's hand. I win. Don't You get it? I win."

"You've won nothing," The Alpha said. "You have merely sealed your own eternal fate."

Apollyon strutted forward, face turned defiantly upward, full of himself. "Really? Well, here I am. Why not just eliminate my life force right now? Come on," he shouted, "do it! Do it and prove to everyone how powerful You are. Well, what are You waiting for? Oh, that's right. You won't. It says it right there in the Archives. Because You wanted beings capable of having eternal relationships, You made us immortal and indestructible . . . just like You. Well, how's Your plan working now?"

Abel cowered behind Steele and Wendly; his head reached only their waists. He peered between and around them toward the incomprehensible scene playing out. Turning his face upward, he strained his eyes to catch a glimpse of The Alpha, but there was nothing there. Just a vast expanse of heavens completely alien to what he had been used to seeing on the Earth.

"Piteous, twisted thing."

The Alpha's voice filled the atmosphere around him, resonating within every fiber of Abel's being.

"You are correct. I will not destroy you," The Alpha continued. "You will do that on your own. And now, away with you. Leave this area and do not return—you and all your twisted followers."

With that pronouncement, Apollyon and his demonic horde vanished from the Void and the landing around the bridge entrance, leaving Abel gasping in confusion and wonder.

The Alpha said, "Well done, My mighty warriors. Return now to your rest. Although some were wounded, remember, it is your wounds that give you prowess and compassion."

He paused, and Abel felt himself surrounded by The Alpha's Presence, much like it had been previously on Earth, but many times more intense.

He fell to his face on the stone landing, saying, "Alpha, I . . ."

"Abel, My beloved child. I want to be the first to welcome you to My outpost in the Spiritual Realm. Although you suffered pain and violence, you will now experience nothing but peace and unspeakable joy. Here, you can find rest. You are the first to cross the bridge and enter RIP City."

"I am so confused, Alpha. I don't know where I am or what has happened to me. And . . . the battle, I'm just—"

"I know. And all will be explained shortly."

While The Alpha had been speaking, Michael and the forces of Shamayim had slowly withdrawn until only Steele and Wendly remained with Abel, about to cross the bridge.

The Alpha said, "Honor Guard, please take Abel to his rest."

Steele picked up Abel as if cradling a frightened child and began walking across the bridge and then, on the other side, toward the paradise he had seen upon arrival before the battle began.

Wendly said, "It's all over, Abel. You're safe now."

Abel glanced downward. "You are very large."

Steele laughed, saying, "We have actually shrunken ourselves to be closer to your size so as not to be too intimidating."

"It's not working," Abel said. "Where exactly am I? This is all so confusing, and I feel completely disoriented. I mean, one minute Cain is caving my head in with a rock or something, then I'm at the entrance to a bridge and this huge battle breaks out, then The Alpha appears and talks to me. It's all a bit much."

Wendly said, "We all talked about that, Abel—about how confusing the transition from death to life would be. Which is why we're here."

"So, I'm dead, and I'm not going back home? I'll never see Mom and Dad and Azura again?"

"No, you won't be going back to that home, but yes, you will see your parents and all your siblings again. Well, except for Cain. He has made his choice and must now face the consequences of that choice."

They reached the end of the bridge and entered a garden so large and verdant it took Abel's breath away.

"Where am I?"

Steele sat him gently onto the thick carpet of sweet grasses. "You are in RIP City, an outpost of Shamayim."

"RIP City? I don't—"

Laughing, Wendly said, "It's something Schindaug came up with. It was originally Peace City, but he decided that since people would be *resting* in peace here."

"Rest in Peace City. RIP City. I get it. Clever."

"Yes, he is nothing if not."

Abel said, "I met him and another angel at the bridge. By the way, if I am dead, then why do I still have a body?"

"Your physical body has been left behind. You are now like us . . . spirit. You have a different body."

"But I can see you." Reaching out his hand, he touched Steele's shoulder. "I can feel you."

Steele said, "There is much to learn. But look: Shamayim is just there across the chasm and beyond the Rainbow Stream."

"It's far in the distance, but I can see it," he said, his eyes filled with wonder. "Can I go there?"

"Not yet. Maybe someday," Wendly said, hoping he was right. "For now, why don't you tell us your story?"

"My story?" Unconsciously, he reached up and felt the back of his head where Cain's weapon had so cruelly wounded him. "All right, but this could take a while."

"Well, as it turns out, there is no time here, so we have a *while*.

Chapter Forty-Eight

Cain knelt by the depression in the earth he had carved out with the very tool he'd used to murder his brother. Sometimes weeping, sometimes wailing, he dug down through the loamy soil until there was a trench deep enough for the body to be completely covered over by topsoil.

Blubbering, babbling, he replayed the horror over and over in his mind. Swinging the weapon and catching Abel first on the shoulder, then his lower back, and finally, the back of his head. His brother falling, pleading for his life. Then, raining blow after cruel blow against his head until there was nothing left. At least, nothing left that resembled anything remotely human.

Falling over onto his back beside the hollowed-out grave, he lifted his voice in lament, sobbing so violently that his stomach finally emptied itself of its contents. But he couldn't empty his mind of what he had done.

He knelt beside Abel's body, trying to gather the strength of will required to roll him into the grave. Reaching out repeatedly, he would draw back at the last instant as if unwilling or unable to touch his body. In the end, he stood and nudged the body over the lip of the trench with his feet, watching as it rolled ingloriously into the hole, settling onto the bottom with Abel's face staring wide-eyed and accusingly at him.

"Oh, Brother," he sobbed, "what have I done? What have I done?"

Kneeling, he began scooping piles of dirt into the grave, his body continuing to be wracked by uncontrollable sobs.

Awan found him like that, approaching silently and cautiously.

"Hello, Cain," she said softly, causing him to leap fearfully to his feet. Appearing from among the stalks, she continued, "I've been looking for you."

As soon as he saw his sister, Cain fell on his knees in front of her, covering his face with his hands and wailing, "I am undone. I am undone."

"Cain," she said, dropping to her knees to wrap her arms around her brother's neck. "I'm sorry I left. I just couldn't stay and—"

"You were right to leave. It was horrible. He ran, Awan, and I had to chase him down, and then when I caught him, I . . ."

Emotion overcame him, forcing him into silence.

Awan moved around him to stare at Abel's partially covered remains. Kneeling, she reached out tenderly, closing his eyelids.

"Oh, Cain. What will we do?"

"I have to finish covering him up. If for no other reason than I can't bear the thought of animals finding him and . . ."

He couldn't finish the sentence as emotion overwhelmed him once again, falling over onto his side beside the grave and weeping violently.

Awan said almost matter-of-factly, "I will finish burying him," and began scooping dirt into the hole.

"I should be doing that. After all, it was I who—"

"No, Brother. Let me do this. I know it sounds foolish, but I feel that it's a way I can honor him in death."

They stared at each other without speaking.

Cain finally said, "I can't believe this. I killed him, Awan. I killed my brother."

"Yes, well," she replied, "I helped you."

"No, you didn't. It was all—"

"He never would have come to you had I not deceived him into doing so. No, Cain, I am as guilty of this death as you."

Cain sat back on his haunches, watching as Awan completed the grisly task.

When nothing but his face was left, she said with a choking sob, "Goodbye, Brother," and shoved the last bit of dirt into the hole. She then stood and tamped it down with her feet.

She was just starting to help Cain to his feet when they heard a voice nearby saying, "Cain."

Color drained from his face as he whispered, "It is The Alpha." Then, he stood the rest of the way to his feet, placing Awan behind him protectively.

"Yes, Alpha, I am here."

Had it been possible, Awan would have crawled into the grave at her feet and pulled the dirt over her. She had never before encountered The Alpha's Presence, and it felt overwhelming.

"Cain," The Alpha's voice spoke, "where is your brother Abel?"

"How should I know? Since when have I been my brother's keeper?"

"What have you done, Cain? Listen . . . do you hear that? Your brother's innocent blood cries out from the ground for justice."

"But, Alpha, I—"

"Henceforth shall you be accursed from the ground—the ground that has opened up its mouth to drink your brother's blood spilled by your own hand. Because of what you've done, from this point on, when you cultivate the ground, it shall no longer produce good crops. You shall be a fugitive, a vagabond, roaming aimlessly on the earth without a home, in perpetual exile . . . a degraded and despised outcast."

Cain staggered backward, wailing sorrowfully. "This punishment is too much for me to bear. You have driven me out this day from the face of the land. From Your Presence, I will be hidden, a fugitive and aimless vagabond on the Earth. I will be hunted and killed because of what I've done."

The Alpha said, "If anyone tries to kill you, I will exact a sevenfold vengeance upon him. See, I am placing this mark on you so that all will know who you are and to avoid you and not to kill you."

Cain felt around on his face, his hands finally coming to rest on his forehead, where he discovered a lumpy disfiguration that hadn't been there before.

"Alpha," he wailed. "Please, have mercy on me."

"This *is* mercy, Cain. Your days will not be foreshortened so that you may spend the rest of your life in bitter regret over what you have done. And you, Awan . . ."

Stepping fearfully from behind her brother, she said in a voice shaking with emotion and fear, "Yes, Alpha. Here I am."

"Since you enabled the murder of your brother, you shall accompany Cain in his wanderings. You, too, shall live out the full measure of your days, each one bearing stark witness of this evil."

Weeping, she fell to the ground beside her brother, her heart feeling as if it would burst asunder within her chest.

"Depart from Me, Cain," The Alpha said sorrowfully. "Your sin has separated you from Me forever."

Head hanging low, weeping bitterly with Awan following close behind, Cain left the manifest Presence of The Alpha, leaving his family, his fields, to wander in exile in the land east of Eden.

When Adam, Eve, and Azura learned the terrible news about what had happened to Abel, along with Cain and Awan's subsequent banishment, their grief seemed almost greater than they could bear.

Adam tore his clothes, turning his face toward the heavens and crying out, "Why, Alpha? Why did this happen. This day, I have lost two sons. Just kill me now and be done with it, for my heart is nearly failing me for grief. Oh, my son, my son," he wailed. "Oh, my precious boys. Gone. Gone. One killed. One banished with his sister. Beautiful Awan, beloved daughter. What have you done?"

The Alpha wanted to draw near to Adam, surrounding him, comforting in the way loving fathers do when their children have been hurt and are crying out in distress. But He could not. The separation caused by Adam's sin prevented that.

Instead, He remained at a distance, speaking words of peace directly into Adam's spirit. "Adam, My son, though you have fallen, I still care for you and adore you as My very own. Though your heart is broken, know that I, who have laid the foundations of the universe and have set in order all its boundaries, am not finished. I will yet redeem that which has been corrupted. And as for you, go your way. Finish your work. Live. Love. Produce offspring. Fill the earth. Even though the memory lingers, this terrible pain will pass. Fix your eyes far beyond this present times. Now, go. Find your wife. She needs you."

Eve lay face down as though dead, recalling the child Abel had once been. His smile. His delight in surprising her with little things he had created. The way he could always make her laugh. The time when, at four years old, he carved a small figure of himself from soft bark and gave it to her so mama would, in his words, "Have something to hug in the night." And then there was Cain and her precious Awan . . . her heart. Her very life. Gone. All three now gone. If her banishment from the Garden had made her feel like dying, this felt as if she were already dead.

Adam found her in one of Abel's stalls, awash in unrelenting waves of grief. So great was her sorrow that she could do little else but remain prostrate on the ground as copious tears flowed from a seemingly inexhaustible reservoir. Finding he had nothing to say that would bring even the slightest relief, his heart was broken as well. Adam lay down beside her, allowing his tears to mingle with hers, dampening the trampled ground beneath them.

"Husband," she said between sobs, "I brought all of this on our family. If only I hadn't been so foolish and selfish and reckless and impetuous and would have kept to The Alpha's precepts, this would've never—"

"Eve," Adam said, placing a finger gently against her chapped and cracked lips, "this is a situation of our own making. Both of us. And though this consequence is terrible to bear—bear it we must, for The Alpha is calling us onward from this place of sorrow."

"Onward to what?"

"To the rest of the life He has so graciously prepared for us."

"I'm not sure I want to experience a life that doesn't include my precious children."

"We will have many more children before we breathe our last."

"But," she cried, "we won't have Abel, or Cain, or Awan."

Cradling her tear-stained face gently in his hands, Adam said, "I know. These consequences are hard. But we will have each other, and remember what we said when we first left the Garden: we will survive. Never forget that, Eve. We will survive."

Azura searched throughout all of Cain's fields, hands grasping her still-heaving abdomen, stopping to retch every so often.

Stumbling.

Falling.

Crawling, yet never wavering in her search.

And when she finally found the freshly dug trench that held the grisly remains of her beloved brother, she prostrated herself on the grave and wept until no more tears would come.

"Oh, my brother," she mourned, "you did not deserve this horror. You were good and kind and caring. Cain was evil and manipulative, his heart hard as stone. You filled this life with joy and laughter. He filled it with jealousy and bitterness." Pausing to run her hand over the freshly turned earth, she said, "It was as if we shared the same heart, you and me. And now *my* heart seems shattered, shard upon shard, just like that cooking pot we broke last week. But though it is in pieces, each and everyone loves you and will cherish your memory. And now, rest well, Brother . . . wherever you are. I hope to see you again."

Having held grief at bay, her resolve crumbled, sending the grief crashing cruelly over her soul like a storm surge raking the shoreline.

"I will never get over this!" she cried as violent sobs wracked her body.

Observing the sorrow and anguish of soul, Apollyon led a wild bacchanal with the Legions of the Fallen following and swarming overhead as he shouted, "I did it! I did it! I told you all I would do it, and I did it. I have won. I have completely destroyed The Alpha's creation by getting them to destroy themselves." Shaking his misshapen, arrogant fist toward the heavens, he taunted, "You lose, Alpha. You lose. I'm better than You. This was too easy. I will now unleash my Legions on those who remain and turn their pathetic lives into misery, and there's nothing You can do to stop me."

The watchers and warriors, heads hung low in defeat, could only watch sadly as the demonic throng swirled around them, taunting, baiting, poking, prodding, as if daring a reaction.

In Shamayim, The Alpha sat on His throne, His great heart breaking over what had transpired.

Two trees.

One rule.

It had all been so simple.

And yet, man—the pinnacle of His creative powers—had been unable to resist, falling to Apollyon's temptation as easily as tripping over an unseen root underfoot. In the end, it was almost as if all the beauty, the majesty He had given them—the power, the dominion, the authority—none of it had been enough. They wanted what they wanted and were willing to sacrifice anything to have it.

But in gaining what they desired most, they lost it all.

The Alpha's great head sagged back against His throne as emotions held in check suddenly burst forth, flooding the throne room. His voice raised in a cry of lament.

The Fiery Stones darkened, and the Merkabah ceased their movement, hovering overhead out of respect for their Creator's grief.

Throughout the City on a Hill, the mournful dirge was taken up by the angelic host, their voices filling the Spiritual Realm in a symphony of sorrow as the Rainbow Stream darkened and the Field of the In-Between faded to solid black.

With the Bright and Morningstar on His right and FireWind on His left, The Alpha said, "Apollyon is now the god of this world, holding the keys to death, Hell, and the grave. Humans will live in his dominion and under his power, right where their choices have placed them. While a few of Adam's seed will choose faith and righteousness over sin, many will not, and Hell will swell with their numbers. Yet a little while until the Solution, until the Redeemer comes. Until then . . . We make ready."

"Until then, We make ready," echoed the *Elohim*.

As creation wept, Apollyon danced with delight, parading arrogantly the keys to death, Hell, and the grave held high for all to see. And at the far end of the bridge over the chasm, using his newly acquired power of Death, the first brick was laid for the expansive maze of an entrance known as the Gates of Hell. Gates and evil contraptions to ensure that all who died in righteousness would remain imprisoned in RIP City, separating the Alpha from His beloved image-bearers forever. The Gates of Hell would become a monument to the victory of Death he had created. The Faithful would be held as captives under his power for all eternity. The massive and complex building project would create a one-way passage to the bridge from the Void using the excruciatingly painful sting of Death. The Gates of Hell project would completely prevent anyone from leaving RIP City—forever, in Apollyon's view. Anyone who attempted to leave RIP City would be met with the sting of his victory over the Alpha.

Apollyon looked at his keys adoringly and slapped his misshapen hands together, saying, "Well, that's the end of that."

But it wasn't.

THE VOID

HELL

Coming soon:

Trouble on Earth

The saga continues with the quest for the Keys.

Acknowledgments

So thankful for my family and friends who have encouraged and cajoled me along in this drawn-out journey.

Special appreciation to Monty, Brandi, and RG, who were inspiring, creative, and well-reasoned in the balancing act between letting imagination blossom between the lines and strict adherence to the Scriptures.

Glossary of Terms and Places

Angels – Eternal beings, ministering spirits sent by The Alpha

Archangels – Superior to angels with greater size, leadership responsibilities, and special access to The Alpha, each with their own lampstand in the throne room

Builders – A small group of angels designated to help The Alpha oversee the extensions of His creation

Cherubim – Specially designated angels with four wings and four faces who, along with the Seraphim, comprise the Merkabah, angels of the throne

Chief Princes – Archangels with special places of authority

Elohim – The Alpha, the Bright and Morning Star, and FireWind. The Trinity.

Legion of the Fallen – Angels who followed Son of the Dawn into The Defection and who were ultimately cast out of Shamayim

Merkabah – An exalted level of angels with no other duties other than continually worshiping before, above, and around the throne of The Alpha

Messengers – Angelic designation for those with the gift of speech

Ophanim – Carrier angels upon which the Cherubim ride

Seraphim – Six-winged angels, also called "burning ones," keepers of the flame on the altar, who, along with Cherubim, comprise the Merkabah, or angels of the throne

Warriors – Special class of angels who defend the realm

Watchers – Angels designated to keep track of those siding with Son of the Dawn after the Defection. There must be two witnesses to legally declare guilt. The Alpha is always one witness. The watchers provide a second.

The Alcove – Where the Scroll of Remembrance rests on a pedestal and whose walls are inscribed with The Encouragements

The Archives – Where the foundations and precepts of the Realms and life are documented and kept

City on a Hill – The place of The Alpha's abode and the place of His Presence

The Curtain – Membrane separating the Physical Realm from the Spiritual Realm

Deep Lake – A lake as deep as Proud Mountain is tall, feeding a series of waterfalls that form Rainbow Stream

Eden – Center of the Physical Realm Project (PRP)

The Encouragements – Five precepts for the angels upon which life in the Kingdom is built

Field of the In-Between – A large field running perpendicular to the Glassy Sea. Many athletic angels proved their prowess here

Fiery Stones – Sentient objects covering the floor of The Alpha's throne room

Glassy Sea – a long rectangular-shaped "Sea of Glass" stretching from the Fiery Stones into the Field of the In-Between

The Heavens – The galaxies, solar systems, and planets created by The Alpha

Hell/Lake of Fire – Place of eternal existence and sometimes torment for Apollyon, his followers, and the unrighteous dead

The North – The area where Proud Mountain and Deep Lake are set

Physical Realm – Earth and all its inhabitants

Proud Mountain – A towering snow-capped peak in The North

Rainbow Stream – A multicolored flowing stream of water separating the Field of the In-Between from Proud Mountain

RIP City – (i.e., Rest in Peace City) An island formed by Proud Mountain resting inverted in Deep Lake after The Defection, where The Alpha's faithful human followers reside after death

Royal City of Light – The name Son of the Dawn gives to The North after he takes over

Scroll of Remembrance – Where things that are important to The Alpha are inscribed

Shamayim – The home of The Alpha's Presence

Shekinah – The overwhelming manifest Presence of The Alpha

Spiritual Realm – The Alpha's first creation. The place of Shamayim, His eternal home

Valley Beyond – The area beyond the Deep Lake and Proud Mountain. The place of the not yet

The Void – The entirety of the underworld that contains Hell and RIP City. The rest of the Void is dark and desolate or nothingness

About the Author

JC is a competitive, adventurous, midwestern-grown follower of Jesus. As a carrier aviator in the Navy, JC flew the A-6 Intruder. JC is fascinated by the Scriptures, and he is a dad, grandpa, snow skier, fitness wannabe, and traveler.

JC finds pleasure in hosting friends and family at his home in the Pacific Northwest. On occasion, you might catch him having a cigar and a glass of Cabernet Sauvignon with a friend. He has a heart for those in recovery. Fishing with his grandsons is a great joy. In his free time, JC naps.

About the Ghostwriter

R.G. Ryan is the author of the *Jake Moriarity* series of thrillers, *The Voices In My Head* (the biography of late Las Vegas entertainment icon, Danny Gans), and the popular *Snapshots At St. Arbuck's* series. He lives with his wife on the coast of somewhere beautiful. Can sing and play a little.